A VEIL OF INNOCENCE
THE INNOCENCE SERIES
BOOK I

C. HOFFMAN

C. HOFFMAN

For my family and friends—
thank you for loving me through it all.

And for my granddaughter—
may you always find your voice.

CONTENTS

Bill and Judy Alexander drove in silence, their truck humming down a dark, desolate country road just outside the tiny town of Fritch, Texas.

Behind them, their camper rattled with every bump in the asphalt.

They usually avoided traveling after dark—safety first—but they'd gotten a late start leaving the last RV park.

Worse, they'd strayed from their original route—something they *never* did.

But a young couple they'd met the night before had convinced them to try a scenic detour.

A beautiful, secluded lake, they'd promised.

And for reasons Judy still couldn't explain, they said yes.

It wasn't like them.

Not at all.

Bill and Judy had spent their lives working diligently, saving every penny, planning for their golden years.

Retirement had been good to them so far—every frugal sacrifice worth it to finally relax and enjoy life on the road.

Now, surrounded by nothing but darkness and the silhouettes of twisted, leafless trees, Judy felt uneasy.

The road was eerily empty.

No streetlights, no traffic.

Just their headlights cutting through the black void ahead.

Then—up ahead—taillights flickered through the dark.

Bill eased off the gas, his hands tightening on the wheel.

Something in his gut coiled.

"This'd be a hell of a place to break down," he muttered.

One glance at his phone—no signal.

Fritch was still ten miles out.

A white 2023 Ford F-250 with its hood propped open—and an older fifth-wheel camper hitched behind it.

Bill recognized it instantly.

The same young couple from the RV park—Zach and Sarah.

The ones who had convinced them to take this detour in the first place.

Zach, a tall blond man in his mid-twenties, was hunched over the engine, looking frustrated.

As Bill pulled up beside them, Zach straightened, a wide grin breaking across his face.

"Oh, man, am I glad to see you guys," he said.

His voice was light. Too casual.

Bill rolled down Judy's window. "Let me pull over and see if we can help."

Zach gave him a grateful nod. "Oh, thanks, man. We really appreciate it."

Then he looked at Judy through the open window—and let his gaze linger. Just a second too long. Long enough to make her skin crawl.

"Sarah's inside if you wanna go keep her company."

Judy's stomach knotted. Something about Zach's stare—and the way he said it—set her on edge.

She hesitated. "Thanks for the invite."

As Bill inched the truck forward to park along the shoulder, Judy turned toward him, her voice low and urgent.

"Honey, something's off with that guy. I don't have a good feeling. We could just head into town and send help."

Bill sighed and flipped on the emergency flashers.

"Let's see if it's something simple first. If not, we'll go with your plan."

Judy bit her lip, eyes drifting to the shadowed camper behind them.

Her fingers curled around the knitting needles in her lap—an old habit when nerves crept in.

The dashboard clock read 9:06 p.m.

Dinner had been nothing but gas station beef jerky.

As Bill stepped out, unease wrapped around her like ice water.

Heavy. Unshakable.

She watched him disappear in the side mirror, swallowed by the shadows behind the fifth-wheel camper.

Her view blocked by their own rig.

Her pulse quickened.

She picked up her needles, trying to calm her hands.

Trying to pretend this was just another night on the road.

But her thoughts wandered—

She gripped her knitting needles tighter, their smooth, familiar shape grounding her—

—and for a moment, her mind drifted back to the night before.

The moment they met Zach and Sarah.

Bill and Judy were walking toward the indoor pool when they noticed a young couple sitting outside their camper.

The tall blond man nursed a beer, while the petite brunette sipped from a bottle of water.

RV living had quickly taught Judy that life on the road was different.

People were unusually friendly—acting like they'd known you forever.

It had been strange at first, but she and Bill had adapted with ease.

So when the brunette waved as they passed, Judy wasn't surprised.

Bill spoke first. "Good evening. How's it going?"

Zach raised his beer. "Doin' good. How about yourselves?"

Judy smiled. "Just heading to the pool for a quick dip."

Zach grinned. "Enjoy."

Bill gave a wave, and they continued inside.

But not long after they'd settled into the pool, Judy noticed the young couple entering the pool room.

Zach called out, "Sounded like a good idea, so we thought we'd join ya!"

Then—without hesitation—he tossed his towel onto a nearby chair and launched himself into the water.

"Cannonball!" he hollered.

A wave of water splashed in every direction.

Instinctively, Judy and Bill turned their heads.

When Judy looked back, she caught a glimpse of Sarah's face.

She looked embarrassed. Maybe even annoyed.

Bill chuckled. "Well, that was a fantastic cannonball."

He extended a hand. "I'm Bill, and this is my wife, Judy."

Zach swam over and shook Bill's hand with exaggerated enthusiasm.

"Nice to meet ya, sir. I'm Zach, and this is my wife, Sarah."

Sarah gave a shy wave and slid into the water with quiet elegance.

She drifted to the far side, arms resting on the pool's edge, legs gently kicking beneath her.

Judy swam a little closer. "Sarah, right?"

Sarah opened her eyes and shifted into a standing position.

"Yes. And your name was Judy?" Her voice carried a soft, distinct Southern drawl.

"Correct. How long have you and your husband been living the RV life?"

Sarah's long brown hair fanned out in the water as she answered,

"Just over a few months. How about y'all?"

Judy smiled, charmed by the accent.

"Six months. We planned for this a long time. Retired, bought the RV, took a few short trips close to home to work out the kinks, and here we are."

Sarah listened—really listened—something Judy rarely saw in young people.

Most just waited for their turn to talk.

She found Sarah... intriguing.

She couldn't say the same for Zach.

There was something about his grin.

It didn't reach his eyes.

It felt more like a threat—dressed up in charm.

As if on cue, Zach leapt from the water and launched himself into another cannonball.

Bill laughed. "That was a ten out of ten!"

Judy glanced at Sarah, her thoughts slipping out before she could stop them.

How is this beautiful Southern belle with that imbecile?

Before she could catch herself, Sarah gave a small, knowing smile.

"He really is wonderful."

Judy's face flushed.

Had she been that obvious?

Sarah continued, "We met almost a year ago and have been married just as long."

Judy's eyebrows rose. "I'd love to hear the story."

Sarah straightened, her posture tinged with pride.

"My grandfather gifted me a trip to Vegas for my college graduation."

She paused, a soft smile tugging at her lips.

"He taught me chess." she added, her voice dipping into something more nostalgic.

"Said it was the best way to learn how people think.

'Watch the board, not the player,' he always told me."

She glanced at Judy again, and when she spoke, her tone had shifted —casual, confident, controlled.

"I was in Nevada for a research project, actually.

Part of my undergrad psych work.

I was studying how people adapt to isolated living—especially the van life and off-grid crowd. I'd read Lake Mead was a hotspot for it."

Sarah let out a light, almost self-conscious laugh.

"I didn't expect to actually talk to anyone, but I stayed out in the sun too long and passed out."

She paused, brushing wet hair from her face.

"Zach found me, brought me to his camper, gave me aloe and water, and took care of me. That night, we had too much to drink and... well, we ended up married."

She shook her head, grinning. "I know. Total cliché."

Judy chuckled. "That's straight out of a movie."

Sarah giggled. "Have you ever been to Lake Mead?"

Judy's eyes lit up. "Yes! We were just there a few weeks ago. We did the dinner cruise that takes you out to the Hoover Dam."

Sarah sighed wistfully. "I wanted to do that, but it was fully booked."

Judy tilted her head. "What did your family say about you getting married so fast?"

For a split second, Sarah's face darkened.

"My grandfather was disappointed," she said quietly. "But he wants me to be happy."

Before Judy could ask more, Zach's voice echoed from across the pool.

"Hey, Sarah—we're having dinner with Bill and Judy!"

Judy glanced toward Bill, who smiled back at her like the decision had already been made.

She turned back to Sarah. "Looks like we'll be seeing more of each other."

Sarah hesitated, then gave a playful shrug.

"If it's a bother, I can come up with an excuse."

She winked.

Judy waved it off. "Not at all. We're grilling burgers. Does that work?"

Sarah's face brightened. "Sounds delicious! What time?"

Judy was already climbing out of the pool. "Six o'clock?"

Zach, now floating lazily on an inner tube, answered for both of them. "Perfect."

Bill dried off beside her and added, "We're a few spots down at number fifteen. See y'all soon."

Dinner went well.

Sarah and Judy got along easily, their conversation light, effortless.

But something about Zach unsettled Judy.

The way he responded to Sarah.

His juvenile antics.

The constant performance.

Something didn't sit right.

She was pulled from her thoughts when Bill spoke.

"What do you think, Judy?"

She blinked. "Oh—I'm sorry, my mind wandered. What were we talking about?"

Zach chuckled. "No worries. I was just telling Bill we're heading to Fritch, Texas tomorrow—gonna spend a few days at Lake Meredith. Sarah loves it there."

Sarah nodded, eyes bright. "It's beautiful."

Bill turned to Judy. "We should go, too. It's not far out of the way and would only delay us a few days."

Judy blinked. Caught off guard. "Oh, I don't know. We—"

Zach cut in. "The back roads are gorgeous this time of year."

Bill nudged her. "Come on, let's live on the edge."

Judy shot him a look. "We'll talk about it."

She stood, collecting plates—a polite signal the conversation was over.

Sarah's smile didn't falter when Judy hesitated.

Instead, she tilted her head slightly.

Patient. Calm.

As if she already knew how this would end.

But Judy noticed it.

The way Sarah stiffened at the tension.

And the way Zach's jaw tightened in response.

He wasn't used to not getting his way.

For the briefest moment, Judy felt it—

An instinct.

A pull.

She wanted to tell Sarah to run.

Sarah stood to help with the dishes while Zach and Bill stayed at the table, cracking open another beer.

Judy's irritation deepened.

Bill wasn't a drinker—and here he was, knocking back beers like he and Zach were old college buddies.

The more Zach drank, the more she disliked him.

Something about the man felt... off.

Too polished. Too familiar.

Too eager.

And Judy trusted her instincts.

A soft tap on her window pulled her violently back to the present.

She jumped, heart hammering, and turned sharply toward the sound.

Sarah stood outside, her face barely visible in the dark—lit only by the distant flicker of hazard lights.

Judy exhaled, startled. "You scared the daylights out of me!"

Sarah offered a small, sheepish smile. "Sorry. I didn't mean to."

Judy chuckled nervously, trying to shake the tension. "How long have you guys been sitting out here?"

Sarah sighed. "Hours. No cell service. We thought about walking into town, but it got too dark. Figured we'd just wait until morning."

She shifted from foot to foot, wrapping her arms around herself.

"Bill sent me up here to ask if you'd grab the wrench from your tool kit."

Judy nodded, unbuckling her seatbelt. "Sure, it's in the camper. Let me grab it."

As they walked toward the camper door, Sarah spoke softly.

"After last night, I didn't think you'd change your plans.

I figured y'all would've stuck to your original route."

Judy hesitated at the steps, remembering the heated discussion she'd had with Bill after dinner.

She hadn't wanted to spend more time with Zach—

he set her teeth on edge.

Sarah, on the other hand, was sweet. Almost endearing.

But something about their dynamic didn't sit right.

"I like having a plan," Judy admitted. "I don't normally stray from it, but Bill convinced me.

Said sometimes going with the flow is rewarding."

She forced a small smile. "So here we are."

Sarah's lips curled into a soft, gentle smile.

"Well, if you hadn't, Zach and I would be stranded with no hope in sight."

She smiled—soft, too soft.

"You and Bill are our guardian angels."

Judy chuckled under her breath. "Hardly."

She turned her back to Sarah and climbed the camper steps—never noticing the shadow that moved behind her.

She stepped inside, the familiar scent of old wood and fabric greeting her.

Her eyes adjusted to the dark.

She took a few steps in, reaching for the tool kit.

Then—

A blinding pain exploded at the back of her skull.

Her vision went white. Her knees buckled.

Warmth trickled down her scalp.

Her hand flew to the back of her head—

wet. Sticky.

Before she could process the betrayal—

another blow.

The world tilted.

Then everything went dark.

Judy came to slowly.

Muffled voices buzzed in her ears.

Her head throbbed, a searing pain radiating from the base of her skull.

She tried to move—but her limbs were heavy.

Lead.

As her vision cleared, the first thing she saw was Bill.

He was slumped over on the couch.

Eyes open.

Vacant.

Body twisted unnaturally.

She sucked in a breath, trying to scream his name—but her voice came out strangled.

Wet.

Broken.

"Bill!"

A cruel voice echoed her cry in a mocking tone.

"Bill! Biiiill!"

Judy turned her head.

Zach and Sarah stood side by side.

Watching her like she was nothing more than a specimen under glass.

Her heart pounded violently against her ribs.

Her eyes filled with hot, desperate tears.

"Why?" she choked out, barely above a whisper.

Sarah took a step back.

Zach stepped forward.

A smirk twisted his lips.

"Why not?" he murmured.

Then—one swift motion.

The blade tore across her throat—fast, brutal, final.

Her eyes widened in shock.

Her hands flew to her neck, pressing against the gaping wound.

A wet, choking gasp escaped her lips as hot blood poured through her fingers.

Her vision blurred.

The world tilted.

Her last thought was of Bill.

She turned her head toward him—

Willing his face to be the last thing she saw.

And then—

only darkness.

Lauren Collins stepped out of the camper, her hands wrapped tightly around a steaming mug of coffee.

The air was crisp, with a gentle breeze brushing against her face and sending strands of her dark brown ponytail fluttering in the wind.

She brought the cup to her lips, savoring the warmth against the chill of the morning. A slow, deep breath filled her lungs with the scent of damp earth, dew, and wildflowers—spring in its purest form.

She descended the creaky camper steps one at a time, pausing at the bottom to stretch her arms toward the sky. Her body ached slightly from the night before, and the stretch offered a momentary release.

She walked barefoot across the cool, packed dirt to the pair of loungers Stefan had set up the night before, and sank into the one facing the lake.

Another sip of coffee.

Another breath.

For a fleeting moment, she allowed herself to just be.

Lake Meredith glistened in the morning light, a mirror reflecting soft pink clouds and the slow rise of the sun. Tiny ripples danced across the surface as fish jumped for insects, sending circles of motion across the stillness.

Lauren sat in silence, letting it wash over her.

The rhythmic crashing of gentle waves against the shore and the occasional birdcall created a symphony that pulled her backward—to a time when mornings weren't filled with tension and calculations.

She had been here before.

Many times.

She closed her eyes and tilted her face toward the sun, letting the warmth kiss her skin.

If there was a happy place in the world, this was it.

It always had been.

She remembered waking up to the smell of coffee and campfire. Her mother would be humming softly by the grill, the hem of her T-shirt twisted into a knot.

Her father would already be waist-deep in the water, casting his line and calling out for her,

"Come see what I caught, kiddo."

Back then, things had felt simple.

Safe.

But even then, Lauren had been watching.

She could tell when her mom's smile was forced.

She'd memorized the weight in her father's footsteps, could sense when tension hung in the air before anyone said a word.

She learned early that silence could be useful.

That listening was survival.

Even at eight, she had understood how to smooth things over with a joke or a distraction—how to make herself small when she needed to be invisible, or bright when she needed to be loved.

Some people learned that kind of skill as adults.

Lauren had learned it long before she should've had to.

There were only a few things that had ever brought her real joy, and this lake was one of them.

A sacred spot.

A rare moment where her mind could settle—if only for a breath or two.

But the clock was ticking.

Their time here was short.

She and Stefan would be back on the road soon.

The thought tightened her chest.

She instinctively rolled her neck, trying to ease the tension that crept into her shoulders like a slow rot.

Even here—in paradise—reality had a way of creeping in.

This place was supposed to be her sanctuary—a reprieve from the chaos of her life.

Life with Stefan meant unpredictability.

Adventure.

A wild, untethered existence.

But it also meant fear.

Violence.

Secrets.

The creak of the camper door pulled her back to the present.

Right on cue.

Her peace vanished, swept away like sand in the wind.

Out stepped Stefan Warren—tall, blonde, muscular, and barefoot.

His six-foot frame filled the doorway as he squinted into the sunlight, frowning at the morning glare.

"It's colder than I thought it'd be," he grumbled. "You said it was supposed to be warm today."

Lauren rolled her eyes behind her oversized sunglasses. "It'll warm up shortly."

He looked at her, waiting for something—a smile, a touch, a reaction she didn't feel like giving.

She shifted just enough to acknowledge him.

Careful. Calculated.

It was muscle memory by now. Nothing more.

"What do you want to do today?" she asked, her voice even.

"I was thinking... maybe a game of chess. Then a long hike?" he replied, stretching his arms.

"That sounds good," she said as she stood. "I'll set up the board and pack some sandwiches and water for the hike. See you inside."

Back in the camper, she took her time, letting her eyes adjust to the dim interior.

She paused at the sink, placing her half-drunk coffee cup down with a soft clink.

Her fingers lingered on the porcelain as her mind spun.

It astonished her how quickly her mood could shift—

how the mere sight of Stefan could pull her down from peace like a magnet dragging metal.

He had that effect.

A storm dressed in a man's body.

And her?

She was the masked guest at a masquerade ball—practiced, polished, and just convincing enough to survive the night.

Several hours later, they sat at the table, the chessboard between them.

Stefan leaned forward, eyes locked on the pieces, giddy with anticipation.

Lauren was losing—and she didn't care.

She moved her pawn lazily, letting him have his victory.

Stefan's smirk widened as he reached for his queen.

"Checkmate, bitch," he said, the words almost musical. Rehearsed.

She could've mouthed the words with him.

He always said the same thing when he won.

She never forgot the first time he said it—

the one and only time she'd won.

His backhand knocked her sideways, twisting midair before she slammed into the camper floor.

Cold linoleum kissed her cheek. Her skull rang.

She barely inhaled before his boot struck her ribs.

Air fled.

Pain bloomed.

Curled on the floor, blood pooling at the back of her throat, she looked up.

Stefan loomed—chest heaving, eyes gleaming.

"Still feel like a winner?" he sneered.

Spittle flew.

"Checkmate, bitch."

The memory clung to her like smoke.

She never challenged him again. Not where it would show.

From that day on, she smiled when she was supposed to, lost when he wanted to win.

Sometimes survival meant making yourself smaller.

Stefan stood from the dinette table.

She flinched—her body reacting before her mind could catch up.

Like the memory had dropped her right back into that awful moment.

But then she realized—

he wasn't angry.

He was just grabbing his hiking gear.

She exhaled and followed suit, packing their sandwiches and tucking them into her backpack.

A strange flutter of excitement filled her chest—an emotion she rarely let herself feel.

For a moment, she let herself relax, just a little, as she trailed behind Stefan out of the camper.

"There's a great trail off this way," she said softly, pointing toward a small cliff that blocked the view of the rest of the lake. "Want to take that trail?"

Instantly, she felt the tension rise in him.

His silence stretched—thick and taut.

He scanned the area, saying nothing, and Lauren cursed herself for suggesting anything.

It was always like this—walking a tightrope, never knowing if there would be a net beneath her when she fell.

But Stefan finally took a deep breath and pointed toward the exact spot she'd indicated.

"I think we should go this way."

Lauren nodded quickly. "That sounds like a better idea."

They took the trail she'd recommended—now cloaked as his.

She used to hike this path with her father when she was a little girl, before the accident.

Life had been easier then.

She had been different, too—softer, maybe.

She remembered walking hand-in-hand with her dad down the familiar trail, while her mom stayed back at their camper, lost in one of her books.

Those were days filled with love, and warmth, and safety—things she hadn't felt in a year.

Things she wasn't even sure she believed in anymore.

They climbed steadily toward the overlook.

The woods stretched wide and silent around them, filled with the distant hum of cicadas.

When they reached the top, Lauren spotted the same dead tree limb she and her father used to sit on.

She smiled inside and quietly took her seat on it, just like she had all those years ago.

From her backpack, she pulled out the sandwiches and two water bottles.

She handed Stefan his sandwich, and before she could pass him the water, he snatched it from her hand without a word.

No please.

No thank you.

Still, they ate in silence.

No harsh words.

Just birdsong and the gentle lapping of waves below the cliff.

It had been a good day, so far.

She tilted her head back and let the sun warm her face.

For just a second, she almost let herself feel happy.

"You think it would kill you if you fell from here?" Stefan asked.

Lauren turned her head slightly, trying to gauge if she was supposed to answer—

or if this was one of those conversations he wanted to have with himself.

He didn't wait long.

"It would kill you," he said, answering his own question.

"I bet you're right."

Her voice was calm.

She didn't move.

She stayed rooted to the dead tree limb like it anchored her.

Eventually, they rose and turned back the way they came, retracing their steps.

As he walked toward the lake, she followed at a measured distance, head slightly bowed.

To anyone watching, she was the quiet girlfriend.

Tired.

Obedient.

But inside, her mind moved like clockwork—

noting his body language,

the weight of his silence,

the time of day.

She'd learned to track his storms like a seasoned weatherman.

Lauren walked behind him, her eyes trained on the ground.

A soft rattle stopped her mid-step.

She scanned the trail, alert.

Her father's voice echoed in her head:

"Always be on the lookout for rattlers, Little One. They'll get ya. You listen and watch. If you hear one near, always look at your feet. That way, you don't accidentally step on one."

She smiled at the memory of him.

A good man.

A gentle father.

He had never raised his voice.

Never lifted a hand to her.

His love had been simple.

Uncomplicated.

She got lost in the memory.

In the version of herself who had once felt safe.

Wanted.

Loved.

The mask stayed firmly in place.

Stefan led—because he always did.

The afternoon sun now hung higher in the sky as they returned from their hike.

Lauren's cheeks were flushed from the sun and exertion,

but a small smile played on her lips.

The hike had been—surprisingly—pleasant.

For a moment, she almost believed they were a normal couple.

She laughed quietly at the thought.

Normal.

Hand in hand, they collapsed into their loungers.

Stefan reached into the cooler between them, grabbed a bottle of water, and began to chug.

"You could've grabbed one for me," Lauren said half-heartedly, her voice light with faux annoyance.

In a blink—

his hand crashed into the side of her face.

Her sunglasses flew off, landing in the dirt.

The sting hit her instantly—like fire spreading across her cheek.

She sucked in a sharp breath, shrinking into herself.

Her hand pressed against her face as she slowly bent to retrieve the sunglasses.

The world tilted slightly.

Her vision blurred.

But she moved calmly. Deliberately.

She knew better than to react.

She slid the glasses back on, shielding the swelling tears behind tinted lenses.

Silence fell over them like a blanket.

After what felt like an eternity, Stefan reached over, resting his hand on her upper thigh.

He squeezed—hard.

"Would you like a bottle of water?" he asked, voice low and mocking.

She nodded.

He handed her the bottle, a smirk creeping into his voice.

"Are you happy now, Sarah?"

Her chest tightened.

The name sent a bolt of fear through her.

Sarah.

Their code name.

Used only when the line was crossed—

when the games turned real.

They hadn't used their hunting names in nearly a year.

Not since the last time.

Not since the last one.

Why now?

There was no time to dwell on the thought.

Not now.

Not with him watching.

"I wouldn't want to be anywhere else," she said, her voice honeyed.

She reached for his hand, squeezing gently.

Behind her sunglasses, her eyes fluttered shut.

Just play the part. Like always.

Stefan stood and pulled her up by the hand.

"I'm going to take a shower. Join me."

Inside, he guided her to the bathroom.

He kissed her cheek—the same one he'd struck just moments ago.

The skin burned under his lips.

He turned her to face the mirror and lifted her chin with two fingers, forcing her to look.

"You made me do that," he said, voice low and sickly sweet.

"You know what pisses me off."

Her reflection stared back at her.

The red mark was already deepening into a bruise.

Her face looked tired. Hollow.

"This is all on you," he whispered.

She said nothing.

She didn't need to.

The routine had played out countless times before.

The violence.

The guilt.

The sex.

He undressed her slowly.

Almost tenderly.

She closed her eyes and tried to remember the feeling of the morning sun on her face.

The sound of the lake.

The way the world felt when he wasn't watching.

But that was a different life.

A fantasy.

Peace, she reminded herself, wasn't meant for her.

3

The sunlight pierced through the slatted blinds, striking Lauren square in the face like a spotlight on a stage she never auditioned for.

She flinched, turning away from it, but the damage was done.

Her skull pulsed in protest, her body curled tight like a question mark.

Pain bloomed behind her eyes, dull at first—then sharp.

Vicious.

It layered itself over the deeper throb radiating from her cheekbone, bone-deep and angry.

She blinked one eye open, then the other—barely.

Her right eye refused to open all the way.

Swollen. Puffy. The color of storm-clouds at dusk.

A slow, deliberate turn of her head sent a crackle of tension down her neck. She winced and forced her gaze sideways.

Stefan was still asleep.

He lay on his back, one arm flung across his chest, the other tucked beneath his pillow.

His breaths came slow and even.

His lips were slightly parted.

A strand of blonde hair curled across his forehead, softening the lines of his face and making him look—unbearably—peaceful.

Almost innocent.

It made her stomach twist.

She shifted carefully, reaching for the nightstand.

Her fingers brushed against the orange bottle, plastic cool under her touch.

She unscrewed the cap with slow, practiced turns, each twist deliberate, each second a risk.

Four pills dropped into her palm. She threw them back dry, then reached for the half-empty water bottle and took a cautious sip.

She closed her eyes.

Not to sleep. Not to rest.

But to beg.

Please.

Let them work fast.

Let the pain dull before he wakes.

Last night came in flashes—

The heat of his breath on her skin.

The sting of his teeth.

The sudden blur as her head snapped sideways.

The belt.

Fast. Merciless. Over and over.

He'd lost control again.

But this time wasn't like the others.

This time felt... strategic.

He hadn't lashed out in a fit of rage.

There was no shouting. No slurred accusations.

No smashed bottles or shattered plates.

He'd been quiet.

Cold.

Measured.

Like a surgeon with a scalpel, not a man with a temper.

He wanted her to remember.

To feel it.

To know her place.

The assault itself was nothing new.

Pain had become part of the rhythm of her life—like background noise or static.

But this...

This was different.

He had broken two rules.

Rules they never spoke aloud.

Rules that had kept them careful, sharp, invisible.

Rules they followed like scripture.

Until last night.

Rule #3: Never use their play names outside the hunt.

And yet, he'd said it.

Low and intimate, like a lover's whisper.

"Sarah," he'd murmured.

Not during a kill.

Not mid-role-play.

Just there—in bed. In the dark.

Her blood had gone cold.

The name wasn't supposed to cross over.

Not into this version of them.

It belonged to the masks.

To the shadows.

To the people they pretended to be.

Not the ones they truly were.

The line between fantasy and reality had always been clear.

Brutal, but clean.

During the hunt, she was Sarah Warren—Zach Warren's wife.

That was their cover story.

But that identity didn't fit here.

Not in the quiet moments.

Not in the truth she lived with.

In reality, she was Lauren Collins.

Stefan Warren's girlfriend.

There was no ring. No ceremony.

Just another role she played.

Now... it was smudged.

And that smudge terrified her.

Rule 6: Never keep trophies.

She'd watched—silent, breath shallow—as he slipped Bill's watch off his limp wrist.

The dead man's arm had flopped like a puppet's, his skin still faintly warm.

Stefan hadn't flinched.

Hadn't looked at her.

Just pocketed the silver band and walked away like it meant nothing.

Later, she'd seen him pry open the hidden floor compartment.

Felt her heart stutter as he knelt, placed the watch inside, and sealed it shut.

That terrified her more than the bruises.

More than the cracked ribs or the thunderclap of his hand across her face.

Because broken rules meant Stefan was unraveling.

And unraveling meant exposure.

Recklessness.

Patterns.

Mistakes.

And mistakes meant prison.

Their rules weren't about morality.

They were about survival.

About staying invisible.

Erasing every footprint, every trace.

It had never been about trust—she never trusted Stefan. Not really.

But she had learned how to anticipate him.

For a while, he'd been predictable.

Clean.

Contained.

Now... he was unraveling.

And cracks let everything spill out.

She knew what that meant.

She'd have to leave soon.

But leaving wasn't simple.

It wasn't impulse.

It was timing.

And timing was everything.

With every ounce of willpower, Lauren pushed herself upright.

She rolled onto her side first, then braced her elbows beneath her.

Her body screamed in protest—

Muscles aflame, her lower back pulsing with ache, the insides of her thighs rubbed raw.

The aftermath was always worse than the act itself.

What he took from her lingered longer than the pain.

She moved toward the bathroom, each step a silent negotiation with her own body.

Like glass trying not to crack.

Inside, she gripped the edge of the tiny sink and lifted her gaze.

The mirror didn't lie.

The swelling around her eye was bad—but not the worst she'd seen.

A bruise had begun its cruel bloom beneath the socket, shifting from shadowed blue to deep violet.

Always the right eye.

Always his favorite side.

Her lower lip was caked with dried blood, a dark line trailing from the split at the corner of her mouth.

Her arms—freckled with finger-shaped bruises.

Grips hard enough to leave his ownership behind.

Her legs bore the unmistakable marks of the belt.

Parallel lines. Red. Angry.

Familiar.

She winced at the memory.

The sound of the belt sliding free—*whip-whip-whip* through the loops.

A prelude.

A promise.

He always folded it in half.

Held the two ends together. Made it snap.

That was his warning:

She was going to pay.

For what, he never said.

He didn't have to.

And then there was the bite.

The one on her collarbone.

It had broken skin.

She could still feel the heat of it—

Not just the pain.

The possession.

She felt bile rise in her throat.

"You are not a victim," she told herself.

"You're a survivor. You're stronger than him. Smarter. Patient."

Grabbing her shower caddy, she tossed in her toiletries, an oversized towel, a change of clothes, her phone, and earbuds.

She slung on her sunglasses despite the dim light — her armor now — and crept across the RV with the precision of someone who'd learned how to walk through fire without making a sound.

She prayed the door wouldn't squeak.

It didn't.

Outside, she paused.

The lake shimmered in the early light like it didn't know — or didn't care — what happened under the cover of night.

The water was glassy.

Unmarred.

Beautiful.

She inhaled slowly.

Deeply.

The tall grass looked like waves in an ocean, blowing in the wind.

He may have ruined yesterday, she thought,

but I won't let him take today.

Step by step, she moved across the gravel path toward the public bathroom, the silence broken only by her feet crunching lightly against the earth.

She walked into the dark shower building.

Her eyes adjusted to the windowless room.

Flicking on the switch, the fluorescent lights flickered to life with a groan.

She reached for the shower door, opened it, and turned the handle, letting the pipes shudder and creak until water finally sputtered out.

She needed it to be hot — scalding.

She needed the kind of shower that could wash away more than just sweat and blood.

As she undressed, she caught sight of herself in the cracked mirror above the sinks.

The bite mark stared back at her, red and raw.

She touched it, wincing.

A brand.

A fucking brand.

She stepped into the stall and let the water run over her, but it was lukewarm at best.

Her shoulders slumped.

Of course.

Nothing ever worked the way she needed it to.

Still, she closed her eyes and stood there beneath the stream, letting the water trace the lines of her body like a pen sketching a map of her pain.

Each droplet found a bruise, a welt, a memory.

And then, without warning, the past came rushing in.

She remembered being here before — this town, this lake, this stretch of sky — when things were different.

Her father had adored her.

Quiet strength. Gentle hands. He called her *Pumpkin* and lifted her high like she weighed nothing.

Her mother was... unpredictable.

One day, singing barefoot in the kitchen.

The next, unreachable.

Lauren had learned to watch. To listen.

To sense the pressure before the swing.

Granddaddy used to say her mama wasn't sick—just not well.

Even as a little girl, Lauren understood that word—*well*—was a fragile thing.

Something hoped for.

Something never quite within reach.

That's why she studied people.

Why she memorized patterns.

Why she got her psychology degree.

Because somewhere deep down, she wanted to understand how a person could break from the inside out—

and what it might take to stop it.

She often wondered what life might have been like if the accident hadn't happened.

If her father had lived.

If her mother had gotten help.

She blinked, dragging herself back to the present.

The memories clung, heavy and warm, like steam on the walls.

She willed them away.

The weight of what she'd lost was too much to carry today.

She washed quickly but thoroughly, careful not to scrub the bruises too hard.

No use drawing attention at the next gas station—or worse, if they ran into someone who remembered her face.

She dressed in silence: black leggings, a black tank top, and her favorite Reputation Tour T-shirt.

As she tugged it down over her hips, a small grin tugged at her lips.

Of all the versions of herself she wore, this one felt the most honest.

"I am in my Reputation era," she said aloud, chuckling at the irony.

She popped in her earbuds and opened the playlist labeled *TayTay*.

The first song to come on was *Lover*.

Her eyes went wide.

"Oh, hell no."

She scrolled furiously and hit play on *Look What You Made Me Do*.

As the sinister beat kicked in, she smirked.

Her bruised face reflected back at her in the mirror, partially hidden by her sunglasses.

She lip-synced along, pulling her towel over her shoulder like a cape.

Lauren Collins.

Survivor.

Performer.

No one saw the cracks behind the sunglasses.

And that was the point.

She stepped out into the sunlight and strutted back toward the RV, every beat in her earbuds syncing with her pulse.

She danced a little as she walked—small steps, careful of the soreness.

The lake sparkled in front of her like it was proud of her.

Like it knew who she really was.

She eased down into the camp chair and stared at the water, bobbing her head to the rhythm of her playlist.

This—this was her happy place.

The lake.

The water.

The quiet before she made her next move.

Across the lake, barely visible through the trees, a man sat in a folding chair.

Still.

Unmoving.

Watching.

Lauren didn't see him.

But he saw her.

And something shifted.

She felt it before she heard anything—if there was anything to hear at all.

Just a change in the air.

A static charge.

Her body went rigid, not from noise, but from instinct.

A tightening in her chest.

A flutter in her gut.

Her instincts were usually right.

They always had been.

But this was new.

Not fear.

Not Stefan.

Something else.

She sat still, listening to her body—not sure what it was trying to say.

A second ripple followed. This one, she knew by heart. The kind that crawled under your skin before footsteps even landed.

Footsteps creaked down the camper steps. Stefan's presence pressed against her back like a shadow taking form. She didn't flinch, but every nerve in her body went on alert.

His fingers settled on her shoulders—too gently. The same hands that hurt her. Now pretending tenderness.

Tension rolled off him in waves, infecting the space around him like smoke in a closed room. Even when he hadn't touched her yet, her body remembered. Muscles clenched. Shoulders braced. Breath caught.

He didn't have to speak. He didn't even have to look at her.

His presence alone was enough to unravel her calm — or at least threaten to.

But today, she held it together. Because she had to. Because timing was everything.

Behind her sunglasses, her eyes rolled so hard they almost got stuck.

She forced her body to relax. She had learned how to become soft when she wanted to scream.

Stefan's voice floated toward her, sugar-laced and careful. "How are you feeling?"

She exhaled slowly, grateful — for now — that this was the version of Stefan she'd gotten today:

Sweet. Doting. The good one.

The one who brought her coffee with a smile.

The one who called her beautiful instead of broken.

He was making his move while she made hers.

She smiled softly, pretending. "I'm good. Just enjoying the view. Listening to music."

This was the careful version of Stefan — syrupy-sweet, but simmering underneath.

She knew that smile. She knew what it cost to keep it in place.

Not every piece had to move first.

Some stayed still.

Close to the danger.

Waiting for their moment.

She removed her earbuds and tucked them into her bathroom bag.

He grimaced slightly. "Taylor Swift again, I'm assuming?"

"You know it," she replied with a giggle.

He smirked.

"What ERA are you in today?"

There was a beat.

Just long enough to panic.

But Lauren was quick.

Always had been.

"Lover," she said with a wink.

Stefan's smile widened like a kid handed candy.

Lover meant they were in a good place.

Lover meant hearts and stars and no bruises.

He liked Lover.

Because in his mind, that meant she liked it rough.

That she wanted it.

Lauren swallowed her disgust.

"Actually..." she said sweetly, "I wanted to ask you something."

Stefan looked pleased.

"You know I'd do anything for you."

Lauren took a breath and adjusted her voice to match his tone — low, warm, trusting.

"My Granddaddy is only about forty-five minutes away... and our account is getting kind of low. If we stopped by, I'm sure he'd release more from the trust. We could fill the tank, stock up—"

He stiffened.

The silence hung thick between them.

Then, with a forced smile, Stefan stood.

"Sure. That sounds like a great idea. Give him a call and see if he's around."

Lauren sprang to her feet — the sudden motion reminding her of every place she ached.

She threw her arms around him anyway, biting her cheek to keep from crying out.

"Thank you, thank you, thank you!" she said, masking pain with gratitude.

He grabbed her and hugged her tighter than necessary, lips against her ear.

"We're not staying long," he whispered, voice low and cold.

"And when I say it's time to leave, we leave. Got it?"

Lauren nodded quickly. "Absolutely."

She turned, eager to escape—

but Stefan grabbed her wrist and yanked her back into one of his too-long kisses.

She fought the instinct to recoil.

When he finally released her, she climbed into the RV and collapsed onto the bed.

Her hands shook as she reached for the bottle of ibuprofen.

She dry-swallowed four more pills and lay still, staring at the ceiling until the tremors in her chest slowed.

Then she rolled to her side and picked up her phone.

There was only one person who mattered anymore.

One person who still saw her.

She dialed.

"Granddaddy?"

Her voice cracked.

"Hey, Pumpkin Pie," he answered.

And for a moment,

Lauren felt something like safety.

4

Lauren's stomach fluttered as the city limits sign for Amarillo, Texas came into view.

She pressed her forehead to the warm truck window, her breath fogging the glass.

The horizon stretched endlessly along either side of the highway — flat, dry, and cloaked in a thin brown haze of dust.

Amarillo wasn't exactly scenic — in truth, it was plain ugly, with few trees and a monotony that could lull anyone into a coma.

But to Lauren, there was a certain beauty in its brutal honesty.

It didn't pretend to be more than it was.

The open sky made up for the landscape.

You could see for miles — and the sunrises and sunsets painted the whole damn world in gold and fire.

No other place had ever made her feel so exposed
and so nostalgic
at the same time.

As they cruised down I-40, her nerves began to tangle in her chest like barbed wire.

It had been almost a year since she'd last seen her Granddaddy.

She missed him.

Missed the safety of his presence.

The gruff affection in his voice.

The way he could make her feel like a little girl again with just a hug and a "Pumpkin Pie."

But this visit wasn't just for nostalgia.

But it came with a cost: the mask.

She'd have to hide the swelling in her cheek and the thin purple line beneath her right eye —

a gift from Stefan after one of his more volatile episodes two nights before.

Granddaddy would notice.

He always noticed.

She wasn't afraid he'd ask questions —

she was afraid he'd see the answers before she gave them.

She'd been rehearsing her excuse for days.

Slammed right into the cooler. Damn camper steps. Clumsy me.

Her tone had to be light, but not dismissive.

Her eyes had to convey embarrassment, not fear.

The mask had to fit perfectly.

Because if it slipped — even for a second —

Granddaddy would know.

And if he knew...

this visit could get complicated fast.

He deserved more than a lie.

But lies were all she had.

To keep him safe.

To keep herself safe.

Her thoughts drifted as the truck rolled into her old neighborhood — a well-manicured pocket of Amarillo that had no business being as green as it was.

Her Granddaddy's house stood proud on the corner.

The same one she'd grown up in.

It looked untouched by time.

Like even grief had been afraid to settle in too long.

The fifth wheel camper, dusty and battered, looked completely out of place parked on the curb in front of the pristine homes.

Stefan's fingers tapped the steering wheel as he pulled to a stop, then he reached over and took Lauren's hand.

He kissed it — not a loving gesture,

but a warning.

His eyes never left the road.

"We're here long enough for him to move the money. That's it," he muttered.

"Then we're gone. Got it?"

Lauren turned toward him, offering a sunny smile that didn't quite reach her eyes.

"Absolutely."

She jumped out of the truck before he could say anything else and sprinted toward the house, her shoes thudding softly against the concrete.

Before her hand even reached the door, it swung open —

and there he was.

LeRoy Collins.

Sixty-five years old and still standing tall, though the silver in his beard had grown thicker.

He stepped out onto the porch and swept her into a strong hug.

Lauren winced inside from the aches, but she never let it show on the outside.

"There's my Pumpkin Pie," he murmured, holding her like he never wanted to let go.

He pulled back just enough to study her face, and his jaw clenched when his eyes found the bruise.

"WHAT THE—"

"Oh, Granddaddy," Lauren laughed, brushing him off and turning slightly to obscure the worst of the damage.

"I fell. Walking down the steps out of the camper. Slammed right into the side of the cooler. You know how clumsy I am."

He didn't buy it.

She knew it,

and he knew she knew it.

Stefan joined them a moment later, smiling like a wolf in Sunday best.

"Hi, Sir. I'm Stefan Warren. It's so nice to meet you."

LeRoy's grip tightened around Lauren's hand before he reluctantly extended his own to Stefan.

"LeRoy Collins." He said short and to the point. "Sure is good to see my Pumpkin Pie."

He gave Lauren a warning glance — one that said *We're talking about this later*.

Lauren squeezed his hand in return — hard.

Not now, her eyes begged. *Please.*

LeRoy dropped it.

For now.

"Come in. Jackie's got lunch ready," he said, gesturing toward the door.

Stefan swept past them like he owned the place.

"Thank God! I'm starving," he said, already halfway to the kitchen.

LeRoy rolled his eyes and gave Lauren a sidelong glance.

"We'll be discussing this."

"Yes, Granddaddy," she murmured, lowering her head as she stepped inside.

The kitchen was immaculate —

a warm, welcoming place that smelled like home.

Steak, potatoes, fresh rolls,

and years of unspoken love.

Jackie, who had worked for LeRoy since Lauren was a teenager, wiped her hands on a towel as she came around the island to greet her.

"Hi, Jackie," Lauren said, pulling her into a hug.

"Well, look at you," Jackie replied, her voice caught somewhere between affection and alarm.

She pulled back, eyes narrowing at Lauren's face, the color draining from her own.

Her lips parted to ask a question, but Lauren quickly shook her head — a silent plea: don't.

Jackie's eyes flicked toward Stefan, who was already piling food onto his plate like a starving man.

Her expression twisted with quiet disdain.

Lauren gave her a grateful pat on the arm.

"Thank you, Jackie. You're amazing."

"Let's eat," LeRoy said, placing a guiding hand on Lauren's back as he led her to the table.

As they ate, Lauren regaled her grandfather with carefully curated stories about their travels — the tourist stops, the roadside diners, the quirky strangers.

She never mentioned the shadows in between.

Never mentioned the hunts.

This was how Lauren had learned to live —

with eyes on her. Always watching.

LeRoy nodded politely as Stefan chimed in now and then,

his charm turned up just enough to seem harmless.

But LeRoy knew better.

He watched every interaction.

Every subtle glance.

Every flinch Lauren tried to hide.

His granddaughter had always been complex —

guarded and clever. A survivor.

And now he saw something else in her:

fear disguised as devotion.

After lunch, they moved into the living room.

Lauren curled up in the corner of the couch, legs tucked beneath her, as Stefan and LeRoy launched into a discussion about baseball.

She smiled and nodded when appropriate, but she didn't care about the Texas Rangers or the Yankees.

"I'm dying for a hot shower," she said, suddenly standing. "Grand-daddy, you mind if I—?"

LeRoy blinked at her.

"Since when do you ask if you can take a shower? Go on."

Lauren noticed the way Stefan tensed.

She walked over and whispered, "Is it okay?"

His fingers closed around hers — a firm but silent yes.

She leaned down, kissed him —

a performance of a lifetime —

then turned to her grandfather and hugged him tight.

"Love you bunches."

"I love you too, Pumpkin," LeRoy said softly, brushing a hand over her hair.

The game carried on in the background while the silence between the two men thickened.

Stefan eventually excused himself and climbed the stairs.

He found Lauren asleep on the bed, wrapped in a towel, her damp hair fanned across the pillow like silk.

He stared at her —

at the bruises that had bloomed across her cheek and the soft rise and fall of her chest.

His thoughts drifted back
to the first time he saw her.
Before she was his.
Before she understood what she was meant for.
It was a brutal, sweltering afternoon near Lake Mead.
The sun sat heavy in the sky, unrelenting and merciless, baking the cracked earth beneath his boots.

The lake glinted in the distance like a shard of glass — still and silent —

an open invitation to predators like him.
As if she was placed there as a gift.
She was alone, sitting on a flat rock at the water's edge,
a blur of sun-kissed skin and tousled brown hair.

Her backpack lay beside her, unzipped, contents spilling lazily into the dust.

At one point, she sat up and dug through it, rifling with vague purpose —

as if checking for something, then thinking better of it.
A small pink canister rolled deeper into the shadows, unseen.
She didn't notice.
She didn't seem to care.

Her arms were bare, shoulders already pink from too long in the sun, but she didn't move to cover herself.

She just stared out at the lake,
like she was watching a memory
or listening to ghosts.
He crouched in the brush, studying her.
Something about her posture struck him —
not fearful, not careless.
Just... empty.
As if she was waiting for something to happen.
Or someone.

She lay back eventually, curling onto her side like a child, and let the heat pull her under.

She fell asleep right there, on the hot rock,

as if she trusted the world to leave her untouched.

That trust made her his.

He waited, letting her cook under the sun just long enough.

Let her skin turn red, raw, tender.

When he finally moved, it was with the precision of a hunter.

No noise.

No hesitation.

But as he stepped closer, she stirred —

not startled,

just aware.

There was a connection.

She felt him before he said anything.

She opened her eyes.

And instead of flinching or screaming, she looked up at him —

squinting through the sun's glare.

Calm.

Curious.

He liked that.

Took it as a sign.

"Hey," she said, voice dry and hoarse.

"Do you have water?"

He blinked, thrown off.

Most people would have panicked.

She sounded like someone asking for directions.

He nodded slowly and reached into his pack, pulling out a bottle.

She took it and drank greedily, wiping her mouth with the back of her hand.

Her lips were cracked, her skin flushed red from the burn.

He offered his hand.

She didn't even ask his name.

She just said,

"Do you have shade?"

And he led her to the camper.

No resistance.

No questions.

39

Just a quiet obedience that wasn't submission —
it was something else.
Something stranger.
She walked beside him like they'd done it before,
like this was part of some unspoken agreement neither of them
needed to explain.
Inside the camper, he gave her a damp cloth, some ointment, and
watched her tend to her burns with slow, deliberate movements.
She didn't thank him.
Didn't speak.
She just looked around, took in the cramped space, and sat calmly on
the edge of the couch.
He was used to control.
Used to dragging them.
Tricking them.
Breaking them.
But this —
this was something new.
She was burned
and silent
and still.
And he was the one growing restless.
He stood over her, expecting the usual cues —
nervous glances, clenched fists, signs of fear.
But there was none of it.
She simply sat there,
skin blazing red
and eyes ice cold.
He reached out, brushing his fingers along her shoulder.
She didn't flinch.
She stood up with confidence.
And then the kiss.
Violent.
Confusing.
Electrifying.

She was different.

Dangerous in a way that mirrored him.

And that scared him more than he cared to admit.

He stood over her, looming, and without hesitation, struck her across the face — hard.

The sound cracked through the small space like a whip.

Her head snapped sideways, her body jerked,

but she didn't cry out.

But she hadn't reacted like the others.

No screams.

No begging.

Just that quiet whisper:

"I'm not going to fight you."

It stopped him cold.

He stared at her, stunned.

Not because of what she'd said,

but how she said it —

calm,

resigned,

unwavering.

Her eyes didn't blink.

Didn't flinch.

She looked at him like she knew him.

Like she'd seen monsters before

and decided they didn't scare her anymore.

For a moment, he forgot how to breathe.

He had always needed the fear —

the begging, the terror, the desperate scrambling.

That's what made it worth it.

That's what gave him power.

But she wasn't playing the game.

And that pissed him off.

He lunged at her, grabbing her roughly by the arm.

Her body rocked from the force,

but she remained still.

Unmoving.

She held her face,

the skin already tender and hot,

and stared at him like a statue.

Solid.

Untouchable.

He should have hurt her right then.

Should have broken her for her defiance.

But instead...

he froze.

Something about her unnerved him.

Excited him.

He leaned in, nose to nose with her, breathing hard —

trying to understand what the hell he was feeling.

She was studying him, he could tell.

Taking him in with those unblinking eyes

like she was dissecting him from the inside out.

And then, like a storm breaking over glass,

she reached up, grabbed his face — hard — and kissed him.

It wasn't soft.

It wasn't romantic.

It was violent.

Possessive.

Her teeth grazed his lip as her mouth collided with his,

and he responded instinctively.

Hungrily.

For a moment,

he was completely lost in it.

In her.

Then his mind snapped back.

What the fuck do you think you're doing?

He pulled back and slapped her again,

this time with open rage.

Her head snapped to the side. Sunburned skin bloomed with his rage.

She didn't cry.

She didn't run.

That only made his erection pulse harder.

He growled, grabbing her by the waist and hoisting her over his shoulder

like she was nothing but a sack of meat.

"I'm in charge, you fucking bitch," he spat, the words low and guttural.

"I'm going to make you scream."

He laughed — a sick, excited sound — and tossed her onto the bed.

She didn't flinch. Didn't speak.

And that silence... that maddening, eerie silence made him want to tear the walls apart.

He would make her scream.

He had to.

A knock at the door snapped him out of the memory.

His arousal still lingered—throbbing, unwelcome.

"Dinner will be ready in thirty minutes," Jackie called through the wood.

Stefan clenched his fists.

Rage surged like bile.

Fucking Jackie.

He shoved Lauren roughly.

"Get up. Dinner in thirty."

He stormed into the bathroom, gripping the edge of the sink.

His reflection stared back—flushed, furious.

He splashed cold water on his face, breathing heavily.

"Get it together, man," he muttered.

He'd be good.

Be charming.

Be the loving boyfriend.

Just long enough to get the money and get the fuck out of here.

Then they'd disappear again.

Just like always.

5

The knock came like a warning shot—sharp, sudden.

Jackie's interruption came like she'd just jammed the pin back into a grenade seconds before it could explode.

Lauren barely registered Jackie's words, and relief crashed over her like cold water.

Her limbs, clenched tight with tension, began to tingle as adrenaline leaked away.

Her hands went numb, then burned—the kind of burn that came after surviving something that hadn't happened... only because it was interrupted.

Stefan swung his legs off the bed and stood.

The mattress shifted again as his weight left it.

The floor rattled with protest beneath his footsteps—sharp, uneven, full of fury.

With each step he took away from her, Lauren allowed herself to exhale—slow and shallow—releasing her muscles inch by inch, like she was peeling herself out of a straightjacket.

She waited, eyes still shut, counting each beat of distance.

One.

Two.

Three.

Then the bathroom door shut behind him.

Only then did she move—swift and silent.

She slipped out of bed, every bruise protesting, and gathered her clothes with practiced precision. Shirt. Leggings. Socks. No hesitation. No wasted motion.

Then she slipped out the bedroom door, down the stairs — every movement fluid, purposeful, like muscle memory etched into her bones.

Her heart thundered in her chest, wild and caged, pounding like it might break free.

No stumble. No pause. Her body knew the rhythm of escape like it knew how to breathe.

At the bottom of the staircase, she stopped.

She could still hear the low hum of the bathroom fan upstairs. Water running faintly through the old pipes.

Her pulse roared in her ears. Her face remained a mask.

She inhaled slowly, drawing breath down into the deepest part of her lungs.

Smoothed her shirt.

Tucked a stray strand of hair behind her ear.

Shifting her mask back into place.

Sweet, obedient granddaughter.

Polite. Composed.

Not the girl upstairs, curled beneath a monster.

Not the girl who tallied bruises like calendar marks.

This was the version she wore in daylight.

The one who laughed at dinner.

The one who played along.

And she'd keep wearing it—

Until she didn't have to anymore.

Her Granddaddy sat in his recliner, a black-and-white Western flickering across the screen. The crackle of static, the distant sound of horses, gunfire echoing in grainy nostalgia — it offered a strange sort of comfort. Something real. Something untouched.

She walked over, leaned down, and kissed the top of his head.

"Hi, Granddaddy," she said softly.

LeRoy looked up, his eyes warm — but edged with something else. Concern. Doubt. A quiet storm building beneath the surface. He saw more than she wanted him to.

"Did you have a good nap?" he asked, voice gentle.

"I did," Lauren replied, giving him a practiced smile. The one she wore when pretending everything was fine.

"I'm sorry I fell asleep. I really wanted to spend more time with you before we go."

He studied her carefully, his brows knitting together. She recognized that look — the one that meant he wasn't buying it. He was weighing something, balancing love, concern, and restraint... against suspicion.

She shifted tactics. "Did the Rangers win?"

LeRoy didn't blink. He squinted at her instead, his eyes flicking briefly to the bruise on her right eye.

"Lauren, that's not gonna work with me today."

His voice was low and even — but it cut straight through her act like a blade.

She swallowed. Knew what was coming. Tried again anyway.

"Granddaddy, I know what you're thinking—"

"Oh yeah?" he interrupted, eyes sharpening. "And what exactly am I thinking?"

She pressed her lips together, chewing gently on the bottom one. An old tell. One he'd picked up on before she even knew what lying felt like. She could deceive the world — but not him.

He watched her carefully, silently. The way she drew her shoulders back. Her eyes flicked sideways, then back to his — a performer hitting her mark. She was putting on a show.

That's what scared him the most.

She'd always been like this. Even as a kid, she was sharper than the rest—studying people instead of playing with them. He used to joke she was born with a chessboard in her brain — always calculating, always watching.

Always seeing the move before it happened.

But this version — soft-spoken, careful, composed — wasn't the Lauren he'd raised.

She looked... contained. Like she was wearing a version of herself instead of being her.

You can lie to the world, Pumpkin Pie, he thought. But not to me.

He thought of the folder again. That one she used to keep hidden on her laptop. News clippings. Photos. Patterns. Unsolved cases she studied late into the night. He'd asked her once why she cared so much.

"Because someone has to," she'd said.

He never forgot that. And now, sitting across from her, he couldn't shake the feeling that she was slipping into the same kind of story she used to collect. A headline waiting to happen.

He wanted to grab her, shake the truth out of her. But she was an adult now. And she was good at this. Too good.

A beat passed. Then she drew in a slow breath — the kind she took before walking into rooms where danger waited behind smiles.

Then she gave her monologue. The one she'd rehearsed, edited, perfected. The one with just enough truth to make the lies feel real.

"You're thinking exactly what you should be thinking. And I love you for it. You've always looked out for me. And I am okay. I promise. I have a plan. I'm in control. I just..." She softened her voice, squeezed his hand. "I just need a little more of my trust fund. Enough to keep us going for a bit. Just until things line up."

She locked eyes with him — steady, unflinching — pouring sincerity into every syllable. Just enough light to disguise the shadows.

He looked back at her, saying nothing. But inside, a slow burn had started.

If she was this polished, this precise, he thought, then something was very, very wrong. He didn't believe her. Not really. But he didn't push. Not yet.

Stefan appeared in the doorway, cutting through the moment like a blade. "What'd I miss?" Stefan asked, his eyes fixed on Lauren like a predator scenting a shift in the wind.

Lauren didn't flinch. She turned toward him, placid smile still in place. If he'd heard what she said—really heard it—there would be no smile. Only fury. In Stefan's world, their money was entitlement. Her independence wasn't freedom—it was betrayal. But he hadn't heard. Not fully. She saw it in his eyes—curiosity, not rage. A close call.

LeRoy didn't miss it either. He didn't like how quiet she went when that bastard was near.

He shifted the narrative with seamless ease, his voice casual. "Lauren was just telling me about your trip. Sounds like a real adventure."

Lauren turned to him, grateful, and picked up the thread. "It's been amazing, Granddaddy. Seeing the country, living on the road—it's hard to put into words."

Jackie stepped into the room, kindness etched into every line of her face. "Dinner's ready," she announced. "Do y'all need anything else tonight?"

LeRoy shook his head, his tone edged with appreciation. "No, thank you, Jackie. We're all set. See you in the morning."

Jackie turned to Lauren, her gaze lingering with quiet care. "Will I see you tomorrow, or will you be gone before I get in?"

Stefan answered for her. "We'll be leaving before sunrise."

Lauren didn't look at him, but LeRoy did. His face fell, the disappointment unguarded. "I'd sure love to have you both longer," he said, the words slower, heavier.

Then he caught Stefan's glance toward Lauren—sharp, controlling, a silent correction. LeRoy's mouth tightened. Another one of his damned signals—another silent leash. He adjusted course, swallowing the fire rising in his chest. "But I understand. More adventure awaits," he said, quieter now.

Son of a bitch.

You think I don't see it?

You think I don't notice the way she flinches when you move too fast?

He cleared his throat. "Where to next?"

Lauren smiled again, vague and light. "Oh, you know... wherever the road takes us."

Another lie.

Don't feed me that, Pumpkin Pie.

You never left anything to chance.

You were born with a plan in your pocket.

He knew his granddaughter.

She didn't drift.

She calculated. She adapted.

The only reason she wouldn't have a plan now was if she was trapped in something she couldn't steer.

Dinner was a quiet affair.

Small talk.

Laughter that didn't reach eyes.

Stefan did most of the talking—long-winded stories about the road, their campsite disasters, the truck's "quirks," the time he fixed a broken water line "with nothing but duct tape and brilliance."

Every anecdote looped back to him.

His adventures.

His resourcefulness.

His sacrifices.

Lauren smiled where she had to.

LeRoy let him talk, nodding occasionally, but saying little.

He was too busy studying. Watching.

Every flick of Stefan's hand. Every glance at Lauren that came with too much edge.

Every time she laughed just a second too late, like she had to remember her cue.

Then Stefan pivoted.

"You know, this lifestyle's not cheap," he said, glancing at LeRoy over his glass. "We've been managing fine, but the trust fund's been a life-saver. Just a little more would really help us get through the next leg."

And there it was.

LeRoy's fork trembled in his tightening grip.

You're sitting at my table, eating my food, smiling at my family—and now you're coming for her money?

You think I'm going to fund you hurting my Pumpkin Pie?

You think I can't see you for what you are?

It took everything he had not to explode.

Not to leap across the table and tear the bastard limb from limb.

Lauren looked at him.

Just for a second.

A glance. Silent. Heavy.

Her eyes met his—calm, but edged with a plea. *Not yet.*

She told him to stop without saying a word.

And he did.

They both saw it.

And they both knew the cost of pretending not to.

The ghost of real conversation hovered between them like smoke—thick, heavy, waiting.

Instead, LeRoy reached for his glass of water, lifting it slowly to his lips, buying himself a moment.

"Hmm," he said, noncommittal. "Didn't realize you were strapped already."

His voice was calm. But his heart was a war drum.

After dinner, they migrated to the living room, but not before LeRoy insisted on helping clear the table. He lingered near the sink, stacking plates, his voice soft with something close to regret.

"You know, we never really got to celebrate your graduation," he said, rinsing a dish. "You met Stefan, and next thing I knew, you were off seeing the world."

Lauren smiled as she wiped the counter. "I know, Granddaddy. But this is a once-in-a-lifetime opportunity. A little adventure before I settle down and open my own practice."

LeRoy's expression softened as he dried his hands on a dish towel.

"I always meant to tell you how much I loved that paper you wrote on the serial kill—"

Lauren stepped in, quick and quiet. "Granddaddy—"

Her voice was soft, but the warning in it was clear.

At that moment, Alexa chimed from the corner of the kitchen, her voice almost too cheerful:

"Your local evening news will begin shortly."

The words hit the room like a spark in dry brush.

Lauren stiffened. Just slightly.

Not enough for Stefan to notice.

But LeRoy did.

She kept wiping the counter, her movements slower now—measured.

LeRoy dried his hands, watching her from the corner of his eye.

She was bracing for something.

And LeRoy was, too.

Stefan, seated at the island, glanced up, then back down at his phone—unmoved. Oblivious.

He hadn't caught the full sentence.

But Lauren had seen the flicker in LeRoy's eyes—the instant he realized why she'd stopped him.

He understood.

Across the kitchen, Stefan didn't help. Didn't offer.

He wasn't there to mingle.

He was there to monitor Lauren —

to police her tone,

to make sure she didn't say too much.

Lauren flashed her brightest smile and raised her voice just enough to carry.

"All done here! Need anything else cleaned up?"

Stefan barely responded. But she could feel him listening now, not just hearing.

She'd dodged a bullet. This time.

Later, in the living room, the news caught their attention.

The words from the television sucked the breath from Lauren's lungs.

She sank into the couch, her hands clasped so tightly her knuckles turned white.

On the screen: Bill and Judy's truck.

Crime scene tape fluttered in the wind like yellow caution against memory.

Stefan turned to face the screen, and his grin bloomed — slow and dark, like a sinister flower.

She felt sick.

"Two deceased individuals... found outside of Fritch... homicide..."

LeRoy's voice cut through the rising tension. "Jesus."

Lauren couldn't move. Her breaths came shallow. Her heart thundered like it was trying to punch its way out.

LeRoy turned up the volume.

The report continued, but she didn't hear anything past *homicide*.

This was different. She had never seen the aftermath of their hunts play out on the news before.

This wasn't whispered recollection or a cold trail in the rearview.

This was real.

Public.

Loud.

She couldn't stop watching Stefan.

Couldn't look away from the way his eyes lit up—like a child on Christmas morning.

She wondered if anyone else could see it.

But she knew better than to ask.

She always knew better.

She was learning to keep track of everything now. Every reaction. Every inconsistency. Every tell.

She wanted to vomit.

Stefan broke the silence with a smooth, calculated tone. "Well, it's been a wonderful visit. We should get to bed. Early morning and all."

He reached for her hand, and like a puppet, she gave it to him.

Her body moved automatically.

Her mind? Shut down. Detached. Protecting her.

LeRoy stood. "I understand," he said softly.

He crossed the room and pulled her into a hug.

Lauren held on, tight. Desperate.

Trying to say everything she couldn't voice in that single, aching squeeze.

Help me. I love you. Don't forget me.

She wanted to reach for his hand like she used to as a child — thumb tucked beneath his weathered palm, safe and certain.

He had always been her shelter in the storm.

But that was a different girl. A different life.

"I'll get that transfer done in the morning," LeRoy said quietly against her hair.

He felt her exhale — a shiver, not a breath.

And then Stefan's hand clamped down on her upper arm.

Firm. Possessive. Controlling.

"We really should get to bed, babe," he said, all syrup and threat.

LeRoy froze.

Did that son of a bitch just tell her when to go to bed? In my house?

He kissed her forehead gently, fighting the urge to knock Stefan through the damn wall.

"I love you, Pumpkin Pie," he whispered.

Lauren looked up at him.

Her mask cracked — just for a second.

A tremble at the corner of her mouth. A flicker in her eyes.

He saw the real her.

The girl who used to sit across from him at the chessboard, eyebrows drawn, lips pressed tight in concentration.

The girl who always knew the right move — until life changed the game.

And just like that, it was gone. Mask back in place.

"I love you, Granddaddy!" she said brightly, kissing his cheek.

God, baby girl... what are you really hiding?

Stefan guided her from the room with a hand that felt more like a

53

leash. He didn't drag her. Didn't shove. But LeRoy saw it for what it was. Control, dressed up as affection.

She didn't look back.

He watched them ascend the stairs, hand in hand. To anyone else, they looked like a normal couple. But LeRoy knew better.

He knew his Pumpkin Pie. She was smart. Independent. Stubborn as sin. She didn't take orders. She didn't flinch.

Until now.

She was scared—he saw it, even behind the smile. That man was hurting her.

He didn't need guesses or gut feelings—he had proof. The bruise on her cheek. The cut by her eye. The way she held herself like every breath came with pain.

And when he hugged her... He felt it. The stiffness. The weight. The unspoken scream beneath her skin.

It took everything in him not to follow them. To rip Stefan limb from limb and carry Lauren out himself.

But she'd asked him not to. Not with words— but with that glance. That impossible, bone-deep glance.

She told him to trust her.

To believe she had a plan.

To let her see it through.

And God help him, he did.

But he wasn't helpless.

He still had control of the trust fund.

And that gave him control of one thing—access.

If he gave too much at once, she could disappear.

But if he gave only what was needed... little by little... she'd have to keep coming back.

She'd have to stay connected.

Stay within reach.

It was the only way he knew to keep her close without driving her away.

Because if he pushed too hard—if he stormed in like the hero—he might lose her forever.

And LeRoy had already lost too much.

He buried his son.

Buried his daughter-in-law.

Two coffins, one cruel accident.

And now the last piece of his world was walking up those stairs with a monster.

He closed his eyes and let out a long, unsteady breath.

Please, Pumpkin Pie. Please know I'm still here.

And I will never stop watching.

6

They left in the middle of the night—fleeing the mess they'd made.

The news story had shattered any illusion of safety. Bill and Judy's smiling photos filled the screen, followed by grainy gas station surveillance footage. They both saw it.

The anchor's voice blurred into static—background noise in Lauren's ears. But the meaning was crystal clear: *They had to go. Now.*

Neither of them said a word. Not as they climbed the stairs. Not as they packed, methodical and silent, like soldiers executing a plan. Not even as they sat side by side on the bed's edge, listening—waiting—for Granddaddy's snores to mark their moment to move.

They moved like ghosts—silent, weightless, slipping through shadows. No shoes. No lights. Just breath and tension—and floorboards Lauren knew how to avoid.

She'd memorized every creak in this house as a child. The loose board by the hall closet. The sharp groan of the step outside her bedroom. She used to sneak out for midnight ice cream—not to flee for her life.

This wasn't how she imagined leaving. Not with Stefan at her side. Not like a criminal. Not like this.

As they crossed the threshold, something inside her snagged—like a loose thread catching on splintered wood.

This house had been her last clean place. The last place where she could pretend—just for a few hours—that she was still someone else.

Still LeRoy's "Pumpkin Pie." Still the girl who played chess on the porch and once kept a secret folder full of unsolved cases on her laptop.

Cases she couldn't stop thinking about. Cases no one had solved.

Now she was walking away from it like it didn't mean anything.

And that was the moment something started to slip.

Her hands shook as she reached for the door handle of the truck. She steadied them before Stefan could notice, but inside, the mask she wore so well had shifted—just slightly off-center. Not enough for anyone else to see. But she felt it. And it terrified her.

Stefan drove. Lauren watched the dark horizon swallow the road ahead.

Texas faded behind them—along with any illusion of distance from what they'd done.

For Lauren, the silence was suffocating. Each mile only deepened her fear that they'd be linked to the murders. That LeRoy had already figured it out. That Bill and Judy's names would somehow be tied to hers.

Stefan, on the other hand, looked proud. Confident. Like they'd pulled off something brilliant.

She saw it in the way he gripped the wheel—one hand loose, cocky. In the occasional smirk that tugged at his mouth when he thought she wasn't looking. He didn't feel guilt. He felt power.

Neither of them spoke as the hours dragged on. Lauren stared out the window as they drove. To where, she didn't know— Only that it was farther from her Granddaddy. Farther from safety. Farther from the last place she still felt like herself.

Her thoughts drifted—uninvited, unstoppable—back to the hunts. There had been many. Too many.

But really, even one was too many. And the guilt... It gnawed at her. Quietly. Constantly. Like rust eating through metal.

The first one came not long after she'd stepped into Stefan's camper for the first time. Back when it was easier to call it studying. Easier to call it survival.

She'd studied him as he stalked his prey. Silent. Focused. Intent. She sat in a flimsy old lounger outside the camper, pretending to relax while her eyes tracked every move.

The woman had been middle-aged. Alone. Traveling in a beat-up van with a tiny white dog. Easy to overlook. Easy to charm. Easy to kill.

Stefan had noticed a leak under her van.

He'd caused it earlier—while she was out for a walk—just to have a reason to approach.

And it worked.

Lauren watched him worm his way into the woman's trust, all smiles and soft laughter.

He was calm. Confident.

Utterly in control.

Like this was something he'd rehearsed a thousand times.

Maybe he had.

She watched him like a textbook come to life. Trying to gauge him. Decode him. For survival.

But part of her knew, even then, she was watching something else.

Something darker.

And that made her complicit.

She remembered thinking—How does someone learn to be that charming? Was Stefan born with it?

Or had he watched others—mimicked them—until he figured out how to fake normal?

Because it wasn't natural. She knew that much from school.

It wasn't real.

Not empathy. Not connection.

It was rehearsed. Reflexive. Calculated.

A weapon dressed in warmth.

People might've called it charm—

But Lauren knew better.

It came from instinct. From need.

Maybe even from something broken.

Something he couldn't shut off.

The dog didn't trust him.

The little thing barked endlessly, hackles up, eyes locked on Stefan like he saw the monster beneath the skin.

The woman finally scooped the dog up with an embarrassed laugh and placed him inside the van, closing the door behind him.

Too bad she didn't realize he was trying to save her life. The dog knew.

He knew better than she did.

And he'd tried to warn her.

But she hadn't listened.

For the next few hours, he kept himself busy—driving into town, picking up what he needed to fix it, playing the part of the helpful stranger.

From the small window, Lauren sat motionless, eyes locked on Stefan knelt by the woman's van and "helped."

Fixing what he'd broken.

Performing concern like it was second nature.

He came back into the camper hours later, sweaty and smug, that infuriating grin stretched across his face.

He was proud of himself.

Pleased.

He had achieved what he set out to do—

He'd planted the seed.

Earned her trust.

Now he just had to harvest it.

That night, they left the campsite and hit the road, heading toward their next destination.

Or so she thought.

Somewhere along the stretch of empty highway, Stefan pulled off onto the shoulder. Shifted the truck into park. Turned on the hazard lights.

Without a word, he got out. Lifted the hood. And waited.

Lauren sat still, hands folded in her lap, eyes fixed on the side mirror.

She knew exactly what this was. She just didn't want to believe it yet.

It didn't take long.

The woman's van roared by moments later.

The van's brake lights flared red in the dark. Lauren held her breath. A pause. Then the van took the next exit and looped around.

She came back, slower now. Pulled in behind the camper and parked. Hazard lights flashing.

Her headlights lit the back of their camper and truck like a spotlight on a stage.

Lauren stared through the windshield. Her pulse thundered louder than the engine.

It was a two-lane highway. Middle of nowhere. Hardly any traffic at all.

The woman got out. Still trusting. Still kind.

She walked up to the passenger side window, smiling as she waved.

Lauren tried to remember what was said between them. What words had been exchanged. But nearly a year had passed, and the dialogue was gone.

Just a blur.

What she remembered—clearly, vividly—was Stefan.

He appeared beside her—casual, smooth—and asked to borrow a wrench.

Then the three of them walked back toward the woman's van.

The woman's little dog barked wildly from inside the van, sensing something Lauren hadn't—yet.

Stefan moved fast. Instant—like a switch had been flipped.

One second he was smiling—

The next, he reached into the van, grabbed the dog by the throat, and twisted.

The snap was sharp—wet and final.

The woman gasped, stumbling back, catching her foot and falling hard to the ground.

Her hand flew to her chest, like she was trying to hold her heart inside her body.

Lauren didn't move.

Stefan turned on the woman with the same violence—

Slapped her hard—a crack so loud it split the air.

She screamed. Rolled. Tried to crawl away.

But Stefan kicked her square in the ribs.

She collapsed again, hands grasping her side, her mouth opened like she meant to speak—but no words came.

Only air. Only panic.

She looked up—straight at Lauren.

Begging. Pleading. A silent cry: *Help me*.

But Lauren couldn't move.

She stood, paralyzed—like her body had disconnected from her mind.

It was too fast. Too much.

Violence and rage—colliding like the final pieces of a bomb snapping into place.

And when it was over—

When the woman lay beaten, breathless, and still—
Stefan stood over her with a kind of pride.
Admiration.
He stared down like she was a masterpiece in a gallery.
Like he had created something.
Lauren's stomach twisted. She wanted to vomit.
She wanted to run—wanted to scream.
But her feet were locked into the earth.
She searched her memory for the woman's name—desperate to reclaim it. But it wasn't there. It had never been.

That was the moment Sarah was born—a silent vow wrapped in guilt and resolve. To know their names. To remember. Because if she couldn't stop him... she could at least make sure no one vanished without a name.

The tension in the truck cab was thick and alive—pressing against Lauren's chest like a weighted blanket she couldn't peel away. Every breath felt shallow. Trapped. Mechanical.

Their plan had been to head to Oklahoma—familiar territory. A place to regroup. But halfway there, it became clear: it wasn't far enough.

Without a word, Stefan took the exit toward Springfield, Missouri.

Lauren didn't ask why. She didn't ask anything. She just stared out the window, her reflection hollow and distant in the glass.

They pulled into the RV park just after sunrise. The sky above was streaked with soft pinks and pale gold, the last shadows of night fading into something that almost looked peaceful.

Stefan stepped out of the truck, holding an ID that read "Zach Warren." The plastic looked real enough—government issued, laminated, forgettable.

Lauren didn't move. She stayed in the passenger seat, her limbs heavy, her body aching from more than just exhaustion. Her silence was complete.

She hadn't said a word since they left. Not one. Silence had become its own language.

Whatever had cracked inside her back in Amarillo... It hadn't stopped. It was still breaking.

Before Lauren, Stefan had a pattern—predictable, primal, like a predator bound to the moon. He hunted monthly—like clockwork. His rage, his cravings, the things he did—they had nearly gotten him caught more than once. His name had floated across FBI desks. Faces of women they hadn't identified, or hadn't been able to save in time. Lauren should've been one of them.

But she wasn't.

She'd flipped the script—if only temporarily. Her presence, somehow, had steadied him. The rage didn't vanish—it just dulled, narrowed into focus. That's when the rules started. He liked structure. Boundaries. He said it helped. And with her around, the mess had shifted. The old patterns—messy, impulsive, obvious—became... cleaner. The violence more controlled. Less obvious. The lines he used to cross without hesitation now gave him pause. She didn't ask for the change. Didn't push for it. But somehow, things were different with her there. It worked. Until now. Lately, he'd been slipping—spiraling. The darkness was closing in again. His temper was unpredictable. His triggers multiplied by the week. Lauren knew it was only a matter of time before something inside him snapped for good. She didn't know if she had the strength to stop it—or survive it.

Stefan returned to the truck and tossed the RV park map onto the dashboard. Without a word, he shifted gears and turned onto the gravel lane. Their assigned site was sandwiched between a million-dollar motorhome and a modest fifth-wheel with four bicycles leaned in a row —two big, two small. A family. Perfect.

Stefan backed the camper in with casual precision. He could've done it blindfolded. Lauren climbed out, her body aching like she was recovering from a week-long flu. They worked in silence, each falling into familiar roles. Tarp. Power. Water. Level. Fifteen minutes. No conversation. Just routine.

Then, wordless, they slipped inside. Lauren collapsed onto the bed like a discarded rag doll. Stefan drained a bottle of water in seconds and joined her without a word. Exhaustion claimed them both. — Lauren awoke to darkness. Her phone buzzed as she reached for it. 8:05 p.m. They'd slept the entire day away. Her body begged for sleep, but her stomach clawed at her insides. She tiptoed into the kitchen, opened the cabinet—empty. Not even a cracker. They had left in such a rush, there hadn't been time to think about food.

She pulled out her phone again and opened her banking app.

Her fingers hovered above the screen, heart pounding as she refreshed it.

The transfer was there—only half of what she'd expected.

A faint smile tugged at her lips.

Granddaddy had done exactly what she'd expected—just enough to keep her safe, not enough to keep her silent.

She'd have to call him soon. That was exactly what he wanted.

Stefan came up beside her. His voice was a low rumble. "What's got you so happy?"

For once, he sounded genuine.

Lauren played along. "Granddaddy sent us some money. We're covered—for now." She paused, weighing the moment. "Wanna go out for dinner?"

He nodded, almost childlike. And for a brief moment, he was almost normal.

Dinner was surprisingly easy. No outbursts. No accusations. No quiet seething beneath the surface.

Lauren didn't trust it.

Back at the camper, they played a slow game of chess at the cramped little table. Lauren yawned.

Stefan glanced up. Usually, that small gesture would be enough to set him off. To spark accusations of boredom. Of ungratefulness. Of disrespect.

But this time...

"You wanna go back to bed?" he asked. "We can finish this in the morning."

She blinked. "Yes, please."

He stood and waited—expecting her to follow.

She hesitated, just long enough to register the risk, then rose.

He led the way down the narrow hall without looking back. No pressure. No snarling commands. Just quiet steps and a door that didn't slam.

Just... sleep.

She lay beside him, stunned. Could this be what normal felt like?

But she couldn't sleep. The quiet was too loud. The peace felt unfamiliar. Unnatural.

Her mind spun with images: Bill. Judy. The look in their eyes before it ended.

And then, her thoughts turned darker.

She slipped out of bed, careful not to wake him. Wrote a note—just in case. She didn't want to tempt fate. Not tonight.

The air outside was cool and crisp. It kissed her skin and cleared her mind.

The RV park was still.

She passed quiet campers, lights dimmed, curtains drawn. Her footsteps echoed faintly through the stillness.

And for the first time in days, she could breathe.

Until she felt it. That prickle on the back of her neck.

Someone was watching.

She stopped. Turned. Looked. Nothing.

The trees swayed gently, as if whispering secrets to each other. But no sound. No breath. Just stillness.

She reached the camper steps, hand poised over the handle—then froze. The unease bloomed again, sharp and insistent.

She turned one last time. Her breath caught.

Someone was there. A tall silhouette stood just beyond the tree line —where the shadows swallowed the light. Still. Unmoving. Watching. Like it belonged to the dark.

She blinked. Gone.

A trick of the light, she told herself. The fog of exhaustion. The trauma. The fear.

But something inside her whispered: Stefan isn't the only one watching anymore.

She turned back to the camper, still shaken.

The door flung open. Stefan stood there—face coiled in fury.

"Where the fuck have you been?"

Lauren stumbled back a step. "I left you a note," she said quickly. "I couldn't sleep—I just went for a walk."

His face softened—but the softness was a lie. The air buzzed with that stillness that always came before pain.

He reached out his hand. She hesitated—then took it.

The moment she reached the top step, he shoved her. Time slowed. She flew backward—weightless—then the gravel rushed up to meet her.

Her head cracked against the ground. Pain exploded. Her breath left her. Her body refused to take in more.

Everything blurred.

As darkness closed in, her last thoughts were of Judy— so this is what it felt like when Stefan struck her.

And the shadow in the trees.

She woke to bright, sterile light and the sharp sting of antiseptic.

Pain pulsed through her skull—deep and rhythmic, like a second heartbeat behind her eyes. The overhead light cut through her eyelids like a blade the moment they fluttered open.

She squinted, then shut them again, groaning softly as nausea curled in her stomach.

Somewhere to her left, a machine beeped steadily. An IV tugged at her arm, the tape itchy and cold against her skin. She was upright— barely—propped by pillows she didn't remember.

The sheets were stiff. The room, unnaturally still. Her body throbbed in dull, rhythmic waves, the world tilting with each breath.

"Where...am I?" she croaked, her voice dry and broken.

Stefan's voice came through the fog.

"You gave me a scare. You fell down the camper stairs, babe. Hit your head hard. Been out for a couple hours."

Lauren blinked, her memory fracturing. She remembered the walk. The anger. The shadow. Then—nothing.

A soft voice entered the room.

"Hi, Ms. Collins. I'm Erin, your nurse. You're at Mercy Hospital. You've got a mild concussion and a small laceration on the back of your head."

Erin smiled gently.

Lauren winced as pain radiated through her skull.

Stefan squeezed her hand—hard.

Not comfort.

A warning aimed at Lauren, disguised as warmth for everyone else.

"You're gonna be okay. Right, Erin?"

Erin nodded. "You'll be just fine. We're moving you upstairs for observation—just for tonight."

Lauren wanted to say no. She wanted to say don't leave me alone with him. But she couldn't. Not yet.

"I'd rather go home," she whispered. "Please."

Erin glanced at Stefan, who was already clenching his jaw.

"I think it's best if you stay," the nurse said gently.

Lauren faked a sob. "Please... don't make me stay alone. I need him."

Erin hesitated, then softened. "Alright, sweetie. I'll get your pain meds."

As she stepped out, Stefan leaned in and whispered:

"Good girl. You did good."

Lauren closed her eyes. Not because she trusted him. Not because she felt safe.

But because the pain medication was coming. And when it hit, it would take her somewhere else— somewhere quiet. Somewhere he couldn't reach her. Even if only for a little while.

7

It had been two days since Lauren left Mercy Hospital.

Normally, they would've packed up and disappeared by now. It was their ritual—commit, escape, erase. But this time, Lauren wasn't in any condition to run.

Her head still throbbed. Her body moved like it was filled with wet sand.

Even her thoughts felt waterlogged, soft around the edges. Like a photograph left in the sun too long.

She didn't remember everything from that night. But she didn't believe she had fallen. And neither did Nurse Erin.

It happened just minutes after she woke up. Stefan stepped out, saying he was going to grab a soda. The door had barely clicked shut before Erin moved closer.

She lowered her voice, kind but direct.

"I have to ask. Those bruises on your face... they don't look like a fall. Do you need help, Lauren?"

Lauren had frozen.

For a second—she almost said yes. Almost reached for the rope being offered. But then...

She imagined the fallout. Stefan turning on her. The stories he'd tell. The way he'd twist everything until she was the monster.

If she turned him in, he wouldn't go quietly. And he'd take her down with him. She'd seen what he was capable of.

And she wouldn't survive prison.

That wasn't part of the plan.

So she met Erin's gaze, summoned a practiced tremble in her voice, and said: "I'm just clumsy. That's all."

Erin didn't believe her, but she nodded anyway. The police arrived an hour later.

Stefan stood his ground. And so did she.

She gave them nothing. No details. No betrayal. Just soft nods and vague words. They left a business card on the bedside table. A lifeline—one she couldn't afford to reach for.

Stefan never left her side after that. He clung to her like a shadow—smiling, touching her shoulder, whispering how proud he was. Like she'd done something noble. Loyal. His perfect girl.

But Lauren wasn't shielding him out of love—she was protecting herself. If she turned him in, he'd drag her down with him—and worse, he might survive it. She wouldn't.

And now... something was off.

At night, her dreams twisted into something darker. The shadow figure returned—always there, just out of reach. No face. No sound. Just presence. Watching.

She woke drenched in sweat, unsure if she'd truly slept at all.

But the worst part? It wasn't just in her dreams anymore.

During the day, sitting outside the camper, she felt it too—that strange, electric current beneath her skin. The sense of being watched. She'd glance over her shoulder. Scan the trees. Nothing. But the sensation lingered. Eyes on her. Movement where there should be none.

The other RVs were mostly empty. No one around but wind, silence, and that crawling awareness that someone might be out there.

At first, she blamed the head injury. Maybe it was the concussion. The pain meds. The trauma.

But deep down, in the part of her that had always known when to run—she didn't think she was imagining it.

Someone was following them. And it wasn't Stefan.

Stefan, meanwhile, played the part of the concerned boyfriend with unsettling precision. He cooked now—carefully, methodically—like he was trying to earn a merit badge. He brought her bottled water before she could ask, placing it just-so beside her chair. He hovered like she was breakable glass.

Not out of love. Out of performance. Out of control.

It wasn't kindness. It was strategy. And that made it worse.

But something in him was coiled tight. Vibrating beneath the surface.

He kept disappearing. "Going to the store," he'd say.

But he never came back with anything. No groceries. Not even snacks.

She didn't know where he was going. Or who he was meeting. And she didn't have the strength—yet—to find out.

Before the "fall," Stefan had been unraveling. That hadn't changed. If anything, his calm now was more terrifying than his rage.

Lauren sat curled in the plastic lawn chair outside the camper, knees to her chest, a blanket wrapped around her shoulders. The afternoon air was still. Too still.

Her eyes swept the tree line again.

She knew Stefan was dangerous.

But now... she was beginning to wonder if someone else was, too.

Lauren had fallen asleep early, the pain medication pulling her under like an anchor into deep, uneasy dreams.

At first, there was only darkness—weightless, numb.

But then, like fog parting, something took shape.

The figure.

This time, it wasn't still.

It was running toward her.

She tried to scream.

Tried to run.

But her legs wouldn't move. Her arms were lead.

Paralyzed.

Helpless.

She stood frozen as the figure closed in—fast, relentless.

Her breath came in shallow gasps.

She wasn't afraid of the figure itself.

Not exactly.

It was the not knowing.

Who—or what—it was.

Why it kept showing up in her dreams.

Why it always watched.

As it got closer, she could make out the vague shape of a man.

Or maybe a woman.

She couldn't tell.

No face. No features. Just presence—heavy and pressing. Suffocating.

It reached out an arm—

SLAM.

A car door snapped her awake.

Lauren bolted upright, heart hammering in her chest, drenched in sweat. Her eyes scanned the camper. Still. Quiet. But the silence felt charged.

Her mind raced, grasping for logic. The dream still clung to her skin.

Had the figure followed her here?

Then—

The camper door flung open.

Stefan stormed inside. His shirt stuck to his body, soaked through with sweat. His breath was ragged, uneven.

The air shifted—heavier.

Lauren flinched.

"Oh my god. Are you okay?" Her voice cracked.

He looked at her. Smiled.

But it wasn't joy. It was satisfaction—cold and dark.

"Why wouldn't I be?" he asked, too casually.

That smile told her everything she needed to know.

Something had happened. Something bad. Something he'd done.

His jeans were damp up to the knees. Dirt streaked across his hands. There was something dark on his boot—thick and smudged. Maybe grease. Probably blood.

He smelled like pine needles and sweat. And something else. Something metallic.

She didn't ask. She couldn't. Because the answer would change everything for her.

The sickness hit fast. Her stomach turned, the bile climbing up her throat like it had claws. She stumbled into the bathroom, collapsing over the toilet as her body revolted.

Everything she'd eaten came up violently.

Her stomach emptied— but the sickness stayed.

Stefan followed.

He didn't touch her. He stood over her. Watching like she was some kind of spectacle. Calm. Still. Like he was proud of her reaction. Like it proved something.

And for the first time since they'd been together, Lauren wanted to cry.

Not because of what he might've done— but because of what he hadn't had to say.

The tears stung behind her eyes. Unfamiliar. Unwelcome.

She had always kept herself together. Never screamed. Never cried. Never begged.

But now?

Now she wanted to do all three.

She was unraveling.

She clenched her eyes shut and forced her breath to steady.

In. Out. In. Out. She swallowed the sob clawing its way up her throat. She bit the inside of her cheek until the metal taste of blood hung on her tongue.

Then—she did what she always did. She put the mask back on.

Without a word, she wiped her mouth, pushed to her feet, and stepped out into the night.

The air was cold. Not cold enough. She sat in her folding chair—the same one she'd been glued to for days—and stared into the trees.

The woods were quiet. But the silence wasn't peaceful. It felt like something was waiting.

She scanned the tree line. Searching for any sign of movement. Something flickered in the shadows—there and gone, too fast to trust. But her spine stiffened anyway, like prey sensing the moment before the strike. Any shift in the dark. Any trace of the figure she'd seen before. Watching. Waiting. Following.

She didn't know if she wanted it to be real—or just a symptom of her fraying mind.

Stefan came out behind her. He didn't yell. Didn't growl or spit cruel words.

Instead, with eerie calm, he simply said: "Pack up. We're leaving."

Lauren nodded. That was it. No questions. No resistance. Just quiet obedience.

She stood and began her silent ritual—folding chairs, coiling cords, securing the camper like a well-trained soldier. Every move was automatic. Practiced. But her eyes kept drifting to the tree line.

She remembered the sound of tires crunching gravel earlier—how Stefan had been gone longer than any grocery run should take. She remembered the way his hands had trembled. His nails caked with something dark.

The memory made her skin crawl.

What had he done this time? Who had he hurt?

Maybe the figure in her dreams wasn't there to harm her. Maybe it was trying to warn her.

She glanced once more into the trees.

Maybe it was still out there—closer than she realized.

Because the truth was, she was breaking.

Piece by piece.

And if she didn't pull herself together—fast—Stefan would take them both down.

It was just after midnight when they pulled out of the campsite,

gravel crunched beneath the tires as they rolled past rows of dimly lit campers.

The old RV groaned as Stefan guided it onto the narrow road leading back to the highway.

Lauren sat in the passenger seat, cheek pressed to the cool window glass, watching the black tree line blur and vanish.

She stared into the woods, searching for something—anything—that might be out there.

The figure.

The presence.

The shadow she had dreamed of.

But there was nothing.

Just trees swaying in the wind.

The faint echo of crickets.

A darkness too familiar to feel safe.

Still, something inside her whispered: Not safe.

Her eyes lingered until the campsite disappeared, swallowed whole by night.

The next few hours passed in a haze. Lauren sat in silence, reliving the past few days like a film stuck on repeat. The hospital. The questions. The stifling weight of pretending. The guilt of what she'd hidden.

She thought of Nurse Erin—her pleading eyes. Her voice when she'd asked, "Do you need help?" — not with suspicion, but kindness. Lauren had ignored the chance. Lied to the one person who might've saved her.

And now? Now she wasn't sure she could fix it.

Her hand twitched toward her phone. She wanted to call her Grand-daddy more than anything— just to hear his voice. Just to feel safe for a second.

He had always been her shelter in the storm.

But she knew she couldn't.

Not yet. Not like this.

Stefan, meanwhile, was in one of his moods. Giddy. Buzzing with energy like a child coming off a sugar high. He tapped the steering wheel and sang along to some obnoxious country song on the radio, shouting the lyrics with too much enthusiasm.

Lauren couldn't stand the sound of his voice tonight— it grated on her skin like sandpaper.

Without a word, she slipped in her earbuds, pulled her hoodie over her head, and queued up her favorite playlist. She tapped shuffle, not caring what came next— as long as it drowned him out.

Taylor Swift's voice filled her ears. "I Did Something Bad."

The irony wasn't lost on her—it pulsed beneath the lyrics like a cruel joke.

She drifted off to the rhythm, the music blurring her thoughts until her body finally gave in to sleep.

It was still dark when the truck gave a soft jolt and rolled to a stop.

Blinking into the faint glow of the dashboard, she turned toward Stefan.

"Where are we?" Her voice came out hoarse, rough with sleep.

He grinned at her like they were on vacation.

"Good morning, sunshine. We're in Branson. Thought we'd grab breakfast and find a place to camp for a few days."

He winked.

"You'll like it here. Lots of tourists, lots of noise. Easy to disappear."

Lauren nodded slowly, rubbing the sleep from her eyes. Her stomach twisted—not from hunger, but dread.

She didn't like how cheerful he was. It meant he had a plan.

And if she'd learned anything, it was that Stefan's plans never ended well for someone.

Still, she muttered, "Okay," and stepped down into the crisp Branson morning.

Her eyes swept the quiet street—already calculating who might be watching.

And whether the shadow from her dreams had followed them here, too.

8

Stefan's eggs sat untouched, but his laughter echoed with sickening satisfaction—sharp, manic, and far too loud for the quiet corner booth of the small-town Denny's. He stirred his coffee with exaggerated cheer, the metal spoon clinking against ceramic in a steady, unsettling rhythm. A performance he didn't even realize he was giving.

His mood was buoyant, uncontainable—like a child who'd gotten away with something forbidden. Lauren didn't need to ask. She could smell it on him, like the lingering smoke of a wildfire that had already consumed everything in its path. He'd hunted—every nerve screamed that he'd extinguished another life.

It was in his dancing eyes, sparkling with cruel glee. In the twitch of his fingers. In the way his lips curled just a little too long after each laugh. She knew that look better than her own reflection.

He had a pattern—before he met her—a methodical, depraved ritual. He'd find a girl: young, soft-spoken, naive. Someone who trusted too easily. He'd draw her in with charm, then isolate her, corner her with promises spun into threats, and finally, break her with pain. Always with that same, chilling line right before the horror began:

"I'm going to make you scream."

Lauren saw it all in her mind—vivid and uninvited. The terror widening the girl's eyes. The confusion. The moment her fight kicked in too late. The breathless pleading. Then silence. That awful, final silence.

Stefan didn't hide the bodies. He didn't care to. He wanted them found. Wanted his name whispered in crime stories and nightmares. This wasn't about lust. It was about legacy.

Lauren's fork dragged through scrambled eggs she had no intention of eating. Occasionally, she lifted a bite to her lips, mimicked a chew, and swallowed bitterness instead of food. Her stomach coiled with nausea. Once, she could stomach it. She could play her role and find equilibrium in the chaos. But now, it tasted like ash and betrayal.

There had been rules. Codes. A balance that kept the darkness contained in a manageable box. Stefan had burned the box.

And worst of all—he had cheated.

Not on her heart. That was never the arrangement. But on their pact. Their control. Their game. And in breaking it, he became unpredictable.

And unpredictable meant dangerous.

That betrayal cut deeper than any bruise ever had. Not because she loved him—God, no—but because it meant she was losing her grip. He was unraveling, and if he wasn't playing by the rules anymore, she wasn't safe.

If he was spiraling, she was standing at ground zero. And Stefan never let chaos land without a target.

She reached for her coffee but paused, hand hovering as a cold shiver traced her spine like an icy fingertip. Her skin tightened, every nerve awake.

She lifted her eyes.

The Denny's hummed with morning life: low conversation, the griddle's hiss, the clink of mugs and forks. Booths filled with locals nursing early breakfasts and yesterday's gossip.

A few tables over, two men in dusty utility uniforms sipped from chipped white mugs, speaking in hushed tones. At the counter, an elderly man was hunched over a folded newspaper, eyes squinting at the print. Nothing out of place. Nothing obvious.

But something felt off. Like being watched from a blind spot—too close to see.

Her eyes drifted to the large front window. The sun had just begun to breach the horizon, casting long golden streaks across the parking lot. And parked at the far edge— A car. Dark. Engine off. A figure in the driver's seat. Unmoving.

Her breath caught. Her pulse thundered in her ears.

Then the passenger door opened, and a waitress in a Denny's uniform climbed in. Just a coworker getting a ride.

Lauren exhaled, her shoulders slumping. Paranoid. You're getting paranoid.

But the feeling didn't leave. Not entirely. It clung to her like static.

She pulled out her phone. The screen blinked to life: 5%. "Shit," she muttered, thumbing frantically through local listings.

She searched for nearby RV parks, desperate to get them somewhere else—somewhere new.

She found one by Lake Taneycomo and, without hesitation, made a reservation under their aliases. Before it died, she turned the screen toward Stefan.

He didn't ask questions. Just glanced at the map, smirked, and tapped his finger on one of the spots.

"That space will be perfect for hunting," he said, tone casual, like he was choosing a place to grill burgers.

Lauren froze. He just killed someone. He's already thinking about the next.

She nodded, said nothing. But inside, she screamed.

They arrived an hour later. The RV park was peaceful—too peaceful. Nestled beside the lake, mist floated over the water like a secret waiting to surface. Birds chirped lazily overhead. A fisherman's boat buzzed across the lake like a distant warning.

It should have felt safe. But it didn't.

Stefan went into the park office, ID in hand, and came back with a map, tossing it onto the dashboard. They set up quickly—no words, no instructions. Just the same routine, repeated too many times to count.

Lauren slipped into the camper, plugged in her phone, and tried to breathe.

Then—voices. Outside.

Stefan, talking to someone. Too friendly.

Her heart kicked. She wasn't ready to pretend again. Wasn't ready to wear the mask. Not tonight. Not ever again.

But she didn't have a choice.

The door creaked open.

"Hey, Sarah, come meet our new friend. He just pulled up across from us."

She stood, straightened her shirt, and muttered her mantra under her breath.

Mask on. Smile on. You can do this.

Stepping outside, sunlight hit her square in the face. She squinted against it, then slipped on her sunglasses and scanned the park. She expected to see Stefan chatting with someone—but the space around their camper was empty.

"Zach?" she called, rounding the front of the truck. "Where did you go?"

"Never mind," he replied from somewhere off to the side. "He had to go. Said he'll meet up with us tomorrow."

Stefan reappeared, sunglasses perched low on his nose. Lauren clenched her jaw but kept her expression smooth, pleasant.

"You need anything?" she asked, the dread already blooming in her stomach.

He paused, tilting his head. The way he lowered his glasses to meet her eyes felt like a warning in itself.

"You okay?"

There it was. That edge. That quiet test.

"Of course," she said softly. "Just still sore from the fall."

Fall. Yeah right.

But the thought had been gnawing at her ever since she woke up in that hospital bed.

Why did he take her there?

Stefan didn't do doctors. Didn't risk hospitals. Too many eyes, too many questions. He'd let her bleed out before putting himself in danger.

And yet... he had taken her.

That part didn't make sense. None of it did.

The question slipped out before she could stop it.

"Why did you take me to the hospital?"

His expression shifted. Cold. Calculating. Dangerous.

She knew she'd made a mistake.

He closed the distance between them in two steps, grabbed her arm, and twisted it sharply. Pain flared up her shoulder. She winced, her face hidden behind her sunglasses.

"You want to start something?" he hissed.

"No," she whispered. "Not at all. I'm sorry. I'm not feeling well. Please forgive me."

She recoiled as she spoke, instinctively shrinking into herself, trying to make her body smaller, less threatening. Less noticeable.

She knew how to vanish without leaving the room.

A metallic clang rang out across the park. A man's voice followed.

"Hey Zach, you got any charcoal?"

Just like that, Stefan let go.

He straightened up, turned his head, and called back with easy charm, "Sure do!"

Then he turned back to Lauren, grinning wide—but his eyes were dead.

"Get back inside. Rest before you piss me off."

She turned away, cradling her arm. As she stepped onto the camper's steps, she glanced across the street.

A black truck with a camper topper.

The back door hung open. Feet were visible beneath it—someone was there. Watching?

Or just unpacking?

Lauren stepped inside, heart pounding.

She'd made a mistake.

And Stefan would make her pay for it.

She just didn't know when.

Later, she lay in bed, one arm curled protectively around her aching ribs, the other scrolling through her now-charging phone. TikTok videos buzzed across the screen—dances, lip-syncs, jokes. It felt like a world that didn't exist anymore. Not for her.

She tried to recall waking up in the hospital—sterile lights, a nurse's voice—but something was off. A flicker in the hallway. A shape. Not Stefan. Not a nurse. A man. Dark hair. Watching from the doorway. She blinked, and the image vanished. Maybe it was just a dream. Or maybe her brain was filling in the blanks. Still, the thought clung to her like static. Someone else had been there.

Outside, she had heard the roar of their truck engine moments before it faded into the distance. Stefan had left. Where to, she didn't care. For now, it was quiet.

And that was enough.

For the first time in days, she was alone. The silence pressed in, heavy but welcome. For a moment, her thoughts slipped somewhere dangerous. What if I ran? What if I poisoned him? What if I stopped pretending, just once?

Her fingers gripped the blanket's edge, knuckles white.

No. That wasn't smart. That wasn't safe. That wasn't her.

She exhaled and let the silence settle over her like a weighted blanket. The camper was still. Too still.

Through the small window beside the bed, the night sky bled deep indigo, stars faint behind a thin veil of cloud. A breeze whispered through the trees, making the branches sway and creak. Somewhere nearby, a dog barked once—sharp and high-pitched. Then, nothing.

She reached into the duffel bag beside the bed, fingers brushing over the familiar worn fabric inside. The little silver pin—her mother's. Bent and scratched, long unused. She never wore it anymore, but she always brought it. A piece of her old life, small enough to hide.

Stefan didn't know it existed.

That was the only reason it had survived.

Her eyelids had just begun to droop when—crack.

A twig cracked beneath a footstep. Slow. Intentional.

Not wind. Not animal.

She froze.

A shadow moved across the window.

Her breath caught. It wasn't Stefan—he didn't move quietly. He stomped, slammed, announced his presence.

This was different.

Heart pounding, she crept toward the window, careful not to let the floor creak beneath her. She peeked out slowly, pulse loud in her ears.

Across the gravel path, the black truck with the camper topper still sat beneath the trees.

A faint light glowed behind the blinds—soft, eerie. Someone was awake.

Then—click.

Darkness.

She waited. Barely breathing. Barely blinking.

The window stayed dark. No movement. No sound.

Just stillness.

Lauren lowered herself back into bed, but her body remained rigid, coiled tight as wire. Her thoughts whirled.

Was someone out there? Or had her mind finally cracked under the weight of fear?

She was afraid of Stefan. That much was clear.

But now... she feared shadows, too.

And maybe—just maybe—paranoia wasn't the problem.

Maybe reality was.

9

Lauren woke drenched in sweat, her heart jackhammering as she jolted upright. Her breath came in ragged bursts, her skin damp and clinging to the sheets. The dream had escalated again—gone from flickering shadows to something far more visceral.

This time, there had been a woman. Faceless. Shattered. Screaming. And Stefan was the one hurting her—again and again and again.

The woman's cries echoed in Lauren's skull like a siren, not just from the dream, but from memories she had buried deep, too deep. In the dream, she had tried to help. She screamed. She fought. But her limbs were bound—held by invisible ropes. No matter how hard she struggled, she remained trapped. Powerless. Helpless. Useless.

And then—from the edge of a blackened forest—a figure appeared. A silhouette. A shadow. Watching. Unmoving. Silent.

She screamed at it, begged for help—for herself, for the woman, for anyone. But the figure didn't move. Didn't flinch. Just stared. Unblinking. Present.

Lauren rubbed her face with trembling hands and whispered, "Just a dream. Just a dream." But even to herself, the words sounded hollow.

She pushed herself out of bed, still disoriented, her legs shaky as she stumbled into the small bathroom. Her ribs still ached from Stefan's last outburst—bruised, tightening with every breath. Each step sent dull pain shooting up her side, but she kept moving. She had to.

Cold water hit her face in harsh, splashing waves. Again. And again.

Until the image of the woman, the forest, and those eyes in the dark blurred into the porcelain sink.

She dried her face on a rough towel, moved barefoot to the kitchenette, and started a pot of coffee. The motions were familiar. Grounding. Caffeine will help, she told herself. It always helps.

But just as the scent of coffee began to drift through the camper, she froze. Something was wrong.

She hadn't heard Stefan come in last night. No heavy footsteps. No slamming cabinet doors. No muttered curses from the kitchenette.

Heart beginning to race, she stepped away from the counter and moved quietly down the narrow hallway toward the bedroom.

The door was slightly ajar.

She pushed it open.

Bed still made. Room still empty.

Her pulse kicked harder.

She spun around, crossed quickly through the living area, and threw the camper door open.

The morning sun hit her hard—bright and disorienting.

Shit.

She had overslept.

The truck was gone.

So was Stefan.

Not even a note.

Her eyes darted across the small RV park, scanning for any trace of him. Nothing.

No familiar crunch of gravel.

No lingering scent of his aftershave in the morning air.

He hadn't come back.

Her gaze snagged on the black truck parked across the gravel drive —the one with the camper topper.

Unmoving. Silent.

It sat like a predator waiting in the shadows.

Something about it tugged at her nerves.

Instinct overruled reason.

She stepped outside in her pajamas, feet bare against the cold grit of dirt and gravel. She didn't care. She needed to know.

She crossed the short distance quickly and knocked on the camper door.

Once.

Twice.

Nothing.

She pressed her ear against the cool metal.

No voices.

No movement.

No sounds at all.

Just silence.

Thick. Artificial. Wrong.

A faint creak echoed from deep inside—too faint to be harmless.

Like a floorboard groaning beneath weight.

Then nothing.

A coil of unease tightened in her stomach.

She backed away slowly, eyes still fixed on the camper.

Only when she reached the safety of her own steps did she turn and hurry inside.

Her fingers trembled as she grabbed her phone off the counter and tapped Stefan's contact.

His photo appeared.

That smug, knowing smile.

A predator pretending to be a man.

It rang.

And rang.

No answer.

"Shit…" she whispered, pacing the narrow floor. Her thoughts spun, panic fluttering in her chest like trapped wings.

What if he hunted again? But that didn't make sense. Stefan didn't act on impulse. Planned. Watched. He didn't go off-script.

Unless something had snapped. Or worse—

What if he got caught? Would he take her down with him? Would he finally say her name? Reveal everything?

She darted to the window, parting the curtain with shaking fingers. The black truck hadn't moved.

That cold lump of dread rose in her throat again, heavier this time. Denser.

Her phone vibrated. She jumped.

Caller ID: Stefan.

Relief hit first—hot and dizzying. Then came the suspicion.

"Hello?"

His voice was quiet. Slurred. "Hey."

Lauren stilled. Something was wrong.

"Are you okay? Did something happen? Did you get in an accident?"

A pause. "No. I'm fine," he said, but it sounded off. Hollow. "Went to the bar. Drank with that guy across the street. He left. I passed out. Woke up to the phone."

Lauren's heart thudded. Passed out?

"You passed out?" she repeated, careful to keep the judgment out of her voice. "That's not like you. You usually handle your alcohol just fine."

"I know," he muttered.

She could hear the faint rasp of his palm dragging over his face, like he was trying to rub the fog out of his head. "My head is killing me. I swear I didn't drink that much."

Her gaze flicked back to the black truck across the gravel. Still there. Unmoved.

"You're sure you were with that guy?" she asked. "The one with the camper topper?"

"Yeah..." A pause. "Pretty sure. We were at the bar. Talked about travel. Cool guy, I think. My memory's fuzzy, like I'm missing pieces."

Lauren's body tensed. Her gut twisted.

Missing pieces. Had Stefan been drugged?

But the truck hadn't moved. Not once. She would've noticed.

"I'm heading back," he added. "Sorry I worried you."

Lauren froze. Stefan never apologized. Not once.

Her thoughts splintered in every direction. A new tactic? A test? A trap? Or something else entirely—vulnerability?

..."It's okay," she said slowly. "I've got coffee waiting for you."

They hung up.

And the silence returned—thicker now, pressing in on the thin camper walls.

She stood there for a long moment, unmoving, staring at nothing.

Her thoughts skidded off track, scrambling for a plan that didn't exist.

She wasn't just paranoid anymore—she was burning from the inside out.

Something was off. With Stefan. With the man across the way. With everything.

The apology.

The headache.

The dream.

She poured herself a mug and stepped outside. The morning was warm and deceptively calm. Birds chirped in the trees like nothing had changed, like the world hadn't tilted slightly off its axis.

Lauren curled up in the lounger, sunglasses shielding the panic in her eyes, her coffee steaming in her lap. Her gaze fixed on the black truck. Unmoving. Unblinking. Like the shadow from her dream—waiting, watching.

And she realized with sudden, icy clarity—

Someone else was in control now.

And it wasn't Stefan.

Her heart thudded slow and heavy. The sun warmed her skin, but her insides felt cold. To anyone else, it was just another parked vehicle. But to her, it felt alive. A silent observer. A held breath.

Who are you? she thought, the words barely forming in her mind. Not about the man across the way, not entirely. Not even just about Stefan.

But about the thing beneath it all. The thing that had been watching, circling, waiting to strike. The presence in her dream. The silence in the trees. The sense that she wasn't just unlucky—she was chosen.

Who are you... and what do you want from me?

The thought rippled through her like a chill, settling into her bones.

She'd always relied on Stefan being the most dangerous man in the room. It made him predictable, manageable. But now... if someone could drug him—slip something past him—then they weren't just dealing with a threat.

They were being hunted. Or worse—studied.

She sipped her coffee slowly, forcing her hand not to shake. Her mind was moving quickly now, flipping through possibilities, cataloging threats. This wasn't the time to panic. This was the time to plan.

Option one: Leave. Grab the essentials. Disappear before Stefan returns. But where would I go? He'd find her eventually. He always did. And what if they—whoever they was—wanted her more than him?

Option two: play dumb. Pretend nothing's wrong, act like she believes Stefan's story. Keep him close. Watch for signs. Use his weakness to her advantage. He's never been vulnerable before. Maybe it's finally my turn to hold the leash.

Option three: confront the shadow. March across the lot and knock on that damn camper again. Force a conversation. Ask questions. Look into that man's eyes and find out what the hell he wants. Too risky. Not yet.

She adjusted her sunglasses, eyes still locked on the truck. What if it wasn't about Stefan at all? What if this was about her?

What if someone already knew what she really was?

A slow, creeping dread twisted through her gut—but along with it, something else: a spark.

Not fear—exactly.

Opportunity.

Because if Stefan was slipping, if he was losing his grip, then maybe she didn't have to wait for the perfect moment to run.

Maybe she could create it.

Her hand trembled slightly, and she tightened her grip on the mug. No one could see her break. Not now.

She looked down into her mug and whispered into the rising steam, "Clock's ticking."

And across the lot, the black truck stayed still.

But somehow, Lauren knew—she was no longer just being watched.

She was being tested.

The shadow in the trees.

10

Lauren sat motionless in the lounger, coffee gone cold in her hands. She waited for Stefan. Waited for whatever came next. Let this version be quiet. Just this once.

The sound of a truck engine broke the stillness—low and grumbling, growing louder as it moved through the narrow drive of the RV park. Her spine stiffened.

She stood, brushing invisible dust from her pajama pants, forcing her expression into something softer. Controlled. Measured.

She'd learned to wear different masks like armor. Smiles became shields. Softness, a strategy.

The truck rounded the bend and pulled into their gravel spot. Stefan stepped out, slow and unsteady, like a man wading through fog. Bloodshot eyes. Pale, drawn face.

For a moment—just a moment—something in her stirred. Concern, maybe. Or pity. Don't.

He looked... disoriented. Unmoored. Not like himself.

And that scared her more than rage ever had. Because vulnerability didn't make Stefan gentle. It made him cruel.

When he cracks, everything around him shatters.

He saw the look on her face—compassion, real or not, didn't matter. To him, it was a crack. A weakness.

His jaw tightened.

The shift was instant. "You think this is funny?" he snapped, stalking toward her. His voice was low, dangerous. Feral. "You think I'm weak?"

"No," she said, instinctively backing up. "No, I—"

His hand shot out. The slap cracked across her face—sharp, practiced, precise. That spot. Always that same spot.

Her head whipped to the side. Her hair flew across her cheek. The coffee mug slipped from her hands and shattered on the gravel. Her sunglasses skidded across the gravel.

Stefan's eyes darted across the RV park. Still. Too still. No one at the picnic tables. No one walking their dog. Just long shadows and quiet.

Lauren's heart thudded hard against her ribs. Not just from fear. From recognition. She'd seen that look before. This version of him—cornered, exposed, teeth bared.

She braced herself. He turned back to her, fury etched deep into his face.

She didn't run. Didn't scream. What was the point?

Without a word, he grabbed her. Scooped her up like she weighed nothing. Slung over his shoulder like a rag doll.

Stay calm. Stay limp. Don't make it worse. He climbed the camper steps and flung the door open without slowing.

Count the steps. Breathe. Stay small. She hated how her body folded so easily into the act—how it remembered what to do before she even gave the command.

Her body tensed as he shifted his grip— then drove his fist into her side.

He carried her to the back, then threw her down hard. Like she was nothing. Discarded luggage.

The mattress groaned beneath her. Pain bloomed in her ribs as she landed—white-hot and familiar.

She barely had time to scramble upright before his shadow loomed again.

Don't look afraid. Don't look strong. Just... neutral. Silent. Forgettable.

The rules she lived by weren't written—they were carved into her by survival.

"You think you've got the power now?" he barked, his face inches from hers. "You think I don't see what you're doing?"

Lauren didn't breathe. Didn't blink. She knew that tone—feral, erratic. This wasn't about her. It was about the script playing in his head.

"I'm not—" she tried, but the words dissolved in her throat.

Too fast. Too loud. Too soon.

He hit her.

Not a slap. His fist.

Her head snapped back. Pain exploded behind her eyes like fire. The room spun. Her ears rang. She tasted blood—sharp and metallic. Her own.

"I'm in control!" he screamed. "Do you hear me? I'm in control!"

Yes, she thought. Loud and clear. You always are—until you're not.

"Yes," she whispered, her voice threadbare. "You are."

He stepped back, panting, trembling with rage.

Then his hands went to his belt.

No.

The sound—snapping free, slicing through the air—made her stomach twist.

Please not again.

She knew what came next. The pain that would ripple through her body for days. The bruises she'd have to hide. The tears she'd refuse to shed.

But then—

The silence broke.

A knock. Sharp. Loud. Sudden.

Stefan froze, mid-motion. His eyes locked on hers. He raised a finger to his lips.

Don't speak.

Lauren nodded, breath shallow, every nerve on fire.

I won't make a sound, she thought. But I hope to God they knock again.

"What?!" Stefan barked at the door, his voice still vibrating with fury. Raw. Unfiltered.

A pause.

Then a calm voice—older, deeper, steady—answered: "Mr. Warren?"

Stefan blinked.

His head tilted. In that moment, something shifted.

He straightened. Ran a hand through his hair. Tugged his shirt down.

And when he turned toward the door, the rage melted from his features like it had never existed at all.

Curtain up. Costume on.

He opened the camper door with a practiced ease, one hand braced against the frame.

Lauren exhaled, barely audible. Her hands were shaking, but her face remained still.

Focus. Don't show it. Don't crack now.

"What?" he said again—softer now. Measured. Controlled.

The violence was gone from his tone, buried beneath layers of charm and calculation.

Lauren lay perfectly still, every muscle trembling, as the camper door creaked open.

She couldn't see him from the back, but she could hear the smile in his voice—

The one that made strangers trust him.

The one that made people believe him.

She could picture it anyway.

The way his shoulders relaxed, just enough to appear casual.

The slight tilt of his head, casual and disarming.

The smile that didn't reach his eyes.

The charmer returning.

But she knew better.

She knew what came before the charm.

She still felt the pain echoing in her ribs.

Still tasted the blood on her tongue.

"Ah—yeah. Sorry about that," Stefan said, stepping outside and pulling the door shut behind him.

"Just a bit of a rough morning. Everything's fine now. Thanks for checking."

Lauren lay frozen in the silence that followed, the world outside muffled through the thin camper walls.

She listened—his voice, calm, almost gentle, a costume stretched over a monster.

He didn't growl; he charmed. And that was always worse.

The voice he used when he wanted to seem harmless.

Warm. Trustworthy. Human.

She'd heard that voice at check-ins.

At gas stations.

At diners.

But this time, she wasn't just surviving it.

She was cataloging it.

Every word. Every pause.

Every shift in tone.

Because one day, she'd need to play it back in perfect detail.

She didn't blink. Didn't breathe too deep.

The bruises would fade.

But the plan—

That would stay.

Lauren lay motionless on the bed, her body throbbing in protest.

Her lip burned.

Her ribs pulsed.

Her ears still rang from the impact.

But she was alive.

And the belt hadn't come down.

She exhaled shakily and stared at the ceiling, Stefan's voice washing over her like acid. He was laughing now. Small talk with the older man. Friendly. Easy. Effortless.

The same man who, moments ago, had threatened to break her apart—now laughing like nothing happened.

Lauren pressed her hand gently to the swelling on her cheek, wincing. She blinked back the tears—not from pain. She knew pain. Pain was expected.

This was different. This was dread. Gnawing. Crawling. Spreading.

Because for the first time, she felt it in her bones—the truth she couldn't keep buried anymore.

One day, she wouldn't be fast enough. One day, the knock would come too late.

Something had shifted. And she needed a new plan. Fast.

He's going to finish what he started, she thought, stomach tightening. Unless something stops him.

Her mind raced. There wasn't time for guilt. There wasn't even time for fear.

Just instinct. Pure and cold.

She remembered the old man she'd seen earlier— Shuffling toward the bathhouse, towel under his arm. Quiet. Alone. Forgettable.

Would Stefan notice him?

Could he?

The thought made her sick. But the alternative was worse.

He'd have to become a piece on the board. One to keep another in check.

The early afternoon sun filtered through the trees in long golden beams, casting a warm glow over the RV park.

Birds chirped.

Lawn chairs sat empty.

Everything looked safe.

But inside—it wasn't.

She heard the door creak open. Then shut with a soft clap.

His boots hit the vinyl floor—

Heavy. Measured. Closer.

She didn't move.

Didn't breathe too deep.

Then he was there.

Framed in the doorway.

Eyes locked onto hers.

She sat still, perched on the edge of the bed.

Her cheek pulsed with pain, but she didn't lift a hand.

His face was calm now.

Too calm.

The kind of calm that came after the storm—but not before the next one.

Lauren forced her voice to stay even. Careful.

"There was an older man out earlier," she said. "Near the bathhouse. Looked like he was scoping it out before heading in."

Just a comment. A passing observation. Nothing more.

Stefan narrowed his eyes. She saw it—

That flicker.

Something catching fire.

"Alone?" he asked.

"Yeah. Late sixties, early seventies, maybe. I think he's staying in one of the older fifth-wheels near the woods."

And then she looked away.

Soft. Passive.

Like the kind of girl who wasn't thinking ahead at all.

The silence stretched tight between them—taut as piano wire, ready to snap.

Then he scoffed and looked her over with open disgust. "Get cleaned up. You look like a mess."

Lauren nodded quickly, avoiding his eyes.

Yes, sir. Just your broken doll. Busted up and obedient.

A mess you created.

Inside, she felt the smallest ripple of relief.

Not because she was safe.

But because—for now—his rage had passed her by.

She could still feel the sting in her cheek, the throb in her ribs.

The bruise beneath the skin of her thoughts.

This is what you made, she thought. This is who you turn people into.

And yet—she stood.

Because whatever came next—

She'd be ready.

The bait had worked.

She had redirected him.

For now.

She pushed herself to her feet.

Every movement sent pain sparking through her body—sharp at the ribs, dull at the base of her spine—

But she kept her expression neutral.

Controlled.

Measured.

No winces. No hesitation.

Nothing he could call weakness.

Don't give him anything.

Slowly, she gathered her shower bag and a towel from the closet.

Her fingers fumbled on the zipper, masked quickly by a controlled breath.

In the bathroom, she flinched as she lifted her shirt.

A bruise was blooming along her ribs—dark and deep, spreading like ink across a page.

She touched it gently, testing the edge of her breath.

That one will last.

The tiny camper shower wouldn't do.

Not for this.

She needed pressure.

She needed heat.

She needed space to breathe—if only for a minute.

A few minutes later, she emerged, posture upright but aching.

Every joint screamed.

But she walked like she was fine.

"I'm going to the shower house," she said, her voice steady. "I'll be right back."

Stefan didn't answer.

He'd moved to the window, fingers slipping between the blinds, scanning the RV park like a predator.

Watching. Calculating.

She didn't wait for permission.

She opened the door and stepped outside.

The warm light hit her face like a spotlight—too bright, too sudden.

She squinted, taking a brief moment to steady herself on the steps. Her eyes flicked toward the black truck.

Still parked.

Still watching.

Who are you?

And what are you waiting for?

Then she turned and walked toward the bathhouse—

Each step stiff. Deliberate.

Like her body moved while her mind hovered above it, detached and distant.

A shell.

A performance.

But still standing.

Inside the camper, Stefan watched her go.

He didn't move for a long moment.

Then he turned back to the window and leaned against the counter.

The park had gone quiet again—wrapped in that eerie stillness that always came just before the dark.

His thoughts twisted.

He hated the way that bitch looked at him now.

Behind the bruises—pity.

Like he was something broken.

Something manageable.

She thinks she can handle me.

Redirect me.

Outmaneuver me.

She was wrong.

But something about last night didn't sit right.

He was never the type to black out.

Not fully.

He knew how to drink, how to push the edge without falling over it.

But he'd woken up slumped behind the wheel of his truck—head pounding, mouth dry, sweat cooling on his neck.

No memory of getting there.

No memory of what had come between rage and nothing.

What the hell happened?

He didn't tolerate blanks.

Gaps made him feel weak.

Exposed.

And he hated that even more than pity.

That man—the nobody at the shower house—might finally serve a purpose.

Stefan needed to hurt something.

Something weaker.

Something easy.

Something to remind the world—and himself—who he was.

He stepped outside, letting the camper door click shut behind him.

The air was humid, thick with the scent of grills and pine needles.

A slow breeze stirred the trees, but it did nothing to cool the weight in Stefan's chest.

He scanned the bathhouse.

Still. Empty.

No sign of the old man yet.

He flexed his fingers. Cracked his neck.

The pressure behind his eyes wouldn't quit.

Then—

Movement.

A hunched figure shuffled toward the concrete building, towel slung over one shoulder, mesh bag swinging from one hand.

Stefan's lips curled into a tight, knowing smile.

There he was.

Fragile. Predictable. Perfect.

He followed at a distance.

Slow. Deliberate.

Gravel crunching beneath his boots in a steady rhythm.

The man reached the bathhouse and disappeared inside.

The door creaked shut behind him.

Stefan stopped near a tree, half in shadow.

Unmoving. Silent.

Pain made sense.

Dominance had rules.

Watching gave him back control.

From here, he could see it— The man's frailty. Brittle bones. Measured steps. Breakable.

He wouldn't strike now. Not yet. He needed to know more. His routine. His caution. Whether anyone would miss him.

Predators didn't strike quickly. They circled. Watched. Waited.

He exhaled slowly, jaw tight. This wasn't about rage anymore. It was about balance. Resetting the scale. The girl thought she could redirect him. Soften him. Manage him. She never would.

He wasn't made to be managed. He was born to break things.

The hiss of the water had stopped, but its echo lingered stubbornly in Lauren's ears.

Steam coiled around her like ghostly fingers as she stepped carefully out of the shower stall. Her muscles throbbed beneath the surface, each cautious movement sending sharp ripples of pain through her ribs, her shoulder, her hip—bitter reminders of Stefan's temper and the mask she would have to wear when she returned to him.

Just get dressed. Just get through this part.

She moved deliberately, wary of jostling her tender body any more than necessary. Reaching for the robe she had hung just outside the stall, she slipped it on. It was warm from the humidity, slightly damp from the heavy air, yet it felt soft and comforting against her bruised skin. She pulled it tightly around her, tying the belt securely at her waist, hugging herself against the chill that quickly replaced the warmth of the steam.

This is the only place I don't have to pretend.

The public bathhouse was empty now. Silence filled the space, broken only by the faint hum of the overhead lights, the gentle squeak of her bare feet on the slick tile floor, and the rhythmic, persistent drip of a faucet long ignored. Sunlight filtered through frosted windows, hazy and muted, painting long shadows across the room.

Lauren padded slowly toward the bench where her shower bag sat exactly as she'd left it—zipped up, untouched. Or at least, so it appeared.

She eased herself onto the bench, wincing as her bruised hip made contact with the hard surface. Her eyes stared unfocused into the distance, thoughts swirling chaotically through her mind—memories of Stefan's hands, his voice cracking with fury, the narrow escape from his wrath leaving her with nothing more than bruises. Her hand moved automatically to her bag, intending only to grab her phone and check the time.

Her fingers brushed something dry, unfamiliar. Paper.

A crease formed between her brows. She hadn't brought any paper.

Lauren's breath quickened, her heartbeat picking up a frantic pace. She pushed aside her small towel, her comb, the little travel-sized bottle of conditioner, her motions becoming more frantic—until she finally saw it clearly nestled at the bottom of her bag.

A single folded slip of paper, neatly tucked beneath her belongings, waiting patiently for her discovery.

A folded square of paper, tucked neatly among her things. The edges were slightly crumpled and soft from the steam.

Frowning, Lauren pulled it out with slow, hesitant fingers. Her breath caught before she even opened it, a cold pit forming in her stomach. Something about it felt wrong. Intentional.

She unfolded the note.

Block letters stared back at her, written in thick, harsh strokes— sharp, angry.

GET THE FUCK AWAY FROM HIM.

Her hands trembled—fingers twitching, knuckles pale. A flash of heat flushed her face, then vanished, leaving only cold sweat. Her stomach turned to ice.

The bathhouse suddenly felt colder, heavier, as if the walls themselves were closing in. Her skin prickled, a shiver sliding down her spine as the room seemed to constrict around her, stealing the last remnants of safety.

Lauren twisted her head sharply, scanning the quiet space, her breath quickening into tight, shallow gasps.

Even the dripping faucet had gone quiet. Just silence. And something beneath it—listening.

Had someone been here?

They must have been.

While she was vulnerable. Naked. Unaware.

Someone had stood mere inches away—close enough to touch her things, close enough to violate her personal refuge and leave behind this stark, terrifying message.

Whoever wrote it had seen the truth. And that meant it wasn't just in her head. It was real. And maybe—just maybe—she couldn't keep pretending anymore. Not for him. Not for survival. The illusion was crumbling, and denial wouldn't protect her. It was time to start acting like it.

Her gaze swept the row of stalls again. Empty, still—but that didn't matter anymore. Someone had been watching, hiding in shadows. Someone had been frighteningly close.

Lauren's fingers tightened around the note, crumpling the paper slightly as panic surged through her veins.

She stared down at her bag, heart pounding in her ears—louder, louder. Each beat sounding like a countdown. Beneath the note lay her phone, exactly where she had intended to reach earlier—now seemingly insignificant yet her only connection to safety.

She grabbed it with trembling fingers and clutched it as if it might anchor her to something normal, something tangible, something safe.

But who would write such a note? A concerned stranger—or someone playing a twisted game? Her mind raced with possibilities, each more unsettling than the last.

There was no signature. No hint of who had left it. No context—just those six words, sharp as glass.

But they were enough to tell her someone else knew. Someone else had seen through her carefully crafted façade, the mask she'd worn so skillfully. Someone else knew about Stefan—and the brutal reality she lived behind closed doors.

And that terrified her.

Because maybe—just maybe—someone had seen the truth—and cared enough to warn her.

Or perhaps the motive was darker—more personal. Maybe they wanted her gone for reasons she couldn't yet name.

With shaking hands, Lauren zipped the bag shut. Her nerves crackled with urgency, each second stretching like wire.

She slipped on her cloths and sandals, her breath catching as pain flared through her bruised body.

Rising slowly, each step toward the exit quickened her pulse. Her muscles clenched, every movement wound tight with fear.

She didn't look back. Couldn't.

The bathhouse silence had turned oppressive—too full, as if a shadow had slipped through unnoticed, its breath still clinging to the air.

Outside, the sunlight struck her like an interrogation light—brighter and harsher. As if judging her for secrets she'd desperately hidden away.

The air smelled sharper now—like ozone and warning. Like something about to break.

The gravel crunched beneath her sandals, loud as gunfire in the quiet. Her pace quickened, reflex overriding reason.

Her breath stuttered—rapid, shallow. Like prey.

Every camper loomed darker now—like hollow sentinels watching, waiting.

She didn't dare look toward the black truck—though its presence pulsed at the edge of her mind.

She could feel it. Heavy. Unmistakable. Its gaze pressing on her skin like a heartbeat gone wrong.

Watching.

Waiting.

She clutched her robe tighter, pulling it closer around her trembling body, as if the thin fabric might somehow shield her from whatever unseen dangers lurked just out of sight. Her heartbeat thundered, the note's words echoing relentlessly—consuming her thoughts like flames devouring dry paper.

Get the fuck away from him.

As if it were that simple. As if escape could be achieved by merely deciding to run—by stepping into a life untouched by violence, untainted by fear. As if freedom were just some easy, uncomplicated choice she'd somehow forgotten to make.

She quickened her pace again, almost jogging now, eyes locked on the gravel. The note burned hotter in her mind. Each hurried step whispered the same mocking question:

Could she even escape now? Or was it already far too late?

12

Lauren stepped into the camper, her chest tight with emotion, thoughts tangled like thorns in her mind. She paused in the entryway, the door clicking shut behind her, sealing her inside with a storm of questions and fears.

A hundred thoughts buzzed like hornets inside her skull, stinging her with doubt and dread. Her heart pounded—too loud, too fast.

Would her face betray her?

She pressed her lips together, forcing her expression into something neutral. Blank. Calm. A mask. But behind it, everything churned.

Should she tell him someone was watching?

No.

Absolutely not.

This was her secret, hers alone. Something about it felt too fragile to share, too dangerous to speak aloud. She needed to hold it close—at least until she had more clarity. She'd rushed into danger before, acted on impulse, and it had nearly destroyed her. She wouldn't make that mistake again. Not with this.

Not with something that felt like it could shift everything.

The weight of old missteps—misjudged people, misplaced trust—pressed on her like wet concrete. Heavy. Suffocating. She had to be smarter now. Sharper.

This was hers to carry. Hers alone.

Across the room, Stefan didn't turn. He stood at the narrow camper window, arms crossed, gaze fixed on the black truck across the lot. It hadn't moved in hours. His posture was rigid, coiled, like a trap set to spring.

He didn't speak.

Didn't glance her way.

Didn't acknowledge her at all.

And for once, Lauren was grateful.

She didn't want to be seen. Not like this. Not with her mask still slipping into place. If he looked—really looked—would he see it? The fear behind her eyes? The tremble beneath her skin?

She wasn't ready to find out.

She turned without a word and slipped into the bathroom, locking the door behind her with a soft, deliberate click. The space was small, humid, claustrophobic—but it offered sanctuary. Temporary, but hers. Safety measured in square footage.

She let out a slow breath and reached into her bag, pulling free the damp towel she'd wrapped around herself at the bathhouse. She hung it carefully on the hook by the mirror, her movements methodical, almost reverent—something to focus on.

Her fingers brushed the worn canvas of her bag again. That's when she saw it.

Her stomach dropped.

The note—wrinkled now, corners slightly damp, but the words still screamed silently from the page.

She stared at it for a long moment, the silence around her pressing inward like a held breath.

It had slipped into the side pocket—nearly forgotten in the frantic rush to get out of the shower room.

Why hadn't she tossed it then?

Why hadn't she trashed it? Flushed it? Burned it? Anything but this.

What kind of fool brings evidence back into the lion's den?

Her breath quickened. The note sat in her hand like a live wire, buzzing with danger. That single slip of paper felt radioactive—irrationally small for something that could detonate her entire world. Her hand trembled as she shoved it down into the bottom of her bag, fingers jamming it beneath clothes, beneath toiletries, beneath the weight of her own fear.

She'd get rid of it later—somewhere safe. Somewhere far away. Somewhere Stefan wasn't.

She carried the bag into the back bedroom, each step silent but deliberate against the worn vinyl floor. She placed the bag inside the closet with practiced care, as if tucking it away might also bury her unease.

Slipping out of her robe, she dressed in soft sweats and an oversized sweatshirt, every movement deliberate, mechanical. Her muscles ached —tight and bruised, reminders of Stefan's last outburst. Her shoulder still throbbed with a dull, persistent ache. She sank onto the edge of the bed, slowly, quietly, exhaling as she tried to settle into the silence.

But there was no peace here.

Not really.

Through the narrow blinds, she stared again at the black truck. Still. Unmoving. Watching.

Where was the driver? Just far enough to avoid suspicion? Close enough to keep her guessing? Her mind spun with possibilities, each one more disturbing than the last.

The door creaked open, and Stefan entered the bedroom. The air shifted immediately—denser, heavier—like it always did when he was near. Her spine stiffened.

"What are you looking at?" he asked, his voice sharp and suspicious.

She didn't turn to him. Instead, she forced a neutral tone and said, "Did you see the elderly man I mentioned earlier?"

Stefan rolled his eyes and let out a sharp exhale through his nose— his version of a laugh with all the joy stripped out. "Yeah. I saw him. Our usual plan won't work."

He gestured vaguely at her face, his voice curling with disdain. "You look like shit."

He said it like a fact. Cold. Unfeeling.

As if her appearance was some inconvenience. As if the bruises he'd left were a failure she owed him an apology for. Something she should've prevented. Hidden. Fixed.

And in his mind, maybe she did owe him that.

Maybe, to Stefan, her pain was just another mess he had to clean up —another problem she created by not being more careful, more obedient. Maybe she was just another broken thing he expected to keep functioning.

To smile. To serve. To endure.

And most of all, to stay quiet.

"I'll handle it myself," he muttered, annoyance simmering beneath the words.

"I'm sorry," Lauren said quietly, still not looking at him. Her eyes remained fixed on the truck. "What can I do to help?"

"I was thinking I'd take a walk," he continued, more to himself than her. "Just happen to run into him. Strike up a little conversation. Maybe offer to buy him breakfast."

Lauren nodded slowly. "Sounds like a great idea," she murmured, barely registering her own words.

A beat passed. Then, Stefan asked, "Want me to whip up something for dinner, or...?"

Her stomach churned at the thought of food, but she'd heard his stomach growl earlier—and knew better than to suggest he skip a meal.

"I'm good," she replied. "But you should eat. I can fix something if you want."

"Nah," he said, moving toward the door. "I was gonna walk to the office and grab one of those pre-made sandwiches. Gives me a reason to look around a bit."

"Got ya," Lauren mumbled, only half-listening.

He paused at the doorway, glancing back over his shoulder. She was still sitting there, still staring out the window like a statue. Like a ghost.

Without another word, Stefan left the camper.

Lauren watched his figure shrink down the road until he disappeared around the bend.

Only then did she exhale—long and low. The breath had been trapped for so long it felt like a stranger in her chest. Her shoulders sagged as the tension in her chest unraveled, just slightly. Not release— just a shift. A temporary loosening of the mask.

The silence returned, coiling around her like a shroud. Still. Suffocating.

She leaned closer to the window, forehead nearly touching the glass, eyes locked on the truck once again.

It was still there—unmoving. Watching. Waiting.

And so was she.

She stayed there, unmoving, forehead nearly brushing the glass.

Why now? Why here?

The truck hadn't moved in hours.

It hadn't mattered before. But now it did.

Because now she knew someone had gotten close—close enough to slip something into her bag, close enough to know the truth.

Her thoughts turned sharp, dangerous.

What had she overlooked? What else had they seen?

Every trip to the bathhouse. Every time she stepped outside alone.

Had they been watching when Stefan raised his voice?

When he didn't raise it—but made her flinch all the same?

Was it a neighbor? One of the retired couples she waved to in the mornings?

Or someone else entirely?

Her mind spun through faces. Voices. Movements.

That truck could belong to anyone.

But it didn't feel random—it felt staged. Planted.

Like a piece positioned before the first move.

13

Edward Wallace sat at the worn picnic table beside his aging RV, hunched over a weathered notebook. The late evening sun stretched golden fingers of light across the gravel lot, warm against his back.

His thinning silver hair stirred slightly in the breeze, and his wire-rimmed glasses had slipped halfway down the bridge of his nose again—something he was too absorbed in thought to fix. He wore a neatly pressed button-down polo tucked into ironed khaki pants, the kind of outfit he'd laid out with care that morning, out of ritual more than hope. No one ever came to visit, but that didn't mean he wouldn't be ready if they did.

He paused at the sound of footsteps—firm, confident strides crunching over the gravel.

A young man approached. Blonde, broad-shouldered, clean-cut, and dressed like someone who hadn't seen many hard days in his life. Edward's face lit up with quiet surprise. It had been a long day of silence —the only conversation he'd had was with the photo of his beloved late wife, Margaret, resting beside his notebook.

"Good evening, sir," Edward called out, his voice kind and steady, the sort that made people feel safe without knowing why.

The young man slowed, turned, and offered a warm smile. "How are you this fine evening?"

Edward chuckled softly, his voice carrying a gentle Southern drawl. "Well, I can't complain. Still on the right side of the dirt, as they say."

The stranger laughed and stepped closer, extending a hand. "That's a good way to look at it. I'm Zach."

Edward reached out and shook his hand, surprised by the strength in his grip—controlled, firm, assured. "Edward Wallace. It's a pleasure to meet you, Zach."

"Likewise, sir." Zach nodded toward the RV office. "I was just heading over to grab one of those pre-packaged sandwiches they keep in the fridge."

Edward made a face and wagged a finger in mock warning. "Oh no, son. You don't want those. They'll send you running for the bathroom—or worse, the ER."

He let out a soft laugh, and Zach joined in, the two men sharing a brief, easy moment in the fading light.

"Darn," Zach said with a playful grimace. "I was hoping to skip cooking tonight. My wife's back at the camper—not feeling too hot."

Edward's heart tugged a little. There was something about hearing that word—*wife*—that still made his chest tighten. "Well now, I'm sorry to hear that." He stood slowly, joints creaking in quiet protest, and began making his way toward the steps of his RV. "Tell you what—I've got leftovers from dinner. Far too much for one old man to finish. I'd be glad to share them with you."

Zach raised a hand politely. "I couldn't possibly ask you to do that."

"Nonsense," Edward said, already halfway up the RV steps. "Help an old fella out, will you? I hate seeing food go to waste."

"And truth be told," Edward added with a gentle smile, "it gets mighty dull cooking for one. I always end up with too much. Habit, I guess—Margaret never could cook for fewer than five. You'd be doing me a favor, really—take some for your wife."

Zach hesitated for just a beat—then smiled back. "Well, when you put it like that, how could I refuse?"

Inside the RV, the air smelled faintly of lemon cleaner and something warm—roast chicken, maybe, or stew. The space was small but homey, lived-in and lovingly kept. A crocheted blanket was draped over the back of the couch, and the walls were filled with framed photographs—snapshots of a life well-lived.

"You're young and spry," Edward said, moving carefully toward the kitchenette. "You need all the nutrients you can get."

"I appreciate it," Zach said, glancing at the photos with genuine interest. "Is this your family?"

Edward's eyes lit up with quiet pride. "Yes sir. That's my Margaret." He pointed to a framed photo of a smiling woman in a flowered dress. "She passed three years ago.

"It started as something small. A cough. Fever. We didn't take it seriously until it was too late." His voice dipped softer. "Still talk to her most days, like she's right here with me."

He smiled, a little wistfully, then motioned to a second frame. "Those are my boys—John and Matthew. Named after the good book. Margaret wanted strong names."

He opened the small fridge and pulled out a Tupperware container wrapped neatly in foil.

"And these here—these are my grandkids." He pointed to a photo of five children, grinning in swimsuits by a lake, water glinting in the sun behind them. "We used to go up to Broken Bow every summer. Best memories I've got."

He held the container up with a smile. "Hope you're hungry. Margaret always cooked like she was feeding a battalion."

"You have a beautiful family," Zach said sincerely, his gaze lingering on the photographs.

"Thank you." Edward's smile faded slightly. "I don't see 'em much anymore. Margaret's passing kind of pulled us all apart." His voice softened. "I think being around me just reminds them of what they lost."

Zach didn't say anything, but his silence felt intentional—respectful. Present. Edward appreciated that more than he expected.

"I bought this RV for Margaret," he continued, his tone shifting into something wistful. "Our dream was to travel once we retired. She had a whole list of places she wanted to see. After she passed, I found that list tucked inside her Bible." He gave a quiet chuckle. "So now I'm doin' it— markin' 'em off, one by one."

"Sounds like you're a man of your word," Zach said. He smiled, but it didn't quite reach his eyes. Something about the way he said it felt slightly off. Like the admiration was a performance he'd practiced.

Edward gave a humble shrug. "Would've been more romantic if I'd done it while she was still here." He tapped his chest lightly. "But I feel her with me. Right here."

He turned back to the small counter and packed the leftovers into a plastic Walmart bag—neatly labeled Tupperware, lids sealed tight. Everything folded, wrapped, and handled with care.

"Here you go, Mr. Zach," he said with a smile. "There's plenty in there for both of you."

"I can't thank you enough, Mr. Wallace. My wife'll really appreciate this." Zach hesitated, bag in hand. "How can we ever repay you?"

"No need," Edward said, brushing it off with a wave. "I appreciate the company more than anything. Gets mighty lonely out here."

Zach stepped toward the door but paused, thoughtful. "Actually... I'd love for you to meet my wife. Her granddaddy died last year, and she's been missing him something awful. I think meeting someone like you might really lift her spirits."

Edward's brows lifted, touched. "That sounds real nice."

"And listen—this might sound strange, but... I'd love to take you to breakfast tomorrow. Just to say thanks."

Edward chuckled, already shaking his head. "You don't have to do that, son. Young folks don't usually take old men out to breakfast."

"I'm not most young folks," Zach said with a wink.

Edward beamed. "Well then. It's a date."

As Zach turned to leave, he noticed the vibrant marigolds blooming in a pot by the steps.

"Nice setup. The flowers—do they mean something?"

"Thank you. Marigolds were Margaret's favorite. I bring them with me wherever I go. Feels like she's still ridin' along."

Zach's eyes drifted to the picnic table outside. The wind had flipped open Edward's notebook, its pages fluttering in the breeze. Before Edward could say anything, Zach stepped forward and picked it up.

"You left your notebook. Want me to bring it in?"

"Yes, please. Much obliged." Edward reached out for it—but paused when he noticed Zach glance down at the open page.

It was a list—cities and states, most of them crossed off. The last entry read:

Branson, Missouri

Beneath it, written in the same careful hand:

Mountain Home, Arkansas.

Zach's lips curled into a faint smile. His eyes sharpened, just for a second. "You been to all these places?"

"Workin' my way through," Edward said with pride. "Tryin' to finish 'em all before I kick the bucket." He gave a half-laugh, but it didn't quite cover the truth behind the words.

"Well," Zach said with an easy grin, "if I were you, I'd finish that list sooner rather than later. Time has a funny way of running out."

Edward nodded slowly, folding the notebook with care. "Ain't that the truth."

Zach stepped back outside, one foot already on the gravel. "Well, I'll see you in the morning, Mr. Wallace. Thanks again for dinner."

Edward nodded. "You take care now."

Zach turned, walking a few steps, then called over his shoulder, "Can't wait for you to meet my lovely wife."

Edward smiled warmly. "I'll be lookin' forward to it."

He watched Zach walk down the road until he disappeared around the corner, his footsteps fading into the quiet. He closed the door behind him with a quiet click and looked at the photo of Margaret on the shelf.

"That was a nice young man, honey," he said softly. His voice was tinged with hope, a trace of something almost childlike.

He glanced at Margaret's photo, then asked gently, "You think he'll show up for breakfast?"

He waited a moment in the stillness, as if waiting for her answer in the hush of the camper. The silence wrapped around him gently, familiar.

"Maybe he will," Edward said, smiling faintly. "Maybe he will."

14

She sprang into action the moment Stefan left for the hunt.

That's what he called it—the hunt. His voice thick with thrill, his eyes gleaming like a kid on Christmas morning. But there was a twitch behind the smile, a sharpness in his tone that hadn't been there before. Like the joy was too forced. Too rehearsed.

"Let's see what the night brings," he muttered, almost to himself, and then let out a low laugh—quiet, but not right. Not sane. He didn't bother hiding it anymore. He enjoyed the chase. The power. The ritual. He'd even whistled as he packed the cooler, murmuring, "Let's see what the night brings," as if it were a game.

To him, it was sport.

To Lauren, it was survival.

She waited exactly three minutes after he faded into the distance. Then, heart pounding and limbs trembling from equal parts fear and pain, she grabbed the note from her bag. Her fingers shook as she bolted from the camper toward the shower house, adrenaline pushing past the ache in her ribs and the fire in her bruised shoulder.

Inside, under the unforgiving glare of fluorescent lights, she tore the note into the smallest pieces her shaking hands could manage. Her palms were damp—not just from nerves, but from something deeper. Shame. Rage. Helplessness.

She dropped the shredded paper into the trash, her chest rising and falling in short, frantic bursts.

But as her fingers hovered above the can, doubt set in.

It wasn't enough.

Her eyes darted around. She yanked a wad of paper towels from the dispenser and layered them over the scraps—just enough to bury them without drawing attention.

Not too tidy. Not too sloppy.

Something forgettable. Something that said this never mattered.

It was just a note, she told herself. *Only ink and paper.*

But it had unspooled something inside her.

A warning.

A lifeline.

A trap.

She still didn't know which.

Someone saw me.

Someone knows.

That should have comforted her.

But instead, it felt like weight pressing against a fault line.

If they were trying to help, they didn't understand the rules.

Help could feel a lot like exposure.

And exposure could get her killed.

Stay quiet, she told herself. *Stay still. Stay small.*

The game hadn't changed.

But someone else had entered the board.

A sound near the entrance made her spin—fast.

Her pulse slammed against her throat. Footsteps. Voices. Was it Stefan?

Had he forgotten something? Had he doubled back?

A full-bodied panic bloomed in her chest. Her knees buckled as she dropped to the floor, feigning a frantic search for something lost—an earring, a contact, anything.

Her mind raced. *If it was him, she'd say she came to wash her face. That she'd dropped something important. That she was alone for two minutes. Just two.*

But it wasn't him.

A woman and her young daughter stepped into the humid room, arms full of shampoo bottles and towels, chatting casually. The girl giggled at something, blissfully unaware.

Lauren exhaled too fast, too hard. Her head swam.

She rose slowly and forced a brittle smile. "Hello," she said.

The word snagged in her throat like a splinter.

The woman said nothing—just gave her a glance, her expression tight-lipped, and tugged her daughter toward the farthest stall.

Lauren's smile faltered.

Something about the woman's silence gnawed at her. Was it judgment? Pity? Fear?

Did she know?

Lauren turned toward the mirror, almost without thinking, eyes scanning her reflection. That's when she saw what the woman had seen.

The bruises had bloomed overnight—dark, blooming clouds of purple and yellow spread across her jaw and under her eye. Her temple throbbed, visibly swollen. Her lip, slightly split.

She looked like she'd been in a bar fight—or worse.

No wonder the woman hadn't spoken. No wonder she'd stared at Lauren like she was contagious. Like she'd fall apart if touched.

Lauren flinched at the reflection.

How had she forgotten to cover them?

She always covered them. Always.

Letting the bruises show meant risking questions—attention she couldn't afford.

The mask had to stay in place.

Perfect. Untouched. Believable.

Even now, when part of her wondered if some things were better seen.

But not yet.

Not here.

Fingers shaking, she pulled her hair down to curtain her face and backed out of the shower house, nausea coiling in her gut as she crossed the gravel back toward the camper.

It was just a note, she told herself. *Just ink and paper.*

But it had unspooled something inside her. A warning. A lifeline. A trap.

She still didn't know which.

Inside the camper, she collapsed onto the mattress with a low whimper, the pain in her ribs stabbing with every breath. Her legs trembled beneath her. Her head throbbed with a hollow, pulsing ache.

She reached for the bottle of Tylenol, twisted off the cap, and swallowed four pills with a swig of lukewarm water anyway, just for the ritual of it.

Outside, the sun had long since slipped behind the trees, leaving only a dark sky smeared with stars.

She lay there, staring out the window, *willing herself to sleep. Willing the thoughts to go quiet. Willing the nightmares not to come.*

But sleep didn't come easy anymore.

She lay in the silence, haunted by jagged handwriting that screamed through her memory:

GET THE FUCK AWAY FROM HIM.

Was it a threat?

A plea?

A promise?

The words flickered in her mind like broken neon, pulsing and relentless.

She imagined the writer's hands—*were they shaking? Calm? Determined? Desperate?*

Was it someone who knew?

Someone who'd seen too much?

Someone who was still watching?

The camper door creaked open, and cold night air slipped in behind him.

Stefan.

She squeezed her eyes shut, her heart freezing mid-beat. *If he saw her awake, there'd be questions. If he saw the fear, he'd feed on it.*

She had to be asleep. Silent. Small.

He was humming. Quiet, satisfied.

Whatever had happened—it hadn't gone wrong.

That meant he wouldn't need to hurt her tonight.

Not physically, at least.

"Hey?" he whispered.

She didn't move.

He hovered for a moment, then walked the short distance to the kitchenette. She heard the click of the microwave door, the soft hum as it began to heat. He was warming up a plate of food—something home-made, something that smelled like it came from someone else's table.

The scent drifted through the camper—roast chicken, green beans, something buttery. It hit her with an unexpected wave of memory.

It reminded her of her parents' memorial service.

Strangers had brought food by the trayful. Casseroles. Pies. Roasted chicken.

As if food could fix the unfixable.

As if grief could be soothed with starch and seasoning.

She didn't want roast chicken.

She wanted her parents back.

But in the haze of loss and polite condolences, she remembered one thing clearly:

Her Granddaddy watching her from across the room.

He saw everything—the strain in her face, the way she stood too still, too quiet.

He crossed the room without a word, lifted her into his arms, and held her tight.

That was what the smell reminded her of.

Not food.

Not grief.

Him.

The one person who had always understood without her having to speak.

The one person who showed up when it counted.

She lay still, resisting the sudden, irrational urge to get up and join him. *To pretend they were normal.*

Where had he gotten a meal like that?

She didn't know.

But the comfort in the smell somehow made it worse—like something good had been dragged into their darkness.

A memory that belonged to safety—hijacked by the hands that hurt her.

She lay still as he ate in silence, each fork scrape a jagged sound against the hush of the camper.

It was almost worse than the violence—this pretending.

This grotesque imitation of normal life.

He thinks this is domestic. He thinks this is peace.

Her body stiffened.

The last time he thought they were playing house, she'd woken up with blood in her mouth and bruises down her spine.

She swallowed the nausea rising in her throat.

That smell—what it meant—was never his to have.

He left the plate on the counter. No cleanup.

Of course not.

After a few minutes, he climbed into bed, set his alarm, and eventually slipped into the slow rhythm of sleep.

But she didn't move.

Not yet.

Only after his breathing stayed steady for a long while did she open her eyes to the dark ceiling above.

Her body ached too deeply for rest.

Her mind was too loud for peace.

She reached down, pulled the blanket up higher beneath her chin, gripping it with aching fingers.

The fabric was scratchy. Too warm. Nothing like the soft flannel throws from her childhood.

Her thoughts drifted to a night long ago—

A thunderstorm had knocked out the power. She'd been seven.

She remembered climbing into her Granddaddy's bed with a flashlight and chessboard, her heart still pounding from the crack of lightning.

He hadn't said a word.

Just set the board between them and moved the first pawn.

They played by flashlight until the storm passed.

Until her breathing slowed.

Until she felt safe enough to sleep.

Now, the storm lived inside her.

And there was no board.

Only silence, and Stefan's steady breath beside her.

Sleep came and went in shattered pieces—each one yanking her back into the same looping nightmare.

The faces of the women they'd hurt, mouths gagged, eyes wide with agony. Their hands reaching out—not to fight, but to beg.

One of them whispered her name.

Not Sarah.

Lauren.

But now there was someone else.

An old man. Lying beside her. Pale. Waxy. Still.

Dead.

His body twisted unnaturally, like Stefan had broken him in too many places.

His eyes were open.

Staring at her.

Through her.

She wanted to look away, but couldn't.

And in the shadows, the figure was there again.

Closer now. Silent.

It never stepped fully into the light, but this time, it held the note in its hand.

Holding it out.

Demanding she look again.

GET THE FUCK AWAY FROM HIM.

She bolted upright in bed, chest rising and falling in wild bursts.

Her heart galloped inside her ribs like a caged animal.

She pressed her fists to her eyes, trying to steady herself.

Trying not to scream.

It was too much.

She reached for her *Reputation* hoodie from the closet and pulled it over her aching frame—soft, worn, hers.

She didn't think about the irony—not now.

She just needed something that could feel like armor.

Then she grabbed the blanket from the foot of the bed and slipped outside into the cool night.

The air kissed her bruised face with the softness of fog.

She wrapped the blanket around herself and curled into one of the loungers, eyes scanning the dark rows of the camper park.

Stillness.

Except...

There. Again.

That faint glow from inside the black truck.

Just a sliver of light in the cab—like someone reading... or watching.

The hair on the back of her neck prickled.

She narrowed her eyes.

She could walk over there.

Right now.

Demand to know who it was.

What they wanted.

Why they were watching.

But her feet stayed rooted.

It wasn't time.

She didn't know how she knew that.

But she did.

That person had left the note.

She felt it in her bones.

And whoever they were—they knew.

They'd seen enough to leave it.

And maybe... just maybe...

They'd seen enough to help her.

She watched the truck, wide-eyed and unblinking, until sleep finally pulled her under like a tide.

But even there, in the depths of her dreams, the figure stood waiting—

silent—and holding the note.

15

Lauren woke to the sound of birds chirping—delicate and far-off—threading through the low hum of a car engine idling at a nearby campsite. The morning air was crisp, but it did little to dull the throbbing ache in her body. Her eyelids felt glued shut—reluctant to face another day.

When she finally pried them open, the muted light of dawn spilled across the campground, softening the outlines of trees and trailers like a watercolor beginning to bleed.

She shifted in the lounger she'd fallen asleep in—and instantly regretted it. Pain surged through her ribs, deep and unforgiving, from where Stefan's fists had landed the day before. She winced and let out a breathless curse under her breath, carefully easing herself upright. Her joints cracked as she stretched—muscles tight, skin tender.

The discomfort was familiar now. Too familiar.

Her eyes flicked toward the black truck. Still parked across the gravel road. Silent. Unmoving. The dim light she'd seen glowing inside the night before was now off. No sign of movement. No shadow in the window.

A chill rippled down her spine—not from cold, but from the stillness. She stared at it for a long moment, heart knocking gently in her chest, before finally making her way back inside the camper. Each step jarred her body, bones aching under her skin.

The air inside was stale, thick with the scent of sweat and leftover tension. She tiptoed down the narrow hallway, holding her breath as Stefan's alarm blared from the back bedroom. She froze.

Sheets rustled. The mattress creaked.

Her pulse spiked.

She peeked through the half-open bedroom door—and found him already awake. Sitting on the edge of the bed, elbows on his knees, eyes locked on her—like crosshairs.

He looked her up and down with cold, deliberate disdain.

"Get ready," he said flatly. "We're taking Edward to breakfast." His eyes flicked to her cheek. "Do something about those bruises."

She gave a quiet nod, grabbing a pair of jeans and a loose hoodie from the closet. It smelled of dryer sheets and campfire smoke—faintly familiar, almost comforting.

As she dressed, her mind drifted—not away from the moment, but deeper into it. Stefan was being careful this morning. Too careful. Smiling. Charming. Playing host.

But it wasn't just the performance that unsettled her.

It was the effort.

He wanted Edward to like him.

Needed it, even.

And that was rare.

Why this one? she wondered, pulling the hoodie over her head. What makes him different?

It wasn't like Stefan to keep someone around this long. The mask usually came off quickly. And when it did, someone paid for it.

She moved slowly. Deliberately. Every joint ached, every limb protested. But she said nothing—she'd learned that lesson long ago.

She didn't know what Stefan was planning—but if Edward ended up hurt, it would be because she didn't stop it.

Once Stefan emerged from the bathroom, she slipped in and closed the door behind her. The light buzzed to life above, harsh and unflattering. She stared at her reflection in the mirror, willing it to lie.

It didn't.

The bruises were worse than she expected—angry swells of purple and blue splashed across her cheekbone and temple like paint hurled in fury. No amount of foundation would hide the raw truth today.

She stepped back, breath catching. *You fell down the steps. That would have to be today's excuse.*

Her fingers moved automatically, applying concealer in practiced strokes. She swept her hair forward, letting it fall like a curtain over the worst of it.

Then she reached for her sunglasses and slid them on like armor—not just to hide the bruises, but to shield herself from the reality of the situation. From the man waiting just outside the door. From the truth that she was playing a role in a lie that would get someone else hurt.

It would have to do.

They left the camper and drove the short stretch to Edward's lot. Stefan climbed out and walked up to Edward's weathered camper door while Lauren instinctively slid into the back seat, away from view.

The morning sun cut across the gravel like a blade, and she squinted against the glare.

Then the old man from the day before appeared. He stepped out slowly, as if the world had to make room for him to move. His plaid shirt was tucked neatly into pressed khakis, his silver hair combed with care. He looked like a relic from a gentler time, and something about that softened a small part of her.

He moved with the weight of years—but his eyes still held something light. Something kind.

Stefan greeted him with laughter, an easy smile stretched across his face.

It wasn't the mask he usually wore for strangers. It looked... real.

Lauren narrowed her eyes. The movement sent a sharp jab of pain across her cheek.

The passenger door opened with a creak. Stefan leaned in slightly and gestured toward her. "Hey, honey, this is Mr. Wallace. Mr. Wallace, this is my wife, Sarah."

Lauren managed a smile, despite herself. "Good morning, Mr. Wallace. It's a pleasure to meet you."

Edward's face lit up. "Please, call me Edward. The pleasure's all mine. Thank you both for takin' me out this morning."

"Didn't think I was serious, did you?" Stefan teased as he helped Edward into the truck.

"If I'm bein' honest, I did not," Edward replied, matter-of-fact. "But turns out I was wrong."

As they drove, Stefan and Edward fell into an easy rhythm, chatting like old pals. Lauren sat quietly in the back, listening with a strange mix of curiosity and detachment.

Stefan—this Stefan—was laughing. Smiling. Leaning toward Edward like he actually admired him. It was jarring. Surreal.

Edward talked about his late wife Margaret, their sons, and his five grandchildren. Lauren chuckled at the appropriate moments, mimicking Stefan's reactions, but her mind was elsewhere. Always elsewhere.

She kept glancing at the mirrors. Out the windows. Half-expecting to catch a shadow in pursuit. A flicker of movement. A presence.

But nothing stood out. Not yet.

The diner was a small roadside spot with a flickering neon sign and booths that had seen better decades. Stefan helped Edward out of the truck, guiding him with unexpected gentleness. Lauren followed, careful not to show how badly she was hurting.

Each step was a silent scream.

Inside, they were led to a booth near the window. Lauren hesitated. She wanted to sit next to Edward—partly to shield him from the worst of her face, partly to put a layer between herself and Stefan.

Stefan, as if sensing her intent, slid smoothly into the seat across from Edward.

Edward smiled kindly. "Do you mind sittin' next to an old man?"

"Not at all," she replied. Then added with a soft laugh, "Do you mind if I keep my sunglasses on? I've had a migraine since yesterday."

Edward nodded gently. "Of course not. My Margaret used to get migraines too. I'm sorry you're not feeling well, dear. You didn't have to come just for me."

Lauren placed her hand on his, grateful for the distraction. "I wouldn't miss it. Zach was really excited for us to meet you. You remind me a lot of my Granddaddy."

Edward's face softened even more. "Zach told me your grandfather passed recently. I'm so sorry to hear that."

The lie hit her like a slap. Her head jerked up to Stefan in disbelief.

Her fingers twitched once—small, almost imperceptible. But real.

He said Granddaddy was dead.

The words replayed in her mind like a scratched record, skipping at just the wrong place.

He wasn't supposed to touch that part of her. Not him. Not ever.

She forced her hands to still. She folded them carefully in her lap. Pretended to read the menu.

But her pulse pounded behind her eyes.

You sick son of a bitch.

He's not dead.

The one person who matters—and you made him part of your story.

Her story.

You buried him with your lies just to make yourself more believable.

Her stomach turned, but she smiled. Just enough to be polite. Just enough to survive.

Let him think it worked.

Let him think she believed the script.

Let him feel safe.

So she could take everything back.

Edward studied her face. Something flickered behind his eyes—just a moment of quiet consideration. He turned the page of the menu slowly, his glance lingering an extra beat.

She hadn't expected that story. Not from Stefan. Not about Granddaddy.

A flash of memory hit her: sitting cross-legged on the porch, chess-board between them, his hand resting gently on her back after her parents died. Him teaching her to be a few steps ahead of the opponent.

He's not dead, she thought again. *And I won't let you bury him.*

Edward, catching the discomfort in her voice, quickly patted her hand. "It's okay, sweetheart. I shouldn't have brought that up."

He changed the subject with practiced ease, flipping open the menu and chatting about pancakes and bacon as if nothing had happened.

Lauren blinked back the heat rising behind her eyes and nodded along, pretending everything was fine.

She barely touched her food. The hum of the restaurant—the clinking of cutlery, the soft conversations, the scratch of menus—faded into background noise.

Across the table, Stefan and Edward talked about the weather. Road trips. The next stop on Edward's RV journey.

And then—

Everything stopped.

A familiar face flashed across the TV screen mounted in the corner. The diner noise collapsed into a low, buzzing static.

Lauren's heart seized in her chest.

Erin.

The nurse from the hospital. The one who'd handed her ice chips. The one who had squeezed her hand like it meant something.

Now her face stared back from the television, beneath a bold, terrible caption:

ERIN NELSON – MISSING.

A hotline number scrolled across the bottom of the screen. The words *Mercy Hospital – Springfield* seared into Lauren's mind like acid.

A photo beside Erin's name showed a group of nurses laughing together—everyone smiling except Erin. Her eyes were locked on the camera. Direct. Unblinking.

Her stomach flipped hard. Her mouth went bone dry.

She turned to Stefan.

Rage cracked open in her chest like a fault line. A dormant volcano waking up.

For one split second, her fury was naked on her face.

Stefan caught it—his brow twitched. Confused. Calculating.

Was it anger he saw? Fear? Recognition?

He couldn't tell.

When he blinked, the look was gone—replaced with something unreadable.

He followed her gaze to the TV. And then... he smiled.

Smiled.

Lauren shoved out of the booth so fast the table rattled. "Excuse me. I'm not feeling well. I—I think I'm going to be sick."

She didn't wait for a response. She barely made it to the bathroom in time.

The door slammed behind her. She dropped to her knees and vomited violently into the toilet.

Her head throbbed.

Her ribs screamed.

Her stomach churned with bile and heartbreak.

When it was over, she slumped against the grimy wall, hands trembling, tears slipping down her cheeks.

And for the first time in ages, she let herself cry.

She cried for Erin. For the nurse who had shown her kindness. For the woman who didn't deserve to be punished for caring. For the life that had likely been stolen in the dark.

If I had known—God, if I had known—I would've stopped it. I didn't see it in time. I didn't.

I'm sorry. I'm so fucking sorry.

She cried, knowing the monster was still out there—sitting at that booth across from her, smiling like he belonged. She cried for the kind, unsuspecting Mr. Edward Wallace—sipping coffee, never realizing the predator sat across from him.

She cried for herself, too.

For the lies.

For the bruises.

For the woman she used to be before Stefan took her apart piece by piece.

And as she sat there on the sticky bathroom floor, the world narrowed around her. One thought screamed through the static in her mind:

I hate him. I fucking hate him.

But beneath the tears, something else stirred.

Not just grief.

Not just rage.

Something colder.

A plan.

16

They pulled into the RV park, the tires crunching over the gravel like brittle bones snapping under pressure.

Edward remained gracious to the end, offering a soft smile despite Lauren's obvious discomfort. She managed to explain—through clenched teeth and a carefully practiced smile—that her migraine had gotten the best of her.

She lied so easily, it made her sick.

Edward, kind as ever, insisted they not worry about him. "Take her back to rest," he said gently. He thanked them for breakfast. For the company. For the conversation.

As if they hadn't just dragged him into their private hell—for sport.

Stefan's silence was sharp. His hands gripped the steering wheel too tightly, his knuckles bone-white, his jaw twitching in restraint. His eyes flicked to Lauren's face again and again, cutting through her like glass.

Edward, oblivious, laughed softly beside him—still trying to ease the tension that hung in the cab like smoke from a fire no one had admitted to starting.

When they reached Edward's camper, Stefan hopped out, plastering on a grin like a mask he no longer enjoyed wearing. He walked around the truck and helped the frail man out gently, like a grandson tending to his beloved grandfather.

It made Lauren's stomach turn all over again.

Edward turned to her before heading inside, his eyes kind, his voice even softer. "Ms. Sarah, it was wonderful to meet you. I pray you feel better soon. Get some rest."

Lauren forced a polite smile, though it felt like it cracked her face apart. "Thank you, Mr. Wallace. I hope to see you again."

Oddly enough... she meant it.

Edward's presence—his warmth—felt like a memory from a life she could barely touch anymore. Something buried under bruises and blood and silence.

Stefan walked him the rest of the way to the camper, the two of them still talking, still laughing, like something had clicked between them.

Edward gave her a kind smile, but as he turned to go, something in his eyes clouded for just a second.

Not doubt, exactly.

Just... something heavy.

Like something didn't sit quite right.

But he couldn't name it.

So he let it go.

Lauren didn't care.

She didn't want to care.

All she wanted was to be anywhere but here. Anywhere beyond the gravitational pull of the monster she lived with.

Erin's face still burned in her mind—clearer now, sharper.

A name to match the ache:

Erin Nelson. A nurse from Springfield. Missing.

She had been real.

Kind.

And now... gone.

Stefan returned to the truck like a storm rolling back to shore. He slammed the driver's side door so hard the rearview mirror trembled. For a moment, he just sat there—his jaw tight, chest heaving, eyes locked straight ahead.

Lauren barely had time to brace before the inevitable.

"You stupid little bitch."

She flinched hard, her arms flying up to shield her face out of instinct.

But the hit didn't come.

Not to her.

Instead, Stefan's fist slammed into the dashboard, rattling the glovebox and sending a sharp burst of air through the vents.

"You couldn't even keep your shit together for a couple fucking hours?" he spat. "You stupid, stupid little bitch. You just wait—this time, I'll make you scream."

Lauren didn't speak. Didn't move. She stared blankly out the windshield like she was watching someone else's life play out in front of her. A stranger's misery.

Maybe he'd kill her this time.

Maybe she wouldn't even mind.

And then they both saw it.

At the same time.

"Would you look at that," Stefan muttered, eyes narrowing.

Lauren's breath caught in her throat.

The black truck was gone.

The spot where it had sat for days—silent, watchful—was now empty. No tire tracks. No headlights. No lingering shadow in the mirrors.

Like it had never been there at all.

Her stomach twisted. She didn't know why—but its absence left something cold behind. Heavy. Unsettling. Was it fear? Relief? Loss?

She couldn't name it. Only feel it settle into her like a weight.

A faint metallic scent drifted through the cab—blood, maybe, or oil. Something sharp. Foreign. It caught at the back of her throat, made her stomach lurch.

Stefan, on the other hand, was livid.

He jerked the gear into reverse, backing toward the camper with enough force to rattle the entire cab. His voice came sharp and bitter— but not to her. Not this time.

"You little piss-ant piece of shit," he growled, eyes locked on the empty gravel. "Not even a goddamn goodbye."

Lauren opened the truck door cautiously, bracing for the rage to turn back on her.

But Stefan didn't even glance her way.

He was too distracted—too fixated on the vanishing truck and its mysterious occupant.

She tiptoed around the front of the truck, keeping herself small. Invisible.

Stefan kicked at the gravel, shouting into the trees.

"I actually liked that guy!"

It didn't make sense—Stefan barely knew the man.

But that was the point. It wasn't about friendship. It was about control. Someone walking away before Stefan was finished with them? That cracked something deep inside him. It was a challenge. A loose end. And Stefan didn't tolerate loose ends.

Then his fury turned physical. He tore through the campsite—ripping open storage bins, yanking hoses free with jerky, violent movements.

Lauren didn't wait for instructions.

Her body didn't need instructions. It already knew what to do. She moved efficiently—unhooking the power, folding cords, organizing supplies with practiced, surgical precision.

Her body throbbed from the night before, every movement pulling at bruised muscles and swollen joints. But she didn't make a sound.

She didn't ask where they were headed.

She didn't need to.

When Stefan packed like this, it meant one thing.

The hunt was back on.

But had Edward been the target? Or just a test?

Or was something changing in Stefan?

Something deeper. More erratic.

Something she couldn't quite put her finger on yet.

I used to know how to read him.

I used to know what was coming before it came.

They pulled away in silence, gravel dust trailing behind them like smoke after a fire.

Stefan's face stayed blank, but she could feel the storm brewing beneath. He hadn't let go of Edward.

He wasn't finished.

That wasn't how this worked.

Lauren leaned her head against the cool glass of the window and let herself drift into a fitful sleep as they turned onto U.S. 160, heading east.

She jolted awake when the engine cut off.

The sun was high now, spilling in through the windshield and blinding her for a moment.

She blinked, disoriented, eyes locking onto the blue and yellow sign in the distance.

Walmart.

She rubbed her eyes, her mind still thick with sleep. "Where are we?" she asked, her voice dry and cracked.

"Mountain Home, Arkansas," Stefan replied. His tone was flat. Calm again—*too* calm.

"We'll get supplies," he said, shifting the truck into park. "Then we're headed to Norfork Lake. It's just up the road."

Lauren nodded. Barely.

Stefan nodded toward the store. "Go get us groceries. I'll fuel up."

Lauren reached for the door handle.

"Deodorant," he added. "A new razor. And grab some of those Little Debbie cakes I like."

She paused, nodded. "Okay. Anything else?"

"No. Now go. And leave those sunglasses on."

His voice scraped like sandpaper. Her cheek throbbed beneath the lenses. She reached up to touch it—gently—and still flinched.

She walked into the store like a ghost, her body on autopilot. Lunch meat. Bread. Cheese. Snacks.

Behind her, the camper shrank with every step, its fiber glass shell gleaming under the sun. It looked so harmless from the outside.

But she knew better.

It wasn't just a home. It was a cage.

And walking away didn't feel like freedom.

Just another version of trapped.

Everything felt distant. Mechanical. Like she was watching herself move.

Her body ached. Her head swam.

Erin's face haunted every aisle.

The news report. The note in her bag.

Bill. Judy. *All ghosts now.*

Halfway down the canned goods aisle, she froze.

Her hand hovered over a can of soup.

Something felt... wrong. *Off.*

She glanced over her shoulder, pretending it was casual.

A man rounded the corner at the end of the aisle, pushing a cart, eyes glazed with boredom. Nothing unusual. But still—her skin prickled.

She moved on.

In the dairy section, the feeling returned—heavier this time. Like a breath on the back of her neck. Too close.

She glanced around, pretending it was nothing.

A woman—wrangling a screaming toddler—reminded her of Nurse Erin.

It wasn't her, of course. But the gentle face, the quick glance of concern... it struck something deep.

Lauren looked away too fast, her chest tightening.

An elderly couple squinting at yogurt.

No one looking at her.

And yet... it clung to her—the sense of being seen.

The pressure clung to her skin—silent, invisible, unrelenting.

Her heartbeat stuttered. She picked up the pace, moving through the rest of the store with a kind of frantic efficiency—grabbing, bagging, checking out.

Just get out. Just keep moving. Just breathe.

At the checkout line, she caught sight of herself in a mirrored panel above the register.

The sunglasses did little to hide the truth.

The bruising bled beneath the frames. Under the fluorescent lights, the swelling looked grotesque.

People could see—if they wanted to.

But no one looked.

No one asked.

They never did.

They never wanted to.

She swallowed hard and kept moving.

So much had happened. Too fast.

Stefan was spiraling—losing control in a way she hadn't seen before.

The violence was worse now. Quicker.

There was no pattern anymore. No warning signs.

She wasn't sure what would set him off next.

As she stepped out into the sunlight, she paused—tilting her face toward the sky. Just for a second. Just to let the warmth remind her she was still alive.

Then she saw it—in the far corner of the lot, parked beside their camper: Edward's truck.

Stefan was leaning against the side, talking to Edward through the open window, smiling like nothing had ever happened.

Lauren's pulse skipped.

What the hell was he doing here?

She pushed the cart slowly toward them, confusion twisting in her gut like a blade.

What the hell was he doing here?

Had he followed them?

Or worse—had Stefan orchestrated this? Lured him here?

But why?

Edward had seemed genuine—soft-spoken, kind, harmless.

So what was this?

A trap? A coincidence?

Or had Edward somehow been watching them too?

The thought felt too big to hold. Her grip on the cart tightened until her knuckles burned.

"Well, hello, Mr. Wallace," she called out—voice too bright. Too brittle. "So glad to see you."

Edward nodded, his smile warm and genuine. "Such a pleasure to see you too, Ms. Sarah. Hope you're feeling better."

"I am," she lied again. "Thank you. I should get these groceries put away."

She turned away, hands trembling on the cart handle. She pulled the camper steps down and disappeared inside.

The moment the door shut behind her, she moved like a machine—putting the groceries away in silence. Every motion measured. Controlled.

But when she stepped back outside, a chill ran down her spine.

The hairs on her neck rose.

Her eyes scanned the lot. Swept over every car. Every shadow.

No black truck.

No camper topper.

And yet—her chest tightened.

Why am I even looking for it?

The thought struck her hard—but it didn't feel new. It felt old. Familiar. Like something buried just beneath all the others. Waiting.

How would he have known where they were going?

She hadn't even known until they'd pulled in.

Stefan wouldn't have told anyone.

And Edward—Edward had said it himself. They were the only people he'd spoken to in days.

So why did it feel like someone had followed them here?

Was it paranoia?

Caution?

Or something worse—an instinct clawing its way to the surface?

She didn't know what scared her more—

The idea of the man in the black truck...

Or the gnawing feeling that she was losing control, piece by piece.

Her grip on reality, on safety, on herself—it all felt just a little too loose.

And then, just as suddenly as it had come, the feeling slipped away.

She blinked. Shook her head. Forced her feet to move.

Not now.

She could come back to it later.

She glanced toward the two men, still chatting like nothing was amiss.

Lauren climbed back into the truck, reached into her backpack, and popped two ibuprofen into her mouth. She chased them with a cold Coke that hit her tongue like metal.

Her eyes never stopped scanning the lot.

Searching. Watching. Waiting for any glimpse of the black truck.

It wasn't over.

Not by a long shot.

She felt it in her bones.

She wanted to believe it was nothing—

A ghost of adrenaline.

A trick of her battered brain.

But deep down, the thought had roots.

And it was growing.

17

The drive from Walmart to the RV park should have only taken fifteen minutes, but it stretched out like a slow-moving fog. Stefan drove like a man unraveling—braking without warning, accelerating only to slam the pedal again seconds later. The truck jerked and sputtered down the road, mimicking the storm building beneath his skin.

In the side mirror, Edward's old pickup followed behind them like a tired hound. Steady. Unbothered. Unaware.

Lauren sat with one hand gripping the door handle, the other pressed lightly to her stomach. Not because she feared a crash—she didn't. Not really. It was the rage pouring off Stefan like heat from asphalt that made her brace herself. It wasn't the driving. It was him.

If the truck wrecked right now, she'd be okay with it. Not because she wanted to die—but because it would be simple. Easier than what waited on the other end of this drive.

Stefan was unraveling in real time, and Edward—poor, kind Edward—was caught in the undertow. Did he even realize how close the current had pulled him?

Her stomach twisted.

Because she had done that.

She had made Edward a target—handed him over like an offering on a silver platter.

In a desperate attempt to get Stefan's focus off of her, she'd served up Mr. Wallace instead.

The guilt sat in her throat like ash.

And yet—she would do it again.

She didn't want to.

She didn't mean to.

But she would.

And if Stefan made Edward the next target—

She'd stop it.

She'd step in.

She'd take the hit, because she'd earned it.

It wouldn't be the first time.

"Come on, old man," Stefan muttered, eyes locked on the mirror, his jaw clenched so tight a vein bulged at his temple. His knuckles were bone-white on the wheel.

They reached a stop sign. Edward paused a little too long.

Stefan slammed his palm against the steering wheel. Smack. "Damn it, old man. Move your ass!"

Lauren bit the inside of her cheek, hard, to keep from laughing. There was something darkly funny about Stefan, predator and puppet master, throwing a tantrum over a kind, gray-haired gentleman who posed absolutely no threat—at least, not yet. The irony made her want to scream and smirk at the same time.

By the time they pulled into the RV park, Stefan had mostly composed himself. He always did. Like slipping into character. He grabbed his fake ID from the glovebox, ran a hand through his hair, and stepped out with that same well-rehearsed confidence—like he had a script he knew by heart.

Normally, Lauren stayed behind. But not today.

She slid out of the passenger seat and followed, letting the camper door click shut behind her. She needed to hear what he said. She needed to see how he sold the lie this time.

The RV park office was cool and carried a faint scent of sunscreen, rubber worms, and stale coffee. Large windows overlooked the lake. Sunlight spilled across the floor in warm stripes. The building doubled as a tiny general store—one shelf of canned goods, another of bug spray and fishing tackle.

Stefan was already at the counter, scribbling on a clipboard, his voice smooth and casual. "One week."

Lauren froze just inside the door.

One week?

Her stomach flipped. That wasn't their pattern. When they were hunting, Stefan never booked for that long. Two nights. Three, max. In, out. Set the trap. Take the kill. Disappear.

But one week?

That meant confidence. That meant he thought the prey was already in the net.

Before she could puzzle through the shift, Edward strolled in behind her, practically beaming. "Would you look at that," he said, glancing around. "Reminds me of the campground we used to take the kids to. Just beautiful."

He gave Lauren a warm, gentle smile and stepped in behind Stefan. "Zach, were you able to get spot 46?"

"Yes sir, I did," Stefan replied without looking up. "We'll be neighbors."

Lauren's stomach knotted again. That was far too close. If Edward was the prey, Stefan had just tethered them together—and too tightly. Too recklessly.

She glanced at Stefan, at the fake name—Zach Warren—on the clipboard. She wasn't surprised by how easily he signed the name—they'd done this dozens of times. What caught her attention was the length of the stay.

Something was off. Something was changing.

And for the first time in a long time, Lauren didn't know what Stefan was thinking.

She glanced up at the small surveillance camera nestled in the corner of the ceiling. "Shit," she murmured under her breath.

There they were—on camera together. Arriving side by side. Talking. Smiling at the clerk. Looking like they belonged. Just another happy couple checking in. A neat little visual alibi that tethered her to him. Too tidy. Too dangerous.

She exhaled slowly and turned toward the wide window behind the counter. Outside, the Ozark woods loomed like sentinels—tall and still and endless. Trees stretched into the heavy sky, their limbs swaying in the sluggish wind.

For one fleeting moment, she imagined stepping into them. No plan. No goodbye. Just walking until the sounds faded—until even the wind and birds and distant traffic disappeared into nothing. Until she disappeared right along with them.

"Let's go!"

Stefan's voice cut through the moment like a blade, sharp and jarring. She barely flinched.

Lauren glanced at her phone. 2:07 PM.

How was it already that late? The day had unraveled fast—hospital, breakfast, rushed packing, groceries, the stop at the lake—and now here they were.

Another trap disguised as a vacation.

Their camper settled into spot 46. Next door, Edward began setting up in 45, moving at his usual deliberate pace, hauling gear with quiet precision. He adjusted cords, tightened awning legs, stacked wood beside his steps.

Stefan watched him for a beat, then—unexpectedly—walked over to help.

Lauren stood in the shade of their awning, arms crossed, sunglasses veiling her tired, bruised eyes.

This relationship between Stefan and Edward puzzled her.

Was Stefan drawing him in for the kill?

This wasn't just bait anymore.

It was different.

And that difference made her uneasy—because unpredictability in Stefan wasn't safer.

It was more dangerous.

There was something unsettling in the ease of their conversation, in the way Stefan tilted his head and genuinely laughed.

Was he luring Edward in, or—God help her—was he actually enjoying the man's company?

Her gaze drifted to Edward again.

Just as she lifted her sunglasses to swipe at the sweat along her brow, she caught it. The change.

The color drained from Edward's face. Laughter slipped away, sudden and silent, like a curtain falling. His eyes darkened—haunted, distant.

He was staring directly at her.

Lauren quickly lowered her arm and slipped her sunglasses back into place, turning her face to the side. But it was too late.

Stefan had seen it too—the shift. The silence.

"You okay, Edward?" he asked, frowning slightly.

Edward blinked. "Oh... yeah."

"You sure? You need to sit down?"

Edward hesitated. His voice came softer, fogged. "Yes. I think I got a little lightheaded."

Lauren's pulse skipped—a hard, jarring beat in her chest.

He'd seen it. The swelling. The bruises. The truth, written all over her face.

And somehow, he understood.

"I'll go make you a sandwich," she said quickly, and without waiting for a reply, turned toward their camper.

Inside, she moved fast—ham, cheese, a bag of chips—rushing like every second counted. Her hands trembled, not from nerves, but urgency. She needed to get out, get to Edward, before Stefan changed his mind or followed.

She rounded the corner in a rush—and slammed straight into him.

"Oh—I'm sorry!" she gasped, stepping back.

He didn't move. Just stood there, blocking the path, eyes narrowed.

His voice dropped an octave, low and dangerous.

"Don't mess this up," he said—low, clipped, and dangerous.

But something in his tone faltered. Not enough to name. Just enough to notice—and it made her skin crawl.

She didn't know what it was. Not fury. Not fear, exactly. But something close.

A fracture. A shift. She nodded and slipped past him, pulse thudding in her ears.

Edward's camper was modest and homey, with frayed curtains, sunfaded upholstery, and shelves lined with photos in mismatched frames. It smelled like cinnamon, coffee, and something older—time, perhaps. Or memory.

He sat at the tiny kitchen table, hands folded neatly in front of him. His face was calm, but beneath it was a quiet storm. A knowing.

"Ms. Sarah," he began.

"Mr. Wal—"

"No, ma'am." His voice was gentle but firm. He gestured to the chair across from him. "Have a seat."

She obeyed, head bowed as her hair fell forward like a curtain.

"Take off the sunglasses."

Not a request. A command.

And she did. Before she could second-guess it. Her fingers shook as she pulled them off, revealing everything.

He drew in a sharp breath. "My dear child..."

"I'm fine," she whispered.

"Stop." His voice cut through her like a bell. "Whatever excuse you're about to give is a lie. You know it. I know it."

He leaned forward.

"We don't have much time, do we?"

She blinked, startled by his clarity.

Her lips parted. Just a breath—she almost told him everything.

But the words caught.

Not yet. Not like this.

"My mother wore that same face," he said softly. "I watched my father do that to her—over and over again."

"I'm okay," she said again. *Quieter. Smaller.* It sounded pitiful even to her own ears.

"No, Sarah. You are not." The words were kind, but relentless. Unyielding. "You don't have to explain anything. But we're going to figure this out. You're not alone anymore."

Something shifted in her chest—a warmth, cautious but real. *Kindness—unsolicited. Undemanding.* It had been so long.

"I know you don't believe me," he added. "But I'm here now."

"And I know what it costs to speak up," he added, more to himself than to her. "I've been silent before. Too many times."

A flicker of shame crossed his features—but he covered it with a smile. "Not this time."

She nodded faintly, then slipped her sunglasses back on. She hadn't realized how cold she was until he said it—not alone. The words should've warmed her. Should've cracked something open. Instead, they landed like soft rain on scorched earth. Not enough to bloom anything yet. But she felt them. Deep enough to sting. Deep enough to hurt.

Because he didn't know. He didn't know she'd put him in Stefan's crosshairs. Didn't know she'd made him the shield. The decoy. Didn't know she might've handed him his death sentence.

And yet he offered her hope anyway.

"I should go," she said, standing.

Her hand was on the door when it burst open. She jumped back with a gasp.

"Hey!" Stefan stood there, smiling too wide. Too bright. "Just checking on you. Got the chess board set up."

Lauren forced a laugh. "You scared me!"

Edward rose to meet the moment. "Thanks for letting me steal your beautiful wife for a bit."

Stefan chuckled, sliding an arm around Lauren's shoulders. "Just don't steal her away from me."

As they walked back to their camper, Stefan's hand gripping her shoulder like a leash, Lauren risked one glance over her shoulder. Edward stood at the window, watching—his shoulders tense, brow furrowed, a silent question etched into his face. He lifted a hand—just slightly—in a quiet wave. And she almost stopped. But Stefan tugged her forward, steering her away with that too-wide grin and eyes that saw everything. Back at their camper, once the door clicked shut behind them, Lauren slipped away to the far side of the bedroom, where Stefan wouldn't see her watching. Edward's camper stood just yards away. Still. Silent. She moved to the narrow window and peeked out—careful, hidden. Through the curtain gap, she spotted him at the kitchen table now, sitting alone, elbows resting on the wood, his face turned toward their camper like he was listening for something unspoken. She pressed her fingers to the glass, just for a second, as if reaching for something she couldn't name—connection, forgiveness, maybe even absolution.

You shouldn't have to pay for my survival.

If it came down to it... she'd let him. And she hated herself for that. After a moment, Edward stirred—just slightly—like some unseen weight had passed between them. He stood and moved toward the window. And just before she stepped back, just before the curtain slipped into place again, Lauren looked up. He met her eyes. Then he bowed his head, eyes closed, lips moving in silent prayer. And he prayed.

18

Lauren woke to the familiar scent of bacon crackling on a hot griddle and the rich aroma of coffee drifting through the air. Her eyes fluttered open, catching the soft golden light filtering through the curtains—thin streaks of morning that painted the small bedroom in a warmth that never reached her bones.

She blinked a few times, letting the quiet linger. The other side of the bed was empty. Stefan was already up.

She didn't move. Not right away. Instead, she lay there motionless beneath the thin blanket, cocooned in the fading wisps of sleep, not quite ready to re-enter the world. Her muscles ached faintly—a dull reminder that tension never truly left her body anymore. Even sleep had rules. Even rest required calculation.

Last night returned in fragments—chess, music, laughter that strained to sound real.

If a stranger had passed by their camper and glanced in, they might've seen nothing out of place. Just a young couple sharing a quiet evening. Peaceful. Normal.

But Lauren knew better.

The stillness unsettled her. Even the thought of peace made her body tense. She didn't trust it. Her shoulders remained tight, as if bracing for a slap that hadn't landed yet.

Every game of chess was a performance. A negotiation. A test.

And, as always, she let him win—not out of mercy, but because she had learned what losing cost her.

Letting him have the final move was safer. Easier.

Checkmate, bitch.

She let him win. Let him say it. Checkmate, bitch.

It was his thing—a ritual he clung to like a badge.

Sometimes with a smirk. Sometimes with venom. But always with the same meaning: he won.

And Lauren always let him.

Because losing was safer than what came next.

Giving him the final move kept the game alive.

What he never saw—what he couldn't see—was that she was playing a different game entirely.

And in her game, she was always three moves ahead.

Stefan liked rituals. He liked rules. Patterns. Predictability. It made him feel in control.

But lately... the patterns were slipping.

He was changing—and that made him dangerous in new ways.

Lauren sighed and forced herself to move. Her bare feet met the cold floor, and she slipped into a pair of black leggings and her favorite oversized Taylor Swift hoodie. Soft at the edges, frayed at the cuffs, and still faintly scented with lavender fabric softener. It smelled like safety—or the closest thing she had to it.

At the window, she pushed the curtain aside. The sun had risen higher, casting shimmering flecks across the surface of the lake—like diamonds scattered across glass. Birds chirped in the trees. A breeze rustled the leaves, making them whisper secrets she couldn't quite catch.

Maybe today, she'd find a quiet moment by the water.

Earbuds in. World off.

In the kitchenette, she poured herself a cup of coffee from the pot Stefan had left on the warmer. It was dark and bitter, just the way he liked it. She added a splash of cream, just the way she liked it. A quiet act of rebellion.

Outside, Stefan stood at the portable griddle beside the camper, spatula in hand, flipping bacon and eggs like a man who had never harmed a soul.

She stepped out, shivering as the crisp morning air kissed her skin.

For a heartbeat, it all looked so ordinary. So civilized.

A bird called from a nearby tree—clear, rhythmic, almost cheerful.

Too cheerful.

It sounded rehearsed—like a line from a play she no longer believed in.

And that, she reminded herself, was always the most dangerous illusion.

"Good morning," she said, the words smooth and easy—another move in their ongoing match.

"Morning," Stefan replied, his tone just as casual, his sunglasses hiding whatever calculations lurked behind them.

Their pleasantries were practiced, mechanical. Not signs of affection, but moves on a chessboard. Opening positions.

A smile here. A soft tone there.

Neither of them fooled.

She curled up on the weathered lounger beside the camper, tucking her bare feet beneath her.

Stefan returned the smile, sunglasses masking his eyes. "Want to go for a hike later?"

She glanced toward the lake, letting the stillness wash over her for a moment before answering. "That sounds nice. It's so beautiful here."

"Yep," he agreed. His voice was light, but his eyes lingered on her a beat too long—like a wolf eyeing a rabbit pretending to sleep.

Then: "Hey—how was Edward yesterday? When you took him the sandwich."

Her heart gave a subtle jolt.

Innocent words—on the surface. But Stefan didn't ask innocent questions. He was watching her. Measuring.

She forced a calm expression. "He seemed tired. Grateful. I think he appreciates having someone to talk to."

Stefan nodded slowly, lips twitching into a half-smile as he turned back to the griddle. He slid the spatula under the eggs and flipped them onto a plate with practiced ease. "Breakfast's ready. Want to see if Edward wants to join us?"

Lauren kept her features relaxed. Casual.

"Sure."

She stood, smoothed out the wrinkles in her leggings, and made her way across the damp grass, the dew chilling her bare feet with every step.

At Edward's door, she knocked gently.

The door creaked open almost immediately.

There he was—Edward Wallace, dressed in his signature pressed khaki pants and a blue plaid shirt so crisp it looked like it had just come off the ironing board. His kind eyes crinkled at the corners when he saw her.

"Good morning, sunshine."

This time, her smile came easily. "Good morning, Mr. Wallace. Stefan made breakfast. We were wondering if you'd like to join us?"

Edward glanced past her, toward the other camper. His gaze landed on Stefan, who stood at the griddle pretending not to be watching. With a faint smirk, Edward raised a hand in a polite wave—an old man's quiet defiance.

"I'd love to join you," he said warmly. "Let me grab my coffee and I'll be right out."

Lauren thanked him and turned back, walking slowly through the grass, sunlight breaking through the canopy above. She liked this place. Despite everything, it had a calmness that wrapped around her like a soft blanket—until Stefan yanked it away.

By the time she returned, Stefan was already seated at the picnic table with his own plate, chewing slowly. The table was concrete—old, rough, and stained by years of rain and sun. It always made her hips ache after a while.

Of course he didn't wait for me. But for Mr. Wallace?

She frowned.

He hadn't waited.

He'd invited someone to breakfast and sat like a stranger—already eating, already checked out.

Moments later, she heard the slow rhythm of Edward's footsteps approaching through the grass. She turned and greeted him warmly. Stefan stood, smiling wide, offering his hand with the same charm he wore like cologne—easy to apply, impossible to trust. The mood was light. Edward matched Stefan's performance, playing his role with practiced grace. Lauren was quietly grateful for his ability to pretend—for his willingness to tuck away the truth he'd glimpsed behind the curtain.

For now.

She fixed a plate for herself and one for Mr. Wallace—fluffy scrambled eggs, a few slices of bacon, a careful portion of everything Stefan had cooked. Hosting. Pretending. Mask on. She brought both plates to the table, along with her mug of coffee, and settled into the morning performance.

They ate under a wide blue sky, the lake shimmering in the distance, birds sweeping low over the trees like strokes of a paintbrush. It looked like a postcard—but felt like a setup.

Stefan carried most of the conversation, every word polished, every smile just a little too easy. But Lauren noticed the flicker in Mr. Wallace's expression—the slight tightening of his jaw, the pause that didn't quite belong.

Stefan had noticed it too.

Edward wasn't quite himself.

"You feeling okay, my old friend?" Stefan asked, his tone light—almost concerned.

Edward chuckled, his voice warm and practiced. "Yes sir. Just one of those days. My bones are complaining, and I think I'll spend the evening with a game of solitaire."

Lauren jumped in, sensing the weight in the air. "I'm not feeling so springy myself, Mr. Wallace."

Her smile was genuine, her eyes softening as she looked at him.

The tension eased, just a little.

As they finished the meal, Edward pushed his plate away with a contented sigh.

"Hate to eat and run, but I think I'll lie down for a bit. Feels like the weather's about to change. My bones always know these things."

He smiled gently. "I appreciate the invitation."

Edward stood slowly, wincing as he straightened.

Lauren rose instinctively. "Do you need anything?" she asked.

But Stefan was already at his side.

"Here, let me help you."

He guided Edward toward his camper, moving at a careful pace as they disappeared around the corner.

Lauren stayed behind. Back at their camper, she began cleaning up—stacking plates, rinsing them beneath the weak stream of water in the tiny sink. Her hands moved mechanically, her mind drifting miles away.

Unease lingered like smoke—thin, sour, impossible to ignore.

Stefan sat outside finishing his coffee, but his attention was elsewhere. His gaze was fixed on something in the distance.

A new camper had arrived.

A small tent was being pitched near the tree line. A compact car parked beside it. A lone figure adjusting the poles—slow, methodical.

He watched. Unblinking.

Then he stood and stepped back into the camper.

"We're going on a hike," he said flatly.

Lauren wiped her hands on a dish towel, forcing her expression to stay neutral. "Let me grab my shoes."

She laced up her hiking boots and pulled on her backpack, slipping in water bottles and a few granola bars—more out of habit than hope.

"All set," she said quietly, not meeting his eyes.

Without another word, they set off down the gravel road and disappeared into the shadows of the trees.

Lauren adjusted the straps on her backpack, tightening them across her chest. The sun had climbed higher now, burning off what remained of the morning chill. Birds called in the distance—sharp, cheerful notes echoing through the canopy. For a moment, she allowed herself to feel something like peace.

Stefan led the way without a word, hands shoved into his pockets, whistling a low, off-key tune that clashed with the peaceful setting. His gait was loose, easy—but Lauren knew better.

He wasn't relaxed.

He was thinking. Watching. Plotting his next move.

The trail wound gently uphill, weaving between tall pines and scattered wildflowers. Lauren reached out as they passed a cluster of purple blooms, brushing her fingers across the petals. She smiled. Just for a second.

Stefan walked ahead, whistling that same low tune, but then—without turning—he spoke.

"You know, I used to hike with a buddy back in high school. We'd sneak out, hit this old trail near the quarry."

Lauren didn't answer. She kept her eyes on the path, her breath steady, each step deliberate.

"One time, he got cocky—racing ahead, showing off. I told him to slow down, but he didn't listen. So when we reached this narrow part near the ledge..."

He let the silence stretch long enough to make her wonder.

"I stuck my foot out. Just a little."

Her stomach clenched, but she didn't look at him. Didn't give him the reaction he wanted.

"He went down hard. Rolled all the way down the slope." Stefan chuckled. "Broke his wrist. Knocked out a tooth."

A beat.

"Called it an accident."

Lauren glanced at the slope to their left—loose gravel, jagged rocks, too steep for running. The other side looked better: a ridge, just high enough to duck behind.

Not that she'd run. Not today.

But it helped to know the exits.

Then Stefan's voice dropped, lower now.

"Sometimes I wonder... if I meant to do it."

And just like that, he moved on. Like nothing had happened.

The trail curved uphill through tall pines, the breeze brushing cool air against Lauren's face. Wildflowers sprouted in the dappled sunlight, untouched and unnoticed.

They reached a small overlook where the lake shimmered far below, framed by pines and slivers of sky. It looked like something from a post-card—still, perfect, unreal.

Lauren stepped forward and caught her breath.

It should have been a moment of peace.

She should have been able to relish it—the hush of the trees, the glint of sunlight on the water, the cool air brushing her skin.

But Stefan's story clung to her, thick, oily residue. It coated everything.

Even this.

What should have felt like freedom only reminded her of the drop. The slope. The ease with which someone could fall—and how easy it was to make it look like an accident.

He turned everything into darkness.

Even beauty.

She took a step back from the edge.

Just in case.

Stefan dropped onto a flat rock near the edge, stretching out like a man without a care in the world. Arms behind his head. Legs crossed at the ankles.

Like he owned the view. Like nothing could touch him.

Lauren stayed standing.

She didn't trust stillness. Not from him. Not here.

She pulled a bottle of water from her pack and took a long drink, her eyes drifting across the shoreline. A couple of boats floated in the distance. Somewhere nearby, a woodpecker tapped a slow, rhythmic beat into the bark of a tree.

Finally, she found her own rock—a few feet away from Stefan—and sat down carefully, tucking her knees to her chest.

For a while, they said nothing.

In another life, Lauren might have believed this was real—a quiet life. One where people drank coffee, made breakfast for old neighbors, went on hikes and didn't flinch at every sound.

A part of her wanted to hold onto the moment. Bottle it. Memorize every detail.

But the feeling crept in anyway—that low hum beneath the surface, like something was out of place. Just slightly. Like a picture frame just slightly off-center. Barely noticeable... but once you saw it, you couldn't unsee it.

A single crow cawed in the distance.

Lauren flinched.

19

As Lauren and Stefan made their way back to the trail, the sounds of nature wrapped around them—the soft rustle of wind in the trees, birds chirping overhead, the crunch of dry leaves beneath their boots. The path ahead was shaded and still, and for a brief stretch, Lauren let her mind drift.

Then—crack.

A sharp snap, like a twig breaking underfoot.

Her heart jumped. She froze, eyes darting to the trees.

Nothing.

Stefan kept walking, oblivious, his voice rising and falling as he rambled about nothing in particular. A memory from a past trip, maybe. She wasn't listening. He didn't pause, didn't turn around. Didn't notice the shift in her breathing.

Lauren gave a soft laugh under her breath—part relief, part self-mockery.

Girl, you can't even enjoy five minutes without getting twitchy, she scolded herself.

The tension in her shoulders eased slightly as she forced the thought away. The forest really was beautiful. The trees arched above like a living cathedral, their leaves swaying in a rhythm that felt older than time. Shafts of sunlight filtered through the canopy, scattering gold across the trail.

She let out a slow breath.

For the first time in what felt like ages, she let herself enjoy it. Just a little.

Nature had always been her refuge. Something steady. Uncomplicated.

Maybe—just maybe—a place like this could be home someday.

The idea made her smile, soft and fleeting. She imagined a life far from all this noise, from Stefan's moods and the games and the lies. A place where she didn't have to listen for footsteps or hide bruises with makeup.

But just as quickly as it arrived, the thought vanished.

She knew better than to dream too much.

As they rounded a bend, her eyes caught movement in the trees. More campers had arrived. Tents and RVs now dotted the edges of the campground, some tucked between trees like quiet secrets. A few kids chased each other in the distance. Smoke curled from a nearby fire pit.

Then she saw it.

A tent—one she hadn't noticed before. Maybe it had been tucked out of sight from the trail earlier. Or maybe... maybe it hadn't been there yet.

It sat deeper in the trees than the others, tucked among the trunks as if it didn't want to be seen. A lounger rested outside the flap, and a small, compact car was parked beside it.

Lauren slowed.

She didn't recognize the tent. Or the car. And yet... something about the setup unsettled her. Not memory—instinct.

The air around it felt charged. Familiar. Like a place she'd stood before. Like eyes had once lingered—not just watching her, but looking through her.

It was déjà vu without the memory.

Like someone had written her name in the dirt and then smoothed it over.

She thought back to Lake Meredith. To the trees. To the unease she'd brushed off back then. She hadn't noticed it at the time—hadn't known what to look for.

But now, she did.

She noticed this tent.

And whatever was inside it... she was certain it had noticed her, too.

Stefan led the way, pushing ahead through the trees, oblivious to the tension clinging to her. Lauren followed close behind, her footsteps crunching over dry leaves and gravel. The quiet of the forest pressed in on her, making her feel strangely exposed—like she was walking across glass.

Each step carried her farther from safety. From the illusion of safety.

When they finally reached the campsite, Lauren dropped into one of the aging lounge chairs beside their camper. The fabric sagged beneath her, but she didn't care. She was just grateful to sit, to breathe, to have a second to not pretend.

Lauren reached into the cooler, pulled out two bottles of water, and held one out to him.

"Here," she said, more command than question.

Stefan took it without a word. Twisted the cap. Drank.

His eyes scanned the trees like he was searching for something—or someone.

Then: "I'm hitting the shower."

It wasn't a suggestion.

Lauren nodded, careful to keep her voice even. "I'll get the chicken marinated."

He paused. Just long enough to make her regret speaking.

"Don't over-season it this time," he said, casually. "Or under-season it."

A smile flickered at the edge of his mouth—but there was no warmth in it.

Then he turned and walked off, brushing his hands on his jeans like she still disgusted him.

She didn't watch him go.

Then—for a beat—there was silence. Not peace. Just hollow.

Lauren sat back in the chair and took a long drink of water, letting the bottle cool her hand. But the unease lingered. Like something had shifted and hadn't snapped back into place.

She stood to head inside.

That's when it hit her.

The feeling.

It hit her gut like a stone—heavy, cold, and paralyzing.

She was being watched.

She froze, her fingers brushing the camper's door handle. Her breath caught. The air thickened—distorted, like it held something just beyond her sight.

Don't turn around, she warned herself.

Because if she did—if she looked—what if someone was there?

What if they were watching her right now?

The thought churned her stomach.

She gripped the bottle tighter and stepped quickly into the camper, closing the door behind her with a quiet click.

Inside the camper, Lauren moved to the kitchen, trying to keep her hands busy. Distraction was strategy. Not salvation.

She peeked out the small window above the sink, scanning the campground just beyond the far side of their camper. Nothing unusual. A few campers milling around. Kids chasing each other between picnic tables. Laughter. Porch chatter. Ordinary things.

But ordinary never comforted her anymore.

She crossed the camper and turned to the window behind the couch, her eyes drifting toward Edward's RV. His door was propped open, screen latched to keep the bugs out.

A sliver of safety—still visible.

She let herself smile—just barely.

Edward had become something she hadn't expected: a quiet anchor. Not loud, not heroic. But present. Steady. A soft voice in a world that had become far too loud.

But even the thought of him couldn't shake the sense that something was off.

It crept along her spine like a shadow with no source.

She shook her head and opened the fridge, pulling out the chicken breasts. She moved quickly, mixing the marinade and coating the meat with practiced care—measured, methodical. Like if she got the seasoning right, maybe something else would settle into place, too.

She slid the tray back into the fridge, then grabbed her shower bag, a clean set of clothes, and a towel.

The walk to the shower house took her along the far edge of the grounds, where the trees pressed in and the shadows grew taller. It should have been peaceful—sunlight filtering through the canopy, the scent of pine and damp leaves—but her body ached with every step, the bruises from Stefan's last rage still blooming under her skin.

She felt every one now—a map of pain etched into her bones.

As she neared the tree line, a sound.

Soft. Quick. Almost imperceptible.

A shuffle. A snap. A presence.

She stopped.

She held her breath, scanning the trees.

"Hello?" she called, voice steadier than she expected.

Silence.

The kind of silence that pressed in from all sides. Thick. Listening.

The only sounds now were the chirping of birds and the wind rustling through the leaves. Peaceful, on the surface. But a shiver still crept down Lauren's spine.

Pull it together, she told herself, but her steps quickened anyway. She glanced around.

Two boys were playing near the swings, their mother reading on a nearby bench. A couple sat at a distance, murmuring softly in front of their camper.

But no one else.

She pressed forward.

By the time she reached the shower house, her pulse had slowed, though the unease hadn't fully let go.

Inside, it was quiet—blessedly so. The stalls were large, clean, and private. Each one had a bench and a row of hooks behind the door.

She stepped into the last stall, locked it with a firm click, and hung her towel over the bench. Her shower bag swung gently from the hook as she pulled out her phone and started her playlist.

Her playlist shuffled to Taylor Swift's "The Archer"—a song Lauren had leaned on during more nights than she cared to admit.

"I've been the archer, I've been the prey..."

The lyrics drifted through the stall, soft and echoing through the steam. Too soft for the space. Too raw for her mood.

She gave a quiet, bitter laugh.

Of course, she thought. *Perfect timing.*

A sudden clang echoed from the far stall. Metal against tile.

She froze. Breath caught.

Nothing moved.

It's just plumbing, she told herself. *Just old pipes.*

But her heart was already racing.

She peeked under the stall wall. No feet. No movement. Just tile and shadows.

Silence again.

Her muscles stayed tight for another few seconds—then slowly, cautiously, began to unclench.

The warm water poured over her skin like a reset.

Steam curled through the air, blurring the edges of the stall—and her thoughts.

Maybe it was nothing, she told herself. Just nerves.

For a few minutes, she let herself believe it.

She rinsed. She sang. She let go.

When she finished conditioning her hair, she turned off the water, breathing in the dense humidity around her. She grabbed her towel and dried off slowly, the warmth of the towel a strange sort of comfort.

She dressed quickly, the fabric sticking slightly to damp skin. Then she brushed her hair back into a loose ponytail, humming softly under her breath.

Still half-lulled by the rhythm of the shower, she unlocked the stall and stepped out into the tiled hallway.

She didn't notice it right away.

But as she turned to shut the stall door, something caught her eye.

The world around her seemed to slow.

The warm steam that had once felt comforting now pressed in like a weight. Her chest tightened. Her vision blurred. Her world tipped sideways.

She clutched the towel in one hand.

And froze.

Her eyes locked onto the mirror.

Her breath caught.

Words had appeared there—written in the condensation, bold and jagged.

GET THE FUCK AWAY FROM HIM.

Her heart slammed against her ribs. The message looked fresh—like it had just been scrawled. Like whoever had written it was still nearby.

Fear surged—hot, cold, all at once.

She stepped forward on shaky legs and wiped the mirror with her towel, her hands trembling as the letters smeared into nothing.

Her reflection blinked back—wide-eyed, pale, unraveling.

She had erased the message, but it was already burned into her memory.

The handwriting was different.

Not like the note.

But the warning was the same.

Someone had followed her. Watched her. Knew.

Unless...

Maybe she was imagining it.

Maybe the exhaustion, the bruises, the lies—maybe it was all catching up to her.

What if there was no one else?

What if her mind was finally... fracturing?

No.

Her jaw clenched.

She wasn't crazy.

Her focus sharpened.

This wasn't random.

It was targeted. Precise.

She was the common thread.

They weren't just watching.

They were waiting.

For what, she didn't know.

But the game had already begun.

They knew exactly who Stefan was.

And they weren't afraid to say it.

She spun around.

Nothing.

The shower house was empty. Still. Quiet.

Lauren's skin prickled. She felt it again—that invisible gaze. That suffocating awareness of eyes she couldn't see. The air buzzed—heavy, electric, alive with it.

She jammed her damp towel into her bag and yanking the zipper closed with shaking fingers.

Her pulse thundered in her ears. She shoved the stall door open—and bolted.

Outside, the brightness of the afternoon slapped her like a shock.

Everything looked ordinary. Too ordinary.

Children squealed with laughter by the playground. A woman on a nearby bench looked up from her book and blinked as Lauren rushed past—barefoot, wild-eyed, hair dripping down her back.

Lauren didn't stop. Didn't look back.

She ran like her life depended on it.

Because this time... it just might.

As she rounded the final corner, her foot caught on an exposed root and she went down hard, skidding across gravel and dirt into their campsite. Her knees and elbows hit first, scraping raw across the gravel.

"Damn it," she hissed through gritted teeth.

Her palms stung. Blood smeared across her jeans. The world tilted slightly—her vision swimming.

For one disoriented moment, she thought she heard footsteps behind her.

A presence.

A shadow closing in—a shadow that might not even exist.

But it was only her breath.

Only her heartbeat, thundering in her ears.

Then came the laughter.

Not the warm kind.

Not the kind that made you feel human.

No. This was cold.

Cruel.

Detached.

She looked up.

Stefan sat in the lounger, a beer in hand, his head tilted back, amusement painted across his face.

"You should've seen the way you skidded," he cackled. "What the hell were you doing?"

Her heart thundered from the sprint, but instinct was louder.

Don't tell him anything real.

Never give him ammo.

Never let him in.

"I... I think a dog was chasing me," she blurted. A flimsy lie. Pathetic.

She hadn't seen a single dog in the RV park. Her voice trembled, and she hated how obvious it sounded.

Still on the ground, she glanced at her knees—scraped, bleeding. Her elbows throbbed.

Perfect. Now my limbs matched my face.

Stefan didn't move. Just sipped his beer, the can swinging lazily from his fingers.

She stood slowly, brushing dirt from her jeans. Her freshly washed outfit was already ruined—streaked with grass stains and gravel dust.

"Gonna try to get these stains out," she mumbled, almost to herself.

He didn't respond.

She slipped into the camper, shutting the door harder than she meant to.

But she didn't head for the bathroom. Didn't grab the stain remover.

She sat.

Dropped into the dinette seat like her bones had given up.

Her body ached, her thoughts spun, and her gaze fixed on the window.

The glass reflected her faintly—ghost-like. Pale. Bruised. Afraid.

The mask slipping—just enough to see the girl underneath.

The words from the mirror rang in her head, louder now.

GET THE FUCK AWAY FROM HIM.

Like a scream carved into silence.

20

The evening came and went in a haze of tension and silence.

Another dinner. Another forced routine.

Another game of chess that ended as they always did—Stefan victorious, smugness coating every syllable as he leaned back and drawled:

"Checkmate, bitch."

But this time, Lauren hadn't lost because she let him win.

She lost because she wasn't there.

Her focus was fractured—scattered like broken glass through her mind. Her eyes kept drifting to the narrow camper window, scanning the dusky shadows for movement. Every gust of wind rustling through the trees made her flinch. A distant bark clenched her gut with panic. When a car door slammed two lots down, she jolted so hard her knee hit the dinette table.

Stefan noticed.

Of course he did.

"Skittish little thing tonight," he said, sipping his beer with casual menace.

She mumbled something about being tired.

The truth? She just wanted the night to end.

She wanted the night to pass without incident.

She wanted to be alone—away from the tension, the lies, the unbearable silence between what she knew and what she couldn't say.

When she finally pleaded for bed, Stefan just shrugged and followed.

He undressed quickly, slid beneath the covers, and was asleep within minutes—like a man with nothing to fear. Like a man who'd done no wrong.

Lauren curled inward, arms wrapped tight around her middle.

Praying for silence. For peace. For something close to rest.

But sleep didn't come.

Hell did.

The moment her eyes closed, the dream returned—more vivid than ever. More brutal.

Erin was screaming.

Her voice—ragged, raw, desperate—echoed through the void.

She was begging Stefan to stop.

Her hands reached for Lauren.

And Lauren couldn't move.

Couldn't scream. Couldn't cry. Her limbs felt like lead, chained by something invisible. Frozen. Powerless.

Just a spectator to the carnage she hadn't stopped.

The scene shifted.

Edward Wallace was beside her now.

His eyes—once kind and full of quiet sympathy—were dull.

Staring. Lifeless.

Blood pooled beneath him—dark, spreading, soaking into the dirt—dry and cracked like parched earth.

And still... always...

In the distance stood that same dark figure.

Unmoving. Unblinking.

Watching.

Waiting.

She woke with a strangled gasp.

Her shirt clung—damp with sweat. Strands of hair stuck to her cheeks. Her breathing came fast, too loud in the small camper. Too sharp.

She lay back down, trying to calm herself—but sleep was merciless. It yanked her under again like a riptide.

No resistance. No reprieve.

The nightmares resumed.

Looping like a cruel reel of memory.

Again.

And again.

And again.

By the time morning light crept through the thin blinds, casting pale slashes across the narrow room, Lauren felt like she hadn't slept at all.

Her mind was thick with fog, heavy and aching—like she'd been dragging her thoughts through molasses all night. Dreams and reality had blurred together, and she couldn't tell if she was waking from a nightmare or still trapped in one.

Her head pounded. Her limbs felt like lead. Every noise in the camper made her twitch.

She was exhausted in a way that went beyond the physical—like her soul had been pacing for hours while her body lay still in a locked room.

Even breathing felt like a task.

What if this never ends?

The thought came fast and cruel. She shoved it down. Not now. Not yet.

She hadn't rested. She'd only survived the dark.

And for a split second, she longed for something simple—Granddaddy's old porch swing, creaking under a summer sky.

Safe. Still.

Before everything.

She sat up slowly, wincing. Her body throbbed. Her heart pounded like it had been running miles without her.

Barefoot, she padded to the bathroom and flicked on the light.

Her reflection made her flinch.

Bruises mottled her cheekbone, already deepened to shades of sickly yellow and violet beneath her eye.

No longer fresh—but still blooming. Still loud.

Her knees and elbows were raw from yesterday's fall—scraped and angry.

Every inch of her felt bruised, broken, haunted.

She splashed cold water on her face.

But it didn't help.

Her mornings had become mechanical. Ghostlike.

She moved through them without thought: setting the coffee pot, rinsing out the old grounds, pouring water from the jug.

The smell filled the camper—familiar, bitter, comforting, in theory.

But it offered her nothing.

She sat alone at the dinette, mug cradled between both hands, eyes drifting to the window.

Outside, the world looked... fine.

Deceptively fine.

Sunlight glimmered off Norfork Lake in the distance. Birds flitted from branch to branch, chirping their oblivious little songs. The breeze stirred the leaves gently, made the trees sway like they were dancing.

Lauren stared through it all.

She thought about sitting by the water. Letting the wind tangle her hair.

Closing her eyes. Pretending.

Just for a moment.

That she was free.

That she was safe.

But that would mean stepping outside.

And out there—beyond the thin walls of the camper—was the unknown.

Someone waiting. Watching. Hunting.

Out there was danger she couldn't name. Chaos she couldn't control.

Inside?

Inside, the monster had a name. A face. A schedule.

She knew Stefan's moods. His rituals. His triggers.

Inside had once been a predictable kind of horror.

Now? Even that was starting to slip.

Outside... was a question she wasn't ready to answer.

She took another sip of coffee, but her stomach twisted.

She hadn't eaten properly in days.

Now, even her body had started to betray her.

And still—her eyes kept drifting to the door.

To the space beyond it.

To the possibility—however fragile—that the shadow in her dream wasn't just a dream.

That someone really was out there, watching.

And maybe... just maybe...

They weren't watching to hurt her.

Maybe they were watching to save her.

The thought barely had time to take root before it was shattered by sound.

Movement from the bedroom—Stefan stirring.

The creak of the mattress. The drag of his feet across old vinyl.

Just like that, the fragile stillness broke.

Her body tensed on instinct.

He hadn't said a word.

He didn't need to.

They'd had such a good day yesterday.

The thought made her laugh—quiet and bitter.

And that was the bar now.

Peace meant he hadn't raised his voice.

Hadn't raised his hand.

The bar wasn't just low—it was buried.

A nearby camper door slammed, and Lauren's heart leapt into her throat—until she recognized it.

Mr. Wallace.

She rushed to the kitchen window, heart pounding, and peered out.

There he was.

Sitting at his picnic table, just like always. Steady. Predictable.

She let out a breath she hadn't realized she was holding.

There was something about his presence—his quiet routine, his gentle pace—that reminded her she wasn't completely invisible.

Not entirely.

She picked up her half-full coffee mug, still warm in her hands, and raised her voice just enough to carry toward the back room.

"Hey, is it okay if I go sit with Mr. Wallace next door?"

Stefan's voice snapped back, sharp and dismissive. "Who the hell cares?"

But she knew better.

He would've cared if she hadn't asked.

That's how the game worked.

She didn't bother responding.

Lauren grabbed her sunglasses, slipped them on, and opened the camper door.

She stepped out into the crisp morning air.

Sunlight filtered through the canopy overhead, drenching the gravel path and grass in gold.

For just a second, she let herself breathe.

Really breathe.

Her eyes scanned the surroundings out of habit—only a few campers were out, going about their routines. No one too close.

"Good morning, Mr. Wallace," she said brightly, even as the smile tugged against the swelling on her cheekbone.

She reached up, fingers grazing the tender spot, and tried to disguise the wince as casual.

Edward Wallace—ever the gentleman—wore his usual khaki pants and a perfectly buttoned plaid shirt. He looked up from his coffee, his eyes warm, his smile easy.

"Well good morning, sunshine," he said. "How'd you sleep?"

Lauren hesitated. The lie sat on the tip of her tongue—fine, great, thanks for asking—but something stopped her.

Something about the gentle steadiness of Edward's presence.

"I hate to complain," she said quietly. "But honestly... I didn't sleep well at all."

Even that surprised her.

She was so used to pretending, to smoothing everything over with a tight smile and hollow words, that honesty felt like a quiet kind of rebellion. But Edward made her feel like she could wear a different kind of mask—one that let her peek through.

The only other person who had ever done that was her Granddaddy. He'd lean back in his chair, give her that long, quiet look, and say nothing at all. And somehow, that silence cracked her wide open. With him, she could let the weight fall off her shoulders. With him, she didn't have to pretend.

Edward reminded her of that. Not in words, but in presence. In the way he didn't press, didn't pry. He just offered stillness. A kind of listening that made her feel less like a problem to be solved and more like a person to be understood.

His warmth was a lifeline, however fragile. She found herself leaning into his words—not for answers, but for the steady hum of someone who saw her. Someone who didn't flinch when he looked at her. Not like Stefan. Not like the others. Just... human. Just kind.

"Oh, I hate to hear that."

A pause.

"Is everything okay? Are you okay?"

Lauren heard the real question underneath.

Did he hurt you again?

She offered the smallest smile. "Everything's been good, actually. We went on a hike yesterday and played some chess. Just a normal, relaxing day."

She left out the mirror. The message in the steam. The invisible grip tightening around her chest.

"Thank you for asking. What about you—what'd you do yesterday?"

Edward leaned back a bit in his seat. "Well, after breakfast I read for a while. Took a drive over to the general store, just to stretch my legs. Talked with a young mom and her kids at the playground. Nice people. Met a young man staying in a tent around the corner—seems quiet. Came back here, napped a bit. Finished off the evening with an old western."

Lauren nodded politely, but the mention of the tent snagged something inside her. A flicker. A chill.

Around the corner.

Quiet.

Too quiet.

She kept her smile in place, but her fingers tightened slightly around her coffee mug.

Lauren could picture it—that calm, simple kind of day.

It felt like a different life.

A different world.

A breeze cut through the trees, sharp and unexpected, carrying the scent of pine and something sweet—honeysuckle maybe. It barely registered. The world still moved. She just... wasn't part of it.

Their conversation paused as Stefan approached, coffee mug in hand, strutting with that easy smugness that always rubbed Lauren raw.

"Well, hello old-timer," he said with exaggerated cheer.

Edward gave a polite nod. "Morning."

Lauren watched the exchange with quiet fascination. Edward no longer even tried to hide his disdain for Stefan—or "Zach," as he knew him. And Stefan—posturing, always performing—just kept playing pretend.

It was almost entertaining.

Almost.

She stood. "I should go make some breakfast. You're welcome to join us, if you're hungry," she added, offering Mr. Wallace a faint smile.

"Thank you for the company," he replied kindly. "But I've already eaten."

Back inside, Lauren busied herself with cooking, movements fluid, automatic. She kept one eye on the kitchen window, watching Stefan and Edward as they spoke. Their words meant little—postcard pleasantries—but their body language said everything.

Edward, calm and measured.

Stefan—posturing, always performing.

A moment passed—

and then, a thud.

A sharp noise just outside the camper wall.

Lauren froze, spatula halfway to the skillet.

Something had brushed against the siding—too close, too sudden.

She stiffened. Her breath caught.

Her mind raced. Was it a branch? A squirrel? Or something worse?

She didn't hear footsteps. But silence didn't mean safety.

She darted to the dinette window, heart hammering.

Nothing.

No shadows. No movement.

Come on, get it together. It's nothing—just nerves. Just—

She rushed to the door, flung it open, and stepped outside.

The breeze stirred the trees. Sunlight dappled the gravel.

But the space around her stood empty.

No one.

Still, the feeling clung to her skin like static. She could feel it. That presence. That pressure.

The notes.

The ones left for her.

The writing on the mirror.

She wasn't imagining those things.

But was she imagining this?

Had the fear finally cracked her wide open?

Was she spiraling? Maybe. She almost wanted to believe it.

She stood frozen in place when Stefan rounded the back of the camper, catching her mid-stare.

"What the hell has gotten into you? You look like you've seen a ghost."

Maybe I have, she thought, staring at him blankly.

"I thought I heard someone."

"Well, you did—it was me and Edward, dumbass." He laughed, mocking, his voice coated in venom wrapped in humor.

She lowered her gaze and slipped back inside.

They didn't speak while they ate breakfast.

Just the scrape of forks on plates, the low hum of tension filling every inch of air between them.

The eggs were rubbery, the toast slightly burnt.

Stefan ate like it didn't matter—like the only flavor was control. Every clink of his fork against the plate felt deliberate, almost mocking.

Lauren pushed her food around in slow, silent circles. Her stomach rebelled at every bite, but she knew better than to leave a full plate. That, too, would be noted. Tallied. Used.

She kept her gaze low, fixed on the syrupy swirl of jelly seeping into dry toast, trying to ignore the way Stefan kept glancing at her. Not openly. Not enough to call out. But often enough that her skin itched with awareness.

Say something, she urged herself. *Anything. Make it normal.*

But her tongue felt glued to the roof of her mouth.

And he didn't want normal. He wanted silence. Dominance. The quiet game where only one of them got to speak.

She swallowed a bite of bacon.

It tasted like ash.

As she stood to clear the table, Stefan extended his leg and tripped her.

The plate flew.

It crashed to the floor with a clatter—eggs and toast scattering across the linoleum.

Time froze.

For a second, she thought maybe it had been a mistake. Maybe he hadn't meant to—

But then came the laugh.

Stefan burst out laughing. "Had to recreate how funny you looked yesterday when you tripped over nothing."

That laugh.

She hated that laugh.

It crawled under her skin, sharp and cold.

She hadn't said anything wrong.

Hadn't done anything wrong.

Yesterday had been peaceful. This morning had been close.

And yet—

She pushed herself up slowly, knees smarting, hands trembling.

She didn't look at him. Didn't speak.

She just cleaned.

Quiet. Controlled. A machine made of bruises.

Kept her head down while he disappeared into the bedroom.

She washed dishes with shaking hands, silence shrieking in her ears.

When he reemerged, dressed in hiking gear, she tensed again.

But then—

"I'm going for a hike," he said.

Relief bloomed in her chest—sharp, sudden, like air after drowning.

"Oh—I'll get ready real fast—"

"I said I'm going."

He didn't yell. He didn't have to.

She swallowed. "Okay."

He grabbed a few bottles of water from the fridge and walked out without another word.

The silence he left behind was deafening—crushing. And beautiful.

Lauren stood, unsure what to do with the sudden emptiness.

Then she moved.

Quickly.

Before courage could slip through the cracks.

She grabbed her phone, earbuds, a small blanket, and a bottle of water. Slipped on her sunglasses like a shield. Scanned the area before stepping outside.

No one.

Just birdsong. Sunlight. The lake glinting in the distance.

She followed the short path to the water.

With every step, her chest loosened—like something uncoiled inside her.

Like the lake had been waiting for her.

She laid the blanket in the grass and lowered herself onto it, earbuds in. Scrolled.

Found her TayTay playlist.

Hit play on *You're On Your Own, Kid*.

The sky stretched wide above her.

The lake shimmered with secrets—but kinder ones.

And for a moment, Lauren wasn't in the middle of a nightmare.

She was a little girl again, lying beside her mother on a patchwork quilt, a library book open in her mom's lap.

It had been one of the good days—rare, precious. Her mom's voice soft and steady as she read aloud, one hand brushing Lauren's hair off her forehead, the other holding the pages like they were sacred.

The sun had been warm, not hot. The breeze gentle.

And Lauren had felt... loved. Truly loved.

Not in a tangled, conditional way. Just purely. Like her mother had finally reached through the fog of everything else and said, *I see you. I know you. You are mine.*

She'd fallen asleep to the sound of her mother's voice, the scent of sunscreen and lake water wrapping around her like a second blanket.

Lauren smiled faintly at the memory—bittersweet, but grounding.

That version of her had been real. That version of love had been real.

Even if it didn't last, it had been real.

And maybe that was enough.

For the first time in days—maybe weeks—sleep came easy.

No nightmares.

No whispers. No threats.

No shadow figures watching.

Just music.

Sunshine.

And silence.

🦋 21 🦋

Lauren stirred as the air shifted around her.

She felt him before she saw him—his heat, his silence, that unnatural quiet.

A shadow fell across her face, blotting out the sun.

The peace she'd found by the water vanished in a heartbeat, replaced with a stillness that pressed against her chest like a stone.

She didn't move.

If she pretended to still be asleep, maybe—just maybe—he'd walk away.

But she knew better.

He stood frozen over her, watching.

Stefan looked down at her, his thoughts spinning.

She lay on the blanket, hair fanned out, the lake glinting behind her just like that first day.

The memory should have been sweet—nostalgic, even.

But it wasn't.

It reminded him of the first time he'd hit her.

And how she hadn't reacted like the others.

No screaming. No crying. No running.

She just laid there—silent, still, unreadable.

It had thrown him off. For a moment.

Not because he cared—he didn't.

But because it made him wonder how far she could bend before she snapped.

How much she could take before she broke.

That was the question now.

Not if.

When.

And how.

She thought she'd flipped the script—thought she was the one in control.

But she wasn't.

She was still just a game. A puzzle he hadn't solved yet.

And today?

Today he'd test the edges.

He'd push until something cracked.

He wanted to see the break.

He needed to see the break—that's when he'd know he'd won.

He'd been enraged when he returned to the camper and found it empty. Possessiveness bloomed into fury—festering like a wound.

And now?

Now he'd rewrite the memory—twist it, control it.

His lips curled into a smile—thin, joyless, dead behind the eyes.

Lauren didn't need to see it.

It crawled across her skin like static.

She smelled his sweat—sharp and sour.

Tasted the tension in the air, coppery and thick.

Her heart pounded behind her ribs.

Still, she didn't flinch. Didn't move.

If he thought she was weak, she was dead.

So she opened her eyes.

Stefan's expression softened—just barely. Almost playful.

He extended a hand.

She stared at it. Her stomach twisted.

He was playing his character. She firmed her mask in place.

Then she took his hand.

He pulled her to her feet with more force than necessary.

She staggered, clutching her blanket and phone, thumbing off the music.

Her sunglasses were somewhere behind her, forgotten in the grass.

His hand closed around her wrist—tight, possessive.

But her mind clung to the ripple of sunlight on the lake, the way it shimmered like glass.

That peace didn't belong here.

Maybe she didn't either.

Without a word, he reached down and laced their fingers together.

To anyone watching from afar, they would've looked like a couple taking a romantic stroll—hand in hand beneath a blue sky. Peaceful. Serene.

Lauren knew better.

She looked toward the tent, but the car that sat next to it was gone. There would be no help from there.

His grip was too tight. Her fingers throbbed, starved of circulation.

She dared a glance around the RV park, scanning for Mr. Wallace—or anyone, really.

But the nearby campers were still. Too still.

She caught movement in the distance. A child, maybe.

Too far. No help. No witnesses.

Each step toward the camper felt like walking into a tomb.

She thought about screaming. Just once. For someone—anyone—to hear.

But who would actually come?

Would they get there in time?

Would he let them live?

No.

Calling for help wouldn't save her.

It would just give him something new to punish.

So she stayed silent.

Bit her tongue.

Folded into herself.

Her mouth was dry. Her breaths, shallow.

Every rustle of leaves, every birdsong, felt like a mockery. Like nature was reminding her it didn't care.

The camper door creaked open as Stefan pulled the handle.

She willing walked inside, what else could she do?

Lauren flinched as it slammed shut behind her.

Click.

The lock echoed through the camper. Final. Unforgiving.

Stefan turned toward her.

His face flushed.

Pupils too wide.

Smile too calm.

Here we go.

That look—she knew it well.

The look he wore when he was drunk on control.

When he'd decided what he deserved.

He stepped closer.

She backed away—instinctively—until her spine met the thin wall behind her.

He shoved her hard.

She didn't move at first—just blinked, disoriented, the world tilting sideways.

Time stuttered.

Her brain scrambled to reframe it—maybe this was just another outburst. A bad joke. A mistake.

But then her shoulder slammed into the corner of the cabinet.

The pain was sharp. Real.

Denial shattered.

This wasn't a warning.

This was Stefan.

And he was done pretending.

His touch came next. Slow. Deliberate. Not seductive. Not even angry. Just performance.

Each article of clothing he removed, he paused. Watched her face. Drank in the fear she refused to spill.

She bit the inside of her cheek until she tasted blood.

I will not beg. I will not scream. I will not fight.

A mantra. A tether.

"I'm going to make you scream," he growled into her ear, breath hot and sour.

She didn't scream. Didn't move. For one breathless moment, her body simply forgot how.

Then everything snapped back into motion.

She counted the seconds. Anything to stay present. Anything to stay sane.

What followed wasn't sex. Not even rage. Just cruelty. A ritual. A show only he enjoyed.

He hurt her in ways she hadn't thought possible. At times, she blacked out—her mind severing from her body just to survive. He strangled her until her vision blurred. Then let her go. Brought her back—just to do it again.

After Stefan was through with her, he kissed her—hard, possessive, violent. "Thank you, babe," he murmured, like she'd done him a favor.

The taste of blood and bile filled her mouth, but she made herself swallow it. She wouldn't give him the satisfaction of spitting it out.

Then he left her—naked and trembling—on the bed and disappeared into the shower.

For him, it was just another night.

For her, everything had changed.

He had violated her.

Strangled her until the world flickered in and out, until her body seized and spasmed against his weight. Until her lungs screamed and her fingernails bent backward trying to fight him off.

Her vision blurred, vanished, then returned—like a cruel trick.

Blood soaked the sheets.

One eye swollen shut.

The other threatened to follow.

Her lips were cracked and bleeding.

Her throat scorched raw from gasping against his grip.

Her ribs screamed with each breath—sharp, shallow, desperate.

But the worst part wasn't the pain.

It was the silence.

She heard him dress. Heard the front door unlock. Open. Close. Lock again.

And then she was alone.

She didn't move.

She couldn't.

Her limbs were foreign—numb and heavy, like they belonged to someone else.

One arm pulsed with pins and needles. The other hung useless at her side.

Her legs ached, but they wouldn't respond.

Everything below her ribs felt distant. Disconnected.

Even her breathing was fragile. Like if she took in too much air, something might crack open inside her.

She lay there for hours—naked, bruised, broken.

And she cried.

Because there was nothing else she could do.

Time passed in jagged fragments.

Minutes stretched into eternities.

Even if someone opened the door, she wouldn't be able to cry out.

The darkness around her thickened.

She told herself: Stay awake. Don't let go.

But the tunnel closed in.

Again.

Lauren woke to silence.

Her ears rang.

She opened her one good eye and saw nothing but dim light filtering through the blinds.

Her mouth was coated in the taste of metal.

Her chest ached with every breath.

She was a broken thing. Discarded.

A deer in the middle of the road.

She thought about Nurse Erin.

About how Erin had probably endured the same hell Lauren just had —with one difference.

Erin hadn't survived.

Lauren had survived.

But barely.

She wondered—

Had Erin fought back?

Screamed?

Begged?

Had she been alone in the dark too, convinced no one was coming?

Lauren's throat tightened—not just from the bruising, but from the shame coiled deep in her chest.

She should've done something.

But she hadn't.

And now Erin was gone.

Lauren was still here—still wearing the bruises, still pretending, still trying to outlast him.

For now.

Stefan could be in the woods right now, digging a shallow grave.

He could come back any minute and finish the job.

And honestly...

Death might be easier.

She thought about the notes.

GET THE FUCK AWAY FROM HIM.

What if she'd listened?

What if she'd run?

What if she'd asked Mr. Wallace to drive her to Granddaddy's house?

So many what ifs.

But one thing had become crystal clear:

If she survived this time—

She was done.

No matter the cost, she was getting away from Stefan Warren.

Even if it meant prison.

Even if it meant a coffin.

And once again, the darkness came for her.

The world went silent.

And the one eye closed.

22

The morning came and went.

Still, no Stefan.

Lauren's fear had curdled into something primal—ancient and marrow-deep. Every second of silence grew louder, heavier—the air thickening around her, pressing down with invisible hands.

Naked and limp, she sprawled across the stained mattress like a discarded rag doll. Every nerve ending pulsed with agony. Bruises bloomed across her skin in uneven constellations. She could no longer tell where the pain began or ended. It simply was. Ever-present. Like breath. Like death.

She shifted.

A sound tore from her throat—not quite human. A strangled, guttural rasp.

The pain that followed was so sharp, so immediate, that the edges of her vision collapsed. Darkness swallowed her whole before she could scream again.

When she came to, the sunlight had moved. A different angle now, slanting through the blinds. Time had passed. How long—she couldn't say. Her thoughts crawled like molasses—slow, thick, unreachable.

She tried to move again. Her shoulder shrieked in protest—still twisted, still wrong. The same one he'd wrenched back and up, nearly dislocating it.

She'd lain face-down for what felt like eternity—twisted into a shape no living body was meant to hold.

Had her bones reshaped themselves to match the violence?

She begged her memories to melt away.

Begged the universe to melt the reel of horror in her head like chocolate left in the sun.

But the images stayed.

Sharp. Clear. Unrelenting.

She drifted.

In and out of consciousness.

Only the sunlight's slow crawl across the wall anchored her.

Each time she woke, the light had moved—higher, lower, stretching longer across the cheap laminate floor.

Until finally, it dipped low.

Turned amber.

Then gray.

The shadows in the camper stretched, lengthened—matching the darkness swelling inside her.

And it was then she realized—

She'd wet the bed.

A fresh wave of shame washed over her—sharper than the pain, deeper than the bruises.

Her breath hitched in her throat. Her body trembled.

A choked sob escaped her lips, and then the tears came—fast, hot, silent.

She felt like meat left out too long—pulverized and useless.

Bloodied, on display.

Waiting to be tossed aside. Or devoured.

And still...

No Stefan.

A part of her wanted him to come back.

Maybe he'd help her.

Maybe he'd clean her up.

Maybe—just maybe—he'd feel a flicker of remorse.

But the other part—the rational part, the one being slowly smothered—knew better.

If he came back, he might finish what he started.

Maybe he'd dig a shallow grave under moonlight and drop her in like the others.

She flinched at the thought.

Then—just as her eyes fluttered shut again—the silence cracked.

The low, familiar growl of the truck's engine rumbled through the stillness like a death knell.

Her heart galloped, wild and erratic—racing the horror clawing its way back to her.

She couldn't sit up. Couldn't even shift without lightning bolts firing through her ribs.

But her mind—her mind was still calculating.

What would he notice first?

The blood? The disarray? The truth, leaking from the corner of her mouth?

No. That wouldn't work.

She blinked—slow, deliberate. Let her eyes soften and swallowed the pain.

Practiced stillness, like a wounded animal that knew movement only made the predator bite harder.

If she looked broken enough, maybe he'd lower his guard.

She heard the camper door unlock.

Click.

That quiet, sealing sound.

She turned her head toward the noise.

Neck stiff. Skin crusted with blood and dried tears.

Only one eye opened—and barely.

Through the narrow slit, she saw him.

Stefan.

He stood in the doorway, silhouetted by the dying light.

She couldn't see his expression.

She didn't need to.

His posture said everything—arms crossed, body relaxed.

Like a man admiring a piece of art he'd created.

His masterpiece.

She could feel him.

The heat of his presence. The weight of it.

Was that pride?

Satisfaction?

Guilt?

No.

Not this man.

Stefan didn't have a single guilty bone in his body.

She turned her head away and stared at the wall, refusing to give him the satisfaction of her face.

Without a word, he stepped further inside.

The floor creaked beneath his boots.

He reached for her.

The moment his hands touched her, she screamed.

Not from fear.

But from pain.

What came out was a rasp—thin and broken.

Her voice was gone.

Her throat had been shredded from being strangled—again and again.

The gasping. The pressure. The way the world blinked out again and again.

There was nothing left to give.

Darkness rushed back like a tide.

And just before it took her, she heard his voice:

"I told you I'd make you scream."

When she came to again, ice-cold water poured over her head.

Her body recoiled on instinct—

and immediately regretted it.

Pain detonated across her chest.

Hot. Blinding.

Like something inside her had cracked and shifted with the movement.

She lay in the camper's tiny shower, slumped like a broken puppet.

The rigid shower floor pressed into her ribs like knives.

Every breath was a battle. Shallow. Stabbing.

The water was more of a drizzle than a stream—lukewarm at best—but it felt like ice carving into her bones.

She whimpered.

Her brain scrambled to track Stefan, but her vision blurred. Her head swam.

Even the act of turning her face sent shockwaves through her ribs.

Something wasn't right.

Something deep.

Broken.

Inside.

She barely turned her face before blackness pulled her under again.

When she opened her eyes again, she was in bed.

She didn't remember getting there.

She didn't remember being clothed—but now she wore one of Stefan's old T-shirts and a pair of clean underwear.

Had he been the one to dress her?

She didn't want to know.

The sheets were clean.

They smelled like detergent.

That faint, clean scent almost made her cry again.

She was too weak to move when Stefan walked back in.

In his hand: a glass of water.

A straw poked out at an angle.

He said nothing.

Just walked over, held it to her lips like she was a child—or a pet.

She tried to drink.

But her body betrayed her.

Half of it trickled down her chin and soaked into the collar of the shirt.

"Damn it."

His voice cracked like a whip.

She flinched without thinking.

He moved—fast.

Retrieved a towel from the bathroom.

When he returned, he wiped her chin. His movements were surprisingly gentle.

Lauren watched through the narrow slit of her eye.

Her body was shattered, but her mind sparked with something small.

Daring.

"Stefan," she rasped.

Her voice came out more breath than sound.

"I need a doctor."

A swallow.

"Please..."

He stared at her for a beat, and then—without emotion—shook his head.

"Don't move. You'll just make it worse."

He turned out the light.

Left her in the dark again.

When sleep came, it dragged the nightmares behind it.

In this one, Nurse Erin was beside her—screaming, kicking, begging for freedom.

They were both held down—bloodied, breaking.

The scene was blurry. Surreal.

As if her mind refused to clarify the worst of it.

Edward wasn't there.

He was just... gone.

Erased from her subconscious like he'd never existed.

But the shadow was still there.

The dark figure.

Only this time, he wasn't just watching.

He was searching.

Digging through the bushes.

Peering behind trees.

Desperate.

Trying to find *her*.

She woke to voices.

Muffled at first, warped by the walls.

Then—recognition.

Stefan's.

And the other... Mr. Wallace.

Her heart pounded.

She tried to move.

To speak.

To make any sound.

She poured every ounce of energy into hope—hope that he might hear her.

Feel her through the walls.

Sense that something was wrong.

But Stefan's voice grew louder.

Louder. More performative.

"I'd let you in to say hi, but I'd hate for you to catch the flu. She's been in rough shape. I promise, soon as she's got her strength back, I'll send her over."

The door shut.

Footsteps faded.

She lay there—jaw slack, body limp.

Even if she wanted to grit her teeth, pain wouldn't let her.

Mr. Wallace wasn't coming in.

And even if he had...

Stefan would've killed him.

No hesitation.

No remorse.

Just like Erin.

Lauren closed her eyes.

A single tear slipped down her temple.

She wouldn't let it happen again.

Not to Mr. Wallace.

Not to anyone.

23

The routine continued.

Not care. Control.

Stefan played the role of attentive partner like it was a script he half-remembered.

He stroked her hair, whispered soft lies—then tugged a handful hard and laughed.

"Just kidding."

He would press a cool cloth to her forehead—then linger just a second too long on the bruises.

Just enough pressure to make her flinch.

Just enough to remind her: he was in control.

It wasn't kindness.

It was a game.

His game.

This was his chessboard, and he would move his knights wherever he wanted.

Sometimes she imagined sweeping the pieces off the board.

Other times, she imagined flipping the whole damn table.

But mostly, she just lay still—watching, calculating. Waiting for her move.

Two days had passed since she'd last heard Mr. Wallace outside the camper.

Two days of agony so severe she couldn't sit up without the world tilting, blackness gnawing at the edges of her vision.

Each trip to the bathroom became a new kind of torture.

Stefan would lift her like she was made of glass—but not gently.

Just carefully enough not to drop her.

Like a collector cradling a broken trophy.

It reminded her of when she broke her collarbone at eleven.

The way her Granddaddy had held her in the ER waiting room—stoic on the outside, but his hand never left hers.

He didn't cry. He didn't panic. He just sat there, whispering steady things like,

"You're okay, little one. You're gonna be just fine."

And somehow, she believed him.

That was his magic.

His calm steadied the chaos around her.

Back then, she kept glancing at the door—hoping to see her mom's silhouette, her dad's worried face.

But they never came.

She'd waited, and waited, until the truth settled in her chest like a stone:

They weren't coming. They couldn't.

They never did.

Her Granddaddy had known that.

That's why he looked at the door the way he did.

That's why he held her so tightly, so fiercely—because he was the only one who ever showed up.

She hadn't understood it then.

She did now.

Sometimes, she passed out while he carried her—slipping under, because it was easier than being awake for his hands on her skin.

Her body betrayed her more each day.

And her mind...

It had started floating somewhere just above the pain,

hovering like smoke beneath the ceiling,

watching everything happen from a safe, unreachable corner.

She hadn't eaten anything solid.

Just sips of lukewarm broth—burning like glass on the way down.

Her throat too raw, too torn.

She used to count the seconds when things hurt—

Twenty for the slap.

Thirty for the choke.

A hundred for the aftermath.

But now time wasn't something she counted.

It was something she endured.

Once—maybe twice—she thought she saw a shift in Stefan's expression.

Not concern.

Not regret.

Something colder.

A flicker of disappointment, maybe.

Annoyance at how broken she'd become.

But it always vanished.

Replaced by that other look.

The one that made her skin crawl: disgust.

Hatred.

Ownership.

She'd begged Stefan to take her to the hospital.

Once. Twice. Then again. And again.

At first she cried. Pleaded.

Swore she wouldn't say a word. Claimed it was her fault too.

He only smiled. That sick, knowing smile.

Shook his head.

"You are pathetic. I thought you were different from the others. But look at you."

Eventually, the begging died.

If help came, it wouldn't come from him.

It would have to be someone else.

She lay in the narrow bed, staring at the thin sliver of sunlight bleeding through the blinds.

She could only see it through one eye—

the left one, though even that was swelling now.

The world was shrinking.

Framed in pain.

Filtered through darkness.

Her shoulder was strapped into a makeshift sling.

Her face a mess of bruises—deep, spreading, rotting beneath the surface.

She'd caught a glimpse of herself that morning when Stefan carried her to the bathroom.

The mirror showed a stranger.

A thing.

She'd flinched, like she was staring at someone else.

Her mind refused to claim the body in the reflection.

It looked like the stuff of horror movies.

But this wasn't makeup.

This wasn't fiction.

This was real.

This was her reality.

She was utterly dependent on the man who had destroyed her.

If he didn't bring water, she stayed thirsty.

If he forgot the broth, she starved.

And when he disappeared—no warning, no explanation—

she was left alone with her thoughts, her nightmares,

her body broken in a prison she couldn't escape.

That afternoon, Stefan brought her a few spoonfuls of broth.

Then, like clockwork, he ate his own lunch, changed into his hiking gear,

and moved about the camper with mechanical precision.

All she could do was listen.

The fridge opened and closed.

A plastic bag rustled.

Boots scuffed the floor.

The front door opened.

Closed.

Then—

the sound that chilled her blood.

The lock. Click.

It didn't sound casual anymore.

Not like it used to.

This wasn't for safety.

This was about control.

It wasn't about keeping people out.

It was about keeping her in.

She stared at the closed bedroom door, willing her body to move.

If she could just make it to the hallway...

To the window...

Maybe someone would see her.

Maybe someone would help.

She shifted—

just enough to try.

Pain exploded through her ribs.

She rose an inch—then collapsed with a muted cry.

The sound barely left her throat.

A whisper of agony.

Hot tears spilled onto the pillow.

She wept for what she'd lost—

her strength, her freedom, her dignity.

She wept for the helplessness that had replaced her rage.

You have to get the fuck away from him.

She repeated it like a mantra.

A lifeline.

She needed to survive.

She needed to escape.

And then—

There it was.

A sound.

Footsteps outside the camper.

Her heart pounded against her ribs.

That wasn't Stefan. He hadn't been gone long enough.

No heavy stomp. No familiar thunder of boots.

And it wasn't Mr. Wallace either. There was no shuffle.

These footsteps were different—lighter, hesitant.

Someone was out there.

Her lifeline.

"Help," she whispered. Her throat burned—like fire devouring the words before they could escape.

It came out too soft. Like a secret never meant to be heard.

But secrets didn't save people.

Tears streamed down her cheeks as she tried again.

"Help... please... help me..."

She forced herself to sit up, ignoring the firestorm erupting in her side.

She made it halfway—clutching the edge of the mattress, breath ragged and fast.

Her lungs bucked against her will.

The edges of her vision darkened.

Please... not now... not now...

And then—blackness.

She slipped under again.

Back into the black void. Back into the place where nightmares breathed.

She awoke hours later.

She knew because the light had moved—what had once been a beam across her pillow now faded into the far corner of the room.

Her mouth was sandpaper dry.

Her body stiff and sore in new places.

But she was alive.

She could hear the world outside.

Birds chirping in the trees.

The gentle lapping of the lake.

Somewhere in the distance, a boat engine roared to life... and then faded.

She tried again to move.

This time, she rolled onto her good side.

The relief—just shifting weight off her back and hips—was blissful.

From this angle, she could see through the narrow window.

More of the world than before.

It felt like mercy.

Then—

footsteps.

Not light.

Heavy.

Boots.

Stefan.

Like hope—

a voice.

Mr. Wallace.

Louder than usual.

Strained.

There was tension in it—tight and sharp.

She couldn't make out the words,

but her body registered the shift.

It went rigid.

The door to the camper burst open, and angry voices flooded in.

"Listen here, old timer. She's sick with the flu," Stefan snapped—his voice low, but sharp.

"When she feels up to it, you're more than welcome to see her. But right now, she's sleeping. Doctor's orders."

Lauren's stomach clenched.

She knew that tone.

Stefan was unraveling.

Please, Mr. Wallace. Don't push him.

Please just call the police.

Please... just make the call...

She repeated it in her head like a prayer.

Outside, Edward Wallace clenched his fists.

You listen here, you little pompous ass...

But he swallowed the words.

"I understand," he said finally, voice softer.

"I'm sorry, Zach. It's just—my Margaret died from complications from the flu. Guess I'm still a little raw."

He hesitated.

Something about the way Stefan stood—just a little too eager to block the door—needled at him.

Margaret's voice echoed in his head from years ago: "*When someone's too polite, check the locks.*"

He wasn't sure what unsettled him more—the smile on Stefan's face, or the fact that he couldn't see the girl he knew as Sarah at all.

"Right," he murmured, almost to himself. "I'll get out of your hair."

Lauren squeezed her left eye shut. Her breath hitched from the pain, and a single tear slid down her temple, disappearing into her hairline. She forced herself not to move.

She wanted to scream.

To shake the walls.

To throw herself at the window.

Mr. Wallace was just feet away—yet utterly unreachable.

She wanted to tell him she was here.

That she was dying.

That she needed him.

But all she could do was listen,

paralyzed by pain and fear,

as Stefan and her only hope balanced on a tightrope of civility—

one misstep away from disaster.

Time was slipping through her fingers.

Then came the shattering sound of her hope... shuffling away.

Was Mr. Wallace really walking off? Or had he paused just out of sight—heart pounding like hers, torn between instinct and uncertainty?

Maybe he was calling someone right now.

Maybe help was finally coming.

Or maybe...

He'd done what everyone else did when faced with uncomfortable truths—

Turned his back. Chose not to see.

That was the worst kind of pain.

Not just being hurt—

But being invisible in the process.

As Mr. Wallace walked away, a faint rustling came from the nearby tree line. A quick, light sound—like someone shifting their weight in the brush.

He paused, eyes scanning the woods.

Nothing.

Just wind, probably. Or a squirrel.

But the air felt too still. Too silent. Too... watched.

The door opened.

The door slammed shut.

The lock clicked back into place.

Silence swallowed the camper.

Lauren lay there trembling,

her heart thundered in her throat.

She stared at the strip of sunlight on the wall—

shrinking, fading.

Her chance was gone.

And she could already hear Stefan pacing.

Muttering. Seething.

She closed her eyes.
Braced herself.
He knows.
He knows Wallace suspects something.
And now—
she would pay the price.

❧ 24 ❧

Lauren listened to Stefan pacing the narrow camper floor, his boots thudding dully against the linoleum. His lips moved constantly, low mutterings barely audible, but the name—Edward—kept cutting through. Over and over again, like a stone skipping across the surface of his unraveling thoughts. His voice rose and fell in unpredictable swells, crashing down with sudden fury before tapering off into breathy curses and frantic whispers.

She lay still in bed, arms pinned to her sides, her breathing shallow and deliberate. Every breath hurt, but the quiet was worth it. She'd seen this before—this twitchy, storm-eyed version of him. When his mind latched onto something, it spiraled. And when he spiraled, someone paid for it.

Usually her.

He circled like an animal guarding a carcass, convinced everyone was coming to take it away. His paranoia thickened the air in the camper, making it hard to breathe. His eyes darted, unfocused, flicking toward the windows as if he expected to see the old man's face staring back. She didn't dare speak. Didn't even shift her weight. Not when the walls felt like they were made of glass and every sound threatened to crack them.

He was so consumed by his obsessive mutterings that he didn't bring her water. Not even broth. Hunger clawed at her belly, sharp and relentless. Her mouth was dry, her lips cracked. But she stayed silent. Drawing attention, even for basic needs, was a gamble—and she wasn't sure she had any chips left to lose.

Eventually, exhaustion outpaced the pain, and Lauren let herself drift into a foggy, restless sleep. She didn't dream. She didn't dare.

She awoke the next morning to movement—a sudden dip in the mattress beside her. The weight shifted, and the thin foam bowed inward, jostling her broken body just enough to send electric jolts of pain up her ribs and through her mangled shoulder. Her face throbbed with the kind of deep ache that didn't fade, only settled like rot into her bones.

A strangled sound escaped her throat—guttural, raw. Half-animal, half-human.

Stefan said nothing.

Of course he didn't.

She didn't expect a glance. Or concern. Or some flicker of guilt.

Those things didn't live in him.

He simply pressed a plastic straw to her lips like he was refueling a machine—mechanical, cold. Unfeeling.

The first drop hit her tongue like salvation.

She drank like an animal at the last waterhole, the coolness slicing through the raw wounds inside her mouth. Each swallow stung, but she didn't stop. She didn't care. The pain of drinking was still better than the ache of being empty.

And just as quickly as he'd appeared, he stood again. His hands were fidgeting, jaw tight, eyes darting to the front window.

"I'm going to the store," he muttered.

His voice was clipped. Detached.

Lauren stared at him for a moment, blinking through the fog of pain. Then she did something she hadn't done in days.

She moved.

She almost reached for him.

Her hand twitched—an involuntary flicker, like her body remembered what it used to mean to seek comfort. But she stopped herself, letting it hover in the space between them.

She couldn't do it.

Not even now.

Not after everything.

Touching him felt like handing him a weapon.

Instead, she swallowed the pain, steadied her voice, and said, "Stefan... please. I need a doctor."

The words were quiet, but they cut like glass. A final shred of dignity, offered like bait.

He didn't speak.

Didn't pull his hand away.

But something shifted in his expression. Just for a second.

And then it was gone.

For a second, he looked at her.

Really looked at her.

And in that second, Lauren felt the heat building under his skin, rising like steam under pressure.

His jaw clenched, muscles twitching in his neck.

"You ungrateful bitch," he spat.

He turned and began pacing at the foot of the bed, fast, erratic. Each step struck like a war drum. His agitation flared with every word that left his mouth.

"I've done everything for you. Feeding you. Cleaning you. Hauling your pathetic ass to the bathroom. Wiping up your piss like some goddamn nursemaid."

Then—he lunged.

His fist came down hard, stopping inches from her face, slamming into the pillow beside her with a dull, thunderous thud. The force rattled through the bed-frame, through her bones.

Lauren didn't flinch.

She couldn't.

Every muscle was locked in place, frozen in survival. She held her breath, braced for the blow that didn't come.

Part of her almost wished it had.

Just to be finished.

To not have to calculate. Or endure. Or breathe through the fire in her ribs.

She was certain this was it—that this was the moment he'd finally end her.

But it wasn't.

He stood abruptly, his breath ragged. The rage rolled off him in waves as he stormed out of the bedroom. The camper shook in his wake. Then—

The front door creaked open.

A gust of cold air slipped inside.

The door slammed shut, the sound cracking through the silence like a gunshot.

Then—click of the lock.

That sound.

So small.

So final.

It didn't say you're safe.

It said you're sealed in.

Lauren let out the breath she hadn't realized she was holding.

Her chest rose and fell—ragged, shallow. Her ribs screamed with each inhale.

But the walls felt closer now. The silence heavier. The air thinner.

The silence pressed against her like a second skin—thick, suffocating, almost alive.

She could taste blood and bile on the back of her tongue.

Something metallic. Something wrong.

The sheets beneath her stuck to her skin, damp with sweat, and every shallow breath scraped across her ribs like broken glass.

Outside, the world moved on—birds chirping, leaves shifting—but in here, it was all stillness and waiting.

Her mind spun, fast and sharp. Stefan was cracking—splintering at the seams. This wasn't just anger. This was collapse. He was slipping into something darker than she'd ever seen before. Something unstable.

Could she exploit the cracks in his armor—twist his unraveling into opportunity?

It would be like walking a tightrope blindfolded, with a storm below. One wrong move and she wouldn't just fall—she'd shatter.

She heard the truck engine rev to life, gravel spitting under the tires as it pulled away.

Silence returned. Thick. Suspicious.

For a moment, she just stared at the ceiling, unmoving. The pain in her ribs throbbed in time with her heartbeat. She let her eyes drift shut, just for a second.

She fought to stay awake, but her body betrayed her again—dragging her under, deeper this time.

In the darkness behind her eyes, her Granddaddy's hands—warm, steady—wrapped a Band-Aid around her scraped knee. "You're tougher than most," he'd said, ruffling her hair. She remembered the porch light, the cicadas, the way he always made her feel like the world couldn't touch her when he was near.

That feeling was gone.

But she chased it anyway. Even now.

Sleep pulled at her like a current.

Not sleep, not really—something murkier. Slippery. Fragile.

A place between waking and gone.

In the darkness behind her eyes, faces flickered in and out—Judy's blank stare, Erin's wide, panicked eyes, Mr. Wallace's gentle concern.

All of them just out of reach.

And behind them—

a shadow.

Always a shadow.

Not threatening. Not yet.

Just watching.

Searching for something. For someone.

She didn't know how long she floated there. Seconds? Minutes?

But then—

Bang.

The camper door crashed open, louder this time, yanking her back to reality like plunging into a frozen lake. Stefan's boots hit the floor like hammers. Sharp. Angry. Final.

His presence filled the space like smoke—acrid and choking.

He returned to the bedroom, looming over her with something clutched in his hand.

A bottle of Tylenol.

It rattled like a threat as he shook it.

"Open," he barked.

She opened her mouth, and he dropped the pills in like she was a broken doll. When he held the glass to her lips, she drank without hesitation. The cool water stung the raw cuts around her mouth, but she didn't care.

She just wanted the pain to go away—even for a little while.

She looked at him through her one good eye.

"Thank you," she whispered, and meant it. Not out of gratitude. Out of survival.

Stefan changed into shorts and a T-shirt, crawled onto the bed beside her, and fell into a dead, dreamless sleep. She dared not move. Dared not speak. She stared at the ceiling, heart pounding, muscles locked in place.

The nightmares came anyway.

Nurse Erin beside her in the dark—their hands bound together in a nightmarish imitation of sisterhood.

Screaming. Bleeding. Dying.

Then Erin, lifeless.

Mr. Wallace, too. His kind eyes frozen in terror, his body soaked in blood.

And always...

the figure in the shadows.

Watching.

Waiting.

Silent.

She woke with a jolt.

Stefan was dressing in his hiking gear. Another day. Another routine. Another dose of Tylenol. She drank the water, muttered her thanks, and watched him walk away again.

The door opened.

The door closed.

And then the lock.

Click.

The lock.

The prison sealed.

He was slipping. The character he played was cracking. She could feel it in his pacing, in the way he barked instead of sneered. That was the trick now—watch the cracks, widen them, twist them into something she could use. The timing had to be right. She didn't have many moves left. But maybe—just maybe—she had one more.

It wasn't long after he left that she heard it—footsteps.

Not Stefan's.

These were soft. Measured. Cautious.

Someone was just outside.

Her heart slammed against her ribs. Hope flared—bright and dangerous—in her chest. She had to try. Even if it killed her.

She inhaled deeply and screamed—or tried to. The sound came out as a rasping whisper, like the last breath of a dying thing.

"Help... help me," she croaked, voice cracking with strain.

The footsteps stopped.

Did they hear me?

Her throat burned. Her lungs ached. But she forced the words again.

"Please—help. I'm in here!"

Pain exploded through her side as she tried to sit up, scrabbling at the air, reaching for the window. If she could just get higher—just be seen.

She made it halfway before the world tilted. Her vision blurred. Her body gave out, slamming back onto the mattress.

She sobbed—loud, furious, helpless.

The footsteps hovered near the window.

A shadow moved across the blinds.

Please.

Please.

She mouthed the words now: *Help me. Please...*

And then, heartbreakingly, the footsteps began to retreat.

Fading.

Disappearing.

Gone.

A broken sob tore from her chest. The shadow was gone. Whoever it had been—gone. No knock. No call for help. Just... retreating footsteps.

It was worse than Stefan's rage. Worse than the bruises.

Because this time, hope had shown up.

And left her behind.

25

The next morning, it wasn't sunlight that roused Lauren from her prison.

It was the steady whisper of rain tapping against the camper roof—soft but unrelenting, like fingers drumming on a coffin lid. A quiet reminder from the sky that the world still turned, even if hers had stopped.

But this time, it smelled different. Cleaner. Sharper. Like wet asphalt and pine sap. Like the world had been washed while she lay forgotten inside.

Her body screamed as she stirred, every inch stiff and swollen from days trapped in the same twisted posture. The pain wasn't surprising anymore. Just cruelly familiar. Predictable—like an old song she couldn't stop hearing.

The rain mirrored her soul: gray, constant, quietly mourning.

She felt like she was dying. Not dramatically. Not all at once.

Just... slowly. Silently.

Waiting for her body to catch up with her spirit.

Turning onto her side felt like peeling herself from glass. The movement tore at her raw skin, and she cried out—not from shock, but from inevitability. Her nerves were flayed, exposed, like live wires. And yet, she did it anyway.

Lying on her back had left her with sores—angry little mouths of pain that joined the chorus screaming through her frame.

She closed her eyes and let herself drift with the rhythm of the rain, pretending for just a moment that she was outside.

Barefoot.

Standing in the mud.

Letting the storm wash her clean.

She thought of the black truck again.

Of the man she wasn't sure existed.

And she whispered a silent plea to the universe: *Come back. Please, come back. Watch me. Follow me. Save me.*

Even the idea of a stalker felt like fantasy now. A delusion, maybe. Or a dream too fragile to hold onto.

But still—if someone had been watching, wouldn't they have stopped Stefan by now?

Killed him?

Killed her?

Either would've been a mercy.

Stefan stirred beside her.

Lauren's heart snapped to attention. She immediately shut her one good eye and steadied her breath, feigning sleep. A practiced trick by now.

He seemed to buy it.

Or maybe he just didn't care enough to look closely anymore.

He got up. She heard the pop of his joints as he stretched, the rustle of clothes, the bathroom door creaking open, then shut. A moment later —metal clanged, boots tapped the linoleum.

But no coffee.

No breakfast.

No sounds of a pan sizzling or water boiling.

Just the quiet thud of him moving through the camper like a ghost in his own shell.

He returned to the bedroom and kicked the edge of the bed.

The jolt ricocheted through her ribs, sharp and immediate. She groaned.

"Yeah!" he barked. "Wake up."

Lauren mumbled something unintelligible, her voice gravel and breath.

"I'm heading into town. Want anything?"

She blinked.

That question—he never asked. Not like that.

Her mind hiccuped. Was it a trap? Would a request provoke him?

"Maybe... a fountain Coke?" she whispered. "That would be amazing."

He grunted. A sound that meant nothing and everything. Then the door opened. Slammed shut.

She listened.

His boots splashed through a puddle. The truck engine roared to life, then rumbled down the road, fading into the gray morning.

Now she was alone.

The silence that followed wasn't peaceful. It was heavy. Pressed against her chest like a weight.

Her body was tired. Her spirit—worse.

She closed her eye again and whispered,

"Please... let me stop breathing."

And then—

Her eye flew open.

Something rewound in her mind.

The routine.

The sequence.

He got out of bed. Stretched. Dressed. Bathroom. Kitchen—no coffee. No fridge.

Came back. Asked a question. Walked away.

Door opened.

Door closed.

Engine.

She froze.

Door. Door. Engine.

Her brain repeated the rhythm, searching.

Door... door... engine.

No *click*.

No *lock*.

Oh God.

He didn't lock it.

Her heart slammed against her ribs. A drumbeat of sudden, wild hope.

He didn't lock it.

Adrenaline surged through her. Fast. Blinding.

Her body already knew what her mind had just realized—freedom might be possible.

She had to move. Now.

If she could just reach the window. The door. Crawl. Scream. Something.

She pushed herself up.

Pain erupted like fire across her chest, her limbs, her spine.

She kept going.

Again.

And again.

Each time, her body folded beneath her like soaked tissue. Her limbs gave out. Her head swam. Nausea came in waves. Her ribs screamed in protest.

Still—she tried.

Still—she screamed.

Not loud enough for anyone to hear.

But loud enough for the walls to remember.

Just for a moment, she imagined the door swinging open—her Granddaddy standing there, arms wide, saying it was over. That she was safe. That he'd found her.

She tried once more, pouring everything she had into the motion.

A spark ignited inside her.

Freedom was right there.

On the other side of the door.

But her body wasn't ready.

Not yet.

The world pitched sideways.

Blackness swallowed her whole.

Lauren woke to the thunder's rage—a violent drumbeat pounding overhead. It echoed inside her, deep and furious. The bitterness. The grief. The failure.

She hated Stefan—for what he'd done, for what he'd taken.

But more than that—

She hated herself.

For thinking she was different.

Different from Nurse Erin. From Bill. From Judy.

From all the names she never knew but would carry with her just the same.

Lightning cracked. The camper walls trembled. The storm outside was biblical—wrathful and wild.

And then—

The door flew open.

She flinched hard. Her heart lurched into silence. Her breath caught.

Was it Stefan?

No footsteps. No voice.

Only wind.

Rain.

Then—

A voice.

Soft as a prayer.

"Sarah?"

Lauren burst into sobs. Broken, breathless sobs.

"I'm here," she whispered hoarsely. "Help me. Help me."

She heard wet soles on slick metal—Mr. Wallace climbing the camper steps with trembling urgency.

"Sarah?" he called again, louder now. Urgent. Breaking.

"I'm coming, Sarah. I got you."

She heard him nearly fall. The lights were off, the storm dimming everything into a sickly gray. But he kept moving. One foot. Then the other. And then—

And then—he saw her.

He stopped.

Froze.

Didn't breathe.

She was grotesquely swollen.

Her right eye completely sealed shut. Her lips cracked and bleeding, her cheeks a canvas of layered bruises. A deep, jagged cut slashed across her nose. Her neck bore the dark purple rings of strangulation. Her shoulder hung limp in a makeshift sling. Her wrists and forearms were covered in bruises—yellow, violet, angry. Her legs—trembling, exposed—were slashed with belt marks. Fresh. Raw.

And in the center of it all—

The brutal outline of a belt buckle, pressed into her skin like a brand.

"My God," he breathed.

217

He dropped to his knees beside her and cupped her face with trembling hands.

He'd seen bruises before—military rescue, late-night dispatch calls, even a few bloody brawls from his younger days. But never like this.

Not on someone so young. So still. So small.

It reminded him of a case from years ago—back when he still worked dispatch. A little girl found under her stepfather's porch. Ribs shattered like twigs. Eyes swollen shut.

The EMTs said she'd survive.

But he'd always wondered if "living" was the right word.

Now, staring at Lauren—no, Sarah—he felt that same helpless surge. That sick twist in his gut.

The rage.

The bone-deep certainty that he should've done more. Should've asked again. Should've knocked harder. Called someone. Anyone.

She had been right there.

Next door.

Dying right under his nose.

And he'd been too polite. Too damn careful.

"Mr. Wallace," she croaked. Her voice barely more than air. "Help me."

His eyes filled.

"I've got you," he whispered. "I'm getting you out of here."

He reached to lift her—

But the moment his hands touched her sides, she screamed.

A sound that tore through the camper like something dying.

He recoiled instantly, horror on his face, hands held up like he'd touched fire.

"I'm so sorry, sweetheart. I..." He tried again but failed. His hands shook. His aging body betrayed him. "Damn it!"

He hovered beside her, useless, eyes darting from her mangled body to the door. Torn. Frantic. Caught between instinct and reality. He'd always been the one to step in, to do something. But now—his knees screamed, his back ached, and the truth settled like concrete in his chest: He couldn't lift her. Not fast enough. Not safely. And God, what if he made it worse?

"I can't leave you like this," he said, voice breaking under the weight of failure. "I can't—"

"You have to," she said. Her voice was thick with tears but anchored with something else. Resolve. "Before he comes back."

She could see the war in his eyes—his need to be the hero. But this wasn't a movie rescue scene. There wasn't time for valor.

"Mr. Wallace," she whispered. "Please."

And that was it. The word. Please. The one that shattered him.

He looked at her—torn apart, trembling.

Finally, he nodded and gently pressed her hand. Even that slight touch made her wince.

She wasn't used to being touched with kindness. Not anymore. It felt foreign. Unnatural. Like her skin had forgotten how to receive gentleness without recoiling.

"I'm going," he whispered. "I'll be right back. Hang tight, Sarah."

She watched him disappear down the hallway. The sound of the camper door opening. Then—

The door closed behind him.

And for the first time in what felt like forever, she was alone... but not abandoned.

The difference was seismic. Not alone. Not forgotten. Someone had seen her. Heard her. Someone knew.

For one fragile moment, her mind clung to something else. Something brighter.

She could see it— Stefan returning to find Mr. Wallace standing tall in the rain, speaking to police. Flashing red and blue lights reflected off slick pavement. An ambulance parked nearby. Paramedics rushing inside the camper, lifting her gently, wrapping her in a warm blanket. The stretcher rolling out. Freedom.

She could taste it. She was so close.

Maybe the storm would open for her. Maybe she'd be the one survivor.

She imagined her Granddaddy's voice breaking through the static— "Hold on now, Pumpkin Pie. You're almost there." She pressed her battered hand to her ribs, as if to hold that hope in place. To anchor it.

She strained to listen—for sirens. For footsteps. For the voice of someone—anyone—coming to help. Every second felt like glass under pressure—fragile, creaking, ready to shatter.

But there was only rain. The steady tap-tap-tap on the roof. Mocking. Waiting.

But then— She heard it. The roar of Stefan's engine.

Please let Mr. Wallace be inside already. Please let him be calling 911. Please, God.

She heard footsteps—wet, fast, splashing through the mud. Then... silence.

Stefan had stopped.

Her stomach twisted into knots. Think, Lauren. Think.

The door creaked open. Slow. Deliberate. As if he already knew.

And she could feel it—he knew. And she knew he knew.

Her stomach dropped, cold and hollow. Her pulse fluttered in her throat like a bird trapped in a jar.

She didn't need to see his face. She could feel it in the air—the shift. That dreadful stillness that came before the storm.

He'd seen the signs. The rearranged blanket. The faint wet prints on the floor.

And now...

He was going to punish her for it.

26

The moment Stefan got out of his truck and made his way toward the camper, he saw them—

Footprints.

Leading straight to the door.

He followed the trail to the steps, eyes narrowing at the smears of mud across them.

Mud that hadn't been there when he left.

His heart slammed against his ribs. He ripped the keys from his pocket, shoved one into the lock, and twisted. The door creaked open.

He froze.

Rage flooded him. Immediate. Blinding.

He had forgotten to lock the door.

Holy shit.

Stefan stepped inside. More mud. The prints led straight to the bedroom. His jaw flexed as he rolled his neck, trying to choke the fury down long enough to think.

Then he turned and stepped back out into the freezing rain.

The footprints continued—away from their camper.

To the one next door.

He'd kill the old man.

He should have done it earlier.

As Stefan rounded the edge of the camper, he spotted Mr. Wallace descending his own steps, drenched and shivering. Stefan ducked behind his truck, mind racing.

He'd already scoped out the RV park.

No cameras faced this direction.

He waited. Watched.

And in the camper next door, Edward Wallace gripped the railing, heart pounding, unaware he was being watched.

The rain soaked through his clothes—cold, insistent—but he barely felt it. His thoughts were still back in that camper—with Sarah.

With the bruises. The broken body. The quiet, desperate girl.

Seeing her had twisted something deep in his gut.

It had ripped open old wounds.

His mother had worn those bruises once.

Black eyes. Broken ribs.

Courtesy of his father's drunken fists.

He remembered tending to her through those nights.

Cold rags. Shaking hands. Helpless.

But Sarah—Sarah was worse off than his mother had ever been.

And she had been left like that.

For God knew how long.

Mr. Wallace hurt for her.

He needed to get her help.

He thought of Margaret—her voice, always soft but steel beneath the surface: "*If you see something, do something.*"

He had done nothing when he was a boy. Watched his father swing fists and spew rage.

Not this time. Not again.

But the storm had knocked out the service.

No bars. No service.

He had tried—frantically—only to be met with dead air and static.

He'd even thought about driving to town.

But leaving Sarah alone felt like betrayal.

He had made her a promise.

And Edward Wallace kept his promises.

Margaret's voice echoed in his head—calm, unwavering: "*Be the man you wish your father had been.*"

He blinked against the rain, steeling himself. He wouldn't fail this time.

He trudged through the rain, his mind spinning for a plan—any plan.

He'd just open the camper door, yell that he was going for help. He wouldn't go inside again. Wouldn't risk startling her. Wouldn't risk hurting her again.

But then he froze.

Zach's truck was back.

The world tilted beneath him.

Panic surged through him. He reached into his pocket for his keys, ready to bolt for his truck—

Behind him, Zach moved—fast and silent as a shadow. A whisper of motion. A shift in the rain.

—and then pain exploded at the back of his skull.

Blinding. Brutal.

He stumbled, reaching instinctively for the wound. His fingers came away slick with blood.

He turned—dazed—and met the eyes of a madman.

Zach.

Soaked to the bone, hair plastered to his face, eyes black with murder.

Mr. Wallace tried to stagger back, but the mud betrayed him. He slipped and crashed to the ground with a wet, heavy splash.

Before he could recover, Stefan was there—towering over him.

He dropped to one knee, grabbed Mr. Wallace by both sides of the head, and yanked it up off the ground.

Edward gasped, his neck straining under the pressure.

Zach's hands trembled with fury.

He was going to slam his head into the mud—crack it open like an egg on stone.

Edward Wallace thought of Sarah.

Her face. The bruises. That whisper of a voice, begging him to get help.

If I die here… she'll be alone again.

No more chances. No more hope.

Zach would finish what he started. No one would stop him.

His hands twitched in the mud, searching for leverage.

Don't black out. Don't give him the satisfaction.

Stay conscious. Stay alive.

For her.

Then he paused.

Footsteps.

Someone was coming.

Zach leaned in, lowering his mouth to Mr. Wallace's ear. So close his lips brushed skin.

His voice, a venomous whisper.

"Say anything... and I'll kill Sarah."

A pause.

"I promise.

Do. You. Understand?"

Mr. Wallace's heart pounded so violently he thought it would burst.

He saw Margaret in his mind.

He saw Sarah—bruised, broken, bleeding.

He had to protect her.

"Do. You. Understand?" Stefan hissed again, tightening his grip.

Tears welled in Mr. Wallace's eyes.

"Yes," he croaked. "I understand."

In an instant, the monster vanished.

Standing in his place was Zach—the charming, helpful neighbor. The man who offered tools and smiled too easily. The one nobody ever suspected.

He smiled gently, as if they were old friends.

Mr. Wallace barely had time to comprehend it before Zach slipped an arm around his shoulders, hauling him upright—just as a young man jogged toward them.

For just a flicker of a second, Mr. Wallace thought the man could've been his own grandson—same build, same eager stride. Hope surged—pure, aching hope—then recoiled, shriveling into something cautious.

Black hair. Stunning green eyes that seemed to cut straight through you.

"You okay?" the young man called out.

Zach answered before Mr. Wallace could speak, laughing like nothing had happened.

"Hey there! Man, am I glad to see you."

Mr. Wallace, dizzy and cold, said nothing. He remained pinned beneath Zach's arm, unable to escape the performance.

The young man eyed him carefully. "Did you fall?"

"Yeah," Zach replied, all ease. "Lost his balance in the mud. Hit his head a little, but nothing bad."

The young man's gaze lingered. "Are you hurt?"

Zach's grip tightened—subtle, deliberate.

"He'll be fine," Zach said quickly. "I got him."

With practiced care, he guided Mr. Wallace up the steps and into his camper.

Inside, Mr. Wallace tried to steady his trembling hands. His skin felt cold, rubbery. His brain fogged with fear.

He needed to tell someone. Anyone.

But the threat still echoed in his mind:

Say anything and I'll kill Sarah.

"Do you have a first aid kit?" Zach asked cheerfully.

Mr. Wallace nodded, mute.

"Good, good. You should change into some dry clothes too," Zach added, with a wink laced with razor-sharp warning.

Mr. Wallace retreated to his bedroom.

He moved like a sleepwalker, until instinct kicked in.

He reached for his phone—

Still nothing.

His stomach twisted.

Outside, he could hear Stefan chatting casually with the young man:

"Dude, what the hell? One night we're drinking at the bar, next thing you vanish."

"Had to work overtime," the young man said lightly. "Got sent to another project."

Zach's voice turned wary. "Man, that night after the bar, I woke up passed out in my truck. Pretty weird, right?"

The young man laughed, clapping him on the back. "You were wasted, man. You don't remember?"

Zach frowned—but let it go.

Maybe he was overthinking it.

Edward stepped back into the living area, clothes dry but hands still shaking.

The young man smiled at him kindly.

Then, turning to Zach, he asked, "What was your wife's name again?"

Before Zach could respond, Edward answered quietly, "Sarah. And she is a sweetheart."

There was a pause—brief, but sharp.

"She is something," Stefan said with a grin that missed his eyes entirely.

His voice carried that too-light tone—the kind people use when they're hiding something.

The young man's eyes flicked between them. Just for a second.

His jaw tightened slightly, a subtle crease forming between his brows.

Something passed across his face—thoughtfulness, maybe. Or doubt.

But he let it go, folding his arms as he shifted his weight, still watching.

Edward didn't speak.

Didn't look at Stefan.

But his silence said everything.

They bandaged his wound together, the young man offering help again and again.

But Stefan brushed him off with practiced ease. Smiling. Redirecting. Always in control.

Then, too casually, Zach turned to Edward. "Old timer, you shouldn't be alone tonight. Why don't you come stay with us? Just for the night."

Edward froze.

He looked at the young man.

Pleaded silently—*Help us. Sarah needs help. This man is a monster.*

But Stefan was already moving. Already packing a bag for him. Already guiding him to the door.

Mr. Wallace turned back once. Just once.

To look at his camper.

At the blanket Margaret had crocheted.

At the chair where she used to sit, reading dog-eared paperbacks.

At the home they had dreamed of retiring in—one last adventure together.

Somehow, he already knew—

He would never see it again.

He closed his eyes and whispered a prayer.

For Sarah.

For a miracle.

For himself.

As the young man disappeared into the night and Stefan guided him across the muddy lot, Edward Wallace prepared himself for whatever hell waited behind that door.

27

Lauren remained silent, barely daring to breathe, her entire body straining toward the voices outside. Every nerve and muscle in her battered frame screamed with tension.

She needed a plan.

She needed to know which mask to wear when the door finally opened and the nightmare flooded back in.

The feeling was familiar—eerily so.

She had felt it before, standing beside her parents' coffins. A little girl in black, clutching her Granddaddy's hand with white-knuckled fingers.

Everyone had stared.

The poor girl whose parents died.

She hadn't wanted their pity. She hadn't wanted their eyes.

All she'd wanted was to disappear. To become invisible.

She'd been helpless then.

And she felt just as helpless now.

Her mind was exhausted—frayed to the edges by the relentless emotional whiplash.

Anger.

Dread.

Hope.

Despair.

Each one shredding her from the inside out.

Dread had once again turned to hope when she heard Mr. Wallace's shuffling steps—slow, familiar, unmistakably his.

But that fragile hope dissolved into deeper, blacker misery at the sound that followed.

A sickening thud. Final.

Like a tree falling in the woods.

Too solid to ignore.

Something twisted violently in her gut.

Another sound. Not a strike—this time, it was a body hitting the ground.

Heavy. Wet. Final.

Like a sack of soaked flour dropped onto the earth.

Footsteps followed.

The door was cracked just enough. Through the narrow slice, she could hear voices—low and muddled through the rain.

Mr. Wallace came first—urgent, trembling.

Then Stefan—sharp, hostile.

She turned her head slightly, wincing at the dull, pulsing pain that screamed through her neck.

Closing her eyes, she tried to sharpen her hearing, to feel the vibrations in the floor beneath her.

The footsteps were wrong.

They weren't Stefan's rage-filled stomps.

They weren't Mr. Wallace's slow, cautious shuffles.

These were steady.

Heavy.

Measured.

Male.

Each one landed with a deliberate weight that made the hair on her arms stand on end.

From the rain came a voice.

Kind. Calm.

Low, but clear—cutting through the storm like a blade through fog.

Lauren's heart kicked hard against her ribs.

She could hear Stefan now too—louder, closer—and there was something strange about the tone between him and the stranger.

Not hostile.

Familiar.

Her stomach twisted tighter.

Who the hell could this be?

She wanted to get up. To see what was happening.

But her body—betrayed by exhaustion and pain—refused to obey.

She was trapped.

Paralyzed inside herself.

Thunder rumbled above—deep and vibrating—rattling the thin camper walls like an angry giant bowling over everything in its path.

The floor shivered beneath her.

The walls groaned.

Lauren strained harder, desperate to hear more, but the voices outside were swallowed by the storm.

The voices faded into the rain.

She was alone again.

Alone with the deafening rain hammering the roof, the rattling windows, the brutal rhythm of her own fear pounding inside her chest.

Tears welled, blurring her vision—

but she blinked them away.

Sheer force of will.

She had to stay sharp.

Had to be ready.

Terror gnawed at her—

for Mr. Wallace.

For herself.

For whatever fresh horror was about to unfold.

Because when Stefan lost control—

he didn't just rage.

He calculated.

Studied pain like it was art.

Delivered it slowly. Precisely.

With the patience of a sadist who had no limits.

No mercy.

And she bore the proof—

etched into her body, buried in her mind.

Lauren waited, clinging to the last threads of hope like a woman suspended above a pit of knives.

Any second now, she told herself.

Any second now, sirens would wail.

Help would crash through the door.

She just had to hold on a little longer.

The rain softened gradually, becoming a whisper instead of a roar.

Birdsong—tentative and trembling—drifted into the gray air.

A pale, sickly light clawed at the clouds, trying to reclaim the sky.

But no sirens came.

No flashing lights.

No rescue.

Only the endless drip, drip, drip of rainwater sliding off the eaves.

Only the dread, thickening with every breath.

Her thoughts shattered—

replaced by the steady drum of footsteps.

Closer. Heavier. Coming straight for her.

She heard Stefan's voice—sharper, more frantic.

Was he alone?

Had he killed Mr. Wallace?

Had he killed the stranger, too—the man with the kind voice?

Lauren's heart slammed against her ribs in blind panic.

He's going to kill me.

The thought was not a fear.

It was a certainty.

Cold. Clear. Final.

And for one terrible, fractured moment,

she wasn't sure which fate was worse—

Death...

or the endless living hell she was already trapped in.

A new sound broke through the silence.

Mr. Wallace's shuffling footsteps.

Alive. Still alive.

And the stranger's voice again—

threading low and steady through the chaos, pulling her back from the brink.

She gripped the edge of the mattress.

Her Granddaddy never shuffled. He moved with quiet command, boots heavy with purpose, even in his oldest years. When he entered a room, you felt it—like gravity deepening.

Mr. Wallace was different.

His shuffle was worn, hesitant—

but still, somehow, it steadied her.

Because it meant he was still standing.

Still fighting.

For her.

Hope flickered inside her.

Faint.

But stubborn.

But it didn't last.

The footsteps began to fade. Shift. Disappear.

Lauren's breathing spiraled out of control.

Panic sliced into her chest like knives.

She gasped for air, desperate, each breath thinner than the last, until her vision shimmered at the edges.

Outside, the storm had passed.

Inside her, it raged fiercer than ever.

Get it together. Mask on. MASK ON.

The mantra pulsed through her battered mind.

The door creaked open.

Mr. Wallace's familiar shuffle scraped across the floor.

Lauren fought to blink away the blur of tears, straining to see through the haze.

All she could do was listen.

And then—

she felt it.

That suffocating shift in the air.

Stefan.

His presence filled the room, pressing down on her like a physical weight.

She froze. Every muscle tensed, bracing for impact.

Lauren willed herself to disappear into the thin blanket wrapped around her broken body.

Her breath stilled. Her limbs turned to stone.

She became nothing but silence and dread.

"You stupid fucking old man," Stefan snarled, his voice like shards of broken glass.

"You couldn't leave shit alone. You nosy old bastard."

Lauren flinched at the venom in his words.

Panic clawed up her throat—

but she swallowed it down.

She heard him pacing.

Sharp. Erratic.

The sound of a cornered animal—panicked and lethal.

She knew that sound.

Knew what came next.

Mr. Wallace's voice—shaky, but stubborn—broke through the tension.

"Zach, we can work something out," he said, the words tumbling over themselves.

Stefan let out a dry, cruel laugh.

"No, sir. We can't."

Lauren squeezed the blanket tighter around herself, every fiber of her being begging to vanish.

Stefan was unraveling.

She could hear it—

in the cracks between his words,

in the way his boots stormed across the floor.

Mr. Wallace didn't know the signs.

Didn't know the tones to watch for, the buttons to avoid.

He hadn't practiced the tightrope Lauren walked every day—

hadn't studied the shifts in Stefan's voice,

the flick of his eyes,

the breaths between rage and eruption.

He didn't know when to speak.

When to shut up.

When to disappear.

"We can," Mr. Wallace insisted, his voice unraveling. "We'll say I found her on a hiking trail. No one ever has to know. Not about you. Not about anything."

Lauren clung to those words like a drowning woman to a shard of driftwood.

But deep down, she knew better.

Stefan didn't negotiate.

He destroyed.

"You think I'm stupid, don't you?" Stefan hissed.

"No," Mr. Wallace said quickly—too quickly. "I don't. I think Sarah needs help, and you did the best you could."

"Give me your phone," Stefan barked.

A beat of hesitation.

"Za—"

"I said, GIVE. ME. YOUR. PHONE!"

Stefan's voice cracked the air like a whip.

A scuffle.

A gasp.

What followed cracked the air—

the unmistakable sound of flesh striking flesh.

Lauren jerked.

An involuntary spasm of fear.

Then silence.

Thick.

Awful.

That seemed to swallow the whole world.

Then—

a sound just outside the bedroom window.

Soft. Deliberate.

Like someone stepping too close... and then pausing.

Her breath caught.

Was it him?

Or someone else?

Tears blurred her vision again, but she didn't move.

Didn't breathe.

Didn't dare.

Every nerve in her body felt it—

Stefan was teetering on the edge.

The air itself was charged—thick with the threat of him.

One wrong move.

One wrong word.

And he would snap.

A knock shattered the silence—sharp, sudden.

Like a gunshot through glass.

Lauren's eyes snapped open.

Her heart slammed into her ribs.

Was it the police?

Was it rescue?

Stefan cursed under his breath, his footsteps scraping across the floor.

Another knock — harder this time.

"Yeah, man, what's up?" he barked, cracking the door open just enough to talk.

That same voice answered —

calm, kind.

Almost absurd against the horror unfolding inside.

"Dude, I was just gonna run into town, grab some groceries. You need anything? I know you got your hands full."

The man's voice faltered.

Lauren could picture it —

him standing there, staring at Mr. Wallace's crumpled body.

"Oh, dude — what happened to him?"

Lauren's stomach twisted into a hard, burning knot.

"Shh," Stefan said, laughing thinly. "Just takin' a nap."

The door closed behind him.

Lauren caught only fragments of their conversation outside —

broken words, strained laughter.

The minutes crawled by.

Each second flayed her raw.

The door opened again.

Stefan's boots thudded heavily across the floor.

He appeared in the bedroom doorway, his face a twisted mask of rage straining at the edges.

"I'll be back," he growled. Low. Menacing.

"I'll deal with you both then. You can count on that."

Move. Scream. Do something.

No—stay down. Stay silent.

You survive by vanishing.

Lauren didn't dare move.

Didn't blink.

Didn't breathe.

The door opened.

The door closed.

And then the lock.

Click.

The lock.

The prison sealed.

Locked in.

Alone.

But not completely alone.

In the next room, Mr. Wallace's body lay crumpled.

Alive or dead—she didn't know.

The not knowing clawed at her mind.

Tears spilled down her cheeks, silent and unchecked.

Hope and terror battled in her chest—two beasts clawing for the same breath.

For a moment, it almost broke her.

The silence.

The weight.

The sheer, unbearable repetition of survival.

She closed her eyes.

Sank into the ache.

The thought crept in like a poison:

Maybe this is how it ends.

But then—

a breath.

A flicker.

A whisper, raw and hoarse, but hers.

"Not yet."

She opened her eyes.

The storm outside had passed—

but inside, it was only beginning.

28

Lauren blinked through the darkness, her mind a blur of panic and pain.

From the living area—

a rustling sound.

A low moan.

Her heart twisted.

"Mr. Wallace?" she called, her voice hoarse and trembling.

Another moan.

Faint.

Broken.

But alive.

"Mr. Wallace?" she rasped again, more desperate now.

She tried to sit up—too fast.

Her battered body revolted.

Pain ripped through her side, and her vision swam.

Before she could stop herself, she collapsed back onto the mattress with a scream that barely left her lips—dry, cracked, aching.

The pain was blinding.

But worse was the helplessness.

Mr. Wallace was out there. Hurt.

Because of her.

Tears blurred her vision.

For the briefest moment, she let herself wonder if she'd survive this.

If she could.

The pain was too much. The odds stacked too high.

And yet—

She thought of Granddaddy.

Strong.

Steady.

Unshakable Granddaddy.

What would he do in this moment?

He would fight.

He would crawl through the dark if he had to.

He wouldn't give up. Not even on the darkest night.

Neither would she.

Instead, she focused on breathing.

Slow. Controlled.

She moved deliberately, testing each part of her broken body.

She couldn't afford another fall.

She needed every ounce of strength she had left.

Her breaths came shallow and sharp as she braced herself on her elbows. The world tilted, swaying violently. She swallowed the bile rising in her throat and forced herself to stay still.

To breathe through the agony.

One breath. One movement. One small victory at a time.

When she leaned too far left, the world dissolved into black static.

When she leaned too far forward, pain shot like lightning from her spine down her leg.

She learned her limits fast.

Survival depended on it.

Finally—painfully—she made it to a sitting position.

Her skin was slick with sweat, every inch of her trembling, slick body sticking to the blanket beneath her.

Her ribs screamed in protest—raw, tearing agony that blurred the edges of her vision.

It felt like she might split open under the weight of the effort.

But she didn't stop.

She couldn't.

Tears streamed down her swollen face.

She could only see from one eye, and even that was clouded—blood pooling at the edges of her vision.

Her lips moved silently in prayer.

Not for herself.

For Mr. Wallace.

Her muscles trembled with exhaustion.

Her hands shook uncontrollably, fingers curled into useless claws.

Her legs spasmed beneath her, the nerves twitching with every heartbeat.

Even her head wobbled slightly, too heavy for her weakened neck to fully support.

She could feel herself slipping—fading—like her body was trying to shut down to escape the pain.

The camper walls seemed to close in, tighter and tighter, a tomb made of thin wood and cheap metal.

Her breath caught in her throat.

Every inch of her screamed to give up.

To let go.

"No..." she croaked, the word barely audible.

She dug her already broken nails into the mattress, forcing her battered body to stay upright.

"Stay awake," she whispered fiercely. "Stay. Awake."

Her voice was a shattered thing, no louder than breath—

but inside her head, it echoed like a battle cry.

Pulling her from the brink of darkness, she heard it—

Not her name.

But the familiar name.

"Sarah," Mr. Wallace groaned from the living area, his voice thin and full of pain.

Relief slammed into her, nearly knocking the breath from her lungs.

She almost sobbed.

He was alive.

Still alive.

"Mr. Wallace?" she breathed.

"Yes..." he rasped. A pause. Then, weaker: "Sarah... you have to stay still..."

Fresh tears spilled down Lauren's cheeks.

She pressed a shaking hand to her mouth to keep from crying out.

"I'm so sorry," she whispered, barely able to get the words past the lump in her throat.

"If it weren't for me—"

"No, no, sweetheart," Mr. Wallace said gently, cutting her off before the guilt could take shape.

"It's not your fault."

Lauren let herself fall back onto the bed, pain crashed over her like a brutal wave.

Good.

She deserved it.

Every shattered rib.

Every ragged breath.

She deserved it.

"Stay strong," he said again. "We're going to get through this."

His words cut deep—because Lauren knew:

If they survived...

he wouldn't say the same if he knew the truth.

If he knew who she really was.

What she had done.

What she had helped Stefan do.

She wanted to tell him.

Everything.

She wanted to confess before it was too late.

If she died tonight,

she didn't want to die with lies on her lips.

She wanted someone—anyone—to know that she was sorry.

That somewhere, buried deep inside her broken, battered heart,

there was still a piece of the little girl her Granddaddy had raised.

"I'm here," she croaked out, the effort almost too much to bear.

"Good..." he whispered.

A long silence stretched between them, broken only by their ragged breathing.

Then Mr. Wallace spoke again:

"I'm tied up, Sarah. I can't move."

Lauren closed her eyes, forcing her thoughts through the pain.

Of course Stefan would've tied him up. He wouldn't risk anyone interfering again.

If Mr. Wallace was bound, he couldn't reach help.

He couldn't reach her.

It had to be her.

It had to be Lauren who moved.

No one was coming to save them.

"How are you feeling?" she asked, the question slipping out instinctively, her heart aching with real concern.

"I'm... banged up," Mr. Wallace said with a weak chuckle that turned into a cough.

"Better than you are, though."

A pause. Then, voice trembling:

"Sarah... I tried. I promise I tried. But there's no service. I couldn't call for help."

Lauren clenched her fists.

Another dead end. Their last hope, shattered.

"It's okay, Mr. Wallace," she said, though it wasn't okay at all.

"We'll figure something out."

She wasn't sure who she was trying harder to convince—him, or herself.

"I tried, Sarah," he said again, and Lauren could hear the helpless guilt in his voice.

The same guilt she wore like a second skin.

"I know," she whispered. "I know you did."

A beat of silence.

Then she asked—softly, urgently,

"Mr. Wallace... who was the man that came up and helped you?"

She needed to know.

Needed answers.

Needed something—anything—to make sense.

"I don't know his name," Edward said weakly. "I saw him before. At the RV park. In Springfield."

A breath. A tremor.

"Zach was about to kill me. That man... he saved me."

Lauren's heart pounded harder.

Springfield.

The RV park.

The black truck with the camper topper.

Her main suspect in the note.

The one her paranoia kept circling back to.

Maybe even the one who drugged Stefan that night at the bar.

None of it felt like coincidence anymore.

"Mr. Wallace... did he drive a black truck?" she asked, trying to keep her voice steady.

"With a topper on it?"

"I think so," Mr. Wallace said after a moment.

"I think that was him. I saw him and Zach together. A few times."

Lauren's mind raced.

Confusion and fear twisted into a knot she couldn't untie.

How had he found them?

He was there in Springfield—

but he'd left before Stefan knew they were heading to Mountain Home.

Unless...

Unless he'd been following them all along.

Her stomach twisted.

Was he a threat?

Or their only hope?

Before she could think it through, Mr. Wallace's voice pulled her back:

"Sarah... we have to get help. Before he comes back."

Lauren shook her head, trying to clear the cobwebs from her brain.

No time to question.

No time to wonder.

Mr. Wallace was right.

If they stayed here, they were dead.

She had to move.

Had to reach him.

Had to untie him before Stefan—

or someone even worse—returned.

She tried to grit her teeth, but pain flared through her jaw.

So instead, she planted her palms on the mattress, steeling herself against the agony she knew was coming.

She would make it.

She had no choice.

Because this time, she wasn't just fighting for herself.

She was fighting for Edward Wallace.

And for the little girl her Granddaddy once believed in—

the girl who refused to die here,

in the dark.

Now it was her turn to make a move.

29

The weight of the world had settled on Lauren's shoulders, and it was crushing her.

If she failed now, there would be no second chance—

she and Mr. Wallace would die.

And Stefan would win.

The thought struck her like a blade.

Her pulse thudded in her ears, and her breath came in shallow gasps as she lay motionless, every inch of her body screaming.

Her muscles trembled beneath the bruises, and her skin was slick with cold sweat.

But she couldn't afford to break down.

Not now.

Her eyes fluttered shut as she took a slow, trembling inventory.

The pain mapped itself across her like constellations of fire—

sharp in her ribs,

burning down her spine,

aching in her hips and shoulders.

Every breath was a battle.

Every twitch of movement sent another scream clawing up her throat.

Get up, she told herself.

You can do this. You have to. You'll fight. You'll survive. And you'll free him.

The camper was quiet, save for the ticking wall clock and the low hum of wind brushing the metal frame.

The silence pressed in—like the calm before the next strike.

"Sarah, how are you doing?"

Mr. Wallace's voice drifted weakly from the other side of the camper.

Strained.

Worried.

Alive.

Lauren didn't want to waste a single ounce of energy on a reply,

but she let out a soft *hmm*—just enough to let him know she was still conscious.

Still trying.

"Take it slow, sweetheart. Try not to overdo it."

She drew a breath and shifted, jaw trembling but still.

Her fingers scraped over the peeling wallpaper as she reached for the wall,

pulling herself into a sitting position.

Her body swayed.

The dizziness hit like a wave—then again, she swayed.

Stay up. Just stay up. Don't fall. Don't you dare fall.

She couldn't lean forward—she barely had control over her spine, let alone her balance.

So she stayed upright, trembling, her hands gripping the wall behind her for support.

Her head hung low, chin barely dipping toward her chest.

Eyes closed. Breaths thin and shaky.

You've done harder. You've survived worse. He's not here. You are. You're still here.

She rode the wave of nausea, willing herself not to pass out.

She looked up, eyes glassy, and stared at the stained ceiling.

The sight of it made her want to scream.

She had memorized every crack, every water spot from the hours she'd spent trapped in this hell.

Every mark, every drip. I know this place better than I know myself. And I hate it. I hate it so much.

With a deep, shaking breath, she braced herself and shifted toward the edge of the bed.

Her head hung low, arms trembling as she gripped the mattress for balance.

It would be easier to quit.

Just lay back down. Close your eyes. Pretend none of this ever happened.

Every part of her wanted to stop.

To lie back down.

To disappear.

But I'm not him.

I don't disappear. I survive.

She inhaled again.

Pushed herself upward.

Her scream was guttural—raw—torn from a place deeper than pain.

The instant her feet hit the floor, her knees buckled.

Pain exploded in her ribs and back, sharp and unrelenting, like bullets tearing through her flesh.

You idiot. You pushed too hard. You always push too hard.

She crumpled beside the bed with a harsh thud, gasping for breath, hot tears spilling down her cheeks.

Her vision blurred at the edges.

Darkness crept in, swallowing the room.

No—no, don't pass out. Not now. Not when it matters.

She was distantly aware of Mr. Wallace calling to her—

"Sarah!"

His voice laced with panic.

Then—

Silence.

Blackness.

A faint ringing pulled her back from the void—

distant at first, like echoes underwater.

Then came a voice.

Muffled. Urgent.

"Sarah? Please, answer me... Sarah!"

Mr. Wallace's voice cracked—thick with fear.

A sound that gutted her followed.

He was sobbing.

Not loudly. Not theatrically.

Just broken. Quiet. Desperate.

Like a man calling out to a ghost, afraid he's already lost her.

No... don't cry for me. Please don't cry for me.

I'm not worth your tears. Not yet. Not until I get us out.

Her eyes fluttered, lids heavy as stone.

Pain yanked her back to consciousness like a rope cinched around her ribs.

A dry sob escaped her throat.

She was still on the floor, cheek pressed to the cold linoleum.

The air reeked of sweat, blood, and cheap cleaner.

God, not again. Not this floor. Not this cold. I can't—

No. You don't get to shut down.

Not now. He's still out there. And he's coming back.

For a moment, she didn't move.

Couldn't.

Every cell in her body rebelled.

I could just stay here. Close my eyes. Fade out.

Let it end the way it always does.

But then what? He wins? Again?

But the memory of Stefan's voice—

cold, calm, and echoing—

"I'll be back. I'll deal with you both then. You can count on that."

—lit a spark in her chest.

He thinks I'm down. Done.

Let him think it.

Let him walk into a storm he never saw coming.

She opened her eyes.

The world tilted, swimming in and out of focus—

but she could make out the faint orange glow of a porch light bleeding through the closed blinds.

Shadows swayed across the walls with each gust of wind.

I'm still breathing.

That means I can still fight.

Her fingers twitched against the floor.

She wasn't dead.

Not yet.

"I'm okay," she whispered hoarsely.

She wasn't sure if Mr. Wallace could hear her.

Hell, she wasn't sure she'd actually said it out loud.

Lie louder, she told herself bitterly. *Maybe you'll start believing it.*

She didn't try to move. Not yet.

The pain was too sharp, too immediate.

Instead, she lay still—cheek pressed to the cold floor, breath shallow.

Tears slid down the bridge of her nose, pooling on the linoleum.

The salt stung the cuts on her face as they trickled down.

Tiny reminders of everything that still hurt—everything that was still real.

You're not dreaming. You're not gone.

You're still here. Still bleeding. Still his.

Unless you make that stop.

It would be so easy to stay like this.

To close her eyes again.

To let the world slip away.

But you didn't come this far to die on the floor.

You didn't survive Stefan just to rot here like one of his secrets.

Slowly—carefully—she inched her good arm toward the wooden bed frame.

Her other still hung limp in the makeshift sling, useless and burning with pain.

Come on. Come on.

Don't let it win. Don't let him win.

Her fingertips scraped along the floor until they found the edge— rough, splintered.

She didn't have nails to dig in anymore.

Only skin. Only grit.

She paused.

Gathered what little strength she had left.

He's going to come back.

You need to be ready. You need to stand up before he puts you down for good.

Then she hooked her fingers over the wood and pulled—

skin tearing slightly as she braced.

Her breath hitched with each inch of movement.

The pain was indescribable—

a wildfire ripping through her chest and spine.

She dragged herself forward, inch by inch.

Each movement was a war—her muscles trembling, her breath hitching with every shift.

She paused, cheek pressed to the floor, panting from the effort.

The linoleum was cold against her skin, sticky with sweat and dust.

Her good arm shook violently beneath her, but she didn't stop.

The narrow hallway stretched ahead—tight, confining, lit only by the soft orange haze leaking through the front blinds.

She wasn't in the living area yet.

But she was getting closer.

From the other side of the camper, she heard Mr. Wallace stir.

The ropes creaked as he shifted against them.

"I'm still here." Her voice cracked, but it was just loud enough to break the silence.

"You're alright, honey," Mr. Wallace said gently.

"That's it. I knew you could do it."

Lauren let the encouragement wrap around her like a lifeline.

One breath.

One pull.

She tried to grit her teeth—

but her jaw throbbed.

She clamped her cut, dried lips tight and dragged herself forward—refusing to stop.

She wasn't upright.

She wasn't strong.

But she was moving.

The hallway pulsed around her.

Her ribs scraped the narrow walls.

Black spots danced at the edge of her vision.

Blood pounded in her ears.

But she kept going.

Because somewhere just ahead,

past the tight squeeze of the hallway—

was a chance.

Stefan's words echoed in her skull:

"I'll be back. I'll deal with you both then. You can count on that."

She let it push her.

It had to push her.

There was no plan.

No finish line.

Only movement.

Only forward.

She braced herself against the narrow hallway wall.

Her fingers trembled as she planted them flat, tried to rise—

Her legs buckled instantly, and she crumpled again, pain slicing through her side like broken glass.

But she didn't stop.

She rolled slightly, forced herself onto her belly again, and crawled.

The hallway was narrow, her world reduced to inches.

Her breath came quick and shallow.

Her ribs scraped the wall with every pull.

But she kept going.

She turned her head, blinking through the haze.

And then she saw him—

Edward Wallace.

He was hogtied on the couch, wrists pulled behind his back, ankles drawn up and bound tight to his hands.

His body faced away from her, toward the wall, spine rigid with strain.

It was how Stefan liked to tie his victims.

How he liked to tie her.

She swallowed hard, bile rising in her throat.

The sight split her open with grief and rage.

Mr. Wallace squirmed, testing the restraints.

The ropes dug in tighter.

She knew that feeling.

"Mr. Wallace," she rasped, voice breaking, "you have to be still. The more you fight the ropes, the tighter they'll get."

He froze at her words.

"Are you... okay?" he asked, voice choked with pain.

She could hear it—he was crying.

His heart was breaking.

"I'm helpless," he whispered.

"No, please don't." Her voice was steadier now. "It's the way he wants you to feel."

Lauren pulled herself upright to a sitting position, using the cabinet to brace her back.

The darkness surged toward her again, seductive and suffocating.

But Lauren fought it. She refused to pass out. Not now.

She stared at the knots binding Mr. Wallace—

brutal, precise.

Stefan had tied them like he always did. With intention. With enjoyment.

She'd never undo them one-handed.

Her gaze swept the camper—

and landed on Stefan's hunting bag, sitting on the kitchen table.

She tried to stand.

Her body refused.

The darkness loomed again, dragging her toward unconsciousness.

So she didn't stand.

She adapted.

Crawling was her only option.

She rolled to her stomach, tucked her injured arm tight against her ribs, and began crawling.

Again.

The linoleum scraped her elbows raw.

But she inched forward.

One slow pull at a time.

She reached for the duffel bag strap.

Just out of reach.

She stretched—fingers grazing the nylon—

It slid farther away.

A scream tore from her throat—

guttural, wild—

the sound of a wounded animal, furious, desperate,

and emptied by soul-deep frustration.

"Sarah," Mr. Wallace called, his voice gentle despite everything.

"What?" she snapped back, teeth clenched.

"Take a moment, sweetheart. Breathe."

She slammed her eyes shut. Her whole body trembled with pain and exhaustion, but she obeyed.

One shaky breath in.

One out.

Calm the storm. Just for a second.

And when she opened her eyes again—

they landed on the kitchen drawer.

And something in her shifted.

The fear didn't vanish.

The pain didn't fade.

But in its place—clarity.

Sharp. Cold. Steady.

She knew what she had to do.

She crawled toward it.

Pulled it open.

And there—

lying like an offering from God—

was a knife.

For a moment, she just stared at it.

Her mind slow to register what her eyes already knew.

A knife.

Not a metaphor.

Not a dream.

A real, solid truth of steel.

Her breath caught in her throat.

Not from fear.

But from something dangerously close to hope.

Her fingers trembled as she reached for it.

"I got it," she whispered. More to herself than to him. "I got it, Mr. Wallace."

"Good job, Sarah," he breathed, relief clear in his voice. "Can you make your way to me?"

"Yes."

It wasn't a promise.

It was a vow.

She let out a short, broken giggle—

not from joy,

but from something else.

Something sharp.

Something dangerous.

She dragged herself forward.

One pull.

Then another.

Until she reached him.

She placed her hand in his, and he gripped it tightly.

"We're going to make it, Mr. Wallace."

He nodded, still facing the couch.

"Sarah..." he whispered. "Cut me free."

She froze.

"Shit," she hissed.

"Sarah," he urged. "Cut—"

The rumble of Stefan's truck drifted in through the thin camper walls.

Lauren's blood ran cold.

"Oh God..."

She scrambled, dragging herself back toward the bedroom—inch by inch.

Panic fueled her.

Pain dragged at her.

The seconds ticked by like gunshots.

"Sarah!" Mr. Wallace cried. "Sarah!"

She heard him.

But she shut it out.

If Stefan found her in the living room—with a knife in her hand—

It would be over.

Her heart ached with guilt. Every instinct screamed at her to cut Mr. Wallace loose. But her survival instinct—honed by too many near-deaths—was louder.

She had to get back in that bed. She reached the edge of the mattress and hauled herself up. A scream tore from her throat—guttural and raw.

But she made it. She threw herself back into position—exactly how he'd left her. The knife slid beneath the mattress, her fingers lingering just long enough to memorize its place. Close. Reachable. Just in case.

She wiped her brow with a trembling hand, forcing her breath to steady. The adrenaline was fading. And the pain... The pain came rushing back like a tidal wave—blinding, suffocating.

The rumble of his truck was deafening—like hope dying in her chest. Her heart stopped. He was back.

Silence dropped like a curtain—thick, heavy, unbreakable. No one moved. Not even the air stirred. The only sounds were the twin rhythms of tightly held breath and racing hearts.

Lauren and Mr. Wallace lay motionless, eyes shut— but their minds churned like stormwater beneath a frozen surface.

30

Two sets of footsteps.

That was all she could hear.

One—steady and even.

The other—heavy, uneven, dragging slightly.

Lauren knew the cadence of his walk.

The weight behind each step.

But tonight, something was off.

His usual deliberate swagger had dulled into a sluggish shuffle.

She tensed, every muscle taut beneath the thin blanket.

Then—a second voice.

Male. Calm. Kind.

Infuriatingly carefree.

The lock.

The door opened just a crack.

The prison door was unsealed.

The door opened, but barely.

Just enough to hear the conversation happening just on the other side of freedom.

"We should check on Edward and your sick wife," the stranger said, his voice light, amused.

She braced for the worst. A slip. A twitch. A shift in Stefan's voice. If he even slightly suspected Mr. Wallace had moved—

One wrong breath. One misstep. And it's over.

"Oh shit. They're asleep. Leave 'em," Stefan mumbled.

His speech was slurred. Barely coherent.

Lauren's eyes snapped open beneath the veil of her lashes.

Her heart jolted.

He was drunk—more than drunk.

Sloppy. Unstable.

But Stefan could usually drink anyone under the table and still stay in control.

Something was wrong.

Had the stranger drugged him?

"Dude, those shots were strong," the man said louder now, as if putting on a show.

"I needed to let go and unwind. Thanks for the invite."

"You seemed bothered, my friend. Glad I could help," the stranger replied.

Casual.

But smooth. Too smooth.

Something in that voice triggered her instincts.

Footsteps approached the camper steps.

Lauren's breath caught.

"Whoa!" Stefan's voice cracked as his foot slipped.

A stumble.

Then—

"I got you, bro," the stranger chuckled. "Here, let me help you inside."

"Nah, man. I got it," Stefan grunted, recovering.

She imagined him clinging to the handle—

like a drowning man refusing rescue.

"Thanks, though. I'm gonna pass out. I'll catch you in the morning. Wanna go for a hike?" Stefan mumbled.

Lauren's brow twitched.

Wanna?

He was asking.

Not telling.

That wasn't like him.

Stefan didn't make suggestions—he made plans. He gave orders. Even drunk or drugged, he didn't invite input.

Something was off. Deeply off.

Lauren's lungs burned as she finally released the breath she hadn't realized she was holding.

If he passed out...

It might buy them time.

She debated screaming for help.

Call out. Just once. Just in case.

But what if he's with Stefan? What if this whole thing is a game and you were the prize?

And if you're wrong? If he was your only shot and you let him walk away?

But her throat stayed closed.

What if the stranger wasn't an ally? What if Stefan snapped mid-scream?

A single mistake could cost them both their lives.

In the other room, Mr. Wallace stayed still—no movement, no reaction. He had to be thinking the same thing.

"You sure?" the stranger persisted. "We should check on Edward."

Lauren pictured Stefan's narrowed eyes. The way his head would turn—over his shoulder, suspicious.

"He's out, man. He is not goin' anywhere," Stefan mumbled. His tone hovered somewhere between lazy... and hostile.

"Alright," the stranger relented. "I'll see you first thing in the morning for that hike."

Footsteps receded.

The door shut with a dull thunk.

Click.

The lock.

The prison sealed.

She lay perfectly still. Listening.

Stefan's footsteps shuffled inside.

Lauren focused on every creak of the floorboards. He wasn't heading straight for the bedroom. He paused.

She could hear him breathing—labored, uneven.

Then—the faint sound of rope shifting. Stretching under strain.

He was checking on Mr. Wallace.

A hand brushed fabric. A muttered curse. Then a sharp tug.

Lauren's heart seized.

Was he tightening the ropes? Testing them?

Mr. Wallace didn't react. He was pretending to be unconscious—
and thank God, he was doing a damn good job of it.

A long pause.

Then Stefan moved away from the couch, stumbling toward the bedroom.

His footsteps dragged, uncoordinated, like each one took more effort than the last.

Lauren held her breath as the mattress dipped under his weight.

He didn't undress.

Didn't even take off his shoes.

He just collapsed—face-first, by the sound of it.

A beat later, a loud, unfiltered snore erupted from the bed.

He was out.

For real.

Lauren's stomach turned—sharp and sudden.

Nausea crept in, low and slow, and she swallowed it down. Her fingers clenched the blanket like a lifeline.

Still, she didn't move.

Her breath trembled in her chest as she listened—

waited—

for any hint he might be faking it.

A twig cracked. Then the crunch of gravel. A faint creak just outside—

or was that her mind again, conjuring ghosts from silence?

She didn't know anymore. Everything felt warped.

Sounds bent. Shadows whispered.

She couldn't risk being wrong.

Then—snores.

Steady. Loud. Careless.

He was unconscious.

Still, she hesitated.

Her fingers curled against the thin blanket, nerves sparking with indecision.

Then, slowly, she tried to push herself up.

Her muscles screamed in protest.

Fire lit in her side where ribs had likely cracked.

Her legs shook violently.

Her arm buckled beneath her.

She fell back onto the mattress with a thud that echoed like a gunshot.

The impact sent a white-hot bolt of pain through her back and shoulders.

Tears blurred her vision.

She bit down on her lower lip until she tasted blood.

No.

She couldn't make it.

Not like this.

She wouldn't be able to crawl across the tiny camper to reach Mr. Wallace—

her body had made that clear.

But she had to try something.

Her lips barely moved as she turned her head toward the living room.

This is what weakness looks like.

Granddaddy always said there's strength in stillness—but this? This wasn't strength. This was failure.

You swore you'd never be this girl again.

And here you are—laid out, helpless. Waiting for someone else to save you.

"Mr. Wallace..."

It came out dry. Barely audible.

She swallowed hard and tried again.

"Mr. Wallace..."

Nothing.

A beat of silence.

Then—

the faintest shift of fabric.

A breath. Controlled. Careful.

"I'm here," he whispered.

The sound was hoarse, but solid.

Real.

A thread of hope in the dark.

Her chest tightened—

not from pain this time,

but something else.

Relief.

He was alive.

Still with her.

Still trying.

"He's out," she whispered.

"I know," Mr. Wallace breathed.

"I heard him snoring. Sounded like a bear tumbling down a hill."

Lauren managed a weak, pained smile.

The closest she'd come to a laugh in days.

"I tried to get up."

"Don't," he said gently.

"You're hurt worse than you think."

She rested her head back against the thin mattress, wincing as every rib protested.

"I thought maybe I could... do something."

"You already did," he murmured.

"You made it this far. That's not nothing."

She closed her eyes and listened.

Stefan's snoring still filled the camper—deep, rhythmic, careless.

Everything else was quiet.

No footsteps.

No creaking.

No voices.

Just her.

Mr. Wallace.

And the question that had been tugging at her mind all night.

"Do you think... the guy who walked him back... do you think he's here to help?"

Another pause stretched.

His voice came low, steady.

"I don't know," Mr. Wallace admitted.

"But if he is... we need to stay ready.

Watch. Wait.

And if a window opens..."

He paused.

"...we take it."

Lauren nodded slowly, even though he couldn't see.

A window.

That's all they needed.

She glanced over at Stefan, his body slack, snoring like the dead.

She stayed frozen, blinking in disbelief.

Stefan never passed out like this.

Not unless—

Her stomach twisted.

The man in the black truck.

The one with the camper topper.

The one she'd started to believe wasn't real.

The only other time Stefan had acted like this... was after spending time with him.

Was it possible?

Had the stranger drugged him again?

And if so... why?

Was he trying to help?

Dare she let herself believe that?

She turned the thought over like fragile glass in her mind—fragile, volatile, lined with sharp edges.

There had been signs. Subtle ones.

He had tried—repeatedly—to enter the camper earlier.

Friendly. Nonchalant.

Just another friendly neighbor.

But too persistent.

Too perfectly placed.

Could it have been him leaving the notes?

If so... the messages weren't threats.

They were warnings.

But if he was here to help...

why hadn't he called the police?

Why remain a shadow just on the edge of things?

Lauren combed through her memory, trying to pin him down.

The black truck.

The camper topper.

They hadn't been in the RV park for days.

She'd studied the layout on her walks.

Everything had seemed normal:

a scattering of campers,

one lonely tent,

the couples,

the retirees,

Mr. Wallace's camper.

That tent.

Her mind caught on it.

A small, single-person setup.

A compact car parked beside it.

She'd barely glanced at it before.

Never saw anyone come or go.

It was positioned just far enough away to feel unimportant—
but close enough to watch.

But if the man with the camper topper was now staying in a tent—
driving a different car...

None of it added up.

Lauren's thoughts spiraled.

Was she losing touch with reality?

Seeing patterns that didn't exist?

Or was her desperation stitching together hope out of scraps?

She didn't know anymore.

All she knew was this:

Something—someone—was circling them.

Too close to be coincidence.

Too careful to be careless.

She let her fingers slip under the mattress, touching the cold steel of
the hidden knife.

It was a promise. Not to win. Not yet. But to go down fighting.

As she drifted toward sleep, exhaustion finally overtaking fear,
one thought rooted itself in her mind:

Would tomorrow be the end for her and Mr. Wallace—
or the start of something worse?

She didn't know what to hope for anymore.

She wasn't even sure if she should.

Either way, the storm wasn't over.

It was just building.

31

Lauren lay helpless on the camper floor, an invisible force tethering her to the ground—an anchor of dread pressing into every limb. She tried to move, but her body wouldn't respond. Paralyzed. Trapped.

She turned her head to the left.

Nurse Erin lay twisted and still, her vacant eyes fixed on the ceiling —staring past water spots and stains into nothingness. Her neck bore the same bruises Lauren now wore. The same violent rings of strangulation. A matching set.

I'm sorry, Lauren tried to whisper. *I tried to tell you.*

But her lips barely moved. No sound came. The apology died in her throat, unheard.

To her right—

Mr. Wallace.

Hog-tied. Pale. Struggling.

His face contorted in pain as he fought against the ropes that sliced into his skin. His eyes locked with hers—panicked, pleading.

Stefan stepped into view.

Hovering. Watching. Waiting.

His smile was razor-thin. The air around him pulsed with calculated rage—tight, deliberate, like a blade waiting to be drawn. He was ready to create more art, and their bodies were the canvas.

Beside him—

The shadow.

Faceless. Still.

Close enough to touch, yet utterly unknowable.

Watching. Watching always.

As if waiting for something.

As if judging her.

Never stepping in. Never acting in a way that mattered.

Lauren tried to scream again.

Nothing.

She tried to cry, but her eyes were dry, stinging from fear and failure.

Erin was gone—beyond saving. But Mr. Wallace wasn't.

And he was here because of her.

She had brought him into this nightmare.

She strained to reach him. To reach the knife that wasn't there. She tried to kick and fight.

But her body remained paralyzed. Heavy. Useless.

She was powerless.

Again.

Still.

She jolted awake with a ragged gasp, her body drenched in sweat, every muscle screaming with pain. Her side throbbed. Her face pulsed. One eye remained swollen shut, crusted at the corners. The air was heavy, thick with mildew and smoke and silence.

Except for Stefan's snoring.

Deep. Steady.

Unbothered.

He hadn't moved since stumbling in and collapsing beside her hours ago, dead weight, with alcohol clinging to his breath like a warning.

Lauren lay still, staring up at the ceiling, where water stains spread like rot across the camper's thin ceiling panels. Her breath slowed. Her pulse steadied. Sleep was gone. Ripped from her like everything else.

Her mind drifted—back to the beginning.

Back to him.

The day she met Stefan Warren.

It had been blistering hot at Lake Mead. The kind of heat that slowed time and softened thoughts. She'd dozed off near the water's edge, her skin kissed by the sun, a novel about survival and second chances resting open across her stomach. The irony wasn't lost on her now.

She'd felt him before she saw him.

That prickle at the base of her neck. The shift in the air. A subtle disruption in the stillness—like a ripple across the surface of calm water.

She opened her eyes—and there he was.

Charming. Confident. Predatory.

Mask already perfectly in place.

He'd smiled like he owned the lake. Like he'd been waiting just for her.

But what Stefan didn't know—what no one ever knew—was that Lauren hadn't come to Lake Mead by accident. She had been running, yes. But also... searching.

She'd always been drawn to stories that didn't make sense.

Girls who went missing.

Killers who changed their methods midstream.

Unsolved patterns that felt... off.

She didn't have a name for it then—what she was doing. What she was chasing.

When she looked up and saw Stefan, something inside her stirred.

Not fear. Not exactly.

Recognition.

She thought she understood what she was walking into.

Thought she knew how the story would unfold.

She didn't.

And she had paid for it—brutally, relentlessly—every single day since.

Lauren turned her head slightly, wincing at the pain radiating from her cheekbone. The room was still dark, still suffocating. But her mind was alert now. Focused.

She'd survived this long by adapting.

By staying quiet.

By wearing the victim mask.

But survival wasn't enough anymore. Not now.

Now... it was about ending it.

When the sun rose, the mask would slip back on.

She would wear it—flawlessly.

She would speak softly, move gently, look grateful, look small.

But not forever.

The plan had started in fragments—

Late at night, when Stefan snored and her ribs ached too much to sleep.

In the silence after painkillers dulled her body but not her mind.

In the gaps between threats, footsteps, and slammed doors.

A real plan.

Quietly rehearsed.

Each detail etched into her memory, each variable mapped and counted.

Backup plans for the backup plans.

And now, the window was opening.

Stefan was slipping.

The cracks were forming.

And she was ready to strike.

Lauren closed her good eye. The corner of her mouth twitched.

Not a smile. Something colder.

The board was set.

The pieces were in motion.

And this time, she wasn't playing to survive.

She was playing to win.

Eventually, exhaustion wrapped around her like a shroud, pulling her into uneasy sleep.

But peace did not follow.

The nightmare returned—louder, bloodier, closer than before.

And this time, when the shadow figure stepped forward,

his eyes locked with hers.

And something inside her stirred.

Stefan stood over Nurse Erin.

Her body was too still.

Her vacant eyes stared into nothing.

Beside Lauren, Mr. Wallace lay hog-tied, his sorrowful gaze locked onto hers.

"Sorry, Sarah. I tried," he whispered, again and again—each word cracking under the weight of his despair.

Tears carved paths through the dirt on his weathered face.

Even in her dreams—even in his final moments—he was thinking of her.

Of his failure to save her.

The weight of it shattered Lauren.

He was here because of her.

A kind, gentle man caught in the blast radius of choices he didn't make.

Her choices.

Then came movement.

From the tree line, a shadow emerged—slow and deliberate, like a predator.

It crept forward, circling the scene with eerie precision, its presence more felt than seen.

Not a blur. Not a man. Not a monster.

A force.

Lauren's heart leapt—not in fear... but hope.

Maybe this was it.

Maybe he would save them.

Just as that fragile hope bloomed within the nightmare, reality tore it away.

She jolted awake.

Pain exploded in her ribs—white-hot, breath-stealing.

Her one good eye blinked open, struggling against sweat and tears.

Stefan loomed above her.

His hand was pressed hard against her side, digging into the break with cruel intent.

Reality didn't trickle back.

It slammed into her like a wave lined with barbed wire—ripping through thought, breath, and bone.

The nightmare in her sleep was no different than the one she lived awake.

She hadn't heard him get out of bed. Hadn't heard the coffee pot click on.

But the scent was everywhere now—thick, sharp, cloying.

Too ordinary. Too wrong.

How long had he been up?

Had he killed Mr. Wallace while she was unconscious?

No. She couldn't think about that. Not yet.

Lauren clenched her jaw and breathed through the pain.

Slow. Steady. Controlled.

She would not scream.

She would not cry.

She could not run—her body wouldn't let her.

But she wouldn't run in her mind either.

Not anymore.

She'd taken her seat at the table.

It was chess now.

And the stakes had never been higher.

Her mask slid into place—flawless and familiar.

Calm. Composed. Calculating.

Stefan didn't know it yet, but he'd already made the first move.

He smiled the kind of smile only monsters knew how to wear—

Part pleasure. Part hunger. Pure venom.

"You got lucky last night," he said, voice low and cold, eyes sharp as shattered glass.

His voice was even.

Too even.

Lauren knew that tone.

She'd memorized its pattern, tracked it like a storm preparing to make landfall.

It always came before the storm.

She braced herself—but this time, she didn't bite her cheek.

She didn't need to ground herself.

She was grounded.

She was in control.

Even if no one could see it.

Stefan pressed harder into her ribs.

She didn't flinch. Didn't wince.

Though the pain was nearly unbearable.

Instead, she glared up at him with the one eye she could still open—

A slow, fierce burn rising behind it.

Defiance. Pure and sharp.

He threw his head back and laughed—loud, cruel, cinematic.

"You're full of surprises today," he said, cocking his head. "You ready to play?"

She didn't answer.

And then it came—

Movement from the living room. A shuffle. Nothing more.

Her mind flickered.

Mr. Wallace.

Her mask cracked.

Just for a second.

Stefan saw it.

His hand came down across her face, fast and brutal.

Her hair whipped sideways, blinding her.

The healing cuts on her lip and nose burst open, fresh blood mingling with old.

She flung her head back, locked eyes with him again.

Unbroken.

If anything—stronger.

Her courage was building. Quietly. Steadily.

Like pressure beneath ice.

Stefan crawled onto the bed, his knees digging into the mattress on either side of her hips, locking her into place.

"I'm gonna make you scream," he hissed, raising his hand again.

She didn't lift her arms.

Didn't flinch.

Didn't give him the satisfaction.

She took the full force of it—open, exposed. A deliberate act of defiance.

The blow landed hard.

Her ears rang.

Her skull throbbed.

The sound echoed off the camper's thin walls like a gunshot.

Darkness crept in at the edges of her vision.

Thick. Inviting.

Stay awake.

Don't you dare lose it.

GET YOUR SHIT TOGETHER.

A cry split the air.

"STOP! Please, STOP!"

Mr. Wallace's voice—raw, broken, shaking.

He fought against the ropes—desperate, frantic.

Friction tore into his wrists as he threw himself off the couch.

A sickening thud as he hit the linoleum, the air leaving his lungs in a broken gasp.

He writhed.

Helpless.

Bound like an animal. Powerless.

He tried to cover his ears.

But it was too late.

He had already heard it.

The sound of flesh striking flesh hurled him backward in time—

Back to childhood.

Back to the echo of his mother's cries.

His stomach revolted.

He vomited on the floor, sobbing.

The sound cut through the camper like a warning shot.

Stefan's head snapped toward the noise.

He turned from Lauren and moved quickly—stalking down the short hallway toward the source.

That's when it came—

BANG. BANG. BANG.

A sharp, firm knock hit the camper door.

Stefan froze.

The silence that followed wasn't natural.

It was loaded.

Listening.

Lauren's heartbeat roared in her ears.

She didn't dare blink.

Outside, nothing moved.

No footsteps.

No voice.

Just waiting.

Stefan glanced toward the door.

A flicker of something crossed his face—

Not fear.

Annoyance. Sharp and sudden.

Like a predator catching the scent of another stalking too close to its kill.

Lauren barely registered the sound—her ears still ringing.

Mr. Wallace's mouth opened to scream.

Stefan rounded the corner and lunged.

His hand clamped around the old man's throat, knife already drawn from the hunting bag.

The blade kissed Edward's cheek.

"Shut the fuck up, old man," Stefan hissed, low and venomous.

"You say a word, I'll kill that man"—he jerked his head toward the door—

"and then let you listen while I kill that bitch in there. You got it?"

Edward nodded quickly, understanding—and horror—etched across his face.

Another knock came.

Harder this time.

Then the door handle jiggled.

"Hello?" a voice called from outside. Another knock followed—calmer now. Softer.

Stefan rolled his neck.

The popping cracked through the camper like dry branches snapping underfoot.

"Yeah, coming!" he called, suddenly chipper.

Just like that, he flipped.

That was Stefan's gift—his monstrosity wrapped in charm.

Cool. Confident. The man Mr. Wallace had once trusted.

Without effort, Stefan lifted Edward back onto the couch, turning his face toward the wall.

He tossed a blanket over him like folding laundry.

"Don't you fucking move," he hissed in Edward's ear.

He grabbed his hiking bag from the counter and moved to the door.

As he opened it just wide enough to slip through, he turned and called inside, voice light.

"Leaving for the hike. Be back in a few hours."

He stepped outside.

The door shut behind him.

Click.

Locked.

Silence settled.

Lauren's lip trembled. Her body screamed.

But her mind?

Sharper than ever.

She waited a beat longer—long enough to be sure they had walked away.

Then, slowly, she reached beneath the mattress, her fingers fumbling through sweat-soaked sheets until they curled around the handle of the knife.

Cold. Solid. Real.

Her breath trembled in her throat.

She didn't pull it out yet—just let her hand linger there.

Felt the weight of it. The promise of it.

The world narrowed to this: a moment.

A blade.

A choice.

For too long, she'd played a pawn.

Crawled across the board while Stefan played God.

But pawns don't stay pawns forever.

Her fingers tightened.

"Your move, asshole."

The queen's still on the board.

And this time, she wasn't playing for survival.

She was playing for checkmate.

32

Lauren lay still, listening.

Two sets of footsteps trailed off outside—one heavier, the other more casual, almost careless.

One... two... three...

She counted them until they disappeared, swallowed by distance.

Her face throbbed—broken on top of broken.

The one eye she could still open was swelling fast. Panic stirred beneath her ribs as she imagined the world going dark.

Don't you dare swell shut, she told herself. *Not yet.*

She cried out, rolling to her side.

A raw, involuntary sound.

Her ribs screamed in protest, stabbing bolts of fire through her chest. The pressure in her jaw pulsed, rhythmic and merciless.

Gritting her teeth—what was left of them—she tried to sit up.

The pain in her jaw spiked so sharply it made the world tilt.

A hot, dizzying wave of nausea swept through her, and she clenched her eyes shut, willing the camper to stop spinning.

She couldn't.

Her arms shook. Her muscles quivered. Her body refused.

Sit up.

She clenched her fists into the mattress, trying to ground herself against the waves of pain.

Her vision blurred.

The room continued to spin.

Her thoughts scattered like leaves in wind.

It felt like drowning—but dry. Silent.

"Mr. Wallace?" she rasped. Her voice barely made it past her bruised throat.

She swallowed hard, choking down the dizziness and the pull of unconsciousness.

"Edward... can you hear me?"

"I'm here, Sarah."

His voice was weak, cracked with fear and guilt.

"Are you—"

A sob cut him off.

"I'm okay," Lauren said quickly—before he could finish the question.

Before he could say what they were both thinking.

"I have a plan," she whispered. "Just give me a minute."

She tried to stand, but her body betrayed her.

Her mind was ready—sharp, feral, alive.

But her limbs collapsed beneath her like wet paper.

Humiliation burned in her chest.

She'd survived. She'd fought.

And now she couldn't even stand?

She shoved the shame aside.

Flat on the floor, she began to crawl—

One pull at a time.

Elbows scraping across the vinyl.

Every inch earned through fire.

She collapsed against the camper wall when she reached the narrow hallway.

Breath shuddered in and out of her chest, uneven but determined.

She listened.

The coast was clear.

Then she remembered.

The knife.

Still under the mattress.

"Damn it," she hissed, her whisper jagged with frustration and fear.

"Sarah? Are you okay?" Mr. Wallace's voice came from the living room, low and trembling.

"Yeah," she replied, barely above a whisper.

She stared up at the ceiling as a single tear rolled down her swollen, discolored face.

It wasn't from fear.

It wasn't from pain.

It was rage.

She had made a mistake—one that would cost her time.

And time was the one thing she didn't have.

She drew in a slow, shaky breath through her nose, willing herself to move.

Then she turned toward the kitchen and began to crawl.

She reached forward, dragging her shattered body across the camper floor, inch by inch.

Her heartbeat pounded in her ears, syncing with every jolt of pain.

She paused again to catch her breath.

From this angle, she could see Mr. Wallace—still facing the wall, bound and bruised.

Still alive.

"I'm here, Edward," she said, her voice rough but steady.

"You're one hell of a strong woman, Sarah," he said, voice hitching.

"Your grandfather would be so proud of you."

The words pierced her.

Not because of what he said—but because of what he didn't know.

The lies they'd fed this kind, gentle man twisted like thorns in her gut.

She wanted to tell him the truth.

That her granddaddy was alive and well.

That her real name wasn't Sarah—it was Lauren.

She wanted to tell him everything.

How she'd ended up here. That she wasn't a helpless victim.

That it hadn't started that way.

But there wasn't time.

Not now.

She prayed she'd have the chance to tell him—after they were free of Stefan Warren.

Lauren lowered herself again and continued crawling toward the kitchenette.

Two more pulls. Just two.

Then her fingertips brushed the base of the drawer.

She reached up and yanked it open—but couldn't reach inside.

Her arm trembled—fingers clawing through empty air.

She had planned for this.

Had imagined it. Rehearsed it.

Using her good arm, she gripped the edge of the counter.

Took a deep breath.

And screamed.

"AHHHHH!"

The cry tore through the camper like a wounded animal—

Raw. Primal. A sound born from agony and fury colliding.

Running on fumes and fueled by sheer will, she pulled herself upright into a shaky kneel.

Her entire body shook. Her vision blurred at the edges.

She couldn't see the drawer's contents clearly—just shadows and glints of metal.

Knives. There were knives in here. Last time she checked.

She reached in blindly, hand thrashing through utensils, cords, and tools.

Fingers scrambling, desperate, wild.

Mr. Wallace had heard the drawer open.

He had heard her scream—raw and unyielding.

It had cut through him like a blade of its own making. Not despair.

Battle.

He heard the rattling of utensils being shoved around.

Metal against wood. Desperate searching.

The chaos gave way to silence—sharp, absolute, and wrong.

"Sarah?" he called out, his voice cracking.

But still nothing.

"Sarah!" he shouted louder, panic taking root.

Still nothing.

With everything he had left, Mr. Wallace rolled off the couch, landing with a hard smack against the linoleum.

Now facing her, his heart froze.

She was lying motionless.

And just when he feared the worst—

Her chest rose. Just barely.

Relief hit him like a flood.

She was alive.

And even in her broken state, she was still trying to save him.

Guilt gnawed at him. He had wanted to protect her.

But she had been the one fighting to the edge of death to save him.

He inched toward her in slow, wormlike movements, his limbs aching, stiff, and still bound.

Every inch was agony—but nothing compared to what she'd endured.

As he got closer, he saw it—

New bruises on her face.

Her cheek flushed and swelling where that monster had struck her.

Her lip split again. Her jaw... off-kilter.

He rested his head gently on the floor beside hers, close enough to feel her breath—thin and shallow.

Then—

Warmth.

Sticky against his skin.

Blood.

Panic surged. His eyes darted, scanning her body for the source.

Then he saw it—

The knife.

Clutched tight in her fist, even in unconsciousness.

As if she were still clinging to hope.

"Sarah... sweetheart. Can you hear me?" he whispered.

No response.

He nudged her gently with his forehead, the only part of his body not bound.

"Sarah, you have to wake up."

Still nothing.

Then, for the first time in his life, Mr. Wallace yelled.

"SARAH!"

The sound shook him—

But it worked.

She stirred.

He closed his eyes.

"Thank you, God."

Lauren heard the voice through the haze.

It cut through the fog like glass.

Her head throbbed. Her ears rang. Her thoughts spun.

She tried to open her eyes, but the darkness was thick, weighted, smothering.

Another shout—closer now.

She winced.

With effort, she peeled her swollen eye open to a thin sliver.

Mr. Wallace lay beside her, eyes locked on hers.

For a terrifying second, she thought it was another nightmare.

A tear slid down her cheek.

Same nightmare. Different cage.

"Sarah, are you okay?" he asked softly.

Reality snapped back.

Pain shot through her hand.

She flinched again, looking down.

Blood.

It seeped through her fingers.

Slowly, she uncurled her grip.

The knife glinted up at her, smeared with red—but solid. Real.

She'd done it.

"Roll over," she rasped.

He didn't ask questions.

He just moved.

She dragged herself closer, blood slick on her palms, making the knife slippery.

She positioned the blade between the ropes binding his wrists and ankles.

With the blade facing her, she began to saw.

Back and forth.

Back and forth.

The motion slow, desperate, clumsy.

The knife slipped more than once, slicing her fingers again.

But she didn't stop.

Couldn't stop.

When the blood made it too hard to grip, she crawled to a lower drawer and pulled out a towel.

Her breathing turned ragged.

Her limbs trembled with exhaustion.

She wiped the blade, cleaned her hands, and quickly wrapped the towel around her bleeding hand, tying it off as tightly as she could.

She turned and glanced at the clock on the wall.

Her pulse spiked.

He'd be back soon.

"You're doing great, Sarah," Mr. Wallace said.

"You can do this."

She nodded once.

Then she worked faster.

Bit by bit, the rope began to fray.

Time ticked louder.

Faster.

Panic surged through her chest like a second heartbeat.

Blood coated her hand.

Coated Mr. Wallace.

Spattered across the floor in chaotic streaks.

And then—

Snap.

The rope gave way.

He was partially free—his legs no longer tethered to his wrists.

Lauren let out a laugh that was half-sob, half-exhale, her face streaked with sweat, tears, and blood.

"We did it," she whispered. "We did it!"

"You did it, Sarah."

Mr. Wallace smiled as he sat up, stretching his aching legs and hips with a grimace.

His wrists and ankles were still bound. He could move—awkwardly, painfully—but he could move.

And now, they had a chance.

It was a small victory.

The first since this nightmare began.

Lauren steadied herself, her breath uneven.

Their eyes met for a split second—no words, just breathless urgency and something deeper.

Gratitude. Trust.

A silent pact to survive.

"We have to clean the floor before he comes back. We can't let him know what we've done."

"Shouldn't you untie me—so I can run for help?" he blurted, panic edging into his voice.

"There's no time," she snapped. "We both won't make it out before he returns."

He hesitated—then nodded.

"Can you stand up?"

"I think so."

He maneuvered himself to his knees.

"Can you reach the counter with your elbows?" she asked.

He didn't answer. He just moved.

With a grunt, he pulled himself upright, pressing his forearms against the counter for balance.

"Got it!" he said, triumphant.

Lauren's voice was steel now. "In the top drawer—get a towel. Get it wet. Hand it to me. Hurry."

Mr. Wallace opened the drawer with stiff, trembling fingers.

The metal handle clinked softly as he turned on the faucet.

Cold water gushed from the tap—loud, startling.

Too normal in this chaos.

He shoved the towel beneath the stream, letting it soak until it was dripping.

With his wrists still bound, he could barely wring it out—water sloshed down his arms, soaking his sleeves.

Then, with effort, he dropped the towel near Lauren.

She crawled forward and grabbed it, her torso screaming with every movement.

Pain pulsed from her ribs, her hand, her face.

No time.

Blood was everywhere—splattered in a grotesque, scattered pattern across the linoleum.

It looked like violence.

It was violence.

She scrubbed furiously, laser-focused, pushing through the waves of agony.

"Give me another wet towel. And a dry one," she snapped.

Her voice was clipped. Commanding. Controlled.

The mask was back on.

The chessboard still in motion.

There was no hesitation.

Mr. Wallace turned back to the drawer, obeying without question.

He didn't waste time responding.

He knew as well as she did—they were out of time.

Every second counted.

The monster would be back soon.

"You've done this before," he said softly, sadness dragging through his voice like an anchor.

She cut him off, her voice sharp.

"Yes."

No room for confessions.

No time for grief.

Not now.

She thrust the bloodied knife toward him.

"Clean this."

Her voice was mechanical.

Her face—locked in an expression of practiced detachment.

The mask was on.

The same one she'd worn while playing house with Stefan.

The one that kept her alive.

She wouldn't take it off.

Not yet.

Not until they were free.

Mr. Wallace leaned heavily against the counter and began washing the knife.

His movements were slow. Labored.

His breath came uneven.

Blood swirled in the water, turning pink before spiraling down the drain.

They worked in silence.

The only sounds:

The splash of water.

The wet drag of towel against floor.

Lauren didn't need to think—her body already knew what to do.

Cleaning her own blood had become muscle memory.

A twisted ritual perfected over their year together.

She could still hear Stefan's voice in her head:

Look at this fucking mess you made.

She could still feel his hands—shoving her down.

Her face pressed near the pool of red spilling from her own body.

The bed.

The shower.

The floor.

Even the damn walls.

Once—the ceiling.

This wasn't just survival.

It was familiarity.

She looked at the cleaned patch of floor and allowed herself the smallest, cruelest smile.

Thank you, Stefan, she thought, venom lining every word. *You made me an expert.*

It would pass inspection.

At least for now.

He wouldn't suspect a thing.

Mr. Wallace grabbed a dirty cup from the cluttered counter.

He filled it with water, lifted it to his lips, and drank deeply.

Then he refilled it and crouched beside her, offering it to Lauren with shaking hands.

"Thank you," she said, her voice hoarse.

Her throat still raw—every swallow a test of endurance. She took small sips, careful not to drink too fast.

She glanced at the clock.

Not much time left.

She turned to him, her expression unreadable.

"You're not going to like this," she said. "But you have to get back on the couch."

His eyes widened. He shook his head slowly, dread washing across his features.

"You have to trust me. He could be back any minute now."

Her voice softened, but urgency underscored every word.

"Take the knife and hide it in the cushion. It'll be there if you need it.

But you need to be exactly where he left you.

We'll wait for the right moment."

Silence settled between them again.

Heavy. Dread-laced.

Edward didn't argue.

He nodded, slow and reluctant.

His movements were stiff as he returned to the floor and scooted toward the couch, every inch a battle against the tight pull of bruised muscles and screaming joints.

His knees screamed. His back spasmed. His ribs flared with heat.

He clenched his jaw, ashamed of the groans slipping through his teeth.

What right did he have to wince—when she was crawling through fire to save him?

He pushed through it.

With great effort, he climbed up and carefully rolled into the same curled position he had been left in, facing the wall.

His body protested every shift, every breath, but he made himself stay still.

Lauren stayed low, tracking each movement like a chess master resetting the board.

"Is the knife hidden?" she asked.

"Yes," he whispered, the breath shuddering out of him.

"Good."

She shoved the dirty towels deep under the couch, hiding the evidence as best she could.

Then, with her injured hand—still wrapped in a blood-soaked towel —she pulled the blanket over him, tucking it around his body with surprising gentleness.

From the center of the camper, everything looked normal.

Everything looked still.

Like nothing had happened.

She turned her gaze toward the hallway—toward the bedroom.

She stared at the hallway like it was a mountain she had to climb.

And then she began—

Inch by grueling inch.

Each movement lit fire through her side, but she pressed forward, pain pulsing with every breath.

She reached the edge of the bed and clawed her way up.

Her body trembled.

Her mind stayed locked on the task.

She pulled herself back into the exact position she'd been in before—

One leg angled off the bed.

Arm outstretched.

Body curled, as if she'd never moved at all.

She allowed her eyes to close.

Just for a moment.

Just long enough to rest before Phase Two began.

Across the camper, Mr. Wallace lay still, listening.

The silence wasn't peaceful anymore.

It was loaded. Thick as fog. Tense as wire.

"Sarah," he whispered.

Lauren's eyes fluttered open.

"I'm here, Edward."

Every time he said that name—Sarah—something in her flinched.

"Thank you," he said softly.

She swallowed hard, pushing tears back into the pit they always tried
to escape from.

"We're going to get through this," she said.

Not a promise.

A vow.

He wouldn't win this round.

And in the quiet that followed, she dared to drift into sleep.

Just for a moment.

As the dangerous thought took root—

They couldn't outrun him.

But she wasn't afraid anymore.

It was his move.

But she still had moves left to play.

33

Lauren woke without screaming.

Her eyes flitted open slowly, lashes heavy with sleep and sweat. For a moment, she didn't move—just breathed. Just existed.

No nightmares.

No bruises carved into her dreams. No hands around her throat. No voices whispering her name like a curse.

No shadows chasing her into consciousness.

Relief seeped through her like warm water down her spine. Her fingers twitched beneath the thin blanket, savoring the moment, almost afraid to believe it was real.

For once, the silence didn't feel like a threat.

It felt... still.

Strange.

Almost sacred.

She let her gaze drift across the dim ceiling—softly lit by the morning sun bleeding through the slats in the blinds. The streaks of golden light traced long fingers across the camper walls, touching her skin without harm.

That felt... kind.

Her body, however, was wrecked.

Every joint stiff.

Every muscle sore.

A dull ache curled in her chest, wrapping tight around her ribs like a belt cinched too tight.

But her mind...

Her mind felt clear. Sharper than it had in days.

No fog. No panic. No claws of fear gripping the edges of her thoughts.

Just breathe.

Stillness.

Focus.

She was broken.

But she was awake.

And that was enough.

She adjusted the blanket around her shoulders, forcing each inhale to smooth out.

The mask had to hold. Cracks could get them both killed.

Her lips parted as she exhaled slowly, savoring the clarity—

like something fragile she might never hold again.

She blinked, then blinked again—adjusting to the soft, golden light filtering in. Dust motes floated lazily in the air. The world outside was quiet, and that quiet seeped into her bones.

The sun slanted in low—warm and watchful.

Morning. Not quite noon.

She shifted beneath the blanket, inch by inch, testing her ribs. The pain was still there. Sharp. Insistent. But this time, it didn't steal her breath.

It didn't command her.

She owned it.

Manageable.

Contained.

Her voice, dry and cracked, rasped from her throat.

"Mr. Wallace?"

A pause. Then—

"I'm here, Sarah. You okay?"

His voice carried from the living room. Quiet. Steady. The sound of someone holding himself together with trembling fingers and frayed resolve.

She let her eyes fall shut for half a second, absorbing the quiet comfort of his reply.

"Yeah," she murmured. "I think so."

She paused.

Listened.

No footsteps.

No shuffling.

No heavy boots or bottles clinking.

Just the low hum of the camper's tired bones—the refrigerator kicking on, the faint whir of the wall clock's second hand.

And underneath it all...

The quiet.

Real quiet.

Not the kind that came before pain.

The kind that came before possibility.

No footsteps.

No shuffling.

No heavy boots thudding across the linoleum.

No beer bottles clinking together like ominous wind chimes.

Just the low, steady hum of the camper's humming core—the rhythmic purr of a tired refrigerator, the faint buzz of power behind cheap wood-paneled walls. It was a sound she had come to recognize. To track. To depend on. A marker that the world was still turning—quietly, mercifully.

"How long was I out?" she asked, her voice barely louder than a breath.

A pause.

Then Mr. Wallace's answer, calm but worn:

"Hard to say. Sun's not overhead yet."

Lauren stared at the pale strip of sunlight slowly creeping across the linoleum like it had nowhere to be. She watched it stretch forward inch by inch, a silent clock she could feel crawling toward noon.

"Can you see the clock?" she whispered, already knowing the answer.

"Not without moving the blanket," he said gently. "Not risking that."

Right. Of course.

Even the smallest shift could unravel everything.

She nodded reflexively, a motion meant for herself more than him—reassurance in the quiet.

"He'll be back soon," she said, her tone flat but certain. "Be ready."

There was a pause on the other end.

But this one didn't feel like fear.

It felt like armor quietly buckled into place.

Like two people bracing for impact.

A shift in the silence—

Not tension.

Something else.

Resolve.

"You think today's the day?" he asked.

Lauren's throat tightened. She turned her head just enough to watch the light creep closer, its slow crawl inching across the floor like a countdown.

"I think..." she said, her voice low and careful, "it has to be."

If not today, then when?

They couldn't survive another night.

Not like this.

Not with Stefan unraveling and the last thread fraying by the hour.

"Did he take anything with him when he left?" she asked, a fresh urgency curling beneath the words. "Food? Water?"

"Nope," Mr. Wallace said. "Rolled out of bed, hit the bathroom, walked in here. Didn't grab a thing."

A pause stretched between them.

The kind that carried weight.

Implications.

Then—lighter. Wry. A flicker of dry humor cutting through the dread:

"Also—not that it matters right now, but—he doesn't wash his hands after going to the restroom."

Lauren blinked. And then—

A sound escaped her.

A real laugh.

Small. Soft. Real.

The kind of laugh that cracked the ice.

That reminded her she was human.

Alive.

Still capable of something that didn't begin and end with pain.

"Yeah," she said through the smile. "I've noticed."

Her ribs ached. Her lips cracked. But for one fleeting second, it didn't matter.

They were still here.

Still fighting.

Still holding onto something that looked suspiciously like hope.

Mr. Wallace smiled faintly, his voice laced with quiet humor that couldn't cover the pain etched in his bones.

"Real classy guy."

It was absurd. Completely ridiculous. A joke that didn't matter.

But somehow—it helped.

Just a little.

Just enough.

For one moment, the fog lifted.

The fear loosened its grip.

Not all the way. Never all the way.

But enough to let in a single, stolen breath of something close to normal.

Lauren laughed again—soft, small, the kind of laugh that escaped before her body could brace for pain.

A sudden bolt of agony shot through her ribs, stealing the breath it had just given back.

Her arm flew instinctively across her side, curling protectively as her face twisted into a wince.

"Ow..."

"Sorry," Mr. Wallace said, though his tone was anything but sorry.

There was a smile behind it—a genuine one, shadowed by pain but real all the same.

Lauren didn't scold him.

Didn't snap.

Instead, she let the ache pass, let the laugh's echo linger like incense after a prayer.

"No..." she whispered. "Thank you."

There was a pause. A shift.

"For what?" he asked, quieter now.

"You made me laugh," she said simply.

Her voice faltered, the words heavier than they should've been.

"I forgot what that felt like."

Silence settled again. Not uncomfortable. Just thick with unspoken truth.

She imagined him nodding on the other side of the camper, lips pressed tight, heart breaking in a hundred invisible ways.

Then, finally—softly—

"Glad I could help."

Lauren let the warmth of that sit with her for just a second longer.

Then, slowly, she moved.

She slipped her injured hand from beneath the blanket, careful not to disturb the rest of her body.

The towel she had used as a makeshift bandage had stiffened—crusted with dried blood, the edges hardened into brittle seams.

The smell of it hit her first—metallic, stale, sunk into the fibers like guilt.

Her stomach turned, but she forced her fingers to move.

The wound had closed.

Not cleanly. Not beautifully.

But enough.

Enough to keep moving.

Enough to keep fighting.

She sucked in a breath through her teeth as the air hit exposed skin, the pain sharp and unforgiving.

Her hand shook as she slid the bloodied towel beneath the mattress —hidden, like everything else.

Then, her fingers moved lower.

Toward the edge of the bed.

Toward the hidden place beneath the mattress where she'd left it.

Her breath hitched as her fingertips brushed cool steel.

It was still there.

Right where she'd placed it.

Untouched.

Undiscovered.

A small, silent victory.

She didn't lift it—didn't risk the sound or the effort.

Instead, she rested her hand there.

Let her palm mold to the shape of it.

Let the weight of it steady her.

This was hers.

Her weapon.

Her choice.

She slipped her hand back beneath the blanket, tucking it protectively against her side.

The knife stayed hidden.

So did her resolve.

If Stefan saw the wound—if he even suspected she'd moved—

He'd punish her.

He always punished her where it hurt the most.

Maybe even finish her.

It came next, as if summoned—

A sound.

The sound.

Footsteps.

Not a dream. Not a ghost.

Real.

Measured. Slow. Close.

Lauren's breath locked in her chest.

She turned her head toward the living room, voice barely louder than cloth brushing skin.

"You ready?" she whispered.

There was a pause.

The kind of pause where fear breathes.

Then came the answer.

Trembling. But steady.

Mr. Wallace cleared his throat—too quickly. His voice cracked when he spoke again, just for a second.

Lauren heard it.

The doubt he tried to swallow. The fear he didn't mean to show.

But he recovered fast, masking it with the same calm he'd always used with her.

And she didn't mention it.

Because she understood.

"I'm ready."

Lauren didn't nod. Didn't flinch. Didn't dare move.

But inside her chest, something shifted.

A coil winding tighter.

She was ready too.

34

Lauren could hear the two voices just outside the door—Stefan and the stranger—their tones light, casual.

It sounded like two old friends catching up over a backyard fence.

Not a sadist and a man standing outside a crime scene.

She rolled her eyes—or tried to.

The swelling around them made even that a chore.

What a load of crap, she thought, disgust simmering low and slow.

She could almost see it—Stefan's crooked smile, the casual tilt of his head, the way he used words like blades wrapped in silk.

He'd play nice just long enough to be dangerous.

That was his specialty.

Pretending the sky had cleared, right before the strike.

Then came the—

Click.

The lock turned.

Metal scraping against metal.

She braced herself. The ritual had begun.

The door opened, but it was the silence behind it that truly terrified her.

She held her breath.

The door creaked open slightly, then stopped—hovering—hesitant.

Lauren's pulse thudded in her ears, slow and thunderous.

"Want a beer or water?" Stefan asked, voice smooth. Too smooth.

Lauren's stomach turned.

That tone—that false, polished ease—made her sick.

As if he wasn't keeping two broken bodies inside.

As if he wasn't a sadistic coward hiding behind charm and fake smiles.

A breeze drifted through the trees, rustling the brittle leaves like whispers.

Somewhere in the distance, a crow cawed—sharp and solitary.

The stranger didn't flinch.

"Sure, I'll take a beer," the stranger replied, laughing like it was game day.

She heard Stefan climb the steps.

The boots. The pause.

And then—

"Here, let me help you," the kind voice offered, closer now.

Lauren listened intently, trying to decipher their tones.

Something was off.

The stranger wasn't just passing through.

His voice wasn't curious—it was calculated.

And for the first time in days, she felt it again—that flicker of cold, strategic fire rising from the ashes.

Her mind was starting to sharpen.

Her mask was beginning to fit again.

"I got it, bro," Stefan cut in—sharp enough to draw blood.

The door swung open hard and slammed shut behind him.

His voice dropped—just half an octave. That was always the tell.

Not the words—

but the drop.

The drag.

Like venom coiled in honey.

Her fingers curled instinctively into the blanket.

One breath. Then another.

The silence thickened.

And then—

the door crashed open.

Lauren went still.

She could hear the subtle creak of his weight as he stood in place—the pop of his knuckles, the deliberate roll of his neck.

It was a ritual she knew too well.

He was resetting.

Letting go of the act just long enough to breathe.

Preparing to step back into the role of domestic monster.

Her fingers curled tighter around the blanket.

Please. Just walk past. Don't look too long. Don't think too hard.

"Well, how are you, old man?" Stefan said, cheerful again—and then:

Thump.

The sound of a fist hitting soft resistance.

A grunt. A cough.

Air driven from lungs that had taken too much already.

A muffled wheeze. Something heavy hit the couch frame.

The silence that followed was worse than the sound.

Lauren tensed.

Every inch of her body stiffened like a sprung trap, her muscles screaming silently.

Had the blanket shifted while she was asleep?

Had the ropes moved just enough to show he'd fought them?

Had Stefan seen it? The lie? The slack that hadn't been there before?

She strained to hear it—

The give of fabric.

The breathless pause.

The hush of suspicion breathing out.

The moment everything might come undone.

Her mind skittered through possibilities.

If he notices...

He'll start with Wallace.

Or worse—he'll come for her first.

She couldn't stop him. Not like this. Not yet.

Please don't notice.

Please just move on.

Lauren held her breath, every muscle locked tight.

She pictured Mr. Wallace lying there—still, focused, playing the part.

The knife was within reach.

But he hadn't used it. Not yet.

Smart.

Too early, and it would all come undone.

Stefan hovered.

The silence stretched so long it became unbearable—every second weighted, every breath a risk.

Lauren's ears strained toward the living area.

Did he see the ropes? Did he notice the slack?

God, please don't let him notice.

And then—finally—he moved.

Boots shifted.

The kitchen floor groaned beneath his weight.

The fridge opened with a low hum, soft but electric against the tension.

Glass clinked—bottles nudged together.

A drawer slid open.

Lauren's stomach twisted.

Then—

Pop.

A sharp crack, like a gunshot in miniature.

Hiss.

The hiss of pressure released.

Like a breath escaping a beast.

She flinched, barely perceptible under the blanket.

He always started with beer.

Sometimes it led to slurred jokes.

Sometimes it led to broken skin.

One bottle.

Then another.

He set them down on the counter with a soft thud—barely more than a breath of sound.

But to Lauren, it was a drumbeat.

A metronome counting down.

A warning.

Then his boots moved again—heavier this time.

Slower. Swaggering.

She heard it in the rhythm of his steps:

The shift.

From predator to peacock.

From rage to charm.

The performance sliding back into place.

He paused at the door.

Glanced back—she could feel it.

That moment where the mask and the monster blended into one silhouette.

"Don't go anywhere, old man," he said, laughter curling around the words.

Quiet.

Hollow.

Rotten.

Lauren didn't breathe until the door shut behind him.

The door opened. The door closed.

No click.

Her lungs screamed as she exhaled—too fast, too sharp.

Her chest ached from the tension she'd carried too long.

Her fingers trembled. Her ribs throbbed.

Every inch of her body buzzed like it had survived an earthquake.

Outside, the easy conversation resumed—like nothing had happened.

Lauren let out the breath she hadn't realized she was holding.

"Edward," she whispered, her voice unsteady. "You okay? Did he hit you hard?"

A long pause.

Then—softly, but with resolve: "Good."

That was all. But it reached her like a lifeline.

Her throat tightened. She closed her eyes, breathing in the relief like it was oxygen.

There was a long pause—then a soft reply:

"Good."

That was all.

But it was enough.

Her stomach growled—loud, sharp, like it had given up waiting for kindness.

It had been over a day since she'd eaten. Maybe two. Maybe more.

But food didn't matter.

Not now.

The hunger clawed at her insides, but it was nothing compared to the war waging in her head.

Dread. Fury. Strategy.

They screamed louder than hunger ever could.

A storm of dread and fury swirled inside her, making it hard to think, harder to stay still.

Outside, the conversation rolled on—

Smooth. Friendly. A cover story in real time.

Stefan's voice rose, spinning some polished version of how he and "Sarah" met in high school.

"We've been inseparable ever since," he added.

Lauren's lip curled.

Inseparable.

Like skin and flame.

Like shackles and bruises.

Like captor and captive.

Then the stranger again—curious, casual:

"How do you afford to travel and live this lifestyle?"

Stefan didn't miss a beat.

"My grandmother left me a trust. Parents died in a hit and run when I was six. Insurance payout. Granddaddy manages it all until I'm twenty-six."

Her fists clenched beneath the blanket.

Her pulse roared in her ears.

You son of a bitch.

That was her story.

Her pain.

Her fucking truth.

And like everything else, he'd taken it.

Stripped it down. Worn it like armor.

He'd worn her pain like a costume—delivering the words with ease, with that charming smirk that people believed.

But that was her inheritance.

Her bloodline.

Her loss.

She was the one with the old-money grandmother.

The one whose power came dressed in quiet pearls and unspoken rules.

The one who got the call in the middle of the night—two parents gone in one instant.

Gone. Just like that.

He stole that too.

He called it their money, but it never was.

It was hers.

Her future.

Her safety net.

Her freedom.

She was the one who'd bought the truck.

Paid for the food.

Kept them afloat when his charm couldn't.

And the camper? That wasn't even his.

He'd confessed it one night, drunk on cheap whiskey, his breath sour with rot and pride.

How he'd killed the man who owned the camper.

Dumped his body off a cliff like garbage.

Took the truck with the camper in tow.

The keys. The life.

And just kept driving—

Until he landed on her.

Like she was a rest stop.

Her stomach twisted, her vision swam.

But she didn't cry.

She didn't scream.

She planned.

Outside, the conversation dragged on.

Stefan and the stranger drinking, laughing, bonding over whatever lies Stefan could string together.

Hours passed. The voices dulled to a distant hum.

White noise with teeth.

Then—

Footsteps.

Lauren's spine straightened, the stillness inside her shattered.

Her body tensed, ears straining.

The camper door creaked open.

Then shut.

Her breath caught.

What did he say?

What did I miss?

Her mind spun, clawing for context—scraping at scraps of conversation that had already slipped through.

Why is he back?

Why now?

For the first time in hours, her focus wavered.

Her thoughts scattered, spiraling outward like sparks from a live wire.

She'd been so careful. So steady.

And now—this.

The sound of a single door had shattered her grip.

And she hated it.

Hated that he could still shake her like this.

She focused on the hallway. Her vision was narrowed by the swelling around her eyes, but she blinked through it.

Made herself look.

Stefan came into view.

He looked at her.

And smirked.

"You look like shit," he said, the words coated in smugness.

She didn't answer.

Didn't flinch.

He glanced at her.

Smirked.

Then turned and walked off toward the bathroom—like she was a stain on the furniture.

The door shut.

Then opened again.

She listened.

Fridge. Bottles.

Pop. Pop.

The sharp sound cracked through the silence.

Then footsteps—measured, slow. He was enjoying this.

He walked back toward the couch.

"You still alive, old fart?" he asked, casual as a bartender.

Mr. Wallace said nothing.

"Answer me," Stefan snapped, his voice dropping—tight, hungry.

"I'm good, Zach. How are you?" Mr. Wallace replied calmly.

Almost bored.

Lauren could've kissed him.

"I bet you are," Stefan muttered. "You hungry yet?"

"Not really."

A pause. Cold. Lingering.

"Hmm."

"No point feeding a man who's about to stop breathing."

Lauren didn't flinch.

She knew this game.

Knew Stefan was winding up—feeding off silence. Stillness. Fear.

That's what he loved.

Not the pain itself.

The anticipation of it.

He wanted to taste it on their breath before he spilled their blood.

Then, without another word, Stefan turned.

Took slow, deliberate steps toward the door.

It opened.

Closed.

No click. No lock.

Just silence—

Long. Tense. Waiting.

A long beat later, Mr. Wallace muttered under his breath, voice dry as dust:

"Disgusting. Didn't wash his hands again."

Lauren bit back a laugh.

"Facts, Edward," she whispered, breathy and raw.

They shared the smallest chuckle.

A flicker of light in all that dark.

Their brief chuckle faded, swallowed by the dark.

Outside, the voice changed.

A shift in tone. Sharper. Direct.

"Dude, why you driving that piece of shit car? What happened to the truck and camper topper?"

Lauren's breath caught.

If her eyes weren't swollen, they'd have flown wide open.

She went still.

There it is.

She knew it.

Her gut had been screaming it for days.

She hadn't been paranoid.

She wasn't unraveling.

The man outside wasn't just some drifter—or beer buddy.

He knew.

He'd been watching them. Tracking them.

The black truck. The camper topper. The shadow.

The silent protector who never stepped in.

Why?

Why hadn't he taken Stefan out?

Why hadn't he barged through the door and ended this?

Why had he waited? Watched?

She lay there, seething.

The rage burned through her ribcage, electrifying her limbs.

The shadow that had haunted her dreams—he was real.

He was right there.

Close enough to end it all.

But he didn't.

And that made him something else entirely.

Not a savior.

Not yet.

She was done surviving just to suffer again.

She wanted answers.

She wanted freedom.

But first—

She had to survive long enough to win both.

Something shifted.

Stefan's voice filtered in from outside—

And this time... it slurred.

His words dragged at the edges, vowels thick and sticky.

His speech slowed, syrup-thick.

Muffled.

Off.

Lauren stilled.

Not drunk.

Drugged.

Her heart pounded.

It's happening.

She counted the seconds between syllables.

One slur.

A pause.

Another.

And then—nothing.

Just silence.

And the thud of her own heart.

She turned her head toward the living area, barely whispering, "Edward?"

"I hear it too," he replied.

And for the first time in forever, his voice held something different.

Hope.

Real hope.

"Ready?" she asked.

There was no need to explain.

No need to speak what they both knew.

She was bracing—

body broken, ribs on fire—

for what came next.

The crawl.

From the bed to the hallway.

From the hallway to the living area.

Back to him.

Back to the knife.

Back to action.

Every inch of it played out in her mind before she moved a muscle.

She pictured the sharp corner of the cabinets. The way the light spilled across the linoleum.

She could already feel the cold floor biting into her skin.

Already hear the rasp of her breath against the silence.

There would be no room for error.

No time to hesitate.

No strength to waste.

Each movement would be a gamble.

Every breath a blade.

But she would do it.

Because she had to.

Because this was the moment the tide shifted—

Or it didn't.

Her fingers curled into the blanket.
One breath.
Two.
The door opened.
The door closed.
The lock turned—slow this time.
Not a slam. Not a threat.
Just a soft click, like a lid sealing a box.
And still... it made her skin crawl.

❦ 35 ❦

Lauren froze.

　　Her entire body locked tight—
muscles coiled beneath skin too thin to contain it all.
She didn't breathe.
Didn't blink.
Every cell inside her screamed run, but there was nowhere to go.
She reached for the knife hidden in the mattress.
Still there.
Right where she left it.
One move. That's all she needed.
She waited for the sound that had haunted her for weeks—
The stomp of boots.
The grunt of anger.
The click of the lock.
The nightmare crashing back in.
He still thought she was cornered.
But even pawns had their uses.
Then—
a voice.
Low. Careful.
Almost... gentle.
"Hello?"
Her heart skipped. Then pounded.

Not Stefan.

Not the monster.

Someone else.

Mr. Wallace's head shot from beneath the blanket like a drowning man breaking the surface.

"We're here! We're here!" he cried, his voice cracking with urgency, relief, fear—everything at once.

Lauren's throat tightened.

Tears surged—hot, helpless.

Not now. Don't cry. Don't you dare break now.

She shoved them down—buried them beneath instinct and adrenaline.

She forced air into her lungs, into her throat—

And screamed.

"HELP!"

It tore from her chest like shrapnel—

raw, jagged, broken—

but full of fire.

The shadow man didn't hesitate.

One swift movement—

And he was inside.

Lauren flinched, her vision swimming.

Panic surged through her like a current.

Was it him?

Was Stefan back?

Was this another trick?

Her stomach dropped, a lead weight pulling her toward the earth.

She blinked hard, trying to clear the sweat, the fear, the tears.

But he was already moving.

Lauren flinched.

Her whole body jerked, instinct overriding injury—

then recoiled just as fast when pain tore through her side like a lightning strike.

Her mind raced, panic crackling like a live wire.

Was it him?

Was Stefan back?

Was this a trick?

Another game?

No.

No—no, he found a way in.

He's here.

It's over.

It's over—

"Go to her!" Mr. Wallace shouted.

His voice cracked, flooded with panic, urgency, desperation.

"Help her! Now!"

Lauren gasped.

Her lungs burned.

Throat raw.

Ribs screaming.

But she moved—

Tried to, anyway.

She clawed at the mattress with her broken nails, her fingers trembling, slipping on the damp fabric.

Splinters tore at her skin. Blood smeared across the sheet.

Her body buckled, every nerve lit with agony, but she didn't stop.

Didn't care.

She was ready to crawl.

To scream.

She dragged herself toward the sound, hope flaring—and dying—in the same breath—

A shadow filled the doorway.

Broad.

Still.

Watching.

Like something dredged from the darkest folds of her nightmares.

Her heart seized.

For one endless second, time fractured—

and she couldn't tell if this was a dream, a memory, or the moment everything would finally break.

But this wasn't sleep.

And this wasn't Stefan.

He was real.

Solid.

Standing there—just feet away—so still, it made the silence scream.

And then—

He moved.

Not like a threat.

Not like Stefan's looming, cruel swagger.

No.

He knelt beside her—

not gently, but deliberately,

like a storm collapsing to its knees,

like something powerful learning how to hold back.

Lauren's breath caught.

Her heart thundered, pounding in her throat, her ribs—everywhere but her face.

She couldn't blink. Couldn't risk the pain.

Her eyes, swollen and raw, denied her even that.

But still—something inside her shifted.

The mask she wore began to crack, just slightly—

Because for the first time in days...

Someone was kneeling for her.

Not over her.

Standing there—just feet away—so still, it made the silence scream.

Tension cracked the air like glass under pressure.

"My God," he breathed. "What the fuck did he do to you?"

Lauren couldn't blink. Her eyes, too swollen and raw, stayed half-closed, crusted at the corners.

But she saw him—

Dark hair. Scruffy jaw. Green eyes.

Him.

He dropped lower, his voice urgent, but not loud.

"Can you move? Can you walk?"

She tried to sit up again, hands clawing weakly at the mattress with shredded nails.

Pain shot through her chest like broken glass scraping her ribs.

"No," she whispered. "I tried. I promise I tried."

And he saw it.

Not just the bruises.

Not just the wreckage.

But the restraint in her voice.

The steel beneath the ruin.

The mask she'd worn for days.

The fire she'd fed with nothing but fear and fury.

He knelt closer, eyes shining—not with pity, but with something else.

Something hotter.

"It's okay," he said, his voice catching. "I got you. Damn it."

His head dropped for a second, jaw tight, as if holding back something primal.

"That son of a bitch... I'll kill him."

But his rage wasn't for her.

That mattered.

She reached toward him—barely a twitch of her fingers—but he noticed.

"I'll be back," he said, rising with purpose. "Gotta cut Wallace loose. Then I'm coming for you."

It wasn't a promise.

It was law.

And she believed him.

"He'll wake up," she warned, panic pounding inside her like a second heart.

"I drugged him," the stranger called back, already in motion. "He should sleep for a while."

"Call for help!" she cried after him, voice cracking.

"No service," he snapped—

not at her,

but at the sky.

At the world.

At the silence.

"There's a knife in the couch," Mr. Wallace rasped, each word thick and pained. "Left side cushion."

Lauren let her head drop back onto the mattress.

Her body was broken.

But something else was rising.

Hope.

But sharper.

Sharper than any blade.

She heard it—

The scrape of the blade sawing through rope.

Tension splitting.

Fibers snapping one by one.

Like bones breaking free.

At last.

The sound she'd been waiting for.

Freedom.

Mr. Wallace let out a low, trembling breath.

She could hear it—his body uncoiling from the knots, his muscles slowly remembering themselves.

Lauren's chest tightened—not from pain this time, but from something raw and shaking and real.

Mr. Wallace was loose.

At least enough to move.

"We're going to make it, Mr. Wallace," she whispered, her voice barely above a breath.

A breath that held everything—fear, relief, and the fragile thread of belief pulling her forward.

"Yes, we are, Sarah," he said.

And this time, the hope didn't sound borrowed.

It sounded like it belonged to him.

The stranger guided him to his feet—slow, careful, one hand braced under Mr. Wallace's arm, the other still clutching the knife like it mattered more than air.

Lauren listened to them from her place on the mattress.

She couldn't move.

Not yet.

Her fingers twitched beneath the thin blanket, brushing against fabric as if searching for the memory of steel.

But her mind—

Her mind was already counting steps.

Rehearsing options.

Preparing the board.

Because this wasn't over.

Not until Stefan was off the board completely.

She heard his footsteps shift.

Closer. Urgent.

Maybe he was coming to check on her.

Maybe he was about to speak.

Maybe—

Boom.

The door burst open.

No warning. No stomp of boots.

Just the sound of wood cracking, air slicing, and hell exploding back into the room.

Stefan.

Eyes wild.

Shirt half-buttoned.

Knife already in hand, raised.

Blood rushing to his face like a storm rising behind his skin.

And everything they'd built—

The hope.

The progress.

The breath between survival and escape—

collapsed in an instant.

Mr. Wallace's eyes went wide with terror as the air shifted—heavy, electric.

Stefan's shadow filled the doorway like a storm swelling to burst.

No charm. No smirk.

The curtain had dropped.

The real Stefan stepped into the spotlight.

What stood in the doorway wasn't Zach.

It was Stefan.

The real one.

Unfiltered. Unhinged. Unstoppable.

"You messed with the wrong motherfucker!"

He exploded forward—rage in motion—

a body made into a weapon, fists already swinging.

The stranger stepped in front of Mr. Wallace, instinct taking over—

But Stefan was already there.

His shoulder slammed into the man's chest, driving him backward into the kitchenette.

A sickening crack echoed as his spine hit the cabinets.

The whole camper shuddered.

The impact jarred the knife from his grip—

It clattered to the linoleum and skidded across the floor with a sharp, metallic shriek.

Grunts and snarls filled the narrow space.

The two men traded blows in a frenzy of violence—
messy, brutal, desperate.

No technique. No control. Just pain.

The stranger landed two punches—one to the jaw, one to the ribs—
but Stefan's wild strength overpowered precision.

He caught the man with a vicious hook.

His knuckles hit flesh.

A sickening crack.

Blood splattered across the front of the mini-fridge, blooming like a signature.

A beer bottle tipped over in the sink and shattered.

Mr. Wallace staggered to the side, searching for space that didn't exist.

The camper was too small.

Too tight.

Nowhere to run.

An elbow whipped through the chaos—wild, accidental—
and crashed into Mr. Wallace's side.

He stumbled.

Collapsed.

His head struck the edge of the table with a sound that stopped time—
a wet, cracking thunk.

Then silence. Just for a second.

A thud followed—his body hitting the floor.

She didn't move. Didn't breathe.

She lay coiled tight beneath the blanket, every muscle drawn like a wire stretched to its limit.

The camper groaned around her.

Every sound warped—muted one second, jarringly loud the next.

A sharp sting pricked her nose—blood, maybe, or sweat.

The metallic tang clung to her tongue.

Her ears rang, or was that something slamming into the floor?

She couldn't tell.

Her breath thundered in her chest.

Outside, the wind picked up—sharp and restless, rattling the camper's thin walls.

A loose branch scraped across the roof in rhythmic, jarring taps.

She listened—to every slam.

Every curse.

Every sickening sound of flesh on flesh, bone meeting bone.

And in that breathless stillness, she longed for a voice—

a whisper, a promise. "It's over. You're safe now."

But no one said it.

No one ever had.

The truth pressed in, cruel and certain.

Stefan was winning.

The stranger—the shadow—was losing.

And time was running out.

There was no rhythm to the fight anymore.

Just chaos.

Desperation.

She could hear it unraveling in the cadence of grunts, the staggered footsteps, the choking gasps that followed each hit.

She heard it.

Not a thud. Not a grunt.

A crack.

Sharp.

Wet.

Final.

Not just a hit.

Not just pain.

A break—the kind that ended people.

The one that had stalked her through every nightmare since Springfield.

The one that marked the moment someone became still.

Her mind jerked back—

To Fritch, Texas.

To Judy.

To that sickening sound of wood meeting bone.

The hit itself didn't kill her.

But it was the moment the fight ended.

The moment Stefan gained the upper hand.

And Lauren had done nothing.

Just watched.

Just waited.

Just... froze.

Lauren's stomach flipped.

The image collided with the sound, and her hope folded in on itself like a house collapsing in slow motion—wood snapping, walls caving, ash settling.

No screams.

Just destruction.

The violence outside the bedroom abruptly stopped.

One dull thud.

A grunt—low, breathless.

No footsteps.

No noise.

Just one man's breathing—heavy, ragged.

Anger and rage tightening the air like a noose.

Then something heavy scraped across the linoleum, dragged inch by inch.

Stefan cursed under his breath.

"Should've stayed out of it," he muttered.

Low. Venomous. Final.

But what followed wasn't gloating.

Wasn't laughter.

Wasn't victory.

It was silence.

It was the wrong kind of silence.

Not the hush of peace.

The hush of satisfaction—

Heavy. Knowing. Final.

The kind that lingered after blood.

The kind that waited before it killed.

Mr. Wallace wasn't moving, but he was still breathing—shallow, rattled, fragile.

Alive.

It wasn't over.

Not yet.

Stefan was already savoring checkmate.

Swaggering in the false comfort of a win.

But she hadn't tipped her king.

Not yet.

Lauren slowly sank back into the mattress, her body curling inward, hiding the slow, deliberate fury rising behind her ribs.

The pain was still there—radiating in her spine, her jaw, her ribs—but it dulled beneath something hotter.

Sharper.

Focused.

There was no room left for fear.

No space for hope.

No space for mercy.

Only rage.

Not the kind that screams.

Not the kind that flails.

The kind that waits.

That hones itself in the dark—watches, learns, measures.

It doesn't lash out.

It calculates.

It gets closer.

And then it ends it.

She wasn't done.

Not like this.

Not ever.

Lauren lay perfectly still.

One breath.

Then another.

Each more deliberate than the last.

Her good hand inched beneath the mattress.

Fingers trembling. Searching.

Finding the cold weight of steel.

And this time—she didn't hesitate.

She held on.

Not just to the knife.

To the truth.

To the plan.

To the end.

❧ 37 ❧

Mr. Wallace believed in second chances. He believed in them when he walked away from his career. And he believed in them — stubbornly, maybe foolishly — when he looked into the eyes of a girl hiding behind a bruised face and a borrowed name.

That was the last thing he remembered believing in.

Now, lying on the cold camper floor, his ears rang. Every breath scraped his throat like gravel. Pain bloomed in his ribs with each inhale, and his vision swam in pulses—too dark, too bright. The camper groaned. Something creaked—wood, bone, maybe both. The air smelled like blood and sweat and something burnt. Every sound came distorted —thick, like it had to fight its way through water to reach him. The silence that followed wasn't peace. It was the eye of a storm.

He was listening.

He didn't know if she was conscious. Or worse—dead. The silence reminded him of the night his mother stopped screaming. Of the awful stillness that followed. He hadn't been able to save her, either.

But this girl—this time—was different. He wasn't a child anymore. He had strength left. And he'd use every broken rib, every ounce of pain, if it meant giving her a second chance.

If she was still breathing—still fighting—then he had something left to believe in. Something worth staying alive for.

He hadn't been able to save his mother. He'd been a child—helpless

—unable to step in, to stop the violence his father unleashed. But this time—this girl—he wouldn't walk away.

He strained to hear any sign of life from the next room. If she's still breathing, I can't give up. Not yet. Not now. It wasn't over for them. Not yet.

Mr. Wallace lay still, pain spiking with every shallow breath. And still, he listened.

Listened to the monster pacing the floor like a caged tiger— wounded, enraged, circling for his next kill.

This version of the man—this snarling, violent storm—was nothing like the young man he'd first met just days ago.

But the memory came back easily. Too easily.

He wished he could go back and change it. Stop it before it started. Undo whatever opened the door to this nightmare.

She looked like she'd been through hell—and still, she held her head up. God help me, I saw fight in her.

And yet... he didn't regret meeting her. The girl. The fighter. Sarah— the one in the next room, bruised and barely hanging on.

This is my fault. I should've called the police the second I saw him. Should've listened to my gut...

He didn't know if help was coming. Didn't know if the stranger had made it out. But he knew this:

If I have to bleed out right here to buy her a minute, I will. I swear to God, I will.

He closed his eyes and listened. One breath at a time. Still alive. Still hoping.

She reminded him of Margaret.

Not the Margaret he'd buried.

The girl Margaret used to be—quiet, gentle, full of fire she didn't yet know how to wield.

That same stubborn light burned in Sarah's eyes, even through the bruises.

He'd been lonely the day this sadistic monster walked into his life.

Desperate, even.

Hell, he'd gone three days without more than a passing wave from the couple in the fifth-wheel up the hill.

He craved conversation the way a starving man craved bread.

You just wanted someone to talk to. Someone who didn't look at you like you were fading away.

So when the blond-haired young man strolled up with a kind smile and easy manners, Edward had been grateful just to be seen.

Most people overlooked the elderly.

But not Zach.

Zach had noticed him.

And that was the first mistake, wasn't it?

He remembered sitting at the picnic table—sunlight warming his arms, the breeze tugging gently at his shirt, the faint smell of bacon or maybe sausage frying in someone else's pan.

Zach had been heading to the general store to grab one of those premade, shrink-wrapped sandwiches.

Edward—ever the wise old man—had chuckled and warned him off it.

Thought I was helping. Thought I was being neighborly. Look where it got us.

They'd bantered. It had felt good. Normal.

He'd even offered Zach his leftovers. A kindness, he'd thought at the time.

A neighborly gesture to help a young man and his "ailing wife."

That had been his second mistake.

You let him in. You opened the damn door. And now look what he's done to her.

He'd opened up that day — told Zach about Margaret's sudden illness, his boys, the grandkids. Their travels, their little rituals. Even the marigolds he carried from campsite to campsite—his quiet offering. A shrine to memory and grief and the love that still clung to him like mist.

Zach had listened — really listened.

He'd asked questions. Remembered details. Reached for things most people overlooked.

He wasn't curious. He was collecting. Cataloging. Setting the stage.

Mr. Wallace clenched his jaw, the pain in his ribs flaring again.

Not because of the blow.

Because of the guilt.

God help me... I liked him. I trusted him.

At the time, it had felt rare. A young man actually listening. Engaging with an old-timer like him.

Now, Edward knew better.

It wasn't compassion. It was calculation.

All of it.

You fool, he thought quietly. You wanted to believe someone saw you. That someone cared.

But it wasn't care. It was a setup.

The man pacing just outside the bedroom didn't give a lick about marigolds. Or memories. Or Margaret.

He cared about control. About power.

About pain.

And Sarah—dear, brave Sarah—had been trapped at the center of it all.

Bruised. Quiet. Enduring.

Edward swallowed hard, his throat raw, as the memory replayed like a scratched reel of film.

The first time he saw her was at breakfast. Zach had invited him— cheerful, charming, all easy charm—and Edward, starved for company, had accepted without hesitation.

She was quiet. Distant. Kept those sunglasses on the whole time, saying she had a migraine.

I believed her, he thought bitterly. Never even questioned it.

But now? Now, every detail came back with sharper edges.

The way her shoulders hunched inward, like she was trying to disappear.

The stiffness in her movements.

The way she flinched when Zach touched her hand.

She wasn't hiding from the sun, he realized. She was hiding from him.

He should've seen it.

Should've recognized the signs.

And then—he remembered the moment she took off the sunglasses.

Just for a second.

Just long enough for him to catch the bruise blooming across her cheekbone.

A dark, purplish mark that hadn't come from clumsiness.

No, he'd seen too many of those to be fooled.

This one was deliberate. Meant. Left behind like a signature.

It had felt like getting punched himself.

Like the breath had been knocked clean out of his lungs.

His stomach had clenched. His hands had curled into fists beneath the table.

But he'd said nothing. Not enough.

A girl her age, he thought.

With eyes like that shouldn't know that kind of fear.

Eyes that flinched before they focused.

That darted to the side before meeting your gaze.

He knew those eyes.

He'd offered her help, hadn't he? A few gentle questions. A softer tone. He'd asked if she was alright, told her she could talk to him.

But maybe that hadn't been enough.

You should've pushed, he thought, bitter and low. Called the police. Reported it to the park manager. Anything.

Instead, he'd let it slide. Let Zach's charm smooth things over.

Because that's what abusers did best—talked circles around concern, wrapped cruelty in calm voices.

They weren't new signs—not to a man who'd lived a full life, who'd seen enough heartache to know what it looked like behind a forced smile.

Behind oversized sunglasses. Behind silence.

You should've pushed. Called someone. Said something.

Made it undeniable. Made it loud.

Instead, he'd let it go.

You looked away, he thought bitterly. And she's the one who paid for it.

He saw his mother in those bruises.

The way she used to flinch at sudden movements. The way she smiled through split lips and—

purple shadows, pretending everything was fine.

The way no one had helped her. Not in time.

He hadn't been able to save Margaret from the flu that took her in three brutal days.

He'd held her hand, wiped her brow, watched her slip away while the machines beeped and the nurses apologized.

But this—this was different.

This girl didn't need comfort.

She needed rescue.

Because that's what he saw now.

Not a man. Not a husband.

A disease.

A cancer that had wrapped its claws around her ribs and called it love.

It didn't stalk—it rotted.

Quietly.

Patiently.

Until there was nothing left.

He could hear him pacing.

Circling just feet away.

Rage simmering. Breath thick with satisfaction.

Like he'd already won.

You didn't win yet, Edward thought. Not yet, you son of a—

He stopped himself. He didn't curse.

Not out loud.

But if ever there was a time.

His whole body screamed to move.

To grab the knife.

To fight.

To end this.

It had skidded during the struggle—he'd seen it—but now it was lost.

Buried beneath towels or kicked under furniture.

Out of reach.

And yet his fingers twitched like they remembered its weight.

If he moved, Zach would notice.

If he didn't, he'd be nothing but a body on the floor when it ended.

Time's running out, old man. Do something.

Then—

Like the thought summoned it—

Hands clamped around his ankles.

Hard.

Yanking.

Edward's eyes flew open, the panic igniting something feral in his chest.

Not yet. Not like this. He fought like hell.

Instinct kicked in — sharp, wild, desperate.

Edward thrashed, legs kicking out in frantic bursts.

Every inch of him roared to survive.

Not now. Not like this. Not with her still in danger. His feet were free, but his hands were still bound.

He twisted hard, spine screaming in protest. The camper blurred around him.

His knees knocked into something sharp — a broken plate or maybe a cup.

He struck out blindly, scraping at the ground, fingertips clawing through debris.

Come on. Come on. Give me something. Shattered dishes. Splintered wood.

Glass glittered like tiny teeth, scattered beneath him.

The floor was a graveyard — but none of it could save him.

"No! No!" he shouted, the sound ripping from his throat raw and jagged.

It wasn't just fear — it was fury.

Fury at himself.

Fury at Zach.

Fury at the years that dulled his edges and slowed his reflexes.

Zach gripped him like he weighed nothing.

Hoisted him with terrifying ease —

a man tossing garbage, not a human life.

Edward twisted, flailed, shoved back with his shoulder, but it was useless.

You're not a young man anymore. Stop pretending you are.

Then —

Crash.

The couch slammed up into his back like a battering ram.

Pain detonated through his ribcage.

Bright. Blinding.

Like fire spreading from the inside out.

His lungs folded.

The air left him in a hollow, voiceless whoosh.

He opened his mouth, but the cry never made it past his tongue.

God—

Choking. Gasping.

For one terrifying moment, there was no air.

Only soundless agony.

Only darkness swimming at the edges of his vision.

And then —

Air.

Blessed. Burning.

It cut through his chest like barbed wire, but it was life.

It was breath.

He blinked hard, his vision tilting sideways.

Sweat dripped into his eyes. His ears rang.

But he was still there.

Still in it.

You're alive, old man. Now act like it.

Across the camper — muffled, distant — he thought he heard her.

Sarah.

Still breathing. Still fighting.

And if she hadn't given up...

"I'm not done," he croaked under his breath, the words barely audible to even himself.

Not yet. Not while she was still counting on him.

"STOP IT!"

The scream tore through the camper — sharp, raw, desperate.

From the bedroom. From her.

Zach froze mid-step.

Edward's heart stuttered.

No—Sarah, what are you doing?

Zach's eyes went wide. Wild.

Something flickered behind them — not hesitation, not fear.

A shift.

Like a compass needle suddenly snapping north.

The rage didn't vanish.

It refocused.

Edward saw it happen — saw the exact moment she pulled the fury off of him. She's drawing him away.

Putting herself in the lion's den. On purpose.

His throat tightened.

You brave, foolish girl. You should be running... but you're not, are you?

. . .

She knew what she was doing.

Calling the monster.

Drawing the crosshairs onto herself so he might live another minute.

You stepped in front of the firing squad... for me.

Zach rolled his neck.

Pop. Pop.

The sound cracked through the silence like bones snapping.

He tilted his head and looked down at Edward—not with anger.

With amusement.

Mocking. Cold.

That smile—

It didn't belong to a man.

It belonged to something older. Meaner. Hungry.

He was calm now.

Too calm.

And calm, Edward knew, was always the worst state for men like him.

Because calm meant control.

Calm meant cruelty.

Stefan turned slowly toward the bedroom.

Each step deliberate. Measured.

Like a man savoring dessert.

Edward felt the words scrape up his throat.

"Be ready!" he croaked. "He's coming."

"Fight, girl," he yelled. You've got grit in your bones—call on whatever's left. It's enough. It has to be.

Zach didn't answer.

He just laughed.

Low. Rotten. Saturated with delight.

And then came the sounds Edward would never forget.

A scream—guttural, blood-chilling, like something primal had been torn loose.

A heavy thud—a body hitting the floor with brutal finality.

And then, the sickening scrape of her being dragged across the linoleum—

slow,

merciless,

inescapable.

Edward's stomach turned.

No, no, no—what did he do to her? What had she tried?

You shouldn't've screamed, girl. You should've stayed quiet—

But he knew that was wrong.

She'd done it to save him.

She'd known what would happen, and she screamed anyway.

You bought me time, he thought bitterly. And now he's making you pay for it.

Zach emerged, dragging Sarah by the ankles.

Her body scraped across the floor—her skin, her bones—like she was trash to be taken out.

But she was fighting.

God, she was fighting.

She thrashed, kicked, twisted in his grip.

A blade flashed in her hand—small, jagged.

A kitchen knife.

Where did she get it?

You brilliant girl.

She swung it wildly, teeth bared, not caring if she missed—just needing to remind the world she wasn't dead yet.

Her scream tore through the air again.

It wasn't human.

It was raw.

Feral.

Primal.

Like something ancient and sacred had been awakened inside her.

Her hair clung to her cheeks—wet, streaked with blood.

One eye was swollen shut, the other burned with something Edward could only describe as holy fury.

That's no girl, he thought. That's vengeance. That's survival wearing bruises like war paint.

"Let her go! Zach! Let her go!" Edward roared, dragging himself upright with trembling arms.

He knew it wouldn't work.

But he had to try.

If she's going down, she's not going alone. Not without someone yelling her name.

Stefan didn't even glance at him.

Didn't flinch.

He dropped one of Sarah's legs—

reached out with the other hand—

and backhanded Edward across the face with brutal, casual force.

The crack echoed through the camper.

Edward's jaw lit with fire.

He collapsed, stars exploding in his vision. Still here, he thought, barely breathing.

Sarah didn't stop. She swung again — and again — but her reach was short. Her fury was wildfire — but it wasn't enough.

Zach caught her wrist mid-swing. Twisted. She screamed — high, piercing — and he wrenched her onto her stomach.

The knife slipped from her fingers. It hit the floor with a cold, metallic clatter. That sound — that small, sharp sound — was worse than any scream.

It was the sound of hope breaking.

Zach didn't rush. He crouched down slowly, plucked the knife from the floor with deliberate care, and slid it into his pocket — like he had all the time in the world.

Sarah went still. Limp. Her cheek pressed into the linoleum, breath shallow and uneven.

And then — his eyes found hers. Bruised. Bloodied. But burning. Still hers. Unbroken.

Tears slid from her lashes, soaking into the floor like rain on scorched earth.

Edward's heart shattered — not from pain, not from fear. For her.

You are fire, he thought. And he's trying to smother you.

He turned his head, straining to see the unconscious man slumped across the floor — the one who'd come so close to saving them. Wake up, he begged silently. Please, God, wake up.

And somehow, Lauren felt it.

The silent prayer. The aching hope. The kind of hope that didn't come with words — just weight. It pressed against her ribs, curled inside her breath.

She turned her face just slightly, the motion sending sharp jolts through her jaw. But she needed to see Edward.

To let him see her.

To show him...

She wasn't done.

Not yet.

Not ever.

Lauren followed his gaze.

And for just a moment — her mask slipped.

Not the one of fear.

Not the one of submission.

The real one.

And behind it — fire.

Not rage. Not panic.

Purpose.

He saw it.

And he believed.

That fire... it wasn't fading.

It was waiting.

And God help the man who thought she was done.

Stefan must've sensed the shift — that silent fire burning behind her eyes — because he pivoted and kicked the stranger square in the face.

The man didn't move.

Then Stefan turned back to Lauren.

He grabbed her by the hair and yanked her upright.

A scream tore from Lauren's throat — raw and jagged — as Stefan dragged her across the linoleum like a rag doll. Her body folded in on itself, every limb buckling in protest. He hauled her upright and propped her against the cabinets like a broken display, her face tilted just enough for Edward to see.

"Hey, old man," Stefan called out, voice suddenly chipper — too chipper. "You wanna know something funny?"

Edward tried to lift his head. Blood dripped from his mouth. His jaw throbbed. But he looked.

Stefan grinned — all teeth, no soul.

Lauren's breath hitched. Her head lolled slightly to the side.

Stefan reached down, gripped her chin with bruising fingers, and forced her face toward Edward.

"My name is Stefan," he said, like he was introducing himself at a dinner party. He turned to her, tilting his head like a game show host.

"Go on, sweetheart. Tell him your name."

Lauren stayed silent. Her breath came in quick, shallow bursts.

"Say it," Stefan screamed, jerking her hair tighter.

Her lips trembled. She looked at Mr. Wallace — then down at the floor.

"Lauren," she whispered. "My name is Lauren."

Edward blinked. What?

"She told me you were alone at the bathhouse," Stefan went on, circling now — slow, predatory. "She told me where your camper was. She gave you to me."

Edward looked at her. Really looked.

And saw the truth written in the way she wouldn't — couldn't — meet his eyes.

Her lips moved again. "I'm sorry." Over and over. "I'm sorry."

Edward's chest tightened.

It wasn't anger. It was grief.

He had let her in. He had believed in her.

And still — even now — he couldn't hate her. Not like this.

His gaze dropped.

There. The knife — the one that had skidded across the floor during the struggle. It rested just beside her now. Inches away. Close... but out of her line of sight.

He looked back up, heart pounding, trying to catch her eye.

She wasn't looking.

"Stefan, please," Lauren whispered. "Please let him go. Please don't."

He said nothing. He didn't need to.

Stefan reached into his pocket. Pulled out the knife — her knife. The one she'd hidden. The one she'd meant to use.

Lauren's breath caught.

"Please..." she whispered, one last time.

Then the blade came down.

A flash of motion.

A wet sound.

And the world stopped.

Edward's hands flew to his throat. Blood poured between his fingers, warm and thick and impossible to stop. His mouth opened in a silent gasp, his eyes locking onto hers.

Lauren looked up just in time.

"I'm sorry," she said aloud.

Her voice cracked.

And then — he nodded.

Forgiveness, in a single breath.

Even as his vision blurred, he turned his head toward the knife beside her.

One final offering.

One last act of defiance.

Lauren followed his gaze.

Her whole body moved with it.

She saw it.

She saw it.

When she looked back —

He was already gone.

Edward Wallace had given everything.

His strength.

His trust.

His final breath.

To give her a chance.

38

Stefan stood over Mr. Wallace's body, his chest rising and falling with the sick satisfaction of a man convinced he'd triumphed.

His pride radiated off him like heat — smug, gleaming, poisonous.

The tension in his frame had vanished, leaking out of him like air from a slashed tire.

He exhaled like a wolf after a fresh kill.

Lauren stared at the lifeless man on the couch.

The man she had betrayed before even knowing his name.

A gentle, soft-spoken soul who'd started as nothing more than a pawn in her game — a distraction, a shield, a calculated risk.

But somewhere between the first shared laugh and the whispered warnings, he had become something else.

Closer to family.

Something earned. Something she hadn't known she needed.

He had begun as a gambit. But he became something far more.

A necessary sacrifice in a game she'd been playing long before they ever met.

But Mr. Wallace hadn't just accepted the role —

he'd rewritten it.

He'd stepped into the fire without hesitation, even after realizing she'd sent him there.

And he still tried to save her.

He wasn't a pawn.

He was a friend.

And with his final breath, he'd handed her the last piece she needed to win.

She watched the last of his blood seep into the fabric of the couch.

And something inside her broke.

Not like glass.

Like chains.

I put you in this. And you stayed anyway.

You knew — and you stayed.

Rage surged — hot, electric, unstoppable.

The mask she had worn — soft, broken, innocent —

peeled from her skin like dead weight.

It didn't belong to her anymore.

It never had.

It was time to play a different piece.

She had been the queen.

She'd maneuvered the king.

Now, she was the knight.

And it was her move.

Lauren shifted her weight — slow, deliberate — every nerve burning with purpose.

Her eyes never left Stefan.

Even blurred through swollen lids, she tracked him.

Measured him.

Saw the man who thought the board was his.

She was done playing by his rules.

Inch by inch, her fingers crept toward the knife Mr. Wallace had pointed out.

Her hand wrapped around the cold steel like it belonged there.

Like it always had.

She slipped it into the pocket of her sweatpants, fingers pressing it flat.

Claiming it.

Owning it.

Stefan didn't notice.

Too busy admiring his work.

He turned to face her, grinning.

"Your sweet old Granddaddy's still out there, isn't he?"

He leaned in, voice low, venomous.

"If he could see you now...

He might wish you'd died instead."

Lauren didn't flinch.

You don't get to use him, she thought. Not anymore.

He stepped forward, grabbed her by the hair, and yanked her down the hallway.

White-hot pain ripped through her skull — sharp, blinding — radiating down her spine with every jerking step.

Her ribs screamed. Her vision swam.

Every part of her wanted to cry out, to collapse.

But she didn't fight.

Didn't scream.

Didn't cry.

She went limp.

Let him think I'm done. Let him think you're broken.

She shoved the scream back down her throat, caged it like an animal.

The pain was unbearable — but the rage burned hotter.

It was the only thing keeping her sane.

The only thing keeping her alive.

Pretending to surrender made monsters careless.

It was the oldest move on the board —

And she was done playing fair.

It wasn't fear that stilled her now —

it was calculation.

Her mind was sharp, focused.

With every dragging step, she kept her hand deliberately pressed to her pocket, anchoring the blade tight against her thigh.

She didn't need to win yet.

She just needed to wait for her moment.

And when it came —

She'd drive the checkmate home herself.

It was her last breath.

Her final advantage.

The last piece she had left on the board.

The one no one ever sees coming.

If she lost it, she lost everything.

Don't show it. Don't let him see.

You've come too far to flinch now.

"Too bad you won't be able to watch when I hunt your Granddaddy," Stefan said.

"When I beat the smug off his face. When I break him."

His tone wasn't furious.

It was calm.

Calculated.

Rehearsed.

He wanted to see her crack.

But she didn't move.

Didn't speak.

Didn't rise to it.

You won't touch him, she thought. You won't get close.

Because you won't walk out of this room.

He tossed her onto the bed like trash.

Pain lit up her ribs — deeper this time.

Sharper.

Something tore.

Her body arched with the impact. A white flash exploded behind her eyes.

She gasped — and the sound came out wet.

Blood splattered across her lips. Her chest seized. Her lungs refused to expand.

She didn't scream.

She couldn't.

But in her mind, one thought pulsed louder than the pain:

You shouldn't have mentioned him. You just sealed your fate.

One hand flew to her mouth, instinct taking over.

The other?

Pressed tighter to her pocket.

Gripping the blade like it was life itself.

She felt the blood coat her palm—warm, thick, metallic.

Her lungs stuttered with every breath, each inhale jagged and thin.

Something vital had ruptured inside her. She knew it.

But fear had no place here.

Not now. Not yet.

Pain didn't matter.

Only the plan.

She wiped her lips with the back of her hand, smearing red across her skin like war paint.

Then, slowly—deliberately—

she lifted her chin.

Reclaiming the power he had stolen.

The same power the hit-and-run driver took when she was just a little girl.

Through the narrow slit of her remaining vision, she locked onto him.

Not the man.

The target.

Don't look away.

He wants fear. Give him calculation.

Stefan peeled off his shirt and let it drop to the floor, revealing a body built to hurt and a smirk built to gloat.

"You've been fun," he said, like he was ending a date instead of a life.

Casual. Grinning. Poison in human form.

"But you've outstayed your welcome."

He stepped closer.

"Want to know something?" he asked.

She said nothing.

Didn't blink.

Didn't breathe too deep.

Her hand slid into her pocket — slow, steady.

The steel nestled in her palm.

It felt right.

Like it had always belonged there.

Wait.

Watch.

Let him believe you're already gone.

"Answer me!" he snapped, voice fraying with impatience.

That was it.

The shift.

The opening.

She didn't flinch.

Just stared — daring him to take one more step.

"What, Stefan?" she said, cool and steady. "What do you want me to know?"

She knew which buttons to push.

She always had.

And the tragic part?

So had he.

Their game had never really been about domination.

It was about control.

And more often than not, Lauren was the one making the moves.

She watched him take the bait — again — like a mouse strolling toward the bait, never realizing the trap had already been set.

He sneered. "I'm going to make you scream."

"You always say that," she said. "But I rarely do."

She'd braced for it.

Knew it was coming.

Let it land.

Because she was waiting.

"Bitch!"

He hit her — his favorite move. Her hair snapped to the side.

Then — he grabbed the waistband of her sweatpants and ripped them down in one motion.

Her hand slid from the pocket as he yanked them down.

The knife was now clutched under her thigh.

Perfect.

She held still, barely blinking.

One wrong twitch, and it would all be gone.

He stared at her. Bruised. Bleeding. Broken.

And still... not begging.

He crawled forward, face inches from hers.

"I'm going to take all your money," he whispered. "I'm going to kill your Granddaddy."

She felt his breath in her ear. He was savoring this.

"But first," he said, "we're going to play a little game."

He leaned back. Moved her hair from her face.

"Look at me," he said.

She did.

The knife pressed into her palm.

Cold. Familiar.

She could almost hear Mr. Wallace—Be ready.

She was.

And then—she struck.

The blade plunged deep into his abdomen.

His eyes widened.

Confused.

Disbelieving.

She watched as the realization hit Stefan.

His lips parted, like he was about to laugh.

But no sound came. Just the slow slide of his breath turning shallow. He gasped — wet and sharp — like his lungs didn't understand what was happening. Blood streamed from his mouth and onto her shirt. He coughed, and blood sprayed her face. This time, it wasn't hers. It was his.

The light in his eyes dimmed — not from fear, but disbelief. He wasn't in control. Wasn't the hunter. Wasn't the god he believed himself to be. He was just a man — bleeding, broken, and too stupid to realize he'd lost long before the knife ever touched skin.

Lauren didn't feel fear. She felt fire. Fury in her chest. Justice in her hands.

This is for Erin. For Judy. For Mr. Wallace. For me.

"Look at me, Stefan," she growled.

He choked. Blood spilled from his mouth — slow and bubbling. His eyes started to roll back.

"LOOK AT ME!" she screamed.

And he did. For the first time in their long, twisted story — he looked at her and saw the truth. Who she was. What she'd become. What she'd always been.

"Checkmate," she whispered. Then smiled through cracked lips. "... Bitch."

She drove the knife upward. Slicing deeper. Twisting. Claiming the win she'd waited for.

Then she pulled it out — clean, final.

Stefan collapsed. Gurgling. Dying. Done.

Lauren exhaled. A long, ragged breath—like releasing a war she'd carried far too long.

For the first time in a year... She inhaled without flinching. She held it. She let it go.

She could finally breathe.

I was never his victim. This was always going to end like this.

39

Stefan's body lay twisted on the bed.

Lauren still held the knife, the sticky handle slipping slightly in her trembling grip as blood dripped from the tip.

Her white T-shirt clung to her skin — soaked through, marbled with deep maroon.

Her bare legs were streaked with blood.

All of it his.

She didn't move. Didn't blink.

She simply stared at the crumpled, broken monster she had finally turned into prey.

The man who had hunted her, broken her, owned her — now lay dead in the sheets they'd shared for over a year.

His blood pooled across the same sheets that once wrapped around her like chains.

Lauren leaned back against the pillows — the ones she had cried into. Screamed into. Prayed into.

The ones that had soaked up her silence. Her surrender.

Now, they cradled what remained of her.

She stared at the ceiling. Her legs stretched out in front of her, the knife still resting in her hand — like a forgotten part of her body.

She felt nothing. Not fear. Not rage. Not even triumph. Just the eerie weight of silence—too tired to scream, too stunned to cry.

Just stillness. Inside and out.

A hush that rang louder than any scream.

It's over, she thought again.

Not for comfort. Not for clarity.

Just to hear the words.

If she kept saying it in her head, maybe it would start to feel true.

Somewhere in the next room, something shifted — a soft sound, like a foot dragging across linoleum.

She didn't flinch.

Her thoughts drifted.

Her mind wandered — to Nurse Erin, to the women who came before, the ones Stefan had buried in shallow graves and left to rot.

She thought of Bill and Judy.

Of the hunts she had once taken part in.

Of the lies she'd helped sell.

The violence she hadn't stopped.

The guilt she'd learned to carry.

She thought of Mr. Wallace — the kindness in his eyes even when he saw through her.

And how he helped her anyway.

He had been her gambit.

A pawn offered in the name of survival.

One more piece sacrificed.

All the lives that had been traded like pieces on a board. And she had placed herself in that game. Willingly. Strategically. Unflinchingly.

Now, every piece was gone. The board was empty. But the game wasn't over — not really.

She was free. But her mind was still shackled.

Haunted by the ghosts. The roles she'd played. The lives she'd traded for survival.

The blood on her hands wasn't just Stefan's — and she knew it. It was theirs. Nurse Erin. Bill and Judy. The women whose names she never learned. And the men who'd died after the pattern changed. Victims she could have warned. Could have saved.

And then there was Mr. Wallace — her friend.

Lauren could have saved them all. But she hadn't. Because somewhere along the line... she stopped pretending she wasn't part of it.

Stefan was a monster — grown from trauma, pain, something

genetic and cruel. But Lauren? She had no excuse. She knew exactly what she was doing. Every step. Every lie. Every silence.

A flicker of movement pulled her attention — light shifting at the end of the narrow hallway. She blinked, but her vision was too clouded to make anything out.

Then — a low groan. A hand slapping against a cabinet. The soft, clumsy sounds of someone trying to rise.

She knew who it was. And she couldn't bring herself to care.

He had waited too long. Stayed in the shadows. Watching. A whisper in the night. A ghost outside the window. He had tried to warn her. Left breadcrumbs. Scratched warnings into silence.

But he hadn't stepped into the light. Not when it counted.

If he'd come sooner... Mr. Wallace might still be alive. She wanted to hate him. But she couldn't. Because the truth was simple. The guilt wasn't his to carry. It belonged to her.

Her breath came in shallow bursts. Her chest rose and fell under the weight of silence.

Something shifted again in the hallway. A creak. A drag. The faintest sound of breath that didn't belong to her. She didn't move. Didn't speak. Didn't care.

A shadow shifted again in the hallway. Light bent. She didn't bother to look up — her right eye had swollen shut, and the sliver of sight she had left was disappearing fast.

A groan. A shuffle. Then a body leaned against the doorframe.

"Oh shit," he whispered. The words weren't just surprise. They were broken.

She didn't move. He stepped around Stefan's dangling legs, careful but stunned — like a man walking through the scene of a dream. Then he dropped to his knees beside her.

"Lauren... My God. What did he do to you? Tell me this isn't all your blood."

She didn't answer. She just stared into the void of the ceiling, her blood-streaked hand still clutched loosely around the blade.

He touched her arm, then her face. She flinched. His hand lingered a moment too long — not checking for injury, but grounding himself. As if he needed to feel something real. Something alive.

He gently pried the knife from her hand. Her fingers didn't resist.

He took the knife from her hand gently, like peeling a memory from her skin. Her fingers didn't close. Not in protest. Not in fear. Just... nothing.

"I'm fine," she said. Not out of strength — just habit.

Each word scraped her lungs raw.

He looked toward the bed — toward Stefan's twisted, lifeless body — and visibly swallowed.

"Lauren... Mr. Wallace is dead."

"I know."

She coughed. Blood trickled from her lips. She didn't bother wiping it away.

"Jesus—Lauren." His voice broke. "Hang on. Just a little while longer."

His hands hovered for a second, unsure where to touch without causing more damage. "You probably have a punctured lung," he said, the words tumbling out, low and panicked. "We... have to get you help. Now."

She nodded. Slow. Barely.

He looked down at her again, like he couldn't believe she was still alive.

"Lauren," he whispered. His voice cracked.

"I'm going for help. I promise I'll come back. Just hang on, okay? Please... just hang on."

She blinked. Wait.

Had he just said her name? Her real name?

He stood. The door opened. The door closed. The engine turned over — the same one that once rumbled toward victims, now roaring away into the night. And just like that — the shadow was gone again.

She was alone. Alone with the silence. Alone with the ghosts that would never stop haunting her.

But even in the stillness, his voice lingered. Not what he said. How he said it.

Lauren. He'd called her Lauren.

And that was impossible. They hadn't exchanged names. They hadn't even spoken — not really. Tonight was the first time she'd seen his face.

And yet... he'd said it like he'd always known.
So how the hell did he know her name?

EPILOGUE

Lauren Warren was exhausted, both mentally and physically. The adrenaline had burned off, leaving only pain — a deep, aching throb that radiated from her ribs all the way down to the marrow of her bones. Her body—a broken chess piece laid on the board. Battered. Scarred. But still part of a game.

The silence pressed in. Stark. Surreal. After a year of chaos, screaming, and survival... the stillness almost felt wrong. Suspicious, even. Like the silence itself was holding its breath, waiting for her next move. She couldn't see — not clearly. One eye was swollen shut. The other blurred with tears she didn't have the energy to cry. But in her mind, everything was crystal sharp. The memories played like film on a loop: Stefan's smirk. The screams that hadn't belonged to her. The quiet cruelty he delivered like gospel. Every manipulation. Every twisted game. She had seen it all coming. All of it.

Except Mr. Edward Wallace.

She hadn't planned to like him. That hadn't been part of the strategy. She had spent a lifetime keeping people at a safe distance — close enough to be useful, never enough to matter. Except Granddaddy. He had always mattered. And now, somehow... so had Mr. Wallace.

He wasn't supposed to become anything more than a helpful neighbor. A tool. A distraction. But he'd looked at her — really looked — and didn't turn away. Even after he saw the bruises. Even after he saw the truth. And still, he stayed.

She hadn't asked for his belief. She hadn't earned it. But when the time came, he handed her the blade. No questions. Just trust.

Sirens rose in the distance. Not close yet — but coming. Real. Inevitable. Like a cue to slip one mask off... and pull another on.

A sliver of red and blue light sliced across the far wall.

It flickered like a warning. Like the final move before checkmate.

Her thoughts shifted to the other shadow.

Not Stefan.

The one who had watched.

Who had warned.

Who, in the end... kept his promise.

Just like Mr. Wallace had.

That was the difference.

Stefan had tried to control her.

Edward had tried to save her.

But the shadow — he had seen through the lies.

And let her finish what she started.

She thought of the knife. The blood. The choice.

She had made it long before tonight.

Before the first scream.

Before the first bruise.

I was never his victim, she thought, her mouth unmoving, her breath thin.

This was always going to end like this.

And it had. Exactly how she planned.

Now, it was time.

She knew what came next:

Police.

Cameras.

Reporters.

The role she'd been perfecting for months.

And Granddaddy — waiting in the distance, wondering what version of her would walk out that door.

She had prepared for this moment the same day she walked into Stefan Warren's camper.

The story she would tell.

The face she would wear.

The performance of a lifetime.

She had ripped off the mask to survive the night —
Torn it away like a veil.
Let him see what lived underneath.
But now...
Now it was time to pull it back on.
Not just to hide.
To win.
The blood had dried sticky against her hands.
Her body screamed with every breath.
But her mind —
Her mind was made of iron.
She drew in a breath.
Held it.
Let it out.
The chess match was over.
She had won.
The board was resetting.
And the next game was already beginning.
She smiled — not with her mouth, but somewhere deeper.
Somewhere colder.
Somewhere permanent.
And without a word,
Lauren slipped the mask back on.
But beneath the surface, something echoed — a truth only she would ever carry beneath the mask... and the veil of innocence.

For the ones still surviving, still hoping, still wearing a mask to cover the bruises; this page is for you.

You are not alone.

Though this is a work of fiction, the pain Lauren endured is real for far too many.

If you or someone you love is experiencing domestic violence, help is available.

Call the **National Domestic Violence Hotline** at **1-800-799-7233** or visit **thehotline.org** for confidential support, 24/7.

You are worthy of safety. Of peace. Of freedom.

And if reading this page puts you at risk, please feel free to tear this page out. Your safety matters most.

ACKNOWLEDGMENTS

A Veil of Innocence began as a creative outlet—but it became so much more. The original idea for this series was born outside my camper at an RV campground, surrounded by family and friends, as we watched strangers pass by and made-up stories about their lives. That spark of imagination turned into something much bigger—and more personal—than I ever expected.

To my husband—thank you for believing in me and giving me the time and space to write, even when it meant letting me disappear into this world for months.

To my daughter—thank you for pushing me to put my ideas on paper. And using you talent of the cover, and wrap design.

To my son—your hugs got me through the hard days.

To my mom—thank you for reading chapter by chapter, always patient, always waiting for more. You believed in my from the beginning.

To my sister and my soul sisters—and to all my coworkers who listened to me talk about this story day in and day out—thank you for your encouragement and curiosity.

To my editor, Alan Ingram—thank you for walking beside me through every scene, every revision, inching me closer to the finish line with care, insight, and heart.

To every survivor of violence who sees a piece of themselves in Lauren—you are not alone.

ABOUT THE AUTHOR

C. Hoffman was born and raised in Amarillo, Texas, and spent countless weekends at the lake near Fritch, where camping trips and quiet waters became her sanctuary. Even then, her imagination was always at work—creating stories about strangers who passed by, wondering what might be hiding behind their smiles.

As an adult, she continued that ritual with her own family. One afternoon, while watching people from her camper, a single question sparked the idea that would become *A Veil of Innocence*.

C. Hoffman has always been drawn to the psychology of what we hide—and why. While her protagonist, Lauren, moves through the world with a mask of control, Hoffman's strength comes from quiet observation. She's always listening for what people are saying without words, watching how silence speaks. Both know how to read a room—and how to survive in one.

She lives in Texas with her husband, children, and grandchild, and treasures her role as "Nana" most of all. Writing is where she reclaims her voice, and the page is where she finally tells the story her way.

instagram.com/authorchoffman

facebook.com/authorchoffman

tiktok.com/@authorchoffman

bookbub.com/authors/bookbub@authorchoffman

goodreads.com/C.Hoffman

ALSO BY C. HOFFMAN

Also by C. Hoffman

• A Veil of Innocence

• Illusion of Innocence (Coming Soon)

Coming Soon — Illusion of Innocence

The storm has passed... but something darker waits beneath the surface.

Lauren escaped the monster—but the real game is just beginning.

Book Two of the Innocence Trilogy: Coming Soon.

THANK YOU

Thank you for stepping into Lauren's world.

Creating her story has been my greatest joy. Sitting outside my camper, imagining these characters into existence and bringing their voices to life on the page has truly been a dream come true.

If you enjoyed this book, please consider leaving a review.

Your feedback means the world to independent authors like me. Even a sentence or two can help others discover Lauren's story.

Book 2 in The Innocence Series — **Illusion of Innocence** — *is coming soon.*

Stay connected at **authorchoffman.com**.

— C. Hoffman